AMBER AND BLOOD

the Dark Disciple

Volume 3

MARGARET WEIS

AMBER & BLOOD
The Dark Disciple, Volume 3

©2008 Wizards of the Coast, Inc.

All characters in this book are fictitious. Any resemblance to actual persons, living or dead, is purely coincidental.

Published by Wizards of the Coast, Inc. DRAGONLANCE, WIZARDS OF THE COAST, and their respective logos are trademarks of Wizards of the Coast, Inc., in the U.S.A. and other countries.

Reprinted from *Plum Village Chanting and Recitation Book* (2000) by Thich Nhat Hanh with permission of Parallax Press, Berkeley, California. www.parallax.org.

Printed in the U.S.A.

Cover art by Matt Stawicki
First Printing: May 2008

9 8 7 6 5 4 3 2 1

ISBN: 978-0-7869-5001-0
620-95548720-001-EN

Library of Congress Cataloging-in-Publication Data

Weis, Margaret.
  Amber and blood / Margaret Weis.
    p. cm. -- (The dark disciple ; v. 3)
  At head of title in a logo: Dragonlance.
  ISBN 978-0-7869-5001-0
  1. Krynn (Imaginary place)--Fiction. I. Title.
  PS3573.E3978A84 2008
  813'.54--dc22

                                       2007051385

U.S., CANADA,
ASIA, PACIFIC, & LATIN AMERICA
Wizards of the Coast, Inc.
P.O. Box 707
Renton, WA 98057-0707
+1-800-324-6496

EUROPEAN HEADQUARTERS
Hasbro UK Ltd
Caswell Way
Newport, Gwent NP9 0YH
GREAT BRITAIN
Save this address for your records.

Visit our web site at www.wizards.com

the Dark Disciple

AMBER AND BLOOD

MARGARET WEIS

DEDICATION

To my daughter, Lizz

Ackowledgement

I would like to gratefully acknowledge Steve Coon
(aka "Frostdawn" on the Dragonlance message boards),
who created the two artifacts of Takhisis and Paladine
used in the book: the *Necklace of Sedition*
and the *Crystal Pyramid of Light*.

I am of the nature to grow old. There is no way to escape growing old.

I am of the nature to have ill health. There is no way to escape ill health.

I am of the nature to die. There is no way to escape death.

All that is dear to me and everyone I love are of the nature to change. There is no way to escape being separated from them.

My actions are my only true belongings. I cannot escape the consequences of my actions. My actions are the ground upon which I stand.

—The Five Remembrances of Buddha

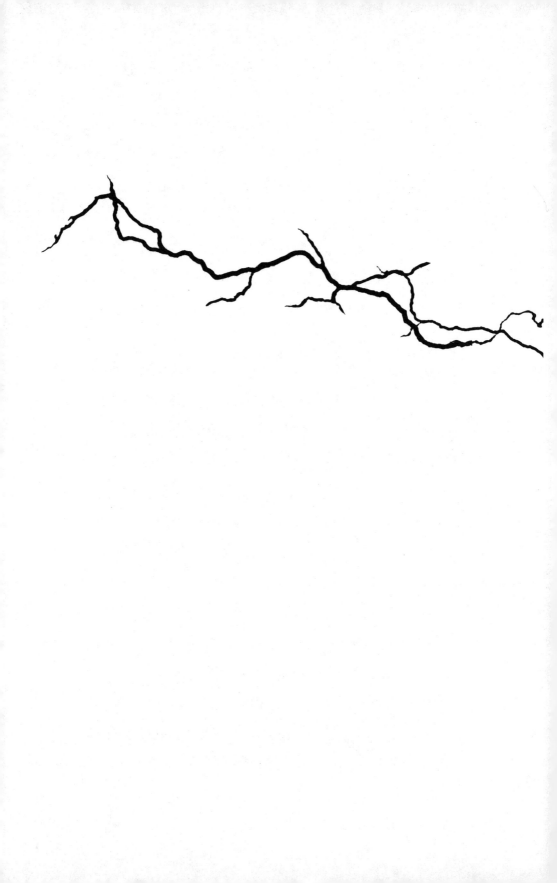

BOOK I

THE

GIFTS

PROLOGUE

What has happened to me?

Where am I?

Who are all these beings, strange and beautiful, awful and majestic, gathered around me? Why do they point at me, and why do they shout with thunderous clamor that makes heaven tremble?

Why are they so angry?

Angry at me?

I have done nothing except give my lover a gift! Chemosh wanted the Tower of High Sorcery that lay beneath the sea and I gave it to him. And now he stares at me with amazement and shock . . . and loathing.

They all stare.

At me.

I am nobody. I am Mina. Chemosh once loved me. He hates me now, and I do not know why. I did nothing but what he asked of me. I am nothing but what he made me, though these others say I am . . . something else . . .

I hear their voices, yet I can make no sense of their words.

She is a god who does not know she is a god. She is a god who was tricked into thinking she is human.

I lie on the cold stone of the castle's battlements, and I see them staring at me and shouting. The thunder hurts my ears. The light of their holiness is blinding. I turn away from the watching eyes and the clamorous voices, and I look down over the walls into the sea far below.

The ever-moving, ever-changing, ever-living sea . . .

The waves rush in and lap the shore, and they swirl back out and rush in again, over and over, unending. A soothing rhythm, back and forth, back and forth . . .

A cradle rocking . . . rocking me to sleep for an eternity.

I was never meant to wake.

I want to go home. I am lost and tired and afraid, and I want to go home.

These voices . . . the quarrelsome squawkings of sea birds.

The sea closes blessedly over me.

And I am gone.

A storm raged on the Blood Sea. A strange storm, of heavenly make, it swirled above a castle that stood high atop a cliff. Clouds boiled around the castle walls. Thunder crackled, and the lightning dazzled and blinded the mortal onlookers—a monk, a kender, and a dog—who were struggling to walk among the sand dunes on the shore far below. The three stood braced against the whipping wind that flung sand into their eyes. They were all three soaked from the spray of salt water, flung up by the waves that came crashing headlong onto the shore. Once there, the waves clutched at the sand with grasping fingers, trying to hold on, but were forced to let go as the motion of the world dragged them back.

Whenever the lightning flared, the monk could see a tower far out to sea. The tower had not been there yesterday. It had appeared in the night, wrenched up out of the depths of the ocean by some catastrophic force, and now it stood with water dripping from its eaves, looking lost, as though wondering, along with men and gods, how it had come to be here.

The monk, Rhys, was almost bent double, his robes plastered

against him, his spare, muscular body fighting for every step against the buffeting wind. He was making headway, but just barely. Nightshade, being a kender and built slighter and smaller than his human friend, was having a more difficult time. He had been bowled over twice and was managing to remain on his feet only by hanging onto Rhys's arm. Atta, the dog, was lower to the ground and therefore was somewhat sheltered by the dunes, but she was having difficulty as well. When the next gust nearly plucked Nightshade from Rhys's grasp and threw Atta into a pile of driftwood, Rhys decided they should return to the grotto they'd just left.

The smallish cave was cheerless and still awash in sea water, but at least they were sheltered from the wind and deadly lightning.

Nightshade sat down beside his friend on the wet rocks and gave a great *whoosh* of relief. He wrung water from his topknot, then tried the same with his shirt, which was considerably worn, its color so faded from the rigors of his travels that he could no longer tell what it had been. Atta did not lie down, but paced nervously, her furry black and white body flinching whenever a loud crack of thunder shook the ground.

"Rhys," Nightshade said, wiping sea water from his eyes, "was that Chemosh's castle we could see up there on the top of the cliff?"

Rhys nodded.

A lightning bolt sizzled nearby and thunder came rolling down the cliff face. Atta quivered and barked at the rumbling. Nightshade huddled closer to Rhys.

"I can hear voices in the thunder," the kender said, "but I can't understand what the voices are saying or make out who is talking. Can you?"

Rhys shook his head. He petted Atta, trying to calm the dog.

"Rhys," said Nightshade after a moment, "I think those must be gods up there. Chemosh is a god, after all, and maybe he's throwing a party for his fellow gods. Though I have to say he didn't strike me as the type to go dancing, what with him being the God of Death and all. Still, maybe he has a fun side."

Rhys watched the dazzling light flash outside the grotto and listened to the voices and thought of the old saying, "When the gods rage, man trembles."

"So many things are happening—so many *strange* things," Nightshade emphasized, "that I'm feeling sort of muddled. I'd like to talk it over, just to make sure that you think happened what *I* think happened. And, to be honest, talking makes the howling wind and lightning seem not so bad. You don't mind if I talk, do you?"

Rhys did not mind.

"I guess I'll start with us being chained up in the cave," said Nightshade. "No, wait. I have to say how we got chained up in the cave, so we should start with the minotaur. Except the minotaur didn't come along until after you fought with your dead brother the Beloved and the little boy killed him—"

"Start with the minotaur," Rhys suggested. "Unless you want to go all the way back to the time I met you in the graveyard."

Nightshade thought that over. "No, I don't think my voice will last long enough for going back *that* far. I'll start with the minotaur. We were walking down the street, and you were really, really angry at Majere and said you were going to quit serving him or any god, when suddenly all these minotaurs came out of nowhere and took us prisoner.

"I cast a spell on one," Nightshade added proudly. "I made him fall down and flop around on the street like a fish. The minotaur captain said I was a 'kender with horns'. Do you remember that, Rhys?"

"I do," Rhys returned. "The captain was right. You were very brave."

"Then the minotaur picked me up and put me in a sack and took us both on board his ship, only it wasn't an ordinary ship. It was a ship that belonged to the Sea Goddess, and it sailed through the air, not the water, and I told you then that you couldn't quit a god . . ."

"And you were right," said Rhys.

Thirty years old, he had been a monk dedicated to Majere for what seemed most of his life. And though not long ago he had lost faith in Majere, the god had refused to lose faith in him. This knowledge humbled Rhys and filled him with thankfulness and joy. He had stumbled and groped through the darkness, taken many wrong turns, ended up in a few blind alleys, but he had found his way back to his god, and Majere had welcomed him with loving arms.

"The minotaur ship brought us here to the other side of the continent where Chemosh built his castle. And the minotaur chained us up in the cave—see, I came to that part."

Rhys nodded again, continuing to pet Atta, who seemed calmer, listening to the kender talk.

"Then we had lots of visitors—a lot more than you'd expect for people chained up in a cave. First Mina came." Nightshade shivered. "That was truly awful. She walked up to you and asked you to tell her who she was. She claimed that the first time she saw you, you recognized her—"

Except I didn't, Rhys thought, troubled. He still did not understand that part of the story.

"—and when you couldn't tell her who she was, Mina got angry. She thought you were lying, and she said if you didn't tell she was going to come back to the cave and kill me and Atta. We would die in torment," Nightshade finished with relish.

"After Mina left, Zeboim popped by. You see what I mean, Rhys? We never had so much company when we were staying in Solace as we did chained up in that cave. Zeboim said for you to tell *her* who Mina was because all the gods were in an uproar over it, and you said you couldn't, and then she got mad and said she would watch with pleasure while Mina killed me and Atta and we died in torment." Nightshade paused for breath and to spit out some sea water. "And after that, you sent me and Atta off to seek help from the monks of Majere in Flotsam, except we never got that far. We only managed to reach the road up there, and that proved very difficult, due to the sand dunes, and I had a talk with your god. I was pretty harsh with him, I can tell you. I told Majere you were going to die because you were being faithful to him and why wasn't he being faithful to you for a change. I asked him to help Atta and me save you. And then two of the Beloved saw us and decided they wanted to kill me."

Nightshade sighed. "It was quite a night for people wanting to kill me. Anyway Atta and I ran for it, but we both have short legs, and the Beloved had long legs and even though Atta has two more legs than I do we were falling behind when I bumped into Majere. Blam. Ran right smack into him. He saw that we were in trouble and he sent grasshoppers after the Beloved and drove them off. I reminded him about you sacrificing your life for him, and he said he couldn't help because there was this strange amber glow in the sky and he had to go do god stuff somewhere else—"

"I don't think Majere said *that*." Rhys was glad the darkness hid his smile.

"Well, maybe not," Nightshade conceded. "Only that's what he meant. Then he gave me his blessing. Me. A kender. Who had spoken quite harshly to him. So Atta and I ran back to the cave where you were still chained up, only to find Chemosh was there. He wanted you to tell him who Mina was, and he said *he* was going to kill you, and he probably would have, only Atta bit him on the anklebone. And then

9

the world shook and knocked us all down—even the god."

Nightshade cocked an eye at Rhys. "Is that right? 'Cause it's here that things start getting strange. Or rather—stranger. Chemosh was extremely angry. He started yelling at the other gods, wanting to know what was going on. Turns out the shaking was caused by that tower being yanked up out of the Blood Sea which caused huge waves to start rolling onto the shore, and these waves flooded the cave, and you were unconscious and chained to the wall and the water was rising up around you, and it was up to me and Atta to save you."

Nightshade paused for breath.

"Which you did," said Rhys, and he embraced the kender.

"I picked the lock on the manacles," Nightshade said. "The first and only lock I ever picked in my life! My father would have been so proud. Majere helped me pick the lock, you know."

A sudden thought struck Nightshade. "Say, do you think Majere would help me again if I wanted to pick another lock? 'Cause there's a baker in Solace who makes these wonderful meat pies, only he closes up shop right after supper, and sometimes I'm hungry in the night and I wouldn't want to wake him and—"

"No," said Rhys.

"No what?" asked Nightshade.

"No, I do *not* think Majere would help you pick the lock on the baker's back door."

"Not even to keep from waking the baker up in the middle of the night?"

"No," Rhys said firmly.

"Ah, well." Nightshade sighed again, this time quite deeply. "I suppose you're right. Though I'll bet if Majere ever tasted those meat pies he might reconsider. Where was I?"

"You had just picked the lock on my manacles," said Rhys.

"Oh, yes! The water was getting deeper and I was afraid you were going to drown. I tried to drag you out of the cave, but you were too heavy—no offense."

"None taken," Rhys said.

"And then six monks of Majere came running into the cave and they picked you up and carried you out. And I guess they healed the bump on your head because here you are and here I am and here's Atta and we're all fine. So," Nightshade said in conclusion, "your brother the Beloved is at peace now. The story's over and we can go home to your monastery, and Atta can guard sheep, and I'll visit my friends in the graveyard, and we'll live happily ever after."

Rhys realized that this was true. The tale was told, the last chapter written.

The night was dark and the storm was wild and ferocious and strange things were happening, but the storm and the night would soon come to an end, as nights and storms always do. That was the promise of the gods. When day dawned, Rhys and Nightshade and Atta would start back home, back to his monastery. The journey would be a long one, for the monastery was located north of the city of Staughton, which was on the west coast, and they were on the east coast of the vast continent of Ansalon and would have to travel on foot. He was not concerned at the distance. Every step would be devoted to the god. He thought of the work he would do to earn his bread, of the people he would meet, of the good he would try to do along the way, and the journey did not seem long at all.

"Did you hear that?" Nightshade asked suddenly. "It sounded like a yell."

Rhys hadn't heard anything except roaring thunder and howling wind and crashing waves. The kender had sharp senses, however, and Rhys had learned not to discount them. He was further convinced by the fact that Atta also heard something. Her head was up, her ears pricked. The dog stared intently out into storm.

"Wait here," said Rhys.

He walked out of the grotto and the wind smote him with such force that even standing upright was difficult.

The wind blew his long dark hair back from his face, whipped his orange robes around his thin body. The salt spray stung his eyes, the sand tore at his flesh. Shielding his eyes with his hand, he peered about. The lightning flashes were almost constant. He saw the black waves with their white, foaming tops and the seaweed being blow along the empty beach and that was all. He was about to return to the shelter of the grotto when he heard a cry, this time sounding behind him.

A gust of wind caught hold of Nightshade, sending him staggering backward for a few feet, then knocking him flat.

Rhys braced himself against the gale and, reaching down his hand, grabbed hold of Nightshade and hoisted the kender to his feet.

"I told you to wait inside!" Rhys shouted.

"I thought you were talking to Atta!" Nightshade yelled back. The kender turned around to the dog, whose ears were flat against her head from the force of the wind. He shook his finger at her. "Atta, stay inside!"

Rhys was hanging on to Nightshade, who was trying to stand against the wind and not having much luck, when he heard the cry.

"There it is again!" shouted Nightshade.

"Yes, but where?" Rhys returned.

He looked at Atta. She was standing at alert, her ears forward, her tail motionless. She was staring out to sea.

The cry came again, shrill and clear, cutting through the howling wind. Squinting his eyes against the spray and sand, Rhys again peered into the night.

"Blessed Majere!" he gasped. "Wait here!" he ordered Nightshade, who didn't have much choice in the matter, since every time he stood up the wind knocked him down again.

In the last flash of lightning, Rhys had seen a child, a little girl, to judge by the two long braids whipping out in front of her, floundering waist-deep in the wind-tossed sea. He lost her momentarily in the darkness and prayed for another lightning strike. A sheet of white-purple light flared across the sky and there was the girl, waving her arms and crying out for help. She was desperately trying to make it to shore, fighting the vicious rip current trying to drag her back out to sea.

Rhys fought against the wind, wiping his eyes free of the spray, keeping his gaze fixed on the child, who continued to struggle toward the shore. She was almost there when a foaming wave crashed over the girl's head and she vanished. Rhys stared at the boiling froth, praying for the child to emerge, but he saw nothing.

He tried to increase his speed, but the wind was blowing off the sea, driving him backward a step for every two he took forward. He struggled on, continuing to search for the child as he fought his way toward the water. He saw no one, and he began to fear the sea had claimed its victim, when suddenly he saw the girl's body, black in the silver moonlight, lying on the shore. The child lay face down in the shallow water, her long braids floating around her.

The wind ceased to blow so suddenly that Rhys, pushing against it, overbalanced and pitched forward onto the wet sand. He looked about in wonder. The lightning had flickered and gone out. The thunder had fallen silent. The storm clouds had vanished, as though sucked in by a giant breath. The red light of dawn glimmered on the horizon. In the dark sky above him, the two moons, Lunitari and Solinari, still kept watch.

13

He didn't like this sudden calm. It was like being in the eye of the hurricane. Though this storm had abated and blue sky could be seen above, it was as if the gods were waiting for the back end of the storm to slam into him.

Recovering from his fall, Rhys ran along the wet shore toward the child, who lay unmoving in the surf.

He rolled her over onto her back. Her eyes were closed. She was not breathing. Rhys remembered with vivid clarity the time he'd nearly drowned after jumping off the cliffs of Storm's Keep. Zeboim had saved him then, and he used her technique now to try to save the child. He pumped the little girl's arms, all the while praying to Majere. The child gave a cough and a gasp. Spewing sea water out of her mouth, she sat up, still coughing.

Rhys pounded her on the back. More sea water came up. The girl caught her breath.

"Thanks, mister," she gasped, then she fainted.

"Rhys!" Nightshade was yelling, running across the sand, with Atta racing ahead of him. "Did you save her? Is she dead? I hope not. Wasn't that funny the way the storm stopped—"

Nightshade came dashing up to Rhys's side, just as the sun cleared the horizon and shone full on the little girl's face. The kender gave a strangled gasp and skidded to a halt. He stood, staring.

"Rhys, do you know who—" he began.

"No time for talking, Nightshade!" Rhys said sharply.

The girl's lips were blue. Her breathing was ragged. She was wearing nothing except a plain cotton shift, no shoes or stockings. Rhys had to find some means to warm her or she would die of exposure. He rose to his feet, the limp child in his arms.

"I'll take her back to the cave. I need to build a fire to warm her. You might find some dry wood behind the dunes—"

"But, Rhys, listen—"

"I will in a minute," Rhys said, striving to be patient. "Right now, you need to find dry wood. I have to warm her—"

"Rhys, look at her!" Nightshade said, floundering along behind him. "Don't you recognize her? It's her! Mina!"

"Don't be ridiculous—"

"I'm not," Nightshade said solemnly. "Believe me, I wish I was. I know this must sound crazy, since the last time we saw Mina she was a grown-up and now she's grown down, but I'm pretty sure it's her. I know because I feel the same way when I look at this little girl that I felt when I first saw Mina. I feel sad."

"Nightshade," said Rhys wearily, "firewood."

"If you don't believe me," Nightshade added, "look at Atta. She knows her, too."

Rhys had to admit that Atta was acting strangely. Ordinarily, the dog would have come leaping to him, eager to help, ready to lick the child's cold cheek or nudge her limp hand—healing remedies known and trusted by all dogs. But Atta was keeping her distance. She stood braced on stiff legs, her hackles raised, her upper lip curled back over her teeth. Her brown eyes, fixed on the girl, were not friendly. She growled, low in her throat.

"Atta! Stop that!" Rhys reprimanded.

Atta quit growling, but she did not relax her defensive stance. She gazed at Rhys with a hurt and exasperated expression; hurt that he didn't trust her and exasperated, as though she'd like to nip some sense into him.

Rhys looked down at the child he held in his arms, took a good, long look at her. She was a girl of about six years of age. A pretty child with long red braids that dangled down over his arm. Her face was pale, and she had a light smattering of freckles over her nose. Thus far, he had

15

no reason to think either the dog or the kender were right. And then she stirred and moaned in his arms. Her eyes, which had been closed, partially opened, and he could see, beneath the half-closed lids, glints of amber.

A cold qualm shook Rhys, and he gasped softly.

"Told you so," Nightshade said. "Didn't we, Atta?"

The dog growled again.

"If want my advice, you'll dump her back into the ocean," Nightshade said. "Only last night she was going to torture you because you wouldn't tell her who she was when you told her you didn't know the answer and she was going to make me and Atta die in torment. Remember?"

Rhys recovered from his initial shock. "I'm not going to dump her in the ocean. A lot of people have red hair."

He continued toward the grotto.

Nightshade sighed. "I didn't think he'd listen. I'll go find firewood. C'mon, Atta."

The kender set off, not very enthusiastically. Atta cast a worried glance at Rhys, then trotted along after the kender.

Rhys carried the child inside the grotto, which wasn't very comfortable and certainly not very dry; the rock-strewn floor was still wet, and there were puddles here and there. But at least they were out of the wind. A blazing fire would soon warm the chill cavern.

The girl stirred and moaned again. Rhys chaffed her cold hands and smoothed back her wet, auburn hair.

"Child," he said gently. "Don't be frightened. You are safe."

The girl opened her eyes, amber eyes, clear amber, like honey, golden and pure. The same eyes as Mina's, except no trapped souls, as he had seen in Mina's eyes.

"I'm cold," the girl complained, shivering.

"My friend has gone to get wood for a fire. You'll soon be warm."

The girl stared at him, at his orange robes. "You're a monk." She frowned, as though trying to remember something. "Monks go around helping people, don't they? Will you help me?"

"Gladly, child," Rhys said. "What do you want of me?"

The girl's face grew pinched. She was now fully awake and shivering so that her teeth chattered. Her grip on his hand tightened.

"I'm lost," she said. Her lower lip quivered. Her eyes filled with tears. "I ran away from home and now I can't find my way back."

Rhys was relieved. Nightshade was wrong. The girl was likely some fisherman's child who'd been caught out in the storm, been swept out to sea. She could not have walked far. Her village must close by. He pitied her parents. They must be frantic with worry.

"Once you are warm, I will take you, child," Rhys promised. "Where do you live?"

The girl curled up in a shivering ball. Her eyes closed and she yawned. "You've probably never heard of it," she said sleepily. "It's a place called . . ."

Rhys had to lean close to her hear her drowsy whisper.

"Godshome."

2

*T*he gods had watched in astonishment and alarm as a mortal, Mina, reached down to the bottom of the Blood Sea, seized hold of the newly restored Tower of High Sorcery, and dragged it up from beneath the waves to present as a gift to her lover, Chemosh.

Obviously, Mina was not mortal. The most powerful wizards who had ever lived could not have accomplished such a feat, nor could the most powerful clerics. Only a god could have done that, and now all the gods were thrown into turmoil and consternation, trying to determine what was going on.

"Who is this new god?" the other gods clamored. "Where does she come from?"

Their fear was, of course, that she was some alien god, some interloper who, striding across the heavens, had come upon their world.

Their fears were allayed. She was one of theirs.

Majere held the answers.

"How long have you known?" Gilean demanded of the Monk God.

Gilean was the leader of the Gods of Gray, the neutral gods, who moderated between light and darkness. The neutral gods were strongest now, their numbers increased due to the self-imposed exile of Paladine, leader of the Gods of Light, and the banishment of Queen Takhisis, leader of the Gods of Darkness. Gilean wore the aspect of a scholarly sage, a middle-aged man of keen intellect and cool, discompassionate eyes.

"Many, many eons, God of the Book," Majere replied.

The God of Wisdom, Majere wore orange robes and carried no weapon. His aspect was generally mild and serene, though now it was fraught with sorrow and regret.

"Why keep this secret?" Gilean asked.

"It was not mine to reveal," Majere replied. "I gave my solemn oath."

"To whom?"

"To one who is no longer among us."

The gods were silent.

"I assume you mean Paladine," Gilean stated. "But there is another god who is no longer with us. Does this have something to do with her?"

"Takhisis?" Majere spoke sharply. His voice hardened. "Yes, she was responsible for this."

Chemosh spoke. "Takhisis's last words, before the High God came to take her, were these: 'You are making a mistake! What I have done cannot be undone. The curse is among you. Destroy me and you destroy yourselves.'"

"Why didn't you tell us this?" Gilean asked, glowering at the Lord of Bones.

Chemosh was a vain and handsome god, with long flowing black hair and dark eyes, empty and cold as the graves of the accursed dead over which he presided.

"The Dark Queen was always making threats." Chemosh shrugged. "Why was this one any different?"

Gilean had no answer. He fell silent and the other gods were also silent, waiting.

"The fault is mine," Majere said at last. "I acted for the best. Or so I believed."

Mina lay so cold and still on the battlements. Chemosh wanted to go to her, to comfort her, but he dared not. Not with all of them watching him. He said to Majere, "Is she dead?"

"She is not dead, because she cannot die." Majere looked at each of them, each and every one. "We have been blind. But now you see the truth."

"We see, but we do not understand."

"You do," said Majere. He folded his hands and gazed out into the firmament. "You don't want to."

He did not see the stars. He saw the stars' first light.

"It began at the beginning of time," he said. "And it began in joy." He sighed deeply. "And now, because I did not speak, it could end in bitter sorrow."

"Explain yourself, Majere!" growled Reorx, smoothing his long beard. The God of the Forge, whose aspect was that of a dwarf, in honor of his favorite race, was not known for his patience. "We have no time for your blathering!"

Majere shifted his gaze from the time's beginning to the present. He looked down at Mina.

"She is a god who does not know she is a god. She is a god who was duped into thinking she is human."

Majere paused, as if to gain control of himself. When he spoke, his voice soft with anger, "She is a god of Light, tricked by Takhisis into serving Darkness."

Majere fell silent. The other gods shouted questions, demanded answers. All the while, Mina lay unconscious on the battlements

21

of Chemosh's castle as the storm of anger and bafflement, accusations and recriminations raged around her. Such was the turmoil that when Mina woke, no one noticed. She stared at the beautiful, radiant, dark and awful beings stalking the heavens, flinging bolts of lightning and shaking the ground with their fury. She heard them shouting her name, but all she understood was that this was her fault.

A memory, a dim memory, from a time long, long passed, stirred in Mina and brought one terrible understanding.

I was never meant to wake.

Mina leapt to her feet and before any one could stop her, she jumped from the battlement and plunged silently, without a cry, into the crashing sea.

Zeboim screamed and ran to the edge of the wall to look into the waves. Storm winds tore at the sea-foam hair of the sea goddess and swirled her green gown about her. She watched the foaming water, but saw no sign of Mina. Turning, she cast a scathing glance and pointed an accusing finger at Chemosh.

"She's dead and it is your fault!" She gestured into the storm-lashed water. "You rejected her love. Men are such beasts!"

"Spare us the drama, Sea Witch," Chemosh muttered. "Mina's not dead. She can't die. She's a god."

"She may not be able to die. But she can still be wounded," said Mishakal softly.

The storm winds ceased. The lightning bolts sizzled and went out. The thunder rolled over the waves and was silenced.

Mishakal, Goddess of Healing, the White Lady, as she was now known on Krynn, for her pure white gown and long white hair, walked over to Majere. She extended her hands to him. Majere took hold of her hands and gazed sorrowfully into her eyes.

"I know you keep your vow to protect one who is now gone," said Mishakal. "You have my permission to speak."

"I knew it!" Sargonnas snarled. The God of Vengeance and Leader of the Darkness strode forward. His aspect had the head of a bull and the body of a man after the minotaur, his chosen race. "This is a conspiracy among the Do-Gooders! We will have the truth and have it now!"

"Sargonnas is right. The time for silence is ended," said Gilean.

"I will speak," said Majere, "since Mishakal has given me leave."

Yet he did not say anything, not immediately. He stood gazing down at the water that had closed over Mina's head. Sargonnas growled impatiently, but Gilean silenced him.

"You said: 'She is a god who does not know she is a god. She is a god who was tricked into thinking she is human.'"

"That is true," Majere answered.

"And you said also, 'She is a god of Light, tricked by Takhisis into serving Darkness.'"

"And that is also true." Majere looked at Mishakal, and he smiled a rare smile.

"Mina's story begins in the Age of Starbirth with the creation of the world. At that time—the first and last and only time in the history of the world—all of us came together to use our power to create a wonder and a marvel—this world."

The other gods were silent, remembering.

"In that one single moment of creation, we watched Reorx take hold of Chaos and forge out of it a great globe, separating the light from the darkness, the land from the sea, the heavens from the earth and in that moment we were one. We all of us knew joy. That moment of creation gave birth to a being—a child of light."

"We knew nothing of this!" Sargonnas growled, astonished and angered.

"Only three of us knew," said Majere. "Paladine, his consort, Mishakal, and myself. The girl appeared in our midst, a radiant being, more beautiful than the stars."

"You should have informed me at least," Gilean said, frowning at Mishakal.

She smiled sadly. "There was no need to tell anyone. We knew what we had to do. The Gods of Darkness would have never permitted this new, young god of light to exist, for she would have upset the balance. Just the knowledge that she had been born would have caused an uproar, threatened to destroy what we had so lovingly created."

"True," said Zeboim coldly. "Very true. I would have strangled the whelp."

"Paladine and Mishakal gave the child-god into my hands," Majere continued. "They bid me cast her into a deep sleep and then hide her away, so that she might never be found."

"How could you bear to lose her?" asked gentle Chislev, Goddess of Nature, shuddering. Her aspect was that of a young woman, lovely and delicate, with the soft eyes of the fawn and the sharp claws of the tiger.

"Our sorrow was deep as the vastness of time," Mishakal admitted, "but we had no choice."

"I took the child," Majere resumed his tale, "and I carried her into the sea. I carried her to the depths of the ocean, to those parts that have never known the sunlight, and there I kissed her and rocked her gently to sleep. And there I left her, sweetly slumbering, with never a dream to disturb her rest. And there she would have remained at peace until time's end, but Takhisis, Queen of All Colors and of None, stole away the world and with it—the child."

"And Takhisis found her," said Reorx. "But how, if she was hidden as you claim, Majere?"

"When Takhisis stole the world, she thought smugly that she was the only god-force in this part of the universe. I do not know for certain how she came to learn of the child's existence, but I think I can hazard a guess based on my knowledge of the Dark Queen. When she first stole the world, she was left dangerously weak. She hid herself away, biding her time, restoring her strength, making her plans. And when she was well-rested and strong again, she left her hiding place. She came out warily, cautiously, probing and feeling about her to make certain she was alone in this part of the universe."

"And she found out she was not," said Morgion, God of Disease, with an unpleasant smile.

Majere nodded. "She felt the force of another god. I can only imagine her shock, her fury. She could not rest until she had found this god and determined what sort of threat the god posed to her. Since god-force within the child shone like a beacon, I doubt if Takhisis had much difficulty in her search. She found the god, and she must have been astonished.

"For she did not find another god who would challenge her. She found a child-god, innocent, unknowing, a god of light. And that gave her an idea . . ."

"Stupid bitch!" Chemosh swore bitterly. "Stupid, stupid woman! She should have foreseen what would happen!"

"Bah!" said Sargonnas. "The Dark Queen was never one to look past her own snout. She would have seen only that this child-god could be of use to her. She would keep Mina under her thumb and use her for her own ends."

"And avenge herself one last time on the gods she had always hated," said Kiri-Jolith, God of Just War. His aspect was that of a knight clad in shining silver armor.

"Takhisis very nearly succeeded," Majere admitted. "She made one mistake and that grew out of her cruel desire for revenge. She decided to give this child-god to her enemy, to the mortal woman Takhisis had always blamed for her downfall during the War of the Lance—Goldmoon. The Dark Queen caused the child-god to be cast up on the shores of the Citadel of Light.

"Formerly a cleric of Mishakal, Goldmoon had brought the healing power of mysticism to Krynn. Now an old woman, she took the child-god, who had the aspect of a nine-year-old girl, to her heart. Goldmoon named her Mina. And Takhisis laughed.

"As Takhisis knew she would, Goldmoon taught Mina about the old gods, for Goldmoon grieved for the loss of the gods. Takhisis came to Mina, who loved Goldmoon dearly, and told her that she would give her the power to seek out the gods and restore them to the world. We all know what happened after that. Mina ran away from Goldmoon and 'found' Takhisis, who was waiting for her. What terrible tortures and torment Mina suffered at the hands of the Dark Queen—all in the name of 'proving her loyalty'—I dare not speculate.

"When Mina was finally returned to the world, she had been shaped and molded in the image of the Dark Queen. Takhisis expected Mina to win victories in her name. All the miracles Mina performed she would think came from Takhisis. Too late, Takhisis realized her mistake. She saw her folly. As do others who tried the same."

The other gods all looked accusingly at Chemosh.

"I did not know she was a god!" the Lord of Bones cried savagely. "Takhisis knew. Witness her final words: 'The curse is among you. Destroy me and you destroy yourselves.' "

"Destroy us!" Sargonnas's laughter boomed raucously through the heavens. "How does a chit of a girl-god pose a threat to us?"

"How does she not?" Mishakal asked sharply. The White Lady

flamed, her beauty and her power daunting. "Even now, you are scheming how to win Mina to your side, to shift the balance in your favor."

"And what about you, Mistress Sanctimonious?" Zeboim flared. "You are thinking the very same thing."

Kiri-Jolith said coldly, "This god is lost to us. She is now a creature of darkness."

Mishakal cast him a sorrowful glance. "There is such a thing as forgiveness . . . redemption."

Kiri-Jolith looked stern and unrelenting. He said nothing, but he shook his head decisively.

"If she is so dangerous, what is to be done about her?" asked Chislev.

The gods looked to Gilean for judgment.

"She has free will," he determined at last. "Her fate is in her own hands. She must decide on her destiny herself. She will be given time to think and consider. And during this time," he added with cold emphasis, "she is not to be influenced by either Darkness or Light."

Which wise judgment, of course, pleased no one.

3

*T*he gods began talking at once. Kiri-Jolith insisted Mina should be banished as Takhisis had been banished. Zeboim protested that this was not fair to the poor child. She offered to take her to her home beneath the sea, an offer no one trusted. She urged Chemosh to support her, but he refused.

He wanted nothing more to do with Mina. Chemosh was sorry he'd ever seen her, sorry he'd fallen in love with her and taken her as his lover, sorry he'd used her to help him create new followers, the undead Beloved, who had been a sad disappointment, ending up being loyal to Mina, not to him. He held himself disdainfully aloof from the argument raging among the pantheon. Thus he was the only one who noticed the three gods of magic, who had heretofore kept silent, now conferring in low voices among themselves.

Solinari, the child of Paladine and Mishakal, was god of the Silver Moon, magic of light. Lunitari, child of Gilean, was goddess of the Red Moon, magic of neutrality, and their cousin, Nuitari, son of Takhisis and Sargonnas, was god of the Black Moon, god of the magic of darkness. Despite their different ideologies, the cousins were close, united in their love of the magic. Together, they often defied their parents and worked toward their own ends, which is what they were undoubtedly doing now. Chemosh drew closer, hoping to overhear what they were saying.

"So it was Mina who raised the tower from the bottom of the Blood Sea!" Lunitari was saying. "But why?"

Lunitari wore the red robes of those dedicated to her service. Her aspect was that of a human woman with inquisitive, always seeking, eyes.

"She planned to give it to the Lord of Bones," said Nuitari. "A love token."

He wore black robes; his face was that of a round moon. His eyes kept his secrets.

"And what of all the valuable artifacts inside it?" Solinari asked in a low voice. "What of the *Solio Febalas*?"

Clad in white robes, Solinari was watchful and careful, walked and spoke quietly, his eyes gray as smoke from the smoldering fire of his being.

"How should I know what has happened to it?" Nuitari demanded testily. "I was summoned to attend. My absence would have been noted. But once this meeting has ended—"

Chemosh did not hear the rest. So that was why Mina had given him the tower! He cared nothing for some old monument to magic. He desired what lay beneath the tower—the *Solio Febalas*.

Long ago, before the Cataclysm, the Kingpriest of Istar had raided the holy temples and shrines dedicated to the gods of Krynn, removing holy artifacts he deemed were dangerous. At first, he took only those from the Gods of Darkness, but then, as his paranoia grew, he ordered his troops into the temples of the neutral gods, as well. Finally, having determined he would challenge the gods for godhood himself, he sent his soldiers to raid all the temples of the Gods of Light.

The stolen artifacts were taken to the old Tower of High Sorcery in Istar, now under his control. He placed the artifacts in what he termed the "Hall of Sacrilege".

Angered at the challenge from the Kingpriest, the gods cast a fiery mountain onto the world, breaking it asunder. Istar sank to the bottom of the sea. If any remembered the Hall of Sacrilege, the survivors assumed it had been destroyed.

As the centuries passed, mortals forgot about the Hall of Sacrilege. Chemosh did not forget, however. He had always fumed over the loss of his artifacts. He could feel power emanating from the relics and he knew they had not been lost. He wanted them back. He was tempted to go in search of them during the Fourth Age, but he was involved at the time in a secret plot with Queen Takhisis, a plot to overthrow the Gods of the Light, and he dared not do anything that might draw attention to himself.

He'd never had a chance to seek them. First he was caught up in the War of the Lance, and then Chaos had gone on a rampage, and later Takhisis had stolen the world. The artifacts of the gods remained lost until Nuitari had decided to secretly rebuild the ruined Tower of High Sorcery that lay at the bottom of the ocean. He had found the *Solio Febalas*, much to Chemosh's jealous ire.

Chemosh had asked Mina to enter the Hall of Sacrilege and bring out his artifacts. But she had failed him and caused the first rupture between them.

Do not be angry with me, my dearest lord. . . . The Solio Febalas *is holy. Sanctified. The power and majesty of the gods—all the gods—are in the chamber. I could not touch anything. I did not dare! I could do nothing but fall to my knees in worship. . . .*

He had been furious with her. He had accused her of stealing the artifacts for herself. Now he knew better. The power of the gods had acted like a mirror, reflecting back to her the divine power she felt burn inside her. How confused she must have been, confused and terrified, and overwhelmed. She had lifted the tower from bottom of the Blood Sea to give to him. A gift.

Thus, by rights, the tower was his. And just now, no one was standing guard. Everyone was yammering about what to do with Mina. Chemosh left the raging argument and sped across the Blood Sea to the rock-bound island on which stood the newly-raised tower.

The Hall of Sacrilege had been located at the very bottom of the tower. Was it still there, or had it been left behind on the sea floor?

Chemosh dove to the bottom of the ocean. An enormous chasm marked where the tower had once stood. The ocean floor had been hauled up with the tower and formed the island on which it now stood. The water was so dark that even immortal eyes could not plumb its depths. Chemosh felt no sense of his own power emanating from the chasm.

The artifacts were still inside the tower. He was certain of it.

The Tower of High Sorcery that had once been beneath the Blood Sea, but which now overlooked it, resembled the original tower. Nuitari had reconstructed it with loving care. The walls were made of smooth, wetly glistening crystal. Water drained from a dome of black marble and ran down the slick walls as the waves hurled themselves in a sullen, petulant manner against the shores of the new-made island. Atop the dome a circlet made of burnished red-gold twined with silver shone in the light of the twin moons it represented. The center of the circlet was jet black in honor of Nuitari. No sunlight could be seen through the hole.

Chemosh eyed the tower narrowly. Two of Nuitari's Black Robes lived inside. Chemosh wondered what had happened to them. If they were still alive, they must have had a wild and terrifying ride. He circled the tower until he came to the door—the formal entryway.

When the tower had been in Istar and after that, at the bottom of the sea, the wizards and Nuitari alone possessed the secret to gaining access. Only those who were invited could enter and this included gods. But now the tower had been wrenched from Nuitari's grasp, stolen from him while his back was turned. Perhaps his magic had been broken.

Chemosh did not bother with the door. He could glide through the crystal walls as though they were water. He started to walk through the walls of shining black but, surprisingly, he found his way blocked.

Frustrated, Chemosh tried pushing open the massive front doors. They did not budge. Chemosh lost his temper and kicked the door with his foot and smote it with his hand. The god could have battered down a castle's walls with the flick of his finger, but he had no effect on the tower. The door shuddered at the blows, but remained intact.

"It's no use. You won't get in. *She* has the key."

Chemosh turned to see Nuitari come walking around the side of the building.

"Who has the key?" Chemosh demanded. "Your sister? Zeboim?"

"Mina, you dolt," Nuitari told him. "And she's sending her Beloved to guard it."

The god of Dark Magic pointed across the sea to the city of Flotsam. Chemosh saw with his immortal vision hordes of people jumping from the docks, plunging into the sea, and either sinking or swimming through the waves which glowed eerily with a faint amber light. These were the Beloved. They looked and acted, walked and talked, ate and drank, like ordinary people with one small difference.

They were dead.

Being dead, they felt no fear, they never tired, they needed no sleep, they had boundless energy. Strike them down and they rose back up.

Cut off their heads and they picked them up and put them back on. Chemosh had been quite fond of them until he had found out they were really Mina's creation, not his. Now he loathed the very sight of them.

"Mina's army," Nuitari stated in bitter tones. "Coming to occupy her fortress. And you thought she was going to give it you!"

"They won't get in," said Chemosh.

Nuitari chuckled. "As our friend Reorx is so fond of saying, 'Wanna bet'?" He gestured. "Once she comes to open the doors and let her Beloved inside, my poor Black Robes will be under siege in their own laboratory. The tower will be crawling with her fiends."

As Chemosh watched, several of the undead creatures dragged themselves up out of the water and headed toward the massive double doors.

"Aren't you the fool!" said Nuitari with a thick-lipped, sneering smile. "You had Mina in your bed and you kicked her out. She would have done anything for you."

Chemosh made no response. Nuitari was right, curse him. Mina loved him, adored him, and he'd cast her off, spurned her because he'd been jealous of her.

Not jealous of another lover. Jealous of her—her power.

The Beloved served her, when they were meant to serve him. Mina had done to him what she'd done to Takhisis. The miracles she had performed in the name of Chemosh had been her own miracles. Men worshipped Mina, not him. The Beloved were subject to her will, not his.

And, if he believed Majere, Mina had done this in all innocence. She had no idea she was the god who had given the Beloved terrible life.

What a fool I've been! Chemosh reproached himself, but even as he did, an idea came to him. He remember the broken-hearted look she had cast him before she had leapt into the sea.

She still loves me. I can win her back. With her at my side, I can supplant that thick-skulled bovine, Sargonnas. I can cast down Kiri-Jolith and thwart Mishakal and thumb my nose at know-it-all Gilean. Mina will gain me access to the Hall of Sacrilege. I will seize all the artifacts. I can rule Heaven . . .

All he had to do now was find her.

Chemosh cast his immortal gaze upon the world. He saw all beings everywhere: elves and humans, ogres and kender, gnomes and dwarves, fish and hounds, cats and goblins. His vision encompassed them, surrounded them, studied them, all simultaneously, all within the splitting of a split second. He found every living being on this planet and all who weren't living in the ordinary sense of the word.

None of them were her.

Chemosh was baffled. Where could Mina be? How could she hide from him?

He had no idea and while he was puzzling this out, he realized that back in his castle, Gilean was asking the gods to swear an oath they would not interfere with Mina. Whatever choice she made about her place in the pantheon, whatever side she might choose, or if she would leave the world altogether, the decision had to be hers.

If I take this oath, Gilean will see to it that the oath is enforced. I will be barred from trying to seduce her.

Chemosh was confident in his power over her. All he needed was to see her, talk to her, take her into his arms . . .

He could not search for her, not at this moment, not while Nuitari was watching him like a snake watches a rat; not while Sargonnas was eyeing him with dark suspicion and Gilean was demanding that each god swear. Chemosh could not search for Mina, but he had someone at his command who could. Fortunately, he had a little time. The Gods of Magic were demanding to know why they needed to swear the oath at all.

Chemosh sent out a call, his thoughts speeding rapidly through the castle to Ausric Krell, the former death knight, cursed by Mina to become human again. Chemosh had to hurry. He had to issue his orders to find Mina before he took the oath. He could not be blamed if Mina came to him of her own free will.

One tiny little shove in his direction would hardly count.

"We should not have to take this oath," Nuitari was arguing. "We were not even born when this child-god came into being."

"We care nothing about Mina," stated Lunitari.

"She has naught to do with magic. Leave us out of this," added Solinari.

"Oh, but she does have something you want," said Morgion, God of Disease, speaking in his soft, sickly voice. "Mina has in her possession a Tower of High Sorcery. And she has locked you out!"

"Is that true?" asked Gilean, frowning.

"It is true," Solinari admitted. "Yet even if we are forced to take this oath, we deem it only fair that we be allowed to try to reclaim the tower, which is rightly ours and which she has basely stolen."

"Losers weepers," said Hiddukel with a chuckle.

"I have as much right to that tower as they do," stated Zeboim. "After all, it is standing in *my* ocean."

"I built it," cried Nuitari, seething. "I raised it up from charred ruins! And you should all of you know," he added with a baleful glance at Chemosh, "that inside that tower, in its depths, is the *Solio Febalas*, the Hall of Sacrilege. Inside that Hall are many holy artifacts and relics thought to have been lost during the Cataclysm. *Your* holy artifacts and relics."

The gods were no longer smiling. They stared at Nuitari in amazement.

"You should have told us that the Hall had been found," said Mishakal, blazing with white flame.

"And you should have told us about Mina," Nuitari returned. He clasped his hands over his black robes. "I say that makes us even."

"Are our blessed objects safe?" Kiri-Jolith demanded.

"I cannot say," Nuitari returned with a shrug. "They were, while the tower under my control. I don't vouch for them now. Especially as the tower was currently being overrun by the Beloved."

The gods turned their gazes onto Chemosh.

"That was not my fault!" he cried. "Those ghoulish fiends are her creations!"

"Enough!" said Gilean. "The only thing this proves is that it is more important now than ever that *all* of us take this oath. Or will each of you risk taking the chance that another might succeed where you fail?"

The gods grumbled, but, in the end, they agreed. They had no choice. Each was forced to take the oath if for no other reason than to make sure the others took it, though each was perhaps privately thinking how he or she might twist it, or at least bend it a little.

"Place your hands on the Book," said Gilean, calling the sacred volume into being, "and swear by your love for the High God who brought us into being, and your fear of Chaos, who would destroy us, that you will neither threaten, cajole, seduce, plead, or bargain with the goddess known as Mina in order to try to influence her decision."

The Gods of Light each placed a hand upon the Book, as did the Gods of Neutrality. When it came the turn of the Gods of Darkness, Sargonnas thumped down his hand, as did Morgion. Zeboim hesitated.

"I'm sure my only concern," she said, dabbing a salt tear from her eye, "is for that poor, unhappy girl. She's like a daughter to me."

"Just swear, damn it," growled Sargonnas.

Zeboim sniffed and put her hand on the Book.

After her, last of all, came Chemosh.

"I so swear," he said.

4

Death had been good to Ausric Krell, and he wanted it back.

Krell had once been a powerful death knight. Cursed by the Sea Goddess, Zeboim, he had known immortality. He could kill with a single word. He was so fearsome and horrible to look upon, in his black armor with the ram's head skull helm, that some poor wretches had dropped down dead of terror at the mere sight of his awful visage.

No longer. When he looked in the mirror, he did not see reflected back the red-glowing eyes of undeath. He saw the squinty pig-eyes of a middle-aged human male with heavy jowls and a sullen brutish face, spindly limbs, flabby flesh, and a paunch. Krell, the death knight, had once reigned supreme on Storm's Keep, a mighty fortress in the north of Ansalon. (At least, that was how he remembered it. In truth, he'd been a prisoner there, and he'd hated it, but not so much as he hated what he was now.)

Of all the undead who walk Krynn, a death knight is one of the most fearsome. Cursed by the gods, a death knight is forced to exist in a world of the living, hating them, even as he fiercely envies them. A death knight is unable to sleep or find rest. He is a prisoner of his own immortality, forced to reflect constantly on his crimes and the wayward passions that brought him to this unhappy state, until he comes to repent and his soul can move onto the next stage of its journey.

That, at least, was the gods' plan.

Unfortunately, with Krell the plan hadn't worked. In life, Krell had been a traitor, a murderer, a thief. He had duped, deceived, destroyed, and betrayed all who had ever trusted him. Possessed of no great intellect, Krell had relied on low cunning, small-minded trickery, a complete lack of conscience, and brute strength to batter his way through life. Krell was a bully and, as with all bullies, he had lived every day in secret terror and died a screaming, craven coward at the hands of the Sea Goddess, Zeboim, who could never forgive him for having slain her beloved son.

Deeming that his torment had been too brief, Zeboim had cursed Krell, transforming him into a death knight, intending he should suffer for eternity. Instead, to her ire, Krell had actually enjoyed undeath. He wielded lethal power with cruel delight. He became the consummate bully, finding pleasure in tormenting and terrorizing and ultimately slaying those mortals who were either foolish or brave enough to encounter him. And he could inflict his punishment without the constant fear that someone bigger and stronger would do the same to him.

True, Zeboim had continued to be a thorn in his skeletal side, but Krell had finally solved that problem. He had sworn to serve Chemosh, Lord of Death, and in return, Chemosh had offered him protection from the Sea Goddess.

And now all that was gone. Death had been snatched from him by that cursed bitch, Mina. He still couldn't understand what had happened. He'd been going to snap her neck. It had all seemed so easy. She had fought him with bestial fury and somehow (he wasn't clear on just how it had happened) she had cursed him by giving him back his life.

Krell was not only alive, he was a prisoner inside his room in Chemosh's castle, fearful of leaving because of the Beloved who roamed the castle and who were thirsting to kill him in a most unpleasant manner. Krell could hear outside his window the rumbling voices of the gods, but he was far too absorbed in bemoaning his own fate to pay much attention to their clamor.

Krell was strong and brutal enough to hold his own against most humans, but he could not fight the Beloved—those heinous undead beings now roaming the castle wailing for Mina. No weapon could kill the Beloved, at least no weapon that Krell had ever found. He had tried to hack them apart with his sword. He had battered them with his fists and even used his formidable magical power on them to no avail. Hacked apart, they put themselves back together and they shook off magic like a duck shakes off water. And now, the Beloved were capable of killing him. Indeed, they seemed to bear him some sort of personal grudge. He'd been forced to throttle a couple of them on his way here, barely managing to escape with his life. Now they lurked about outside his door, keeping him a prisoner in his own bedroom. All this while, outside his window, the gods raged.

Something about Mina being a god . . . Krell snorted, thought it over. True she had done this to him, taken away his power, but he was certain Zeboim was behind it. The two females were in this together. It was a conspiracy against him. He'd get back at the Sea Goddess, and that Mina-bitch, as well.

Such were Krell's brooding thoughts, as he sat in the room, wrapped in a blanket for warmth, for his wonderful, shining, magical armor had vanished. He was thinking with cruel pleasure what he would do to Mina when he finally managed to lay his hands on her when a voice interrupted his blood-drenched day dreams.

"Who's there?" Krell snarled.

"Your master, you dolt," said Chemosh.

"My lord," said Krell, but he said it with a sneer. Once he would have groveled, but he was in no mood to play the toady. Let Chemosh polish his own boots. What had the god done for him? Nothing. Perhaps the Lord of Death had even been in on the plot to destroy him.

"Stop sitting there feeling sorry for yourself," Chemosh said coldly. "You must find Mina."

No one wanted to find Mina more than Ausric Krell. He almost jumped at the chance, but then he checked himself. The Krell of low cunning was back. He could hear in his master's voice an underlying hint of urgency, perhaps even of desperation. Krell could take advantage of the situation to do a little bargaining. He was in a position of power, after all. He had nothing left to lose.

"They say this Mina is now a god, my lord," Krell pointed out. "And *I* am a poor, weak mortal." He gnashed his teeth as he spoke.

"Do this for me and I will make you one of my clerics, Krell. I will give you holy powers—"

"Cleric!" Krell snorted in disgust. "I don't want to be one of your sniveling clerics, running about in a black dress and a fright mask."

"Do not push me, Krell—"

"Or you'll do what to me?" Krell roared angrily. "You came to *me* for help, my lord. If you want my help, change me back into a death knight."

"I can't just 'change' you into a death knight," Chemosh said testily. "It's not like changing one's clothes. It's far more complicated, involves a curse—"

"Then go find Mina yourself," Krell said sullenly.

42

Hunched in his blanket, he stumped over to his bed and sat down.

"I cannot change you into a death knight, but I will grant you the powers of a Bone Acolyte," Chemosh offered.

"A bony what?" Krell asked suspiciously.

"I don't have time to explain! I'm rather busy at the moment. I'm being forced to take a godly oath. But you will be powerful. I promise."

Krell thought this over. Chemosh would have to be true to his word if he wanted Krell to succeed.

"Very well," said Krell grudgingly. "Make me into this Bony Acolyte. Where do I find Mina?"

"I have no idea. She jumped off the battlements into the sea."

"Then you want me to recover her body, my lord?" Krell was disappointed.

"She's a god, you idiot! She can't die! By the Skull, I think I would be better off giving orders to the bed post! I have to leave now—"

"Then where should I start my search, my lord?" Krell demanded, but he received no answer.

Krell had an idea, however. Mina's monk, the one he'd found inside the grotto. Krell had first thought the monk was her lover. Now he wasn't so sure. Still, she seemed to have taken an unusual interest in him. She'd sneaked out of Chemosh's castle to meet up with him in secret in a grotto. Perhaps she'd gone back to find him. The last Krell had seen of the monk, he'd been chained to a wall in the grotto. Not likely he would be going anywhere.

Krell stood up, then realized that he couldn't very well confront Mina wrapped in a blanket.

"My lord!" Krell shouted. "A Bone Acolyte! Remember?"

Chemosh did remember. He granted Krell the powers of a Bone Acolyte and, though he wasn't quite as formidable as he had been when he was death knight, Krell was pleased with the results.

5

*N*ightshade entered the grotto staggering beneath a load of driftwood. He dumped it down on the floor and then stood staring at the girl, who lay unmoving on the cold stones as Rhys chafed her chill hands, trying to warm them. Atta trotted inside, sniffed at the girl, growled, and retreated to a far corner.

"We need tinder to start the fire," said Rhys. "Perhaps some seaweed. If you could hurry . . ."

Muttering under his breath, Nightshade summoned Atta and the two went back out. Rhys hoped he would be quick about his task. The girl's skin was cold and clammy to the touch, her heartbeat slow and sluggish, her lips and fingernails blue. He would have wrapped her in his own robes, but they were as wet as her cotton smock.

He glanced around the grotto that had once been a shrine to Zeboim. An altar to the goddess stood at the far end. He had paid it scant attention when the minotaur had first brought him here. He'd had far more urgent matters to think about, such as being chained to a wall and threatened with torture and death. Now, hoping he might find something of use, he left the child and went back to look at it more closely.

The altar was crudely carved out of a single piece of red-and-black striped granite. A conch shell had been placed reverently on the altar that was adorned with a frayed, sea-green piece of silk. Breathing a prayer of thanks to Majere and another prayer asking forgiveness of Zeboim for defiling her altar, Rhys lifted up the shell, removed the cloth, then carefully put the shell back.

Rhys took off the child's sopping-wet smock, rubbed her dry with the silk cloth, and wrapped her up in it, winding it around her much like the cocoon from which the fabric had been spun. The girl ceased to shiver. Some color came to her pallid cheeks, the blue faded from her lips.

"Thank you, Zeboim," said Rhys softly.

"You're *not* very welcome," said the Sea Goddess, sharply. "Just make certain you scrub my cloth and put it back when you've finished."

Zeboim entered the grotto quietly, subdued—for her—with a only a moderate breeze stirring the blue-green dress that frothed about her bare feet. She cast a bored glance at the girl on the floor.

"Where did you dredge up the kid?"

"I found her washed up on the shore during the storm," Rhys replied, watching the goddess closely.

"Who is she?" Zeboim asked, though she didn't seem to much care.

"I have no idea," Rhys replied. He paused, then said quietly, "Do you know her, Majesty?"

"Me? No, why should I?"

"No reason, Majesty," said Rhys, and he breathed a sigh of relief. Nightshade must have been mistaken.

Stepping over the girl, Zeboim came to Rhys and knelt down before him. She reached out with her hand, caressed his cheek.

"My own dear monk!" she said in dulcet tones. "I am so glad to see you safe and sound! I've been consumed with worry for you."

"I thank you for your concern, Majesty," said Rhys warily. "How may I serve you?"

"Serve me?" Zeboim was dismayed. "No, no. I came merely to inquire about your health. Where is your friend, the . . . um . . . dear little kender. And that mutt. Dog. I mean, dog. Sweet dog. Oh, my dear monk, you're so cold and wet. Let me warm you."

Zeboim fussed about him. Drying his robes with a touch of her hand, she lit the pile of driftwood with a flick of her finger. All the while, Rhys waited in silence, not fooled by her blandishments. The last he'd seen of the Sea Goddess, she had told him she would watch in glee as Mina put him to death.

"There, isn't that better?" Zeboim asked solicitously.

"Thank you, Majesty," Rhys said.

"Is there anything else I can do for you—"

"Perhaps tell me why you've come," Rhys suggested.

Zeboim looked annoyed, then said abruptly, "Oh, very well. If you must know, I'm looking for Mina. It occurred to me she may have come to you, seeing that she found you interesting. I'm sure I don't know why. *I* think you're as dull as dishwater. But Mina couldn't stop talking about you, and I thought she might be here."

She glanced about the grotto, and shrugged. "It seems I was mistaken. If you see her, you will let me know. For all the grand times we had together—"

As she started to leave, her gaze fell again on the child wrapped in the altar cloth. Zeboim halted, staring.

The girl lay on her side, curled up in a ball. Her face was hidden by the cloth, but her tangled red braids were clearly visible in the firelight. The goddess looked at the girl, then she looked at Rhys.

Zeboim gasped. Swooping down on the girl, the Sea Goddess grasped hold of the altar cloth and dragged it from the child's face.

Zeboim grasped the girl's chin and wrenched her face to the firelight. The girl woke with a cry.

"Stop it!" said Rhys sharply, intervening. "You're hurting her."

Zeboim laughed wildly. "Hurt her? I couldn't hurt her if I drove a stake through her heart! Did Majere do this? Does he think he can hide her from me with this stupid disguise—"

"Majesty—" Rhys began.

"Ouch!" Zeboim cried, snatching back her hand. She glared down at the child in shock. "She *bit* me!"

"Come near me and I'll bite you again!" the girl cried. "I don't like you! Go away."

She wrapped herself more snugly in the altar cloth, curled into a ball, and closed her eyes.

Zeboim sucked her bleeding hand and regarded her intently.

"Don't you know me, child?" she asked. "I'm Zeboim. We're friends, you and I."

"I never saw you before," said the girl.

"Majesty," said Rhys uneasily, "who is this girl? You seem to know her."

"Don't play games with me, monk," said Zeboim.

"I am not playing a game, Majesty," said Rhys earnestly.

Zeboim shifted her gaze to him. "You're telling the truth. You truly don't know." She gestured at the slumbering child. "She is Mina. Or rather, she *was* Mina. I have no idea who she thinks she is now."

"I do not understand, Majesty," said Rhys.

"You're not alone," the goddess said grimly. "Where did you find her?"

"She was in the sea during the storm. She nearly drowned—"

"In the sea?" Zeboim repeated, and she added in a murmur. "Of course! She jumped from the wall into the sea. And she came to you, the monk who knew her . . ."

"Majesty," said Rhys, "you need to tell me what is going on."

Zeboim eyed him. "My poor monk. It would be immense fun to walk out and leave you floundering in ignorance, but not even I am *that* cruel. I don't have time to go into details, but I will tell you this much. This girl, this child, this Mina is a god. She is a god who does not know she is a god, a god who was tricked by Takhisis into thinking she was human. What's more, she is a god of light who was duped into serving darkness. Are you keeping up with me so far?"

Rhys stared at her, dumbstruck.

"I can see you're not." Zeboim shrugged. "Well, it doesn't much matter. You're stuck with her. To continue my story, poor Mina had the misfortune to fall in love with Chemosh and—just like a man—he broke her heart. Mina tried to win him back by giving him a gift. She dragged the Tower of High Sorcery up out of my sea and stuck it on that island out there. We were all very impressed. That was the first hint most of us had that she was a god. Majere, of course, already knew."

"I don't believe . . . I *can't* believe . . ." Rhys paused, recalling the name of the place she had referred to as home. "If what you say is true, Majesty, how did she come to be like this? A child?"

"The gods only know," said Zeboim. "No, wait. I take that back. We gods haven't a clue. You think I'm lying, don't you?"

Rhys was embarrassed. "Majesty—"

She grasped hold of his arm, digging her nails through the fabric of his robes into his flesh. Staring into his eyes, past his eyes, into his very soul, she hissed at him.

"Believe me or not, as you choose. As I said, it doesn't matter. Mina came to you. What I want to know is . . . why? Did Majere send her to you? We took an oath, all of us. We're not supposed to interfere. Did Majere break that oath?"

Rhys realized in that instant that Zeboim was telling the truth, and a shudder ran through him. He looked past the goddess at the forlorn little girl, wrapped in a frayed altar cloth, asleep on the cold, damp floor of a cave, and he remembered her floundering in the waves of the god-driven storm. He did not understand the workings of heaven, but he did know something of the suffering of mortals.

"Perhaps she came because she is alone and afraid," said Rhys, "and she needed a friend."

Zeboim tore Rhys apart with her gaze, studied the pieces, then hurled him away from her, sent him staggering back against the stone wall.

"Good luck with your new little friend, then, Monk."

The Sea Goddess vanished in a blast of wind and rain.

Shaken, Rhys gazed down at the child.

"Majere," he prayed, troubled, "is it your will that I undertake this task?"

"Rhys!" yelled a voice, and Rhys was momentarily startled. Then he realized the voice belonged to Nightshade.

"Rhys! Is it safe to come in?" the kender yelled from outside the grotto. "Is Zeboim gone?"

"She is gone." For the time being, Rhys added mentally, certain this was not the last they would see of her.

Nightshade entered cautiously, staring hard into the shadows as though certain she would jump out at him. Then he saw the fire and he snapped his fingers.

"Oops, I knew I forgot something. I was supposed to go fetch tinder—"

"No need now," said Rhys, smiling.

"Yeah, I can see that. I guess I forgot about the tinder because I was so excited about finding something else. I didn't want to bring it in if you-know-who was still here. But since she's gone, I'll go get it."

He darted out of the grotto and returned carrying a long, slender piece of driftwood. He held it out proudly.

"I found it washed up on shore. Doesn't it remind you of your old staff? The emetic or whatever it was you called it? Anyway, Atta and I thought you might be able to use it."

"Emmide," said Rhys softly. He took hold of the staff, clasped his fingers around it. A pleasant warmth stole into his arm and spread throughout his body. And it was in this warmth that he heard the god's voice, knew Majere's answer.

Rhys rested the staff against the wall and spread the girl's wet smock near the fire to dry. She slept deeply, her breathing even and quiet. He sank down onto the floor and leaned back against the wall. He was exhausted, mentally and physically. He couldn't remember the last time he'd slept.

"I heard Zeboim yelling at you. What did she want?" Nightshade asked.

"You and Atta were right. This little girl is Mina," said Rhys. He closed his eyes.

"Whoo boy!" breathed Nightshade.

He removed his pouches, then took off his boots and emptied out the water and arranged them close to the blaze to dry off.

"My boots still smell of salt pork," he said. "Which reminds me. It's been a long time since dinner. I wonder if there's any of that pork left."

He went over to the barrel of salt pork the minotaur had left them for food and peered inside. Atta watched him hopefully. He shook his head, and the dog's ears drooped.

"Oh, well. I guess we can wait until lunch, can't we, girl?" Nightshade said, giving her a pat. "Say, Rhys, did Zeboim tell you how Mina turned into a little kid? I've heard of people aging ten years overnight, but never the other way around. Did the goddess have something to do with that? Did she? Rhys?"

The kender poked him. "Rhys, are you asleep?"

"What?" Rhys woke with a start.

"Sorry," said Nightshade remorsefully. "I didn't mean to wake you."

"That's all right. I didn't mean to fall asleep. What was your question?" Rhys asked patiently.

"I was asking if Zeboim did this. She seems fond of shrinking people." The kender was still bitter over the time the goddess had reduced him to the size of a khas piece and stuffed him inside Rhys's pouch, then sent them both off to fight a death knight.

Rhys shook his head. "The Sea Goddess was shocked to see Mina as a child."

"So what did she say happened?"

"According to Zeboim, Mina is a god who doesn't know she's a god. A god who was tricked by Takhisis into thinking she was human. Mina is a god of light, duped into serving Darkness."

Nightshade regarded Rhys with narrowed eyes. "Did you hit your head again?"

"I'm fine," Rhys assured him.

"Mina a god." Nightshade snorted. "If you ask me, it's all a bunch of hooey. Zeboim did this. She turned Mina into a little kid and sent her to us just to annoy us."

"I don't think so," Rhys said quietly. "Mina woke up while you were gone. She told me she had run away from home and she asked me to take her back."

Nightshade found this news cheering. "See there? Where does the kid want to go? Flotsam? It's not far, just up the coast. She probably got swept out to sea—"

"Godshome," said Rhys.

Nightshade's brow wrinkled. "Godshome? That's not a place. No one lives in Godshome except the—"

He gulped, and his eyes got round, and he gave a low whistle that made Atta's ear twitch.

"I don't think Zeboim told her to say *that*," Rhys added with a sigh.

Nightshade looked at Mina and chewed his lower lip. Suddenly, he brightened.

"I'll bet you heard her wrong. I'll bet she said 'Goat's Home'."

"Goat's Home?" Rhys repeated, smiling. "I have never heard of such a place, my friend."

"You don't know everything," Nightshade stated, "even if you are a monk. There are lots and lots of places you've never heard of."

"I *have* heard of Godshome," Rhys said.

"Stop saying that!" Nightshade ordered. "You know we're not going there. It's not possible."

"Why?" Rhys yawned again.

"Well, for one reason because nobody knows where Godshome is, or even *if* Godshome is. And for two reasons, if Godshome is anywhere, it's close to Neraka, and that's a bad place, a *very* bad place. And for three reasons, if Godshome is close to Neraka, that means it's far from here—clear on the other side of the continent—and it would take us months, maybe years, to travel . . ."

Nightshade stopped. "Rhys? Rhys! Are you listening to my reasons?"

Rhys wasn't. He sat with his back against the wall, his head slumped forward, his chin resting on his chest. He was asleep, fast asleep, so deeply asleep that the kender's voice and even a couple of pokes on the arm could not wake him.

Nightshade sighed and then he stood up and walked over to the little girl and squatted down to stare at her closely. She certainly didn't look like a god. She looked like a drowned rat. He felt again the overwhelming sadness that he had felt when he'd seen Mina, the grown-up Mina. He didn't like that, and so he wiped his eyes and nose on his sleeve and then glanced back surreptitiously at Rhys.

His friend was still asleep and would probably sleep for a good long time. Long enough for Nightshade to have a talk with this kid—whoever she was—and tell her that where she really wanted to go was the thriving metropolis of Goat's Home and that she should travel there on her own, and she should leave now very quietly so as not to disturb Rhys.

"Hey, kid," Nightshade whispered loudly, and he reached out his hand to shake her awake.

His hand hung, poised, in midair. His fingers started to tremble a little at the thought of actually touching her, and he snatched his hand back. He continued to squat there, gazing at Mina and chewing on his lip.

What did he see when he looked at her? What made her different in his sight from other mortals? What made her different from the dead he could see and talk to? What made her different from the undead? Nightshade looked intently at the child, and tears again flooded his eyes. He saw beauty, unimaginable beauty. Beauty that shamed the most radiant, glorious sunrise and made the glittering stars seem pale and plain in comparison. Her beauty made his very soul stand still in awe, for fear the slightest whisper might cause the wondrous sight to slip away from him. But it wasn't her beauty that wrenched his heart and caused the tears to roll down his cheeks.

Her beauty was clothed in ugliness. She was smeared with blood, cloaked in the shroud of death and destruction. Evil, dread and horrible, was a pall over her.

"She *is* a god," he said under his breath. "A god of light who's done really horrible things. I've known it all along. I just didn't know I knew it. That's what made me feel all weepy inside."

Nightshade didn't think he could explain this to Rhys, because he wasn't sure he could explain it to himself. He decided to talk it all over with Atta. He'd found that telling things to a dog was a lot easier than telling things to humans, mainly because Atta never asked questions.

But when he turned around to discuss Mina with Atta, he saw that the dog had rolled onto her side and was deep in slumber.

Nightshade slumped against the wall beside Rhys. The kender was sitting there, thinking mind-boggling thoughts, and listening to Rhys's soft breathing, and the girl's soft breathing, and Atta's soft breathing, and the wind's soft breathing, sighing over the sand dunes, and the waves coming to shore and leaving the shore and coming back to the shore and leaving the shore . . .

55

6

Nightshade woke suddenly, jolted awake by Atta's bark.

Atta was on her feet. Her legs were stiff, her hackles raised, and she was staring intently at the opening of the grotto. Nightshade could hear the sounds of crunching, as of heavy footfalls walking in their direction.

They were close and getting closer.

Atta gave another sharp, warning bark. Mina stirred at the sound and drew the cloth over her head and went back to sleep. The heavy crunching noise stopped. A shadow fell over the entrance, blotting out the sun.

"Monk! I know you're in there."

That voice was muffled, yet Nightshade had no trouble recognizing it.

"Krell!" he yelped. "Rhys, it's Krell!"

Nightshade was as immune to fear as the next kender, but he was also blessed with a good deal more common sense than most kender; a fact which he attributed to spending a lot of his time conversing with the dead. And so, instead of rushing out to greet the death knight, as any other kender would have done, Nightshade scuttled backward on all fours and yelled again for Rhys.

"I am awake," said Rhys calmly.

He was on his feet, the emmide in his hands.

"Atta, silence. Here."

The dog trotted over to stand beside him. She no longer barked, though she continued to growl.

Krell swaggered into the grotto. He was no longer wearing the accursed armor of a death knight. His armor was that of death. His helm was a ram's skull. The horns curled back from his head, and his eyes were visible inside the skull's eye sockets. His breastplate was made of bone—the top part of the skull of some gigantic beast. His arms and legs were encased in bone, as if he wore his skeleton on the outside of his body. Bony spines protruded from his hands and elbows and shoulders, and he carried a sword with a bone hilt.

He was a formidable sight, yet the eyes that glared out from behind the ram's skull did not burn with the terrifying fire of undeath. His eyes were dull and flat. He did not stink of death. He just stank; he was sweating under the weight of his armor. His breath rasped, for the armor was heavy, and he'd been forced to walk all the way from the castle.

Nightshade quit crawling and sat back on his heels.

"Krell, you're alive!" said Nightshade, though he was not sure this was an improvement. "You're not a death knight anymore."

"Shut up!" Krell snarled. He looked searchingly around the grotto, glanced without interest at the sleeping child, glared at the kender, then turned back to Rhys. "I've come for Mina. In the name of my lord Chemosh, I demand to know where she is."

"Not here," said Nightshade promptly. "We don't know where she is. We haven't seen her, have we, Rhys?"

Rhys was silent.

Krell's eyes narrowed. Though dimly lit, the grotto wasn't very big and there were no nooks or crannies where someone could hide.

"Where's Mina?" Krell asked again.

"You can see for yourself," said Nightshade loudly. "She's not here."

"Then where is she?" Krell demanded. He kept his gaze on Rhys. "Remember the last time we met, Monk? Remember what I did to you? I broke almost every bone in your hand. Now I won't waste time breaking bones. I'll just cut your hand off the wrist—"

Krell drew his sword and took a step toward Rhys.

"Atta, stop—" Rhys began, but he was too late.

Atta lunged at Krell and sank her teeth into his calf muscle, a part of his leg left unprotected by the bone shin-guards.

Krell howled in pain and, twisting around, he peered down at his leg. Blood oozed from two rows of tooth marks. He snarled in rage and tried to slash at the dog with his sword. As Atta leaped deftly out of the way, Rhys blocked Krell's blow with his staff.

Krell snorted in derision and hacked at the staff with his blade, thinking to snap it. Rhys swiftly raised the staff and slammed it into Krell's hand, knocking the sword from his grasp. Krell wrung his fingers and glared at Rhys, who had taken a step backward.

Krell bent down to retrieve his blade.

"Atta, guard," said Rhys.

Atta crouched over the sword. Her lip curled back from her teeth, and she snapped viciously at Krell's hand. He snatched it back, his fingers bloody.

"I think you should leave now," Rhys said. "Tell your master that the Mina he seeks is not with me."

"You're a rotten liar, Monk!" Krell said. His breath from the skull helm was foul. "You know where she is and you'll tell me. You'll be begging to tell me! I don't need a sword to kill you in any number of nasty ways."

Rhys did not feel fear, as he had felt before in the presence of the death knight. He felt disgust, revulsion.

Krell was not driven to kill by a holy curse. Krell killed now for small, mean reasons. He killed because he reveled in the pain and fear of his victim, and because he liked holding the power of life and death in his grubby hands.

"Atta," Rhys said calmly, "go to Nightshade."

The kender grabbed hold of the growling dog and clamped his hand over her muzzle.

"Let Rhys handle this," he whispered.

"I just have to say a word to Chemosh, Monk," said Krell. "And he'll flay the flesh from your bones, for starters—"

Rhys gripped his staff firmly, holding it upright before him, his hands clasped over it. He had no idea if this staff was blessed as had been his other staff. Perhaps it was. Perhaps not. He knew Majere stood with him. He could feel the god as a core of peace and calm and tranquility.

The gleam in Krell's eyes turned ugly.

"You'll tell me."

He walked over to the girl, who had slept through the commotion, and reaching down, grabbed hold of the child by the hair and yanked her from her slumber.

Mina gasped and cried out. Wriggling in Krell's grasp, she tried to free herself.

Krell gripped her tightly and put his huge hand to her throat.

Mina gave a little whimper and went rigid and stiff in the man's grasp.

"I always did like 'em young," Krell chortled. "Here's a hint of what will happen to the girl if you don't talk, Monk."

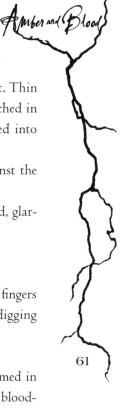

Krell dug long, yellow, skeleton-like nails into Mina's throat. Thin trails of blood trickled from the cuts in her flesh. Mina flinched in pain, but she didn't make a sound. Her amber eyes hardened into fixed resolve.

"Uh-oh," said Nightshade, and he dragged Atta back against the wall.

"I'll cut deeper next time. Where is Mina?" Krell demanded, glaring at Rhys.

But it was Mina who answered.

"Right here," she said.

She seized hold of the bone bracers on his arm and dug her fingers into them. The bracers split and cracked and fell off. She kept digging deeper and blood started to well up from beneath her fingers.

Krell grunted in pain and tried to wrench his arm free.

Mina gave his arm a twist. Bones snapped, and Krell screamed in agony and, moaning, sagged to his knees. The jagged edges of blood-covered bone could be seen jutting out from blue-tinged, bloody flesh.

Mina glared at him.

"You hurt me. You're a bad man." She wrinkled her nose. "And you smell. I don't like you. My name is Mina. What do you want with me?"

"This is some sort of trick—" he snarled.

"Answer me!" Mina kicked him on his armor-covered thigh. The bone armor split in two.

Krell groaned. "Chemosh sent me . . ."

"Chemosh. I don't know any Chemosh," said Mina. "And if he's a friend of yours, I don't want to know him. Go away and don't come back."

"I don't know what's going on," Krell said savagely. "But that doesn't matter. I'll let the master figure it out."

With his good arm, he seized hold of Mina's hand and roared, "Chemosh! I have her—"

Rhys leaped, swinging his staff at Krell's head. The emmide whistled through empty air. Rhys lowered the staff, staring about in amazement. Krell had vanished.

"Rhys," cried Nightshade in strangled tones. "Look up."

The kender pointed.

Krell hung upside down, suspended from the ceiling of the grotto from a length of rope tied around his boot. His ram's skull helm had fallen off and now lay on the floor at Mina's feet.

Krell's eyes bulged. His mouth gaped open and shut. His broken arm dangled helplessly. He struggled, kicking his foot, but only succeeded in twisting round and round in midair.

Mina looked up at Rhys.

"I'm not sleepy anymore. It's time to go."

Rhys gazed up at Krell, twisting and turning on his god-spun thread, demanding, begging Chemosh to come save him. Rhys looked at Nightshade, who was staring at Mina with awestruck eyes—and it is not easy to strike awe into a kender.

Mina reached out and took hold of Rhys's hand.

"You're going to take me home, Mister Monk," she reminded him. "You promised."

Rhys could not answer. A smothering sensation in his chest made it hard to breathe. He was starting to realize the enormity of the task that he had undertaken.

"C'mon, Mister Monk!" Mina tugged at him impatiently.

"My name is Rhys Mason," Rhys said, trying to speak in normal tones. "And this is my friend, Nightshade."

"P-pleased to meet you," said Nightshade faintly.

"What's the dog's name?" Mina asked. She reached down to pet

Atta, who cringed at the god-child's touch and would have crawled off, but Nightshade had hold of her. "She's a nice dog. I like her. She bit the bad man."

"Her name is Atta." Rhys drew in a deep breath. He knelt down, putting himself at eye-level with her. "Mina, why do you want to go to Godshome?"

"Because that's where my mother is," Mina answered. "She's waiting for me there."

"What is your mother's name?" Rhys asked.

"Goldmoon," said Mina.

Nightshade made a choking sound.

"My mother's name is Goldmoon," Mina was saying, "and she's waiting for me at Godshome, and you're going to take me to her."

"Rhys," said Nightshade, "could I have a word? In private?"

"Aren't we going now?" Mina asked impatiently.

"In a minute," said Rhys.

"Oh, all right. I'll go play outside," Mina stated. "Can the dog come with me?" She ran to the entrance of the grotto and turned to call, "Atta! Come, Atta!"

Rhys made a sign with his hand. Atta cast him a reproachful glance, then, her ears drooping, she slunk out of the cave.

"Rhys"—Nightshade pounced on him—"what in the name of Chemosh, Mishakal, Chislev, Sargonnas, Gilean, Hiddukel, Morgion and . . . and all the other gods I can't think of right at the moment, what do you think you're doing?"

Rhys picked up Nightshade's boots and held them out to him.

Nightshade shoved the boots aside.

"Rhys, that little girl is a god! Not only that, she's a god *who has lost her bloody mind!*" Nightshade waved his arms to emphasize his words. "She wants us to take her to Godshome—a place that maybe doesn't even exist to meet Goldmoon—a woman who's been dead for years! That girl is crackers, Rhys! Cuckoo! Looney! Off her rocker!"

"Chemosh," Krell was howling. "You son-of-a-bitch! Come get me out of here!"

Nightshade jerked his thumb upward.

"What happens when Mina gets mad at *us?* Maybe she'll shoot us off to a moon and leave us stranded there. Or pick up a mountain and drop it on top of our heads. Or feed us to a dragon."

"I made a promise," said Rhys.

Nightshade sighed and, sitting down, he pulled on one of his boots and tugged.

"You made that promise before you knew all the facts," Nightshade stated, pulling on the other boot. "Do you even know where Godshome is—that is, *if* it is?"

"Legend holds that Godshome is in the Khalkist mountains, somewhere near Neraka," Rhys replied.

"Oh, well, that's all right," Nightshade grumbled. "Neraka is the most horrible, evil place on the continent. Not to mention that it's on the *other side of the world.*"

"Not quite that far," said Rhys, smiling.

They left the grotto, where Krell was still hanging from the ceiling, twisting and swearing. Chemosh appeared to be in no hurry to rescue his champion.

"In my opinion, you were hoodwinked," Nightshade continued. He halted at the entrance, looking up at his friend. "Rhys, I want you to consider one thing."

"What's that, my friend?"

"Our story is over, Rhys," said Nightshade earnestly. "We had a happy ending—you and me and Atta. Let's close the book and go home."

The kender gestured to Mina, who was running among the sand dunes, laughing wildly. "This is god-business, Rhys. We shouldn't be getting mixed up in it."

"A wise person once told me, 'You can't quit a god,' " said Rhys.

"The person who said that to you was a kender," Nightshade returned grumpily. "And you know you can't trust them."

"I trusted one with my life," said Rhys, resting his hand on Nightshade's head. "And he did not let me down."

"Well, then, you got lucky," Nightshade muttered. He shoved his hands in his pockets and kicked at a rock.

"My story is not finished. No one's story is ever really finished. Death is just the turning of another page. But you are right, my friend," Rhys said with an involuntary sigh. "Traveling with her will be dangerous and difficult. Your story may not be finished, but perhaps now you should turn the page, take a different path."

Nightshade thought this over. "Are you sure Majere won't help me pick locks?"

"I cannot say for certain," Rhys replied, "but I really doubt it."

Nightshade shrugged. "Then I guess I'll stay with you. Otherwise I'd starve."

He grinned and winked. "I'm only fooling, Rhys! You know I'd never leave you and Atta. What would you two do without me? You'd get yourselves killed by crazy gods!"

That may yet be the end of our tale, Rhys thought. Chemosh will not be the only god seeking Mina.

He kept the thought to himself, however, and, whistling to Atta, he gave his hand to Mina, who came skipping up to him.

7

Mina set off, but she did not head toward the road. She started walking toward the sea.

"I thought you wanted to go to Godshome," said Nightshade, who was not in a good mood. "What are you going to do? Swim there?"

"Oh, we'll go to Godshome," said Mina. "But first I want you to come with me to the tower."

"Which tower?" Nightshade asked. "There are lots of towers in the world. There's a very famous tower in Nightlund. I've always wanted to visit Nightlund, because it is filled with the roving spirits of the dead. I can talk to roving spirits, if you ever—"

"That tower." Mina added proudly, *"My* tower."

She pointed to the tower that stood in the middle of the Blood Sea.

"Why do you want to go there?" Rhys asked.

"Because she's crazy," Nightshade said in a low voice.

Rhys gave him a look, and the kender lapsed into a gloomy silence. Mina stood gazing out across the sea.

"My mother will be mad at me for running away," Mina said. "I want to bring Goldmoon a present so she will forgive me."

Rhys recalled Revered Son Patrick, cleric of Mishakal, telling the story of Goldmoon and Mina. After Mina ran away, Goldmoon had grieved for the lost girl and hoped someday she would return. Then came Takhisis, the One God, and the War of Souls began with Mina leading the armies of darkness. Hoping to turn Goldmoon, who was now an elderly, frail woman, to the side of Darkness, Takhisis gave Goldmoon youth and beauty. Goldmoon did not want her youth back. She was ready to die, to proceed on the next stage of her life's journey where her beloved, Riverwind, waited for her. Though Mina tried to persuade Goldmoon to change her mind, Goldmoon defied Takhisis and died in Mina's arms.

Goldmoon must have died in sorrow, Rhys realized, believing the child she had loved was lost forever, bound to evil. No wonder Mina had obliterated that memory.

He determined he should at least make the attempt to help her understand the truth.

"Mina," said Rhys, taking hold of the child's hand, "Goldmoon is dead. She died many, many months ago—"

"You're wrong," said Mina serenely, speaking with unwavering certainty. "Goldmoon is waiting for me at Godshome. That's why I'm going there. To beg her not to be mad at me anymore. I will take her a present so she will love me again."

"Goldmoon never stopped loving you, Mina," said Rhys. "Mothers don't ever stop loving their children."

Mina looked back at him, her eyes wide. "Not even if they do bad things? Really, really bad things?"

Rhys was caught off guard by her question. If this was truly madness, it held a strange and terrible wisdom.

He rested his hand on her slender shoulder. "Not even then."

"Maybe so," said Mina, though she sounded doubtful. "But you can't be sure, and so I want to take Goldmoon a present. And the present I want to take her is inside that tower."

"What sort of tower is it?" Nightshade asked, his curiosity getting the best of him. "Where did it come from?"

"It didn't *come* from anywhere, stupid," Mina scoffed. "It's always been there."

"No, it hasn't," argued Nightshade.

"Yes, it has."

"No——" Nightshade caught Rhys's eye and changed the subject. "So who built it, if it's been there all this time?"

"Wizards built it. It used to be a Tower of High Sorcery. But it's my tower now." Mina flashed Nightshade a defiant glance, daring him to disagree. "And Goldmoon's present is inside."

"A Tower of High Sorcery!" Nightshade gasped, his jaw sagging. "Are there wizards inside it?"

Mina shrugged. "I guess. I don't know. Wizards are stupid anyway, so it doesn't matter. What are we waiting for? Let's go."

"The tower is the middle of the sea, Mina," Rhys said. "We don't have a boat——"

"That's right!" Nightshade struck in happily. "We'd love to visit your tower, Mina, but we can't. No boat! Say, is anyone else hungry? I hear there's an inn in Flotsam that makes a really good meat pie——"

"There's a boat," Mina interrupted. "Behind you."

Nightshade looked over his shoulder. Sure enough, a small sailboat rested on its keel on the shore, not fifteen paces from where they were standing.

"Rhys, do something," said Nightshade out of the corner of his mouth. "You and I both know there wasn't a boat there a second ago. I don't want to sail in a boat that didn't used to be there . . ."

Mina began tugging Rhys excitedly toward the sail boat. Nightshade, sighing deeply, followed, dragging his feet.

"Do you even know how to sail this thing?" he asked. "I'll bet you don't."

"I bet I do," she answered smugly. "I learned at the Citadel."

Nightshade sighed again. Mina climbed inside the boat and began to rummage around, sorting out a tangle of ropes and instructing Rhys on how to raise the sail. Nightshade stood beside the boat, his lower lip thrust out.

Mina regarded him thoughtfully for a moment. "You said you were hungry. Someone might have left food in the boat. I'll look." She felt about under one of the wooden plank seats and came up holding a large sack.

"I was right!" she announced, pleased. "See what I found."

She reached into the sack and took out a meat pie, and handed it to Nightshade.

He did not touch it. It looked like a meat pie and it certainly smelled like a meat pie. Both his mouth and his stomach agreed this was definitely a meat pie, and Atta added her vote, as well. The dog eyed the pie and licked her chops.

"You *said* you were hungry," Mina reminded him.

Still, Nightshade hesitated. "I don't know . . ."

Atta took matters into her own hands—or rather into her mouth. A leap, a snap, a couple of gulps, and the meat pie was a grease smear on her nose.

"Hey!" cried Nightshade indignantly. "That was mine."

Atta slurped her tongue over her nose and began to hungrily paw the sack. Rhys rescued the remainder of the pies and handed them out. Mina nibbled on hers and ended up feeding most of it to Atta. Nightshade ate his hungrily and, finding Rhys could not finish his, the kender ate it for him. He helped Rhys hoist the sail and, acting under Mina's direction, pushed the boat out into the waves.

Mina took the tiller and steered the boat into the wind. The waves had calmed. A light breeze caught the sail, and the boat glided over the waves, heading out to sea. Atta crouched at the bottom, nosing the sack hopefully.

"For a god-baked pie, that wasn't bad," Nightshade remarked, falling down onto the seat beside Rhys when the sailboat took an unexpected lurch. "Maybe a little less onion and more garlic. Next I think I'll ask her to cook up some beef steak with crispy potatoes—"

"We should be very careful *not* to ask for anything," Rhys suggested.

Nightshade mulled this over.

"Yeah, I guess you're right. We might get it." The kender shifted his gaze to the tower. "What do you know about Towers of High Sorcery?"

Rhys shook his head. "Not much, I am afraid."

"Me neither. And I have to say I'm not really looking forward to the experience. Wizards don't like kender for some reason. They might turn me into a frog."

"Mistress Jenna liked you," Rhys reminded him.

"That's true. All she did was slap my hand."

Nightshade caught hold of the gunwale as the boat gave another sudden lurch. They were sailing quite fast now, bounding over the waves, and the tower was coming nearer. It looked extremely dark. Not even the bright sunlight shining on the crystal walls seemed to be able to brighten it.

"I suppose most kender would give their topknots to visit a Tower of High Sorcery, but then I guess I'm not most kender," Nightshade remarked. "My father said I wasn't. He said it came from spending my time in graveyards talking to the dead. They were a bad influence on me." Nightshade looked at little downcast at this.

"I think most kender would give their topknots to be able to do that," Rhys told him.

Nightshade scratched his head. He'd never considered this. "You know. You might be right. Why, I remember once meeting a fellow kender in Solace, and when I told him I was a Nightstalker, he said—"

Nightshade stopped talking. He stared out to sea. Blinking, he rubbed his eyes, stared again, then tugged on Rhys's sleeve.

"There are people out there in the water ..." Nightshade cried. "Maybe they're drowning! We have to help save them!"

Alarmed, Rhys risked standing up in the rocking boat to gain a better view. At first all he could see were sea birds and the occasional frothy white cap. Then he saw a person in the water, and then another, and still another.

"Mina!" Nightshade cried. "Steer the boat over to those people—"

"No, don't," Rhys said suddenly.

The people were far from shore, yet they were swimming strongly, not floundering or flailing. Hundreds of them, swimming, far from shore, heading for the tower ...

"Rhys!" Nightshade cried. "Rhys, they're Beloved and they're swimming to the tower. Mina, stop! Turn the boat around!"

Mina shook her head. Her amber eyes gleamed with pleasure, her lips were parted in a smile, and she laughed for no other reason than pure joy. The sail boat traveled faster, seeming to leap over the waves.

"Mina!" Rhys called urgently. "Turn the boat around!"

She looked at him and smiled and waved.

"Those people are dangerous!" he cried, and he jabbed his finger in the direction of the undead, some of whom had reached the tower and were crawling onto the shore. He could see many more clustering around the entrance. "We must turn back!"

Mina stared at the Beloved in bewilderment, which quickly changed to dismay and then to anger.

"They have no business going to my tower," she said and she steered the boat straight toward them.

"Rhys!" Nightshade howled.

"There's nothing I can do," Rhys said, and for the first time he truly understood the dire peril of their situation.

How could he control a six-year-old girl who could suspend a minion of Chemosh by his heels from a ceiling, summon up a sailboat, and produce meat pies on a whim?

He was suddenly angry. Why didn't the gods themselves deal with her? Why dump this in his lap?

The boat shifted suddenly. The emmide, which had been lying on the seat beside him, rolled up against his hand. He grasped it and, though the staff was wet and slick with salt spray, he felt again a comforting warmth. One god, at least, had his reasons . . .

"Rhys! We're getting closer!" Nightshade warned.

They were quite close to the tower now. The Beloved had already overrun the island, which was not very large, and more were arriving all the time. Some swam. Some crawled up out of the sea as though they had walked along the ocean floor They climbed over the rocks, sometimes slipping and falling back into the water, but always returning. They were mostly human, young and strong, and all of them were dead, yet horribly alive, chained to a world of unendurable pain, victims of Mina's terrible kiss. Rhys's heart ached to see them.

"What are all you people doing there?" Mina cried angrily. "This is *my* tower."

She gave the rudder a twitch, took the boat out of the wind. The sail sagged and flapped, and the boat glided on its own momentum into

73

the rock-bound shore. Rhys feared for a moment they would crash, but Mina proved a deft sailor, and she guided them to a safe landing among the rocks and coral and dripping seaweed.

"Hand me that line," Mina said, jumping lightly onto shore, "so I can tie up the boat."

"Rhys! What are you doing?" Nightshade cried, aghast. "Cast off! Sail away! We can't stay here! They'll kill us!"

The emmide was still warm in Rhys's hand. He remembered his thought: her madness held a terrible wisdom. This was something she needed to do, seemingly. And he had promised. She was in no danger. She could not die. He wondered if she understood that he and Nightshade could.

From his vantage point, Rhys could see his reflection in the tower's glistening black crystal walls. The entrance to the tower was only about a hundred paces away and the door stood open. Many of the Beloved must already be inside. Several hundred Beloved remained on the island, milling about aimlessly. Some of these, catching sight of the boat, turned to stare with their empty eyes.

"Too late!" Nightshade groaned. "They've seen us."

Rhys hurriedly tied up the boat and, taking his staff, went to stand beside Mina. Nightshade helped Atta out of the boat, then he grabbed a boat hook and slowly and reluctantly followed Rhys.

"I could be in some nice graveyard about now," the kender said dolefully, "visiting with any number of *pleasant* dead people . . ."

"Mina!" One of the Beloved cried out her name and "Mina!" said another. The name spread among them. The Beloved began running toward the boat.

"How do they know me?" Mina quavered. She shrank back fearfully, pressing up against Rhys. "Why do they stare at me with their horrible eyes?"

The Beloved thronged around her, reaching out their hands to her, calling her name.

"I hate them! Make them go away!" Mina pleaded, turning away and burying her head in Rhys's robes. "Make them go away!"

"Mina! Mina, touch me," the Beloved begged her, stretching out their hands to her. "You made me what I am!"

One of the Beloved grabbed Mina's arm, and she shrieked in a frenzy of panic. Rhys could not keep hold of Mina and, at the same time, fight off the Beloved. He had all he could do to retain the writhing, screaming child. He flung the emmide to Nightshade.

"It's blessed by the god!" Rhys cried.

The kender understood. He dropped the boat hook and caught the staff. Swinging it like a club, he brought it down with all his might on the Beloved's wrist.

At the staff's touch, the flesh on the Beloved's hand blackened and dropped off from the bone, leaving behind a skeletal hand that unfortunately retained its grasp. Bony fingers still clawed at Mina's arm.

"That was a big help!" Nightshade shouted, casting the heavens an irate glance. "I should think a god could do better than that!"

More Beloved began crowding about. Nightshade struck at them with the staff, trying to beat them off and not having much luck. The fact that globs of flesh were turning black and falling off their bones didn't seem to bother them in the least. They kept coming and Nightshade kept swinging. His arms were starting to ache, his palms were sweating and he was sick to his stomach at the gruesome sight of fleshless hands and arms flailing about him.

Atta snapped and barked and made darting runs at the Beloved, sinking her teeth into any part of them that came within her reach, but the dog bites had less effect on them than the staff.

"Back to the boat!" Rhys gasped, endeavoring to keep hold of Mina and fend off the Beloved. They paid no attention to him or the kender or the dog. They were desperate to seize Mina.

Her piercing shriek, right in his ear, startled Nightshade so that he dropped the emmide.

Skeletal fingers grabbed Mina's wrist. Rhys smashed the Beloved in the face with the heel of his hand, breaking its nose and shattering its cheek bones. Mina stared in horror at the bony fingers digging into her flesh, and, screaming shrilly, she struck at the Beloved with her fist.

Flame—amber, incandescent—consumed the Beloved utterly, leaving nothing, not even ashes, behind. The heat of the blast washed over Rhys and Nightshade and then was gone.

"Rhys," quavered Nightshade, after a moment, "do I have any eyebrows left?"

Rhys managed to cast him a reassuring glance, but that was as much as he had time to do. Mina, keeping hold of Rhys's hand, turned to face the Beloved.

The heat of Mina's holy rage had driven them back. They no longer tried to grab her. They still surrounded her, watching her with empty eyes and repeating her name over and over. Some spoke "Mina" in soft and sad and pleading tones. Others snarled "Mina," desperate, angry.

"Stop saying that!" Mina screamed shrilly.

The Beloved hushed, fell silent.

"I'm going to my tower," said Mina, glowering. "Get out of my way."

"We should go back to the boat," Nightshade urged. "Make a run for it!"

"We'd never reach it," said Rhys.

The Beloved would not allow Mina to leave. They had been waiting here for her. Perhaps it was her command that had driven them to this island.

"Our lives are in her hands," Rhys said. Moving slowly, he reached down and picked up his staff.

Nightshade groaned and muttered, "No meat pie is worth this."

77

Mina, tugging Rhys with her, walked forward. The Beloved drew back, giving her room to pass. She walked through the throng of the dead, watching them warily with frightened eyes, clinging to Rhys's hand so tightly that her fingertips left red marks. Nightshade crowded close behind them, tripping on Rhys's heels. Atta kept near Rhys's side, her body quivering, her lip curled back from her teeth, a constant growl rumbling.

"Tell me again why we're doing this," Nightshade said.

"Shush!" Rhys warned. He had seen the empty eyes shift from Mina to the kender and the flash of sunlight off steel. The Beloved did not attack, however. Rhys guessed they would not, as long as they were with Mina.

"Rhys," whispered Nightshade, "she doesn't remember them! And she created them!"

Rhys nodded and kept walking. The Beloved had been wandering about the island in their aimless fashion until catching sight of Mina. After that, they saw nothing else. They gathered around her, speaking her name in reverent tones. Some reached out to her, but she shrank back from them.

"Go away!" she said sharply. "Don't touch me."

One by one, they fell back.

Mina kept walking toward the tower, holding onto Rhys's hand. When they reached the tower entrance, they found the double doors locked.

"All this way and she forgets the key," Nightshade muttered.

"I don't need a key," said Mina. "This is my tower."

Letting go of Rhys's hand, she walked up to the great doors and, pushing on them with all her strength, gave them a shove. At her touch, the massive doors swung slowly open.

Mina bounded inside, looking about her with a child's wonder and curiosity. Rhys followed more slowly. Though the tower was constructed of crystal, some magic in the walls blocked the light. The morning sun could not even enter the door, but was swallowed up at the threshold. Inside, all was darkness. He halted just inside the doorway.

Slowly, as his eyes grew accustomed to the cool, damp darkness, he became aware that the tower's interior was not as dark as it had first seemed. The crystal walls diffused the sunlight, so that the interior was illuminated with a pale, soft light, reminiscent of moonglow.

The entrance hall was cavernous. A spiral staircase carved into the crystal walls wound round the interior, leading upward, out of sight. Globes of magical light were placed at intervals along the stairway, to guide the way of those who walked it. Most of the globes flickered like guttered candles, as though their magic was starting to wane. Some had gone out completely.

Long ago, the entry hall of the Tower of High Sorcery of Istar must have been magnificent. Here the wizards of Istar would have welcomed fellow wizards and other guests and dignitaries. Here, they must have waited for the Kingpriest, handing over to him the keys to their beloved tower, agreeing in sorrow to surrender rather than risk the lives of innocents in battle.

Perhaps the Kingpriest was the very last mortal to walk this hall, Rhys thought. He pictured the Kingpriest, splendid in his misguided glory, taking a triumphant victory lap, congratulating himself on having driven out his enemies before he locked and sealed the great doors behind him. Locked and sealed Istar's doom.

Nothing of glory or magnificence was left. The walls were wet and grimy, covered in sand and silt. The floor was ankle-deep in sludge, dead fish, and seaweed.

"Ugh! Your tower stinks, Mina!" said Nightshade loudly. Catching hold of Rhys's sleeve, the kender added in low, urgent tones, "Be careful! I thought I heard voices whispering. Over there." He jerked his thumb.

Rhys looked intently into the shadows in the direction Nightshade had indicated. Rhys saw nothing, but he could feel eyes watching him and he could hear someone sucking in gasping breaths, as though he or she had run a long distance.

Exertion did not bother the Beloved. Whoever was lurking in the shadows must be a living being. Rhys had assumed the tower to be vacant—after all, it had been dragged up from the bottom of the sea. He started to think his assumption was wrong. Nuitari had built the tower of his magic; he would have almost certainly found a way for his wizards to inhabit it, even though it had rested on the bottom of the ocean.

Rhys looked at Atta, who usually warned him of peril. She was aware of something in the shadows, for she would occasionally turn her head to glare in that direction. The Beloved represented the greatest danger to her, however, and her attention was fixed on them. She barked a sharp warning.

Rhys turned to see the Beloved crowding around the open door. They did not enter, but hesitated, dead eyes watching Mina.

"Keep them out!" she told Rhys. "I don't want them in here."

"The brat's right," snarled a high-pitched, nasal whine from the shadows. "Don't let those fiends in! They'll murder us all. Shut the doors!"

Rhys would have liked nothing better than to obey the command, but he had no idea how the doors operated. Constructed of blocks of obsidian, red granite and white marble, the double doors were four times the height of a man, and must each weigh as much as a small house.

"Tell me how to close them," he shouted.

"How in the Abyss should we know?" a deeper voice boomed irascibly. "You opened the blasted doors! You shut them!"

But Rhys had not opened the doors. Mina had, and she was too terrified of the Beloved to go back. The Beloved continued to mass around the entrance, but they could not find a way inside, and that appeared to be frustrating them.

"Some force seems to be blocking them," Rhys called out to the strangers in the shadows. "I presume you two are wizards. Do you have any idea what the force is or how long it will last?"

He heard snatches of a whispered consultation, then two wizards dressed in black robes emerged from the shadows. One was tall and thin with the pointed ears of an elf and the face of a savage mongrel. His hair was ragged and disheveled, his robes were tattered and filthy. His slanted eyes darted about like the head of a striking snake. Once, by accident, the eyes met Rhys's gaze and immediately slithered away.

The other wizard was a dwarf, short of stature with broad shoulders and a long beard. The dwarf was cleaner than his companion. His eyes, barely visible beneath shaggy brows, were cunning and cold.

Both wizards appeared to have gone through some traumatic ordeal, for the half-elf's face was bruised. He had a black eye and he had tied a dirty rag around his left wrist. The dwarf's head was swathed in bloody bandages and he was limping.

"I am Rhys Mason," Rhys announced. "This is Nightshade."

"I'm Mina," said the girl, at which the dwarf gave a perceptible start and stared at her narrowly.

The half-elf sneered.

"Who gives a rat's ass who you are, twerp," he said in loathing.

The dwarf cast him a baleful glance, then said, "I am called Basalt. This is Caele." He was speaking to Rhys, but he kept staring at Mina. "How did you get into our tower?"

"What is the force blocking the door?" Rhys persisted.

Basalt and Caele exchanged glances.

"We think it might be the Master," Basalt said reluctantly. "Which means he allowed you to come inside and he's keeping the fiends out. What we want to know is why he let you in here."

Mina had been staring at the wizards. Her brow furrowed, as though trying to recall where she'd seen them before.

"I know you," she said suddenly. "You tried to kill me." She pointed to the half-elf.

"She's lying!" Caele yelped. "I never saw this brat before in my life! You have five seconds to tell me why you are here or I'll cast a spell that will reduce you to—"

Basalt thrust his elbow into his companion's ribs and said something to him in a low voice.

"You're daft!" Caele scoffed.

"Look at her!" Basalt insisted. "That could be why the Master—" The rest was lost in whispering.

"I agree with Mina for once," said Nightshade. "I don't trust these two as far as I can stand the stink of them. Who's this Master they're talking about?"

"Nuitari, God of the Black Moon," Rhys answered.

Nightshade gave a dismal groan. "More gods. Just what we need."

"I have to find the way downstairs," Mina told Rhys. "You two stay here, keep an eye on them."

She pointed at the wizards, then, casting them one last baleful glance, started walking about the great hall, poking and peering into the shadows.

"If it is Nuitari, I wish he'd just shut the door," Nightshade stated, watching the Beloved, who were watching him back.

"If he did, we might not be able to get back out," said Rhys.

Caele and Basalt had been conferring all this time.

"Go on," Caele said, and he gave Basalt a shove. "Ask them."

"You ask them," Basalt growled, but in the end he came shambling up to Rhys.

"What are those fiends?" he asked. "We know they're some sort of undead. Nothing we tried seems to stop them. Not magic, not steel. Caele stabbed one through the heart and it fell down, then it got back up and tried to strangle him!"

"They are known as the Beloved. They're undead disciples of Chemosh," Nightshade explained.

"Told you," Basalt growled at Caele. "That's her!"

"You're full of it," Caele muttered back.

"How did your tower come to be here in the Blood Sea?" Nightshade asked curiously. "It wasn't here yesterday."

"You're telling us!" Basalt grunted. "Yesterday we were in our tower safe at the bottom of the ocean, minding our own business. Then there was an earthquake. The walls started shaking, the floor was the ceiling and the ceiling was the floor. We didn't know if we were on our heads or our feet. Everything broke, all our vials and containers. Books went flying off the shelves. We thought we were dead.

"When everything stopped shaking, we looked out and found ourselves stuck on this rock. When we started to crawl out through a side door, those fiends tried to murder us."

Rhys thought of the power that had wrenched this tower from the bottom of the sea and he looked at the little girl, wandering about, searching behind pillars and tapping on the walls.

"What's she doing? Playing hide-and-seek?" Nightshade cast a nervous glance at the Beloved and another at the two wizards. "Let's get out of here. I don't like this talk about stabbing people in the heart—even if it *was* a Beloved."

"Mina—" Rhys began.

"Found it!" she announced triumphantly.

She stood beneath an arched entryway, hidden in the shadows, that led to another, smaller spiral staircase.

"Come with me," ordered Mina. "Tell the bad men they have to stay here."

"This is our tower!" Caele snarled.

"Is not!" Mina retorted.

"Is so—"

Basalt intervened, clamping his hand over Caele's arm.

"You're not going anywhere without us," Basalt said coldly.

Caele growled in agreement and snatched his arm from his partner's grasp.

"Atta and I will keep an eye on them," Rhys promised, thinking it better to have the wizards where he could see them rather than having them skulking along behind.

Mina gave a nod. "They can come, but if they try to hurt us, I'll tell Atta to bite them."

"Go ahead. I like dog," Caele sneered. His lip curled. "Baked."

Mina entered the archway and started to descend the stairs. Nightshade followed after her, with Atta at his heels. Rhys came last, keeping watch out of the corner of his eye on the two wizards. The half-elf was talking rapidly into his cohort's ear, making jabbing gestures with his hand, emphasizing a point by stabbing it with a dirty finger. The dwarf didn't like whatever the half-elf was proposing, apparently, for he drew back, scowling, and shook his head. The half-elf whispered something else and the dwarf appeared to consider this. At length, he nodded and called out.

"Wait, Monk! Stop! She's leading you to your death," Basalt warned. "There's a dragon down there!"

Nightshade missed his footing, slipped on a stair, and landed hard on his backside.

"Dragon? What dragon?" The kender rubbed his sore tailbone. "I didn't agree to a dragon!"

"The dragon is the guardian of the *Solio Febalas,*" said Basalt.

"The Solo Feebleness?" Nightshade repeated. "What's that?"

Rhys could not believe he had heard right.

"*Solio Febalas,*" Rhys said with a catch in his voice. "The Hall of Sacrilege. But . . . that can't be. The Hall was lost during the Cataclysm."

"Our Master found it," said Basalt proudly. "It's a treasure trove, filled with rare and valuable holy artifacts."

"They're worth a king's ransom. Which is why the dragon is guarding it," Caele added. "If you try to enter, the dragon will kill you and eat you."

"This just gets better and better," said Nightshade glumly.

"Pooh, the dragon won't eat anyone," Mina said calmly. "She didn't eat me and I've been down there. The dragon's name is Midori. She's a sea dragon and old. Very old."

"Rhys," said Nightshade, "I'm sure there are lots of kenders who would really love to be eaten by a sea dragon. I don't happen to be one of them."

"There speaks a man of sense! You and the monk should come back upstairs," Caele urged. "Basalt and I will go with the . . . er . . . little girl."

"What a great idea!" exclaimed Nightshade, starting to head back up the stairs.

Rhys caught hold of him, turned him around.

"We will stay with Mina," he said, and he continued on down, bringing Nightshade along with him.

There was more whispering behind him.

"The Master won't like us going down there," he overheard Basalt say.

"He won't like it if they rob us blind, either," Caele retorted.

Basalt clamped his hand down on Caele's wrist.

"Don't be a fool," said the dwarf, adding something in a language Rhys did not understand.

Caele grunted and twitched his sleeve back in place, but not before Rhys had caught the glint of steel.

Rhys turned away. The two were clearly up to no good and he guessed this had something to with the *Solio Febalas*, the Hall of Sacrilege. If they were telling the truth and Nuitari had found the lost Hall, then what the half-elf had said about it being worth a king's ransom was true. Ransom enough for a hundred kings! Artifacts, relics, potions blessed by all the gods were said to have been confiscated by the soldiers of the Kingpriest. Truly a treasure trove for anyone, even two followers of Nuitari.

These artifacts had been forged in the Age of Might, when the power of clerics was unsurpassed. Priests of all the gods would pay dearly to acquire holy and powerful relics long thought lost. Most prized of all, most desired, would be artifacts blessed by Takhisis and Paladine. Though the two gods were gone from the pantheon, their ancient artifacts might still retain their power. The wealth of nations would be a small price to pay for such a treasure.

I want to bring a present to Goldmoon . . .

Rhys halted suddenly. That's why Mina had come to the tower. She was going to the Hall of Sacrilege.

Nightshade, hearing him stop, twisted his head around.

"The stairs are slick," said the kender. "You should be careful. Not that it matters if we fall and break our necks, since we're all going to be *eaten by a vicious sea dragon!*" he added loudly.

"No, we're not!" Mina yelled. She came bounding back up the stairs. "The dragon's gone."

"Gone!" Caele sucked in a breath.

"It's ours!" Basalt gasped.

The two wizards shoved past Rhys, jostling each other in their clamorous haste to reach the bottom.

9

The wizards rounded a turn in the spiral staircase and vanished. Rhys hurried after them, leaving Nightshade scrambling to catch up. Rhys found Basalt and Caele teetering precariously on the final stair, staring in dismay.

To keep thieves away from the valuables inside the Hall of Sacrilege, Nuitari had housed the *Solio Febalas* inside an enormous globe filled with sea water. The Hall was guarded by sharks, sting-rays, and various other types of lethal marine life, including an ancient sea dragon.

But now all that remained of Nuitari's ingenious aquatic strongbox were mounds of wet sand glittering with shards of broken glass.

The tower's upheaval had shattered the globe. The sea water had poured out, carrying the sea monsters with it. Midori, rudely awakened by the shock, had apparently decided enough was enough and gone off to find more stable housing. The destruction stretched as far as the eye could see.

"No! Atta, stop!" Nightshade cried, grabbing the dog by the scruff of her neck as she started to venture out onto the sand. "You'll cut your paws to ribbons! Where's the Feeble Soloness?" he asked Mina.

She pointed silently and unhappily into the midst of the wreckage.

"Oh, well. I guess we can't go there," Nightshade said cheerfully. "Say, I have an idea. Let's sail to Flotsam. I know an inn that serves beefsteak and crispy potatoes with a side of green peas and—"

"Nightshade," Rhys admonished.

"I didn't *ask* her for it!" the kender said in a defensive whisper. "I just happened to mention beef steak in case she was hungry."

"It was all so beautiful," said Mina, and she began to cry.

Basalt stood staring glumly at the mess.

"I don't care what the Master says," the dwarf stated. "I'm *not* cleaning this up." He heard a snicker from Caele and glowered. "What are you looking so damn pleased about? This is a disaster!"

"Not for us," Caele said, with a sly grin.

Seeing that the monk was occupied with the sniveling brat, Caele crept back quietly back up the stairs, motioning Basalt to come with him. When they were out of earshot of the others, Caele whispered, "Don't you realize what this means? The dragon's gone! The Hall of Sacrilege is no longer guarded! Our fortunes are made!"

"*If* the Hall's still there," Basalt returned. "And *if* it's still intact, which I doubt." He gestured at the debris. "And how do you plan to reach it? The dragon might as well be here. Those glass shards are sharper than her teeth and just as deadly."

"If the Hall survived the Cataclysm, it certainly survived this. You'll see. As for reaching it, I have an idea on that."

"What about Mina and her friends?" Basalt asked.

Caele grinned. Sliding up his sleeve, he revealed a knife attached to his wrist.

Basalt snorted. "Remember what happened the last time you tried to gut her? You ended up a prisoner in your own tomb!"

"She had that bastard Chemosh with her," Caele said, scowling. "This time, all she's got is a monk and a kender. You kill those two and I'll—"

"Leave me out of this!" Basalt snarled. "I've had enough of your plots and schemes. They only ever get me into trouble!"

Caele paled in anger. A flick of the wrist and the knife was in his hand. Basalt was prepared, however. He had always assumed some day he would end up killing the half-elf and this day was as good as any. He began to chant a spell. Caele chanted a counter-spell. The two glared blackly at each other.

Mina was staring in bleak amazement at the ruins of the crystal globe. "I wanted to swim in the sea water again. I wanted to talk to the dragon . . ."

"I'm sorry, Mina," said Rhys, not knowing what else to say to her.

He had his own worries. If the *Solio Febalas* was truly in the midst of the debris, he should find it, make certain it was safe, the contents secure. He could hear the two Black Robe wizards plotting and though he could not make out their words, he had no doubt that they were making plans to steal the sacred artifacts.

If he had been alone, Rhys would have gladly risked his own life trying to find a way through the broken glass, but he could not venture forth and leave his friends and his dog behind, not with the Beloved massing outside the tower, being held at bay by the gods alone knew what force. Nor did he trust the two Black Robes.

Rhys's main concern was Mina. As a god, she could have walked across acres of razor blades without being harmed. But she was a god who did not know she was a god. She shivered from the cold, cried when disappointed, and bled when nails scratched her flesh. He dared not take her with him and he dared not leave her behind, either.

"Mina," Rhys said, "I think Nightshade is right. We should start our journey home. You cannot cross this sand without hurting yourself. Goldmoon will understand—"

"I'm not leaving!" Mina stated petulantly. She had quit crying and now she was sulking. Her lower lip thrust out. She stood kicking the wet sand with the toe of her shoe. "Not without my present."

"Mina . . ."

"It's not fair!" she cried, wiping the back of her hand across her nose. "Why did this have to happen? I came all this way . . ."

She paused. Reaching down, ignoring Rhys's warning to be careful, she picked up a small shard of broken glass. "This *didn't* have to happen."

Mina flung the glass shard into the air and it was joined by a million other shards, sparkling like rain drops in the sunshine. The pieces of glass fused together. Sea water, instead of draining out, flowed back inside.

Rhys suddenly found himself inside a crystal globe, submersed in fathoms of blue-green sea water, and he was drowning.

Holding his breath, Rhys stared about frantically, trying to find a way out. Nightshade was nearby, flailing his arms and kicking his feet, his cheeks puffed out. Atta paddled wildly, her eyes wide with terror. Mina, unaware of their predicament, was swimming away from them.

Rhys had only moments of life left. Atta was already sinking to the bottom. Rhys sliced through the water with his arms, kicked his feet, trying to reach Mina.

He managed to grab hold of her ankle. Mina twisted around. Her face was bright with pleasure. She was enjoying herself. The pleasure faded when she saw her friends were in trouble. She stared at them helplessly, seeming to have no idea what to do. Rhys's lungs were going to burst. He was seeing dazzling stars and blue and yellow

spots and he could no longer bear the pain. He opened his mouth, prepared to suck in death.

He gulped salt water and, though the sensation was not pleasant, he didn't die. He floundered, shaken to find he was breathing water as easily as he had once breathed air. Nightshade, his mouth gaping, his eyes bulging, was spent. He floated limply in the water.

Mina caught hold of Atta, who had ceased to struggle. Mina petted the dog and kissed her and hugged her and Atta's eyes flew open. The dog looked around frantically, panic-stricken, until she found Rhys. He swam over to her and was joined by Nightshade, who grabbed hold of his arm and tried to talk. All that came out were bubbles, but though Rhys couldn't hear him, he understood the kender's general meaning, which was, "You have to do something! She's going to get us all killed!"

Rhys considered this was quite likely, but as for preventing it, he had no idea what to do. An ordinary six-year-old who misbehaved could be swatted or sent to bed without her supper. The idea of swatting Mina who, as Nightshade had said, could drop a mountain on their heads, was ludicrous. And, to be honest, Mina hadn't misbehaved. She hadn't deliberately tried to drown them. She'd made a simple mistake. Since she could breathe water as easily as air, she had assumed they could, too.

Mina swam underwater as though she'd been born to it, darting around them like a minnow, urging them to hurry. Rhys had learned to swim in the monastery, but he was hampered by his robes and by his staff, which he did not want to leave behind, and by his concern for Nightshade.

The kender had never learned to swim. He had never *wanted* to learn to swim. Now, given no choice in the matter, he thrashed about wildly, making no progress in any direction. He was about to give swimming up as hopeless when Atta passed him, churning the water with her front paws. Nightshade watched the dog and decided to emulate her. Not having paws, he used his hands and arms to paddle, and soon was able to keep up with the rest.

Mina swam excitedly on ahead, motioning for them to hurry. When they reached her, she was floating in the water, making small swirling motions with her hands, hovering above what appeared to be a child's sand castle.

Simple in design, the castle was constructed of four walls four feet in height and four feet long, with a tall tower at each corner. There were no windows and only one door, though that door was a marvel.

Three feet tall and not very wide, the door was made of myriad pearls that shimmered with a purple luster. A single rune carved out of a large emerald glowed in the center.

Mina motioned to Rhys, and as he swam awkwardly near her, pushing the staff ahead of him. She gestured at the sand castle and eagerly nodded.

"The Hall of Sacrilege," she mouthed.

Rhys stared in astonishment.

The infamous Hall of Sacrilege—a child's sand castle. Rhys shook his head. Mina frowned at him and, reaching out, she grabbed hold of his staff and pulled him through the water. She pointed to the emerald rune embedded in the door. Rhys swam closer and caught a watery breath in awe. Carved into the rune was a figure 8 turned on its side, a symbol with no ending and no beginning, the symbol of eternity.

Rhys propelled himself backward. Mina regarded him, puzzled. She pointed at the door.

"Open it!" she commanded in a flurry of bubbles.

Rhys shook his head. This was the *Solio Febalas*, repository of some of the most holy artifacts ever created by gods and man, and the door was shut and the door was sealed. He was not meant to enter. No mortal was meant to enter. Perhaps not even the gods themselves were meant to enter this sacred place.

Mina tugged at him, urging him. Rhys shook his head emphatically, and drew back. He wished he could explain to her, but he could not. He turned and started to swim off.

She swam after him and grabbed hold of him again. Childlike, she was determined to have her way. Rhys had the feeling that if they'd been on dry land, she would have stamped her foot.

Rhys would have continued to refuse, but at that moment, the decision was taken away from him.

Even deep below the sea, he could hear the one single word dreaded throughout Krynn by anyone traveling with a kender.

"Oops!"

"Hey!" Caele cried, alarmed. "Where did they go?"

The two Black Robes, intent on killing each other, had been muttering arcane words and fumbling about in their pouches for spell components when they realized they were alone. Kender, kid, dog, and monk had disappeared.

"Damn their eyeballs!" Caele swore, seething. "They've found a way inside!"

The half-elf dashed down the stairs, skidding to a halt when he reached the bottom. The shards of broken glass were still there, sticking up out of the sand.

"If you hadn't been so eager to slit my throat, we'd be in there helping ourselves to the riches." Basalt shook his fist at the half-elf.

"You're right, of course, Basalt," said Caele with sudden meekness. "You're always right. Give the Master my regards."

The half-elf raised his hand in a flourish and vanished.

"Huh?" Basalt blinked. "What—"

The dwarf suddenly understood. He sucked in a huge breath and let it out in a roar. "He's gone after them!"

Basalt did a quick mental run-through of his spell catalog and began a feverish rummage through his pouches of spell components to see what he had on hand. He'd come prepared to do battle, not for traveling to an unknown destination across a sea bottom covered with broken glass. He wondered what magic Caele had used, decided most likely the half-elf had cast a spell known as Dimension Door, a favorite of Caele's, for it required only spoken words, no spell components. Caele disliked casting spells that used components, mainly because he was too lazy to gather them.

Basalt was familiar with the Dimension Door spell himself, but it had one drawback. In order to cast the spell, the wizard had to know where he was going, for he had to visualize the location. Basalt had no idea where the Hall of Sacrilege was or what it looked like. He had never been inside the water-filled globe that protected it.

Caele, on the other hand, had been inside the globe. He had been sent—under duress—to the dragon, Midori, to collect a small amount of her blood which Nuitari had used in the Dragon-sight bowl, allowing him to spy on his enemies. Caele had never mentioned seeing the Hall, but the half-elf was a sneaking, cunning, lying bastard, and Basalt guessed that Caele had done some snooping about while he was down there and simply not mentioned it.

Picturing Caele in the Hall, scooping up treasures right and left, Basalt gnashed his teeth in anger. He glared irately at the broken glass blocking his way and thought wistfully about how wonderful it would be if he could just float over it, and that brought a spell to mind.

Basalt didn't have the requisite pure components on hand, but he could make do. The spell required gauze; he tore the bandage from his forehead and, using his knife, cut off a piece. He generally carried a bit of candle with him, for flame or wax always came in handy. The candle was beeswax, one he'd made himself and he was quite proud of it, for it was magical.

Holding the gauze in one hand and the candle in the other, he spoke the command word and the candle burst into flame. He held the gauze in the flame until it caught fire, let it burn a moment, then blew it out. A thin wisp of smoke trailed up from the blackened fabric. Basalt spoke a magical word and waited a tense moment to see if the spell would work.

He felt a strange and unpleasant sensation, as though flesh and bone, skin and muscle were being magically rendered into a liquid state and then he oozed away, leaving behind a gaseous, insubstantial form. Basalt had not used this spell in some time and it occurred to him—belatedly—that he wasn't sure how one managed to get one's body back again. He would worry about that later, however. Right now he had to catch up with Caele.

Drifting along with the air currents, the gaseous form of Basalt—looking like a hairy cloud of black smoke—wafted over the broken glass and entered what was left of the crystal globe.

97

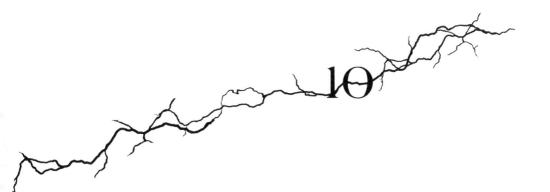

Nightshade had been understandably miffed at Mina for dunking him in sea water and then nearly drowning him, but, after a while, he forgave her. He liked the novelty of being able to breath under water and swim like a fish—or rather, like Atta. He was paddling along through the sea, enjoying the view, wondering if he had gills on his neck and if they were pulsing in and out, and feeling his neck to see if he did, and being disappointed to discover that he didn't, when he came to the sand castle.

Rhys and Mina were arguing. Mina apparently wanted Rhys to go inside, and Rhys was having none of it, which Nightshade, as a kender with common sense, approved, for he guessed immediately this building must be the Solo of the Feeble-minded or the Hall of Sacred Litches or whatever it was called.

Nightshade paddled about, waiting for the argument to end, and soon grew bored. There was nothing to do down here except swim. He wondered how fish stood it. There being nothing to look at except the sand castle, he decided to look at it, and he noticed the castle had an extremely interesting door made up of pearls and the largest, most beautiful emerald the kender had ever seen. He swam over for a closer look.

Nightshade was never certain what happened afterward. Either his common sense decided to pack its pouches and take a holiday or the kender side of him rose up, struck common sense a blip on the head bone, and knocked it out cold.

Not that it made any difference.

The fact was that the emerald was the largest and most beautiful emerald Nightshade had ever seen, and the closer he swam to it the larger and more beautiful it grew, so that in the end the kender part of him that was really there, despite what his father thought to the contrary, simply had to reach out his hand, take hold of the emerald, and try to pry it loose.

Two things happened, one which was unfortunate and the other more unfortunate.

Unfortunately the emerald did not come loose.

More unfortunately the door did.

The door flew open. All the kender had time for was to yell one startled "Oops!" then the sea water rushed inside the sand castle and took Nightshade with it.

The door slammed shut.

Nightshade was tumbled about in the rushing water and for several tense moments he had no idea if he was on his head or his heels, and then the water dropped him down on a solid surface and went on without him. He lay still for a moment gasping at the suddenness of it all. When he was over his shock, he noticed that he was breathing air, not water, for which he was grateful. He'd been going over in his mind what he knew about a fish's diet and thinking sadly that he was going to have to live on worms.

After gulping in few deep, reassuring breaths, he decided to get up and take a look around.

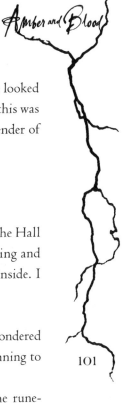

He looked around and looked around again and the more he looked the more he was certain, with a quaking feeling in his gut, that this was somewhere he should not be and there was only thing for a kender of common sense—even a kender with horns—to do.

"Rhys," Nightshade wailed, "help!"

Rhys turned just in time to see Nightshade sucked inside the Hall of Sacrilege and the door slam shut on him. Mina was laughing and clapping her hands. "Now, Mister Monk, you'll *have* to go inside. I win."

She grinned and stuck out her tongue at him.

Rhys had never been a parent himself, and he had often wondered how any adult could bear to spank a child. He was now beginning to understand.

Mina swam to the door, and brushed her hand across the rune-carved emerald. As the door swung slowly open, sea water carried Mina and Rhys inside and bowled over Nightshade, who had been beating on the door with his fists.

Rhys picked himself up. He looked back through the open door onto the desert-like landscape of rippling wet sand.

Atta stood outside the door in the wet sand, shaking off the water, starting with her hind end and working her way to the front. When Rhys called to her, she slunk warily through the door. She clearly did not want to be here. Pressing her body up against his, she stood there, shivering.

Nightshade didn't want to be here either.

"Rhys," he said in a shaking voice, "this is it. This is that Hall place. It's . . . it's pretty scary, Rhys. I don't think we're supposed to be here."

The *Solio Febalas*, the Hall of Sacrilege—the repository of the King-priest's arrogant determination to defy the gods. Nightshade's instincts (and Atta's) were right. Mortals were not meant to be here. The hall was sacred to the gods, to their wrath.

"You're not mad at me for making you come inside, are you, Mister Monk?" Mina asked wistfully, and she slid her hand into his.

Looking at her, he did not see a god. He saw a child with the mind of a child—unformed, with imperfect knowledge of the world, and he wondered, suddenly, if that was what the gods saw when they looked upon mankind.

Rhys no longer felt the gods' wrath. He felt their sorrow.

"No, Mina," he said, "I am not mad at you."

The Hall was immense, perfectly round in shape, with a high, domed ceiling. The walls were notched with alcoves carved into the stone, each sacred to one of the gods. A single rune adorned the wall of each alcove. In some instances, the runes shone with light. There was the steadily beaming light of Majere, the blue-white flame of Mishakal, the almost blinding silver glare of Kiri-Jolith.

Alcoves on the opposite side of the hall were dark, fighting to extinguish the light. The dread symbol of Sargonnas, God of Vengeance, was darkness on darkness. The alcove of Morgion was a noxious black green, Chemosh was ghastly bone white.

The alcoves in between, separating darkness and light, striving to hold each in check, belonged to the neutral gods. In the center was the alcove sacred to Gilean. A book lay open upon the altar. Red light shone upon a set of scales, perfectly balanced, that stood in the center.

On either side of the altar of Gilean, one on the left and one on the right, were two alcoves that were neither dark nor light, but were both shrouded in shadow, as though a veil hung over them. Once,

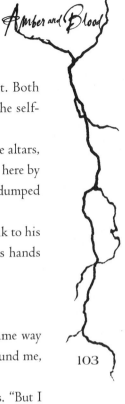

one had been impenetrably dark, the other unbearably light. Both were empty now—the altars of the banished Takhisis and the self-exiled Paladine.

The Hall was filled with holy artifacts, stacked on top of the altars, or jumbled in piles, or tossed carelessly onto the floor. Brought here by the soldiers of the Kingpriest, they had been unceremoniously dumped into his storehouse of shame.

Rhys could not speak. He could not see for his tears. He sank to his knees and, laying his staff carefully at his side, he clasped his hands in a prayer.

"Mister Monk, come with me—" Mina began.

"I don't think he can hear you," Nightshade said.

Mina gave a small sigh. "I know how he feels. I felt the same way when I came here—as though all the gods were gathered around me, looking down at me. And I was so very small and all alone."

She paused, then glanced trepidatiously back at the alcoves. "But I still have to get my present for Goldmoon and I don't want to go alone." She turned to the kender. "You come with me."

Nightshade cast a longing glance at the altars, at the vast assortment of the strange and beautiful, horrible and wonderful.

"I better not," he said at last, regretfully. "I'm a mystic, you see, and it wouldn't be right."

"What's a mystic?" Mina asked.

"It's a . . . well . . ." Nightshade was confounded. He had never been called upon to define himself before. "It means I don't believe in the gods. That is, I do believe in gods—I have to, I met Majere once," he added with pride. "Majere even helped me pick a lock, though Rhys said that a god picking a lock was a one-time occurrence and I shouldn't expect him to do it again. Being a mystic means I don't pray to the gods like Rhys does. Like he's doing right now. Well, I guess I did pray to

Majere, but that prayer wasn't for me. It was for Rhys, who couldn't pray because he was almost dead."

Mina looked confused, and Nightshade decided to cut his explanation short.

"Being a mystic means I like to go my own way without bothering anyone."

"Fine," said Mina. "You can go your own way with me. I don't want to go back there by myself. It's dark and spooky. And there might be spiders."

Nightshade shook his head.

"Please!" Mina begged.

Nightshade had to admit he was tempted. If only she hadn't mentioned spiders . . .

"Dare you!" Mina taunted.

Nightshade wavered.

"Double dog dare you!" Mina said.

That did it. Nightshade's honor was at stake. No kender in the long and glorious history of kender had ever refused a double-dog dare.

"Race you!" he cried, and darted away.

Caele had never actually seen the Hall of Sacrilege, but he had been able to visualize it for his spell. The dragon, Midori, had once described it to him. Caele had not paid much attention to her description at the time; the dragon had rambled on about it simply to torment him. Midori knew he was terrified of her and she found it entertaining to keep him within snacking distance.

Caele had been sick with fear the day the dragon had spent a horrible half-hour rambling on about the sand castle and how clever Nuitari had been in building it to house the holy artifacts and how it was too bad he—Caele—would never live to see it. Caele remembered almost nothing from that conversation, but he did manage to dredge up the words "sand castle" from his memory and, with that image in his mind, his magic carried him to this location.

He materialized in the doorway and immediately froze, not daring to move until he'd assessed the situation. The monk was on his knees, blubbering. The dog crouched at his side. The kender and the brat were off looting an altar. No sign of Basalt.

Caele had been planning to kill the monk immediately, but the deadly spell he was going to cast slipped from his mind as his stunned gaze went from one altar to another. He had never imagined in his greediest dreams the unfathomable wealth. And it was just lying here, unguarded, simply begging to be taken off and sold to the highest bidder. Caele was so moved he could have blubbered like the monk.

He snapped back to business. First he had to get rid of the competition. Caele knew any number of spells which would kill people in a variety of unpleasant ways. He was reaching for the magical lodestone that would cause the monk to disintegrate into oozing globs of flesh when he caught sight of movement near one of the altars.

Caele stared hard in that direction. He wasn't certain which god the altar belonged to, nor did he care. One of the objects glittering on the altar was a chalice encrusted with jewels. Caele had already marked it as being particularly valuable, and he realized someone else had noted its value as well. A shadowy form crept near it— a shadowy, hairy form reaching out his hand.

"Basalt!" Caele snarled.

The dog sprang to her feet with a bark.

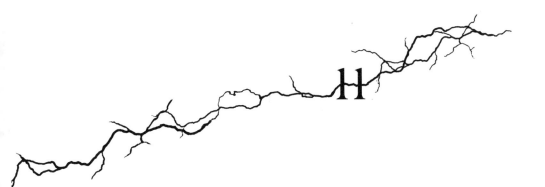

*N*ightshade stood with his hands jammed into his pockets, concentrating hard on keeping them there. He'd never before seen so many interesting and curious and wonderful objects all collected together in one place. Everything he looked at seemed to cry out to him that it wanted to be touched, picked up, poked at, prodded, sniffed, unlocked, unlatched, unhooked, unstoppered, unrolled, or at the very least stuffed into a pouch for further study.

Several times Nightshade's hands made an effort to leap out of his pockets and do all of the above mentioned. He managed by a great effort of will to keep his hands under control, but he had the feeling his will was growing weaker and his hands were growing stronger.

He wished Mina would hurry.

Unaware of the struggle going on in the kender's pockets, Mina wandered back and forth between the two altars, both of them in deepest shadow, looking at the objects stacked up around them. Her lips were pursed, her brow wrinkled. She was apparently trying to make up her mind, for sometimes she would reach out to an object, then draw back her hand and move on to something else.

Nightshade was in agony. One hand had already crept out of a pocket and he'd used the other hand to grab the first and wrestle it back. He was just about to yell at Mina to make up her mind, when Atta's bark—sounding unnaturally loud in the utter silence of the Hall—caused the kender to nearly leap out from under his topknot.

"Mina!" Nightshade cried. "It's one of those bad wizards! He's here!"

"I know," said Mina with a shrug. "They're both here. There's another one sneaking around over there by the altar of Sargonnas." She gave a sly grin. "The dwarf thinks he's clever. He doesn't know we can see him."

At first Nightshade didn't see anything, then, sure enough, a dwarf came into view, skulking about one of the altars. He was eyeing a jeweled chalice that had a foot piece formed in shape of a minotaur's head standing on its horns.

Atta was barking at the other wizard, lurking about in the doorway. Rhys was on his knees, his entire being given to his god. Caele had his hand in one of his pouches, and Nightshade knew enough about wizards to consider it unlikely he was reaching for a peppermint.

"Mina, I think he's going to try to kill Rhys!" Nightshade said urgently.

"Yes, probably," Mina agreed. She was still mulling over her choices.

"We have to do something!" Nightshade said angrily. "Stop him!"

Mina sighed. "I can't decide which one Mother would like. I don't want to make a mistake. What do you think?"

Nightshade didn't think. Caele was pointing something at Rhys and chanting.

Nightshade started to shout a warning, but the shout changed to a gargle of astonishment. A rope made from hemp and twined with holly leaves that had been coiled up on the altar of Chislev, darted like a striking snake and wrapped itself around Caele's arms, pinning them to his side. The words of the half-elf's spell ended in a shriek. He fell to the floor, rolling about, trying to free himself from the binding rope.

At that moment, Basalt grabbed hold of the chalice, and—to Nightshade's astonishment—used it to strike himself in the head. Basalt howled in pain and tried to rid himself of the chalice, only to end up hitting himself again. He kept bashing himself with the chalice, unable to stop. Blood poured down his face. He staggered about groggily, moaning in pain, then toppled over, unconscious. Only then did he quit hitting himself.

Nightshade gulped. His hands, still in his pockets, were now quite comfortable there, expressing no desire to touch anything.

"I think we should leave this place," said Nightshade in a tight, small voice.

"I will take this," said Mina, making up her mind at last.

"Don't touch anything!" Nightshade warned, but Mina paid no attention to him.

She picked up a small crystal carved in the shape of a pyramid from the altar of Paladine and stood admiring it. Nothing happened.

Holding the small crystal, Mina went to the altar of Takhisis and, after a moment's indecision, chose a nondescript-looking necklace made of shiny beads.

"I think Mother will like these," she announced.

"What are they?" Nightshade asked. "What do they do? Do you even know?"

"Of course I know!" Mina said, offended. "I'm not a dummy. I know everything about everything."

Nightshade forgot for a moment that she was a god and she probably did know everything about everything. He made a rude noise, expressive of disbelief, and challenged, "What is that necklace then?"

"It is called 'Sedition,'" said Mina, smug in her knowledge. "Takhisis made it. The person who wears it has the power to turn good people evil."

Nightshade almost said, "You mean like you?" but he thought better of it. Even though Mina had nearly drowned him, he didn't want to hurt her feelings.

"What about the little pyramid?" he asked.

"This was sacred to Paladine." Mina held it up to see the crystal sparkle in the blue light from the altar of Mishakal. "The jewel shines the light of truth on people. That's why the Kingpriest had to hide it away. He was afraid people would see him for what he really was."

Nightshade had a an idea. "Pooh, I don't believe you. You're making that up."

"It's the truth!" Mina retorted angrily.

"Then show me," said Nightshade. He held out his hand for the crystal.

Mina hesitated. "You promise you'll give it back?"

"Cross my heart and hope to die if I don't," Nightshade vowed.

Since he'd sworn this terrible oath, sacred to childhood the world over, Mina agreed. She placed the pyramid-shaped crystal into the kender's hand.

"What do I do?" he asked, regarding it curiously and now a bit warily. He was wondering, suddenly, if the artifact might take offense at being used by a mystic.

"Hold it to your eye and look at something through it," said Mina.

"What will I see?"

"How should I know?" she demanded. "It depends on what you're looking at it, ninny."

Nightshade held up the crystal and looked at the dwarf wizard lying on the floor. He saw a dwarf wizard lying on the floor. He looked at Caele and saw Caele. He looked at Rhys and saw Rhys. He looked at Atta and saw a dog. Thinking that this was a pretty sorry excuse for an artifact, Nightshade turned the crystal on Mina.

A white light shone down upon her, shone round about her, illuminating her from within and without. Nightshade blinked his eyes, for he was half-blinded. He tried to brave the light, to stare into it, to see more clearly, but the light grew ever more brilliant, ever more radiant. Bright and blinding, the light intensified, forcing the kender to close his eyes to try to block it out. The light expanded and grew; the light of a myriad suns, the first light, the light of creation. Nightshade cried out in pain and dropped the crystal and stood rubbing his burning eyes.

Once, when he was a little kender, he'd stared straight at the sun because his mother had told him not to. For long minutes after, all he'd been able to see were dark splotches like small black suns, and that was all he could see now. He wondered for a brief and terrifying moment if that was all he was ever going to be all to see. And after what he had seen, he wondered if maybe that was all he was going to *want* to see.

Mina snatched up the fallen crystal.

"Well," she said. "What did you see?"

"Spots," Nightshade said, rubbing his eyes.

Mina was disappointed. "Spots? You must have seen something else."

"I didn't!" Nightshade returned irritably. "Maybe it's not working."

"Maybe you just didn't know what you were looking at!" Mina chided.

"Oh, I knew," said Nightshade. Thankfully the spots were starting to fade. He wiped the sweat from his forehead. It seemed odd to be sweating when he could still see the goose-flesh on his arms.

Mina stuffed the artifacts into her pockets and then smiled at him. "Your turn," she said.

"For what?"

She waved her hand. "You came with me. You can pick out an artifact. Any one you want."

Nightshade could see Basalt lying bloody on the floor and he could hear Caele's shrieks of terror. Nightshade thrust his hands into his pockets.

"No. Thank you, though."

" 'Fraidy cat," scoffed Mina.

Walking over to the altar of Majere, she picked up something shiny and held it out to Nightshade.

"Here," she said. "You should have this."

In her hand was a gold cloak pin in the shape of a grasshopper. Nightshade remembered the time he and Atta had been set upon by two of the Beloved, only to be saved by an army of grasshoppers. The cloak pin had rubies for eyes, and was so skillfully crafted it looked as if it could have jumped away at any moment. Nightshade was quite charmed with it, and he wanted it more than anything he'd ever wanted in his life. His hand quivered in its pocket.

"Are you sure Majere won't mind if I take it?" he asked. "I wouldn't want to do anything to make him mad."

"I'm sure," said Mina, and before Nightshade could protest, she fastened the pin onto his shirt.

Nightshade stiffened in fright, half-expecting the pin to fly up his nose or knock him on the head. The grasshopper sat quite tamely on his shirt. It seemed to Nightshade, as he marveled over it, that the red eyes winked at him.

"What does it do?" he asked.

"It's a hopper, ninny," said Mina. "What do you think it does?"

"Hop?" Nightshade ventured a guess.

"Yes," she said, "and it will make you hop, too. As high and as far as you want to go."

"Whoo, boy!" Nightshade breathed.

Rhys had not heard or seen anything. The dwarf howled and Caele swore and Atta barked and Rhys was oblivious. The only sound he heard was the voice of the god.

And then Rhys felt a hand tapping his shoulder and he raised his head. The voice of the god ceased.

"Mister Monk, I have my presents for Goldmoon," Mina said, showing him the two objects. "We can go now."

Rhys stood up. He had been kneeling on the floor a long time, seemingly, for his knees hurt and his legs were stiff. Looking about, he was astonished to see the two Black Robes lying on the floor—one trussed and shrieking, the other bloody and unconscious.

He looked to Nightshade for an explanation.

"They made the gods mad," the kender replied.

Rhys was considerably mystified by this pronouncement, but before he could ask, Mina shouted impatiently that she was ready to leave.

"What do we do with weasel-face and furball?" Nightshade asked.

"Leave them here," Mina said, glowering. "Seal them up inside to die. That will teach them a lesson."

"We can't do that!" Rhys said, shocked.

"Why not? They were going to kill us," Mina returned.

Rhys looked down at Caele, bound up in the blessed rope, wriggling about on the floor. The half-elf's fury warred with his fear. One moment he gnashed his teeth and snarled threats and the next he was whining to be saved. The other wizard, Basalt, had regained consciousness and moaned that his head hurt.

"I know how he feels," Nightshade said with a glance at Mina. "She does have a point, Rhys. The weasel was going to kill you with a magic spell if whatever god that is with the rope hadn't stopped him. We shouldn't turn them loose."

"I'm not going to leave anyone to die," Rhys said sternly, in a tone that brooked no argument. "We can at least carry them out of here. You grab that end."

"Ugh!" said Nightshade, wrinkling his nose as he picked up Caele's bare feet. "I never thought I'd say this, but I'm sorry there's no more water in here."

While Mina watched in disapproval, Rhys and Nightshade hauled first Caele, then Basalt, out of the Hall of Sacrilege and dumped the two wizards down onto the damp sand.

"Atta, guard!" said Rhys, pointing at the wizards.

"I don't think that will be necessary." Nightshade said in a low voice. "I think someone's coming to fetch them."

A man clad in sumptuous black robes walked across the wet sand. The man's moon-round face was pallid with fury, his eyes cold and glinting. Mina grabbed hold of Rhys's hand. Atta slunk behind Rhys and Nightshade deemed it prudent to return to the Hall. The man's wrathful gaze skipped over all of them, rested briefly on Mina, then landed full force on the wizards.

Caele saw what was coming and began to blubber.

"Master Nuitari, it wasn't my fault! Basalt forced me to come—"

"I forced you!" Basalt began, but his shout made his head hurt and he moaned. "Don't believe him, Master. It was that mongrel elf—"

The moon face contorted in rage. Nuitari stretched forth his hand, and the two wizards vanished.

The God of the Dark Moon turned to Rhys. "My apologies, Monk of Majere. These two will not bother you again."

Rhys bowed.

"Excuse me, Nuitari," Nightshade called from the safety of the doorway, "to make up for the fact that your wizards tried to kill us, could you get rid of the Beloved? I don't mean to complain, but they've invaded your tower and they won't let us leave."

"This is no longer my tower," Nuitari replied and, with a cold glance at Mina, he disappeared.

"Then who was keeping them at bay?" Nightshade asked, perplexed.

"Probably Mina," said Rhys. "She just didn't know it."

Nightshade grumbled something unintelligible, then said, "So what do we do about the Beloved?"

"As long as Mina is with us, I don't think the Beloved will harm us," Rhys said.

"And what happens when Mina tries to leave?"

"I don't know, my friend," Rhys said. "We must have faith that—"

He paused, his eyes narrowed. "Nightshade, where did you get that golden pin?"

"I didn't take it," the kender said promptly.

"I'm sure you didn't *intend* to take it," Rhys hinted. "I imagine you found it lying on the floor—"

"—where a god dropped it?" Nightshade grinned at him. "I didn't steal it, Rhys. Honest. Mina gave it to me."

He looked down with pride at the grasshopper. "Remember when Majere sent the hoppers to save me? I think it's his way of saying thank you."

"He's telling the truth," Mina volunteered. "The god wanted him to have it. Just like the gods wanted me to have my gifts for Goldmoon. Which reminds me, could you carry them for me?" Mina held the two artifacts them out to Rhys. "I'm afraid I'll lose them."

"Whatever you do," Nightshade warned, *"don't put on the necklace!"*

"I think Goldmoon will like them," Mina continued, handing first the crystal pyramid, then the necklace, to Rhys. "When the gods left, Goldmoon told me she was very sad. Even though years and years had passed, she still missed the gods. I promised her I would find the gods and bring them back to her. And I did."

Mina smiled, pleased with herself.

Rhys shivered. Mina had not found a god. The god, Takhisis, had found her. Takhisis lied to Mina and corrupted her and made her a slave of darkness when she should have been rejoicing in the light. Had Mina been an unwitting victim, or had she known right from wrong and deliberately chosen the darkness? And now, was she blotting out the memories, trying to forget the terrible crimes she had committed? Or had she truly forgotten? Was this play acting? Or was it madness?

Perhaps even Mina did not know the answer. Perhaps that was why she going to Godshome. And he was to make this strange journey with her, guard her, guide her, protect her.

Rhys placed the artifacts—the prism and the necklace—in his scrip. If anyone discovered he was carrying such valuable treasures, he and those with him would be in deadly peril. He thought of saying something to Mina and Nightshade, warning them that they must keep the artifacts secret. He discarded that idea, decided the less fuss he made over them the better. Hopefully, both kender and child would forget about them.

That is exactly what Mina appeared to do. Now that she was free of her burden, she began to tease Nightshade, asking him with a giggle if he'd like to go swimming again. When he said loudly, "No!" she punched him in the arm and called him a baby, and he punched her in the arm and called her a brat, and the two ran off, kicking at each other's ankles, trying to trip each other. Atta, at a gesture from Rhys, dashed after to keep an eye on them.

The shards of glass had disappeared, as had the sea water, presumably at Mina's command.

Rhys lingered near the Hall, reluctant to leave. Majere had spoken to him in the *Solio Febalas*, spoken not to his head, but to his heart. He saw clearly the road he must walk and it was a long one. Mina had chosen him to be her guide, her teacher. He did not understand why, for not even the gods understood. His position was difficult and dangerous for he was a guardian whose charge was far stronger and more powerful than he was. He was a guide who could only follow, for Mina alone had to find the road she must walk. He had accepted the trust placed in him and prayed that he would not be found wanting.

"Mister Monk, hurry up!" Mina shouted impatiently. "I'm ready to go to Godshome now!"

The door to the *Solio Febalas* swung slowly shut. The green emerald glowed with a soft radiance. Rhys bowed in profound reverence, and turned and hastened off to catch up with Mina.

Nuitari lurked about the Hall of Sacrilege. The God of the Dark Moon had one heavy-lidded eye on the door that was now sealed and locked and the other eye upon his fellow god, Chemosh, Lord of Bones, who was also hanging about the Hall.

Both gods had been forced to wait until Mina opened the door to enter the tower, which Nuitari had found particularly galling, since this was, by rights, his tower. His cousins had agreed that he should have it. He had given up the Tower of Wayreth and the Tower of Nightlund to obtain it. And since the *Solio Febalas* was located inside the tower, he considered the Hall belonged to him, as well. After all, sunken treasure belonged to whoever found it.

True, the Hall of Sacrilege was not a ship that had gone down in a storm, but to his mind the law of the sea applied. Chemosh could not be made to accept this perfectly logical view of the matter, and he was proving to be a damned nuisance. His holy artifacts were his, Chemosh claimed, and he wanted them back.

Neither god had been able to enter while Mina was inside with her rag-tag monk and kender. The latter had both gods in agony, envisioning valuable artifacts capable of producing untold miracles disappearing inside the kender's pouches and pockets, to be lost along the way or traded for six pine cones and a trained cricket.

Each had experienced a profound sense of relief to see Mina and company depart with apparently only two artifacts, and a gold bug of small value.

When the monk left, the door had swung shut. Chemosh suspected Nuitari of having shut it and Nuitari suspected Chemosh. Both gods waited for the other to make the first move. At last, Nuitari could stand it no longer.

"I will take a look inside to make certain the kender didn't rob the place blind."

"I will go with you," said Chemosh immediately.

"No need," Nuitari said in oily tones.

"But I insist," Chemosh replied.

Both gods hesitated, eyeing each other balefully, then both headed for the door. Both reached out their hands to grab open the door of the castle made of sand.

An immortal voice, stern and angry, spoke to each of them.

"Once each grain of sand was a mountain. Thus, all things of seeming might and importance are reduced to insignificance.

All things."

A wave rolling forward from the beginning of time smashed into the *Solio Febalas,* washed over it, and, withdrawing, carried it into the vast ocean of eternity.

Shaken to the core of their immortal beings, the gods shrank into the wet sand, neither daring to move or look, lest he draw down upon him the wrath of the High God. Finally Chemosh lifted his head and Nuitari opened his eyes.

The Hall of Sacrilege was gone, washed away.

Chemosh stood up and brushed the sand off his lace sleeves and stalked off with what dignity remained. Nuitari rose to his feet and shook out his black robes. He did not leave, but lingered, gazing at the smooth sand where the Hall had once stood. He had spent years studying the history of and cataloging every one of the artifacts. He knew them all, knew what each did, knew how dearly the other gods would have paid to obtain them. Not in gold or steel or jewels, of course; Nuitari had little care for that. But in other ways. Zeboim would have been convinced to leave his tower unmolested. Kiri-Jolith's blasted paladins would have quit harassing his black robes. Sargonnas would have been forced to allow his minotaurs to practice magic freely, and so on.

But the High God, who never spoke, had spoken. Perhaps it was just as well. The artifacts and the Hall itself belonged to a time and a place that were now long gone. The world had moved on. Better to leave them in the dust of the past. Still, Nuitari could not help but wonder sulkily why Mina had been permitted by the High God to enter the Hall while he and the others had been barred.

The God of Dark Magic withdrew from the place where the Hall had stood, but he did not leave. He conceded the *Solio Febalas* to the High God.

In return, Nuitari wanted his tower back.

12

Mina led the way, for Rhys and Nightshade had lost all sense of direction. She was happy and laughing, skipping along ahead of them, turning around to scold them for being slow. The distance from the Hall to the tower was not far and a short walk brought them back to the stairs.

Mina would have dashed up immediately, but Rhys laid a restraining hand on her shoulder, holding her back.

"What's the matter?" she asked, gazing up at him. She pointed up the stairs. "This is the way out."

"It is best to be cautious," he said. "Let me go first. You follow with Nightshade."

"But you're too slow," Mina complained, as they began to climb the winding staircase. "I have my gifts. I have to get to Godshome right now."

"Godshome is a long way off," Nightshade grumbled. The stairs had not been built for short kender legs, and he was having to work to climb each step, with the result that various parts of him were starting to ache. "A *long*, long way off."

"How long?" Mina asked.

"Miles," said Nightshade. "Miles and miles and miles."

"How long will that take?"

"Months," said Nightshade grumpily. "Months and months."

Mina stared at him, dismayed, then she laughed. "Don't be silly!" she said, adding impatiently, "You both are too slow. I'm going on ahead."

"Mina, wait! The Beloved—" Rhys cried and made a grab for her, but she wriggled out of his grasp and dashed up the stairs.

"I'll wait for you at the top!" she promised.

"Atta, go with her!" Rhys ordered and, as the dog ran off, he turned back to assist Nightshade, who was groaning with every step and rubbing his aching thighs.

"Assuming we get past the Beloved alive—which is an awfully big assume—where do we go now?" the kender asked.

"We have to find Godshome," Rhys replied.

Nightshade scrunched up his face and eyed Rhys intently. "You were having a long conversation with Majere back there in the Solo Flabbiness. Didn't he tell you where to find Godshome?"

Rhys shook his head and cast a worried glance up the stairs.

"Majere should have given you a map. Or pointed out landmarks," Nightshade persisted. "You know: 'Take the left fork at the crossroads and walk twenty paces and turn right at the lightning-struck tree.' That sort of thing."

"He didn't," said Rhys. "Godshome is not a place one can find on a map."

"Oh, I get it," Nightshade said gloomily. "This is one of those whatchamacallit journeys. You know—the kind that's supposed to teach you something."

"Spiritual journey," said Rhys.

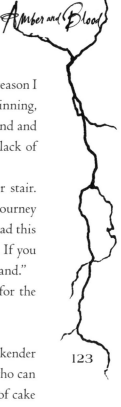

"Right. Gods are very big on spiritual journeys. Yet another reason I became a mystic. When I go on a journey, I like it to have a beginning, a middle, and an end. And I like for there to be an inn at the end and something good to eat. Spiritual journeys are noted for their lack of good things to eat."

Rhys gripped his friend's arm and hoisted him up another stair. "You are wise, as always, Nightshade. And you are right. The journey is going to be long and it could be dangerous. You and I have had this talk before, but now you understand how dangerous it can be. If you want to take your road and leave us to take ours, I will understand."

"I would leave in a heartbeat," stated Nightshade, "except for the free food."

Rhys sighed. "Nightshade—"

"Rhys, Mina can magic up meat pies! Just like that!" The kender snapped his fingers. "I'd be crazy to walk away from a person who can do that, even if she is a god and nutty as a fruitcake. Speaking of cake reminds me, it must be way past dinnertime."

They rounded a curve in the staircase and saw the landing, but no sign of Mina or the dog. Rhys halted, hushed Nightshade when he would have spoken. They both listened.

"The Beloved," said Nightshade.

"I'm afraid so." Rhys grabbed the kender and hustled him along.

"Maybe Majere will help us escape them."

"I'm not sure he can," Rhys replied.

"What about Zeboim? I'd even be glad to see her right now and I never thought I'd say that!" Nightshade said, gasping for breath.

"I do not believe any of the gods can help us. We witnessed their failure in Solace. Remember? Kiri-Jolith's paladin could not kill the Beloved, nor could the magic of Mistress Jenna. The Beloved are bound to Mina."

"But she doesn't remember them!" Nightshade waved his arms wildly and almost took a tumble down the stairs. "She's terrified of them!"

"Yes," Rhys agreed, steadying him. "She is."

Nightshade glared at him.

"I'm sorry, my friend," said Rhys helplessly. "I don't know what to tell you. Except that we must have faith—"

"In what?" Nightshade demanded. "Mina?"

Rhys patted the kender's shoulder. "In each other."

" 'Don't borrow trouble,' my father used to say," Nightshade muttered, "though dear old Dad borrowed everything else that wasn't nailed down—"

They were interrupted by a shrill scream and the sound of pleading voices.

Mina came tumbling back down the stairs. "Mister Monk! Those horrible dead people are up there! Someone opened the door—"

"Someone?" Nightshade growled.

"I guess I may have opened it," Mina admitted. Her face was pale, her amber eyes wide. She looked plaintively at Rhys. "I know you told me to stay with you. I'm sorry I didn't." She took hold of his hand, clasping it firmly. "I'll stay with you now. I promise. But I don't think the dead people are going to let us out," she added with a quiver in her voice. "I think they want to hurt me."

"You should have thought of that before you made them dead!" Nightshade shouted.

Mina stared at him in bewilderment. "Why are you yelling at me? I don't know anything about them. I *hate* them!" She burst into tears and, flinging her arms around Rhys, she buried her head against his stomach.

"Mina, Mina . . ." the Beloved called.

They were gathering on the landing, massing beneath the arched entryway. Rhys could not count their numbers. None of them were looking at him. None looked at Nightshade or Atta. The Beloved's dead eyes were fixed on Mina. The dead mouths formed her name.

Mina peeked out from the folds of Rhys's robes and, seeing the Beloved staring at her, she cringed and whimpered. "Don't let them take me!"

"I won't. Don't be afraid. We have to keep moving," Rhys said, trying to speak calmly.

"No, I won't!" Mina clung to Rhys, dragging him back. "Don't make me go up there!"

"Nightshade, take my staff," said Rhys. He reached down and picked up the girl. "Keep tight hold."

Mina flung her arms around his neck and wrapped her legs around his waist and hid her face against his shoulder. "I'm not going to look!"

"I wish I didn't have to look," Nightshade muttered. "You wouldn't want to carry me, too, would you?"

"Keep walking," Rhys said.

They climbed the stairs, moving slowly, but steadily. One of the Beloved took a step toward them. Nightshade froze, sheltering behind Rhys. Atta barked and lunged, jaws wide, teeth flaring. Mina screamed and hung onto Rhys so tightly she nearly choked him.

"Atta! Leave it!" Rhys commanded sharply, and the dog fell back. Atta padded along at his side, growling a warning, her lip curled back to show her fangs.

"Keep moving," Rhys said to the kender.

Nightshade kept moving, crowding close behind Rhys. The Beloved paid no attention to monk, kender or dog.

"Mina!" cried the Beloved, reaching out to her. "Mina."

She shook her head and kept her face hidden. Rhys placed his foot on the last stair. He raised himself slowly. Ascending the last stair, he stood on the landing beneath the archway.

The Beloved blocked his way.

Nightshade closed his eyes and hung onto Rhys's robes with one hand and the emmide with the other.

"We're dead," said Nightshade. "I can't look. We're dead. I can't look."

Rhys, holding Mina in his arms, took a step forward into the throng of Beloved.

The Beloved hesitated, then, their eyes fixed on Mina, they fell back to let him pass. Rhys heard them move in behind him. He continued to walk at a slow and even pace, and they passed beneath the archway and into the main hall. He halted, overwhelmed with dismay. Nightshade made a choking sound.

The Beloved had invaded the tower. The spiral staircase continued upward to the very top of the tower and the Beloved stood on every stair. The Beloved massed in the hallway, their bodies pressed against each other, jostling and shoving, as each tried to glimpse Mina. And more Beloved were pushing their way through the entrance, shoving their way inside.

"There are thousands!" Nightshade gulped. "Every Beloved in Ansalon must be here."

Rhys had no idea what to do. The Beloved could kill them even without meaning to. If they surged forward to seize Mina, the press of bodies would crush them.

"Mina," said Rhys, "I have to set you down."

"No!" she whimpered, clinging to him.

"I have to," he repeated firmly and he lowered her to the floor.

Nightshade handed Rhys the emmide. Rhys took it and held it out horizontally in front of them.

"Mina, get behind me. Nightshade, take hold of Atta."

Nightshade caught the dog by the scruff of her neck and hauled her close. Atta snarled and snapped whenever the Beloved drew too near, leaving her tooth marks in more than one, but they paid no heed. Mina pressed against Rhys, clinging to his robes. Rhys stood in front of them, holding his staff in both hands, keeping the Beloved at bay. He started walking toward the double doors.

The Beloved surged around him, vying with each other to try to touch Mina. Her name resounded through the tower. Some whispered "Mina," as though the name was too holy to say aloud. Others repeated "Mina" over and over frantically, obsessively. Others wailed her name in pleading tones. Whether they whispered her name or spoke it, the voices seemed laden with sorrow, lamenting their fate.

"Mina, Mina, Mina." Her name was a mournful wind sighing in the darkness.

"Make them stop!" Mina cried, her hands covering her ears. "Why do they call my name? I don't know them! Why are they doing this to me?"

The Beloved moaned and surged toward her. Rhys struck at them with his staff, but it was like trying to beat back the endless waves. The mournful lamenting had taken on a different tone. It was now tinged with anger. The eyes of the Beloved had at last turned to him. He heard the scrape of steel.

Atta yelped in pain. Nightshade struggled against the massing bodies and pulled the dog out from under trampling feet and hauled her up in his arms. Atta's eyes were wide with terror, her mouth open, panting. Her paws scrabbled against his chest, trying to keep hold.

The air was fetid, stank of decay. Rhys's strength was flagging. He could not hold the Beloved back much longer and once he dropped the staff, he would be overwhelmed.

Light flared off a knife blade. Rhys struck at the blade with the end of the staff and managed to deflect the killing stroke, though the knife raked over Nightshade's arm, slicing a deep cut. Nightshade cried out and dropped Atta, who crouched, quivering at his feet.

Mina stared at the blood, and her face went ashen. "I don't want to be here," she said in a trembling voice. "I don't want this to be happening . . . I don't know them . . . We'll go away, far away . . ."

"Yes!" cried Nightshade, clasping his hand over his bleeding arm.

"No," said Rhys.

Nightshade gaped at him.

"Mina, you do know them," Rhys told her in stern tones. "You can't run away. You kissed them and they died."

Mina was at first bewildered, then understanding lit the amber eyes.

"That was Chemosh!" she cried. "Not me! It wasn't my fault."

She glared at the Beloved and clenched her fist and screamed at them, "I gave you what you wanted! You cannot be hurt. You can never feel pain or sickness or fear! You will always be young and beautiful—"

"—and dead!" Nightshade cried. He thumped himself on the chest. "Look at me, Mina. This is life! Pain is life! Fear is life! You took all that from them! And worse than that. You locked them up inside death and threw away the key. They have nowhere to go. They're stuck, trapped."

Mina stared at the kender in perplexity, and Rhys could picture what she was seeing—he and Nightshade, disheveled, bloody, sweating, gasping for breath, shoving at the Beloved with the staff, keeping a grip on the shivering dog. She could hear the kender's voice shake with terror and exasperation, and his voice filled with desperation, and she could hear, by the contrast, the empty, hollow voices of the Beloved.

The little girl dissolved before Rhys's startled eyes and the woman, Mina, stood before him as he had seen her in the grotto. She was tall and slender. Her auburn hair was shoulder length and framed her face in soft waves. Her amber eyes were large and shining with anger, peopled with souls. She wore a diaphonous black gown that coiled around her lithe body like the shades of night. She turned to face the Beloved, gazed out at the restless, dreadful sea of her victims.

"Mina . . ." they chanted. "Mina!"

"Stop it!" she cried.

The sea of dead moaned and wailed and whispered.

"Mina . . ."

The Beloved closed in around Rhys. He struck at them with the staff, but there were too many, and he was slammed back against the wall. Nightshade was on his hands and knees, trying to avoid the tramping feet, but his hands were bloody and his nose was bleeding. Rhys could not see Atta, though he could hear her whimper in pain. The heaving mass gave another surge, and he was smashed between the wall and the bodies and could not move; he could not breathe.

"Mina! Mina!" Rhys heard her name dimly, as everything started to fade.

Mina clenched her fists and raised her head and shouted into the echoing of her own name.

"I made you gods!" she screamed. "Why aren't you happy?"

The Beloved went silent. Her name ceased.

Mina opened her hands and amber flames flared from her palms. She opened her eyes and amber flames shot from the pupils. She opened her mouth and gouts of flame poured out. She grew in size, taller and taller, screaming her frustration and pain to the heavens as the fire of her wrath blazed out of control.

One moment Rhys was being crushed beneath bodies and the next moment searing heat washed over him and the bodies were incinerated, leaving him covered in greasy ash.

Blinded by the blazing light, Rhys coughed as smoke and ash flew down his windpipe. He groped about for his friends and grabbed hold of Nightshade at the same time the kender grabbed hold of him.

"I can't see!" Nightshade choked, clutching at Rhys in a panic. "I can't see!"

Rhys found Atta and dragged her and Nightshade back through the archway and into the stairwell, away from the heat and flames and the greasy black ash that swirled about the tower in a horrid blizzard.

The kender rubbed his eyes, as the tears streamed down his cheeks, making tracks in the ash that smeared his face.

Rhys watched the wrath of an unhappy god destroy her failure.

The burning went on a long time.

Finally, the amber light grew dim and went out, Mina's rage exhausted. Ashes continued to drift down in a gray cloud. Rhys helped Nightshade to his feet. They left the stairwell and plowed their way through horrible black drifts that nearly buried the dog. Nightshade gagged and covered his mouth with his hand. Rhys held his sleeve over his nose and mouth. He looked for Mina, but there was no sign of her and Rhys was too shaken to wonder what had become of her. He wanted only to escape the horror.

They fled through the double doors and stumbled out into sunlight and the blessed fresh air blowing off the sea.

"Where have you been?" Mina said accusingly. "I've been waiting and waiting for you!"

The little girl stood in front of them, staring. "How did you get so dirty?" She held her nose. "You stink!"

Nightshade looked at Rhys.

"She doesn't remember," Rhys said quietly.

The sea was unusually calm, he noticed, the waves subdued, as if in shock. Rhys washed his face and hands. Nightshade rinsed off as best he could, while Atta dove into the water.

Mina set the sail on the small boat. The wind blew strong and favorably, as though eager to help them get away, and the boat went bounding over the waves.

They were nearing shore and Rhys was poised to lower the sail, when Nightshade cried out.

"Look, Rhys! Look at that!"

Rhys turned to see the tower being sucked slowly down beneath the waves. The tower sank lower and lower until all that was left were the small crystal fingers at the top, like a hand reaching up to heaven. Then those, too, vanished.

131

"The Beloved are gone, Rhys," Nightshade said in an awed voice. "She set them free."

Mina did not turn around at the kender's shout. She did not look behind. She was concentrating on sailing the boat, steering it safely to shore.

I made you gods.

I made you gods. Why aren't you happy?

BOOK II
THE
JOURNEY

*T*hough they were all exhausted from their ordeal in the tower, Rhys did not deem it wise to remain long in the vicinity of Chemosh's castle. He asked Mina if the small sailboat could make it to Flotsam and she stated that it could, provided they did not venture too far out to sea. They sailed up the coast, north to the harbor city of Flotsam.

They made the journey in safety, with only one brief scare, when Nightshade suddenly toppled over and lay in the bottom of the boat, where he was heard to faintly murmur the words: "meat pie". Deeply concerned, Mina searched the boat and, sure enough, discovered more pies tucked away in a sack. Nightshade revived wonderfully upon smelling the food and, taking one pie with him, retired to the rear of the boat to eat, thereby avoiding Rhys's reproving gaze.

They spent several days in Flotsam, resting and recovering. Rhys found an innkeeper willing to give him work in exchange for floor space and blankets in the common room. While he mopped floors and washed mugs, Nightshade and Mina explored the city. Rhys had at first prohibited Mina from leaving the inn, thinking that a six-year-old girl should not be roaming around Flotsam even if she was a god. But after a day spent trying to do his work and keep Mina from pestering the guests, infuriating the cook, and rescuing her after she tumbled down the well, Rhys decided it would be less dangerous if she went off exploring with Nightshade.

Rhys's main concern was that Mina would go blabbing to strangers about the holy artifacts. Nightshade had described the nature of the artifacts' miraculous powers, which were truly formidable. Rhys explained to Mina that the holy artifacts were immensely valuable and because of that, people might want to steal them, might even kill to possess them.

Mina listened to him with grave attention. Alarmed at the thought she might lose her gifts for Goldmoon, she promised Rhys solemnly and faithfully that she would keep them a secret. Rhys could only hope she meant it. He took Nightshade aside and impressed upon the kender the need to keep Mina from talking, then sent them both off, with Atta to guard them, to take in the sights of Flotsam so that he could get some work done.

Once, Flotsam had been a swaggering, rollicking, boisterous and free-wheeling rogue of a city. With a reputation for being disreputable, Flotsam had been a haven for pirates, thieves, mercenaries, deserters, bounty-hunters, and gamblers. Then came the Dragon Overlords, the largest and most terrible of which was an enormous red dragon named Malys. She seemed to take delight in tormenting Flotsam, periodically swooping down on the city to set parts of it ablaze, killing or driving off many of the inhabitants.

Malys was now gone and Flotsam was slowly recovering, but the wild child had been forced to grow up, and was now a sadder, though wiser, city.

Most of the ships now in the harbor belonged to the minotaur race, who ruled the seas from their islands to the north to the conquered lands of the former elven nation of Silvanesti to the south and beyond, for the minotaur nation was reaching out to humans, working hard to try to gain their trust. Well aware that their economic survival depended on trade with human nations, the minotaurs were ordered by their commanders to be on their best behavior while in Flotsam. The people of Flotsam, meanwhile, were conscious of their own economic survival and signs welcoming the minotaurs were posted in nearly every tavern and shop in town.

Consequently a city once known throughout Ansalon for its chair-breaking, table-hurling, mug-smashing, bone-crushing bar fights was now reduced to a few bloodied noses and a cracked rib. If a fight did break out, it was quickly squelched by either the local citizenry or minotaur guards. Offenders were hauled away to prison or permitted to sleep it off below decks.

As Nightshade would soon discover, Flotsam was in line to become a model citizen. Crime was down. There was no longer even a Thieves Guild, for the members hadn't been able to raise enough cash to pay the dues. A settlement of gnomes located outside the city offered the only chance for excitement, but the mere thought of Mina among gnomes made Nightshade shudder.

"Might well bring about the end of civilization as we know it," he told Rhys.

The kender was pleased, however, to find people interested in his abilities as a Nightstalker. A great many people had been killed by the dragon, and Nightshade's ability to speak to the departed was much in demand. He lined up a client the second night they were in Flotsam.

Mina was eager to go with Nightshade to the graveyard "to see the spooks" as she put it. Nightshade, considerably offended by this undignified term, told her quite sternly that his encounters with *spirits* were private, between him and his clients, not to be shared. Mina sulked and pouted, but the kender was firm, and that night after dinner, he went off by himself, leaving Mina with Rhys.

Rhys told her to help him sweep up. She gave the kitchen floor a couple of swipes with the broom, then she tossed it aside and sat down to pester Rhys about when they were going to start for Godshome.

Nightshade returned late in the night, bringing with him a set of cast-off clothes and new boots for himself and for Rhys, whose old boots were cracked and worn through. As it turned out, the kender's client was a cobbler and he'd taken the boots in payment. Nightshade also brought a meaty bone for Atta, who accepted it with relish and proved her gratitude by lying on his feet as he related his adventures.

"It all started when I was visiting the graveyard last night and chatting with some of the spirits when I noticed a little boy—"

"A real little boy or a spook?" Mina interrupted.

"The proper term is spirit or ghost," Nightshade corrected her. "They don't like to be called 'spooks'. It's quite insulting. You believe in ghosts, don't you?"

"I believe in ghosts," said Mina. "I just don't believe *you* can talk to them."

"Well, I can," said Nightshade.

"Prove it to me," Mina said slyly. "Take me with you tomorrow night."

"That wouldn't be right," Nightshade returned. "Being a professional, I keep my client's communications confidential." He was pleased at having uttered several large words in a row.

"You're telling us about them now," Mina pointed out.

"That's different," said Nightshade, though for a moment he was flummoxed as to how. "I'm not using their names!"

Mina giggled and Nightshade went red in the face. Rhys stepped in, told Mina to quit teasing Nightshade, and told Nightshade to go on with his story.

"The little boy *ghost*," said Nightshade with emphasis, "was really unhappy. He was just sitting there on this tombstone, kicking it with his heels. I asked him how long he'd been dead and he said five years. He was six when he died, and he was eleven now. That struck me as odd, because the dead usually don't keep track of time. He said he knew how old he was because his father came to visit every year on the little boy's birthday. That seemed to make him sad, so to cheer him up, I offered to play a game with him, but he didn't want to play. Then I asked him why he was still here among the living when he should be on his soul's journey."

"I don't like this story," Mina said, frowning.

Nightshade was about to make a stinging remark when he caught Rhys's eye and thought better of it. He went on with his tale.

"The little boy said he wanted to leave. He could see a wonderful, beautiful place and he wanted to go there, but he couldn't because he didn't want to leave his father. I said his father would want him to go on with his journey and I told him that they'd meet up again. The little boy said that was the problem. If he did meet his father again, how would his father recognize him after so much time had passed?"

Mina had been fidgeting, but she was quiet now, sitting cross-legged on the floor, her elbows on her knees, her chin in her hands, listening intently, her amber gaze fixed on the kender.

"I told him his father would know. The little boy didn't believe me and I said I would prove it.

139

"I went to the cobbler and I told him I was a Nightstalker and I'd talked to his son and that there was a problem. At first the cobbler was kind of rude, and there might have been a small scuffle when he tried to throw me out of his shop. But then I described his little boy to him, and the cobbler calmed down and listened.

"I took the cobbler to the graveyard, and his son was there waiting for him. The cobbler told me that he thought about his son every day, and he imagined what he would be like as he was growing up, and he said that was why he came to visit on his birthday. That he could see his little boy growing up in his mind. When the little boy heard this, he knew that no matter how much he changed, his father would know him. The boy quit kicking the tombstone and gave his father a hug and then he left on his journey.

"The father couldn't see his little boy or hear him, of course, but I think he did feel the hug, because the father said I'd lifted a weight from his heart. He felt at peace for the first time in five years. So he took me back to his shop and he gave me the boots and he said I was a—"

Sitting up straight, Mina said abruptly, "What if the little boy hadn't died? What if he'd lived and grown to be a man and he'd done things that were wicked? Very, very wicked. What would happen then?"

"How should I know?" Nightshade said crossly. "That has nothing to do with my story. Where was I? Oh, yes. The cobbler gave me the boots and he said I was a—"

"I'll tell you," said Mina solemnly. "The little boy must never grow up. That way, the father will still love him."

Nightshade stared at Mina in astonishment. Then, leaning close, he said in a loud whisper, "Is that why she's a—"

"Go on with your story," Rhys said quietly. He reached out his hand and gently smoothed Mina's auburn hair.

Mina gave a fleeting smile, but she did not look up. She sat gazing into the fire.

"Uh, anyway, the cobbler gave me the boots," Nightshade said, subdued. He sat looking uncomfortable and then remembered. "Oh, I have something else!" He went to retrieve a large cloth bag and plunked it down triumphantly.

Rhys had noticed the bag, but had been careful not to ask questions, not being truly certain he wanted to know the answers.

"It's a map!" Nightshade stated, pulling out a large, rolled-up sheet of oiled paper. "A map of Ansalon."

He spread out the map on the floor and prepared to show it off. Unfortunately, the map kept wanting to roll back up again, and he had to anchor it down with two ale mugs, a soup bowl and the leg of the stool.

"Nightshade," said Rhys, "a map like this costs a lot of money—"

"Does it?" Nightshade frowned. "I don't know why. It looks kind of beat-up to me."

"Nightshade—"

"Oh, all right. If you insist, I'll take it back in the morning."

"Tonight," said Rhys.

"The minotaur captain won't miss it until morning," Nightshade assured him. "And I didn't take it. I asked the captain if I could borrow it. That was right before he passed out. My minotaur is a little rusty, but I'm pretty certain *"Ash kanazi rasckana cloppf[1]*," means 'Yes, of course you can, my friend'."

"We'll *both* return the map tonight," said Rhys.

"Well, if you insist. But first, don't you want to look at it? This shows the way to—"

"—to Godshome?" cried Mina, jumping up eagerly.

---

1 Translation: "Shove off before I gut you, you little turd!"

"Well, no, Godshome's not on here. But it does show Neraka, which is somewhere near where Godshome might be."

"Which is where?" Mina asked, squatting down beside the map.

Nightshade hunted a bit, then placed his finger on a mountain range on the western side of the continent.

"And where are we?" Mina asked.

Nightshade placed his finger on a dot on the eastern side of the continent.

"That's not far," said Mina happily.

"Not far!" Nightshade hooted. "It's hundreds and hundreds of miles."

"Pooh. Watch this!" Mina stepped on the map, almost squashing Nightshade's fingers. Placing her feet close to each other, she walked heel, toe, heel, toe from one side of the map to other side. "There. You

see? That was about three steps. Not far at all."

Nightshade gaped at her. "But that's—"

"This is boring. I'm going to bed." Mina walked over to where she had her blanket stashed. Spreading it out, she lay down and immediately sat back up. "We're starting for Godshome tomorrow," she told them, and then laid back down, curled up, and went to sleep.

"Three steps," Nightshade repeated. "She's going to expect to get there by tomorrow night."

"I know," said Rhys. "I'll talk to her." He gazed somberly at the map and sighed. "It *is* a long way. I hadn't realized just far we had traveled. And how far we have to go."

"We could book passage on a ship," Nightshade suggested. "We might find one that would allow kender—"

Rhys smiled at his friend. "We might. But would you put yourself into the hands of the Sea Goddess again?"

"I hadn't thought of that," Nightshade said with a grimace. "I guess we walk."

He plopped down on his stomach and continued to study the map. "It's not a straight line from here to there. How will we remember the route?"

He rolled over comfortably on his back, propped his head on his arms. "The minotaur won't miss his map until morning. If we had something to write on, I could copy it. I know! We could cut up my old shirt!"

He brought the shirt back along with a pair of shears he borrowed (legitimately) from the innkeeper and a quill pen and some ink. Nightshade then settled down happily to make a copy of the map and plot out their route.

"Do you know anything about all these different countries?" he asked Rhys.

143

"I do know something of them," Rhys said. "The monks of my order often leave the monastery to travel the world. When they return, they tell tales of where they have been, what they have seen. I have heard many stories and descriptions of the lands of Ansalon."

A sad note in Rhys's voice caused Nightshade to look up from his work. "What's the matter?"

"All those of my order are urged to make such a journey, but it is not required," Rhys replied. "I had no intention of leaving my monastery. I did not think I needed to know any more of the world than what I could see from the green pastures where I tended the sheep. I would have remained in the monastery all my life, but for Mina."

He looked over at the child, who was asleep on the floor. Mina's sleep was often restless. She cried out, whimpered and cringed, and now she had tangled herself up in her blanket. Rhys rearranged the blanket, tucked it around her, and soothed her until she grew more peaceful.

When she was breathing more evenly, he left her and returned to where Nightshade was still studying the map.

"It occurs to me that the head of my order may know something about Godshome. Although it is out of our way, I believe it would be worth our while to first seek guidance at the Temple of Majere in Solace—"

"Solace!" Nightshade repeated excitedly. "My favorite place in the whole world! Gerard's there, and he's the best sheriff in the whole world. Not to mention chicken and dumpling day at the Inn of the Last Home. Is that Tuesday? I think it was Tuesday. Or is Tuesday pork chop and green beans day?"

The kender returned to his work with renewed vigor. Drawing on his own information (gleaned from fellow kender and therefore not entirely to be relied upon) and Rhys's knowledge of the lands through which they would have to travel, he eventually determined the route.

"We walk overland along the northern coast of the Kyrman Sea," Nightshade explained, when it was all finished. "We go past the ruins of Micah, which, according to the map is about thirty miles, then we travel another seventy miles through the desert, and on to the city of Delphon. What do you know about the humans of Khur? I've heard they're very fierce."

"They are a proud people, renowned warriors, with strong loyalties to their tribes that often lead to blood feuds. But they are noted for their hospitality to strangers."

"That never seems to include kender. Still, with all those blood feuds, they must have a lot of dead people hanging about. Perhaps they'll need my services."

Taking this hopeful view, Nightshade went back to his map. "There's a road from Delphon that leads west through the hills to the capital city of Khuri-Khan. Then there's another big stretch of desert and another hundred miles or so after that, and we come to Blöde, home of the ogres."

Nightshade heaved a sigh. "Ogres like kender—for supper. And ogres kill humans or make them their slaves. But that's the only way."

"Then we must make the best of it," said Rhys.

Nightshade shook his head. "If we get through Blöde alive—which is a big 'if'—we come to the Great Swamp. A Dragon Overlord named Sable used to live there, but she's dead and the curse she cast on that land died with her. Still, the swamp is a nasty place, with lizards and man-eating plants and poisonous snakes. After that, we have to find a way across the Westguard River, then we go west a bit, go south a bit, skirt the coastline of New Sea, travel through Linh and Salmonfall and we finally reach Abanasinia.

"Once there, we cross the Plains of Dergoth, then travel through Pax Tharkas and into what used to be Qualinesti past the Lake of Death. I have to admit I'm kind of looking forward to that part. I've heard there are lots of wandering spirits in the lake. Elf ghosts. I like elf ghosts. They're always very polite. After that, we cross the White Rage River and then venture into Darkenwood, which isn't all that darken anymore, from what I've heard. Then we head out over the Plains of Abanasinia, pass through Gateway and finally trek north to Solace. Whew!"

Nightshade wiped his brow and went off to fetch a mug of restorative ale. Rhys sat in his chair by the fire, contemplating the map, envisioning the journey.

A monk, a kender, a dog, and a six-year-old god.

Walking deserts, mountains, swamps, plains, forests. Encountering civil wars, border skirmishes, tribal battles, blood feuds. As well as the usual hazards of the road: washed-out bridges, forest fires, torrential rainstorms, bitter cold, sweltering heat. And the usual dangers: thieves, trolls, ogres, lizard-men, wolves, snakes, the odd wandering giant.

"How long do you think the trip will take us?" Nightshade asked, wiping foam from his lips.

A lifetime, Rhys thought.

2

hey left Flotsam the next morning, and for the first several miles
the trip went well. Mina was entertained and diverted by the new
and interesting sights. Farmers from outlying districts bringing
goods to market exchanged friendly greetings. A caravan of wealthy
merchants with men-at-arms guarding them took up the entire
road. The men-at-arms were stern and business-like, but the merchants waved at Mina and, seeing the monk, asked for his blessing
on their travels and tossed him a few coins. After that, a noble lord
and lady and their retinue rode by; the lady stopped to admire Mina
and give her some sweetmeats, which Mina shared with Nightshade
and Atta.

They met several parties of kender, who were either leaving Flotsam
(forcibly) or heading in that direction. The kender stopped to chat
with Nightshade, exchanging the latest news and gossip. He questioned
them about the road ahead, and received an enormous amount of information, some of it accurate.

Their most interesting encounter was with a group of gnomes
whose steam-powered perambulating combination threshing machine,

dough-kneader, and bread-baker had run amuck and was lying in pieces on the side of the road. This meeting caused considerable delay as Rhys stopped to tend to the victims.

All this excitement occupied the better part of the day. Mina was happy and well-behaved and eager to meet more gnomes. They made an early stop for the night. The weather being fine, they camped outdoors, and Mina thought that was great fun at first, though she didn't think much of it around midnight when she discovered she'd made her bed on an ant hill.

Consequently, she was cross and grumpy the next morning, and her mood did not improve. The farther they traveled from Flotsam, the fewer people they met along the road until eventually there was no one but themselves. The scenery consisted of empty stretches of vacant land enlivened by a few scraggly trees. Mina grew bored and began to complain. She was tired. She wanted to stop. Her boots pinched her toes. She had a blister on her heel. Her legs ached. Her back ached. She was hungry. She was thirsty.

"So when are we going to get there?" she asked Rhys, lagging along beside him, scuffing her feet in the dust.

"I'd like to cover a few more miles before it grows dark," Rhys said. "Then we'll make camp."

"No, not camp!" Mina said. "I mean Godshome. I'm really tired of walking. Will we be there tomorrow?"

Rhys was trying to think how to explain that it might well be a year of tomorrows before they reached Godshome when Atta gave a sharp bark. Her ears pricked, she stared intently down the road.

"Someone's coming," said Nightshade.

A horse and rider were heading in their direction, traveling at a fast pace to judge by the pounding hoofbeats. Rhys took hold of Mina's hand and hurriedly drew her to the side of the road, to get out of the way of the horse's hooves. He could not yet see the rider, due to a slight dip in the road. Atta remained obediently at Rhys's side, but she continued to growl. Her body quivered. Her lip curled.

"Whoever's coming, Atta doesn't like them," Nightshade observed. "That's not like her."

Accustomed to traveling, Atta tended to be friendly with strangers, though she kept herself aloof and would submit to being petted only if there was no way to avoid it. She was warning them against this stranger, however, even before she saw him.

The horse and rider topped the ridge and, sighting them, increased speed, galloping down the road toward them. The rider was cloaked in black. His long hair streamed behind him in the wind.

Nightshade gasped. "Rhys! That's Chemosh! What do we do?"

"Nothing we can do," Rhys replied.

The Lord of Death reined in his horse as he drew near. Nightshade looked about wildly for someplace to hide. They were caught out in the open, however. Not a tree or a gully in sight.

Rhys ordered Atta to be quiet and she obeyed for the most part, though the occasional growl got the better of her. He drew Mina close to him, holding his staff in front of her with one hand, keeping his other hand protectively on her shoulder. Nightshade stood stolidly by his friend's side. Reminding himself he was a kender with horns, he assumed a very fierce look.

"Who is that man?" Mina asked, gazing at the black-cloaked rider curiously. She twisted her head around to look up Rhys. "Do you know him?"

"I know him," Rhys replied. "Do you know him, Mina?"

"Me?" Mina was amazed. She shook her head. "I never saw him before."

Chemosh dismounted his horse and began walking toward them.

The horse remained unmoving where he left it, as though it had been changed to stone. Nightshade edged closer to Rhys.

"Kender with horns," Nightshade said to give himself courage. "Kender with horns."

Atta growled, and Rhys silenced her.

Chemosh ignored the dog and the kender. He flicked an uninterested glance at Rhys. The lord's attention was focused on Mina. His face was tight, livid with anger. His dark eyes were cold.

Mina stared at Chemosh from behind the barricade formed by the monk's staff and Rhys felt her tremble. He tightened his hold on her reassuringly.

"I don't like this man," Mina said in a shaky voice. "Tell him to go away."

Chemosh came to a halt and glared down at the little red-haired girl sheltering in Rhys's arms.

"You can end this game of yours now, Mina," he said. "You have made me look the fool. You've had your laugh. Now come back home with me."

"I'm not going anywhere with you," Mina retorted. "I don't even know you. And Goldmoon told me never to talk to strangers."

"Mina, stop this nonsense—" Chemosh began angrily, and he reached out his hand to seize her.

Mina kicked the Lord of Death in the shin.

Nightshade sucked in a breath and closed his eyes and waited for the world to end. When the world kept going, Nightshade opened his eyes a slit to see that Rhys had pulled Mina behind him, shielding her with his body. Chemosh was looking exceedingly grim.

"You are putting on a very fine show, Mina, but I have no time for play-acting," he stated impatiently. "You will come with me, and you will bring with you the artifacts you basely stole from the Hall of

Sacrilege. Or I will shortly be seeing your friends in the Abyss—"

Lashing rain drowned out the rest of Chemosh's threat. The sky grew black as his cloak. Storm clouds boiled and bubbled. Zeboim arrived in a gust of wind and pelting hail.

The goddess leaned down and presented her cheek to Mina.

"Give your Auntie Zee a kiss, dear," she said sweetly.

Mina buried her face in Rhys's robes.

Zeboim shrugged and shifted her gaze to Chemosh, who was regarding her with an expression as dark and thunderous as the storm.

"What do you want, Sea Bitch?" he demanded.

"I was worried about Mina," Zeboim replied, bestowing an affectionate glance on the girl. "What are you doing here, Lord of Rot?"

"I was also concerned—" Chemosh began.

Zeboim laughed. "Concerned with how royally you screwed things up? You had Mina, you had the tower, you had the *Solio Febalas*, you had the Beloved. And you've lost it all. Your Beloved are a gruesome pile of greasy ash lying at the bottom of the Blood Sea. My brother has the tower. The High God has claimed the *Solio Febalas*. As for Mina, she's made it painfully clear she wants nothing more to do with you."

Chemosh did not need to hear the litany of his misfortune recited back to him. He turned his back on the goddess and knelt down beside Mina, who regarded him in wary amazement.

"Mina, my dear, please listen to me. I'm sorry if I frightened you. I'm sorry I hurt you. I was jealous . . ." Chemosh paused, then said, "Come back to my castle with me, Mina. I miss you. I love you . . ."

"Mina, my pet, don't go anywhere with this horrid man," said Zeboim, shoving the Lord of Death out of the way. "He's lying. He doesn't love you. He never did. He's using you. Come live with your Auntie Zee . . ."

"I'm going to Godshome," said Mina, and she took hold of Rhys's hand. "And it's a long way from here, so we have to get started. Come on, Mister Monk."

"Godshome," said Chemosh after a moment's astonished silence. "That is a long way from here." He turned on his heel and walked back to his horse. Mounting, he gazed down at Rhys from beneath dark and lowering brows. "A very long way. And the road is fraught with peril. I've no doubt I'll be seeing you again shortly, Monk."

He dug his heels into the horse's flanks and rode off in ire. Zeboim watched him leave, then she turned back to Rhys.

"It *is* a long way, Rhys," said Zeboim with a playful smile. "You will be on the road for months, perhaps years. If you live that long. Though now that I think of it . . ."

Zeboim bent swiftly down to whisper something in Mina's ear.

Mina listened, frowning, at first, and then her eyes widened. "I can do that?"

"Of course you can, child." Zeboim patted her on the head. "You can do anything. Have a safe journey, friends."

Zeboim laughed and, spreading her arms, she became a whipping wind, which then dwindled to a teasing breeze and, still laughing, wafted away.

The road was empty. Rhys sighed in relief and lowered his staff.

"Why did that silly-looking man want me to come with him?" Mina asked.

"He made a mistake," said Rhys. "He thought you were someone else. Someone he used to know."

The time was only midafternoon, but Rhys, worn out from the strain of the encounter with the gods and a day of putting up with Mina, decided to make camp early. They spread out their blankets near a stream that wound like a snake through the tall grass. A small grove of trees provided shelter.

Nightshade soon recovered his spirits and began to badger Mina into telling him what the goddess had said to her. Mina shook her head. She was pondering deeply over something. Her brow was creased, her lips pursed. Eventually she shook off whatever was bothering her and, taking off her shoes and stockings, went to play in the creek. They ate a frugal meal of dried peas and smoked meat, then sat around the fire.

"I want to see the map you drew," Mina said suddenly.

"Why?" Nightshade asked suspiciously, and he clapped his hand protectively over his pouch.

"I just want to look at it," Mina returned. "Everyone keeps telling me Godshome is such a long way away. I want to see for myself."

"I showed you once," Nightshade said.

"Yes, but I want to see it again."

"Oh, all right. But go wash your hands," Nightshade ordered as he removed the map from its pouch and spread it out on top of his blanket. "I don't want greasy finger marks on it."

Mina ran down to the stream to wash her hands and face.

Rhys had stretched out full-length on the ground, resting after the meal. Atta lay beside him, her chin on his chest. He stroked her fur and gazed into the heavens. The sun stood balanced precariously on the rim of the world. The sky was a blend of soft twilight hues, pinks and golds, purples and oranges. Beyond the sunset, he could feel immortal eyes watching.

Mina came running back, to exhibit moderately clean hands. Nightshade anchored the map with rocks and then showed Mina the route they were going to be taking.

"This is where we are now," he said.

"And where is Flotsam where we started?" Mina asked.

Nightshade pointed about a whisker's width away.

"All this walking and we've only come that far!" Mina cried, shocked and dismayed.

She squatted beside the map and studied it, her lower lip thrust out. "Why do we have to go all over the place—up and down and round about? Why can't we just go straight from here to here."

Nightshade explained that climbing extremely tall mountains was quite difficult and dangerous, and it was much better to go around them.

"Too bad there are so many mountains," he added. "Otherwise we could go straight as the dragon flies and it wouldn't take long at all."

Mina gazed thoughtfully at the dot that was Flotsam and the dot that Nightshade said was Solace, where they would find his great friend, Gerard, and the monks of Majere who would tell them where to look for Godshome.

Rhys was drifting off in a pleasant haze of twilight forgetfulness when he was jolted wide away. Nightshade let out a screech.

Rhys jumped up so fast he startled Atta, who yelped in aggravation. "What is it?"

Nightshade pointed a quivering finger.

The map was no longer lines and squiggles drawn on the back of the kender's old shirt. The map was a world in miniature, with real mountains and real bodies of water that shimmered in the dying light, and real windswept deserts and boggy swamps.

Thus the gods might see the world, Rhys thought to himself.

Nightshade screeched again and suddenly the kender was floating up into the air, light as thistledown. Rhys felt himself grow buoyant, his body losing weight and mass, his bones hollow as a bird's, his flesh like a soap bubble. His feet left the ground, and he sailed upward. Atta floated toward him, legs dangling helplessly beneath her.

"Straight as the dragon flies," Mina said.

Rhys recalled the near-drowning incident in the tower. He recalled the meat pies and the fiery conflagration that had consumed the Beloved, and he knew he had to put a stop to this. He had to take control.

"Stop it, Mina!" Rhys said sternly. "Stop it at once! Put me down this instant!"

Mina stared at him, her eyes round and starting to glisten with tears.

"Now!" he said through gritted teeth.

He felt himself grow heavy, and he fell back down to the ground. Nightshade dropped like rock, landing with a thud. Atta, once she was down, slunk off hurriedly to curl up beneath a tree, as far from Mina as possible.

Mina drifted very slowly out of the air to land in front of Rhys.

"We are walking to Solace," he said, his voice shaking with anger. "Do you understand me, Mina? We are not swimming or flying. We are *walking!*"

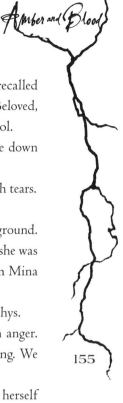

Mina's tears spilled over and ran down her cheeks. She flung herself on the ground and began to sob.

Rhys was trembling. He had always prided himself on his discipline and here he was, yelling at a child. He was suddenly, deeply ashamed.

"I didn't mean to shout at you, Mina—" he began wearily.

"I just wanted to get there faster!" she cried, raising a tear-stained and dirt-streaked face. "I don't like walking. It's boring and my feet hurt! And it's going to take too long, forever and ever. Besides, Aunt Zeboim told me I could fly," she added with a quiver and a hiccup.

Nightshade nudged Rhys in the ribs. "It *is* a long way and flying might be kind of interesting at that—"

Rhys looked at him. Nightshade gulped.

"But you're right, of course. We should walk. That's why the gods gave us feet and not wings. I'll just go to bed now. . . ."

Rhys knelt down and took Mina in his arms. She wrapped her arms around his neck and sobbed on his shoulder. Gradually her sobs lessened, she grew quiet. Rhys, looking down at her, saw that she had cried herself to sleep. He carried her to her blanket that he'd spread on a soft bed of grass beneath a tree and laid her down. He was tucking another blanket around her when she woke up.

"Good night, Mina," he said, and he reached out his hand to gently smooth back the hair from her forehead.

Mina grabbed hold of his hand and gave it a remorseful kiss.

"I'm sorry, Rhys," she said. It was the first time she'd ever called him by his name and not 'Mister Monk'. "We can walk. But could we walk fast?" she added plaintively. "I think I need to reach Godshome quickly."

Rhys was bone-tired, or he might have thought twice before he agreed that, yes, they could "walk fast".

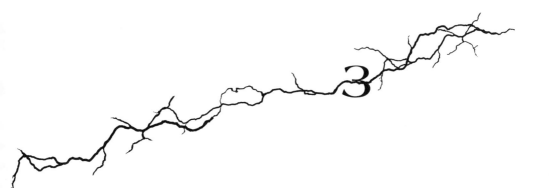

3

*T*he next day, they were in Solace.

"After all," pointed out Nightshade, when he had recovered from the trip, "you *did* tell her we could walk fast."

The morning had started well. Mina was in a chastened mood, quiet and docile. Wisps of fog rose lazily from the stream bed. They set out early with Rhys walking as fast as he thought Mina could manage. When he first saw the trees and grasslands start to slip past him, the increase in speed was so gradual that he thought his eyes were playing tricks on him.

But then the landscape began to slide past him at an incredible velocity. He and Nightshade, Mina and Atta continued to walk at what seemed a normal pace. Fellow travelers flashed past. Clouds raced across the sky. One moment the weather was sunny and the next rain storms soaked them, and the next moment it was sunny again. They sped through the desert. The city of Delphon was a blur of color, the city of Khuri-Khan a blast of noise and heat.

The ogres of Blöde were there, and then they weren't. The Great Swamp was muggy and stifling and foul-smelling, but not for long.

They skimmed across the Westguard River and saw the sun sparkle on the waves of New Sea and then it was gone and the Plains of Dergoth were so much emptiness. The Lake of Death lay in eerie shadow, the White Rage River thundered past. They were in and out of Darkenwood, racing over the Plains of Abanasinia, speeding through Gateway, and here was Solace, and then everything slowed down and stopped.

Rhys was dizzy with the rapid motion and grabbed hold of a post to keep from falling. Nightshade staggered about on wobbly legs for a few moments, then gave a plaintive "Oof!" and collapsed. Atta flopped down on her side and lay there panting.

"We walked all the way!" Mina said proudly. "I did what you told me!"

Her amber eyes were clear and shining. Her smile was eager and happy. She truly believed she had done something worthy of praise, and Rhys did not have the heart to scold her. After all, they had been spared a long, difficult, and dangerous journey, and arrived safely at their destination. He could not help but be relieved. As Rhys came to realize, Mina didn't think she'd done anything extraordinary. For her, strolling across a continent in a day was something everyone could do if he just put his mind to it.

Rhys helped Nightshade to his feet and assured Atta that all was well. Mina was looking eagerly about. She was delighted with Solace.

"The houses are built in trees!" she cried, clapping her hands. "There's a whole city up in the trees! I want to go up there. What is that place?"

She pointed to a large building nestled in the branches of a giant vallenwood.

"That's the Inn of the Last Home," Nightshade stated, eagerly sniffing the air. He was feeling almost back to normal. "Boiled cabbage.

Which means today must be corned beef and cabbage day. Wait until you meet Laura. She owns the Inn and she does the cooking and she's the best cook in all of Ansalon. Then there's our friend, Gerard, the sheriff. He's—"

"Mina," Rhys said, interrupting, "would you run over to that well and fetch some water for Atta?"

Mina did as she was bid, running excitedly off to the public well, taking the panting dog with her.

"I don't think we should tell Gerard the truth about Mina," Rhys said to Nightshade when Mina was gone. "We don't want to strain his credulity."

"Is that like noodles?" Nightshade asked, puzzled. " 'Cause I know you have to strain them."

"I am afraid he would not believe us," Rhys clarified.

"That she's a god whose gone crazy? I'm not sure *I* believe us," Nightshade said solemnly. He put his hand to his forehead. "I'm still kind of dizzy from all that walking. But I see what you mean. Gerard knew Mina, didn't he? The old Mina, I mean. When she was a soldier during the War of Souls. He told us about meeting her that one night when he started talking about what happened to him during the war. But she's a little girl now. I don't think he'd be likely to connect the two. Do you?"

"I don't know," Rhys said. "He might recognize her if he hears her name and sees her. Her looks are extraordinary."

Nightshade watched Mina hurry back toward them. She was carrying water in a pail and sloshing most of it onto her shoes.

"Rhys," said the kender in a whisper, "what if Mina recognizes *him*? Gerard was her enemy. She might kill him!"

"I don't think she will," said Rhys. "She seems to have blotted out that part of her life."

"She blotted out the Beloved too, and it all came back to her," Nightshade reminded him.

Rhys smiled faintly. "We must hope for the best and trust that the gods are with us."

"Oh, they're with us, all right," Nightshade grumbled. "If there's one thing we're not short on, it's gods."

After Atta gulped her water, Rhys and his companions joined the people standing in line, waiting for a table in the popular inn. The line wound up the long, curving stairway that led to the front door. The last rays of the setting sun turned the sky golden red, gleamed off the leaves of the vallenwood and shimmered in the stained glass windows. People in line were in a good mood. Happy to be finished with the day's work, they were looking forward to a hearty meal and an evening spent in the company of friends.

"Goldmoon told me stories about the Inn of the Last Home," Mina was saying excitedly. "She told me how she and Riverwind were brought here miraculously by the blue crystal staff, and how they met the Heroes of the Lance, and how the Theocrat fell into the fire and burned his hand and the staff healed him. And then the soldiers came and—"

"I'm starving," Nightshade complained. "And this line hasn't moved one little bit. Mina, if you could just whisk us to the front—"

"No!" Rhys said severely.

"But, Rhys—"

"Race you!" Mina cried.

Before Rhys could stop her, she had dashed off.

"I'll go get her!" Nightshade offered, and he bolted before Rhys could grab him.

Reaching the stairs, Mina pushed past indignant patrons. Nightshade caused further disruption trying to catch her. Rhys hastened after both of them, apologizing profusely as he went. He collared Night-shade at the door, but Mina was too fast and had already darted inside the Inn.

Several good-natured customers told him he could go ahead of them. Rhys knew he was condoning bad behavior, and also knew he should have scolded both girl and kender and marched them to the back of the line. But, frankly, he was too tired to lecture, too tired to put up with the arguing and the wailing. It seemed easier just to let it go.

Laura, the proprietor of the Inn, was vastly pleased to see Rhys again. She gave him a hug and told him he could have his old job back if he wanted it, and added that he and Nightshade could stay as long as they liked. Laura had another hug for Nightshade, and she was charmed when Rhys introduced Mina, whom Rhys described vaguely as an orphan they had befriended along the way. Laura clucked in sympathy.

"What a state you're in, child!" Laura exclaimed, looking with dismay at Mina's dirt-streaked face and tangled hair, her tattered filthy clothes. "And those rags you're wearing! Mercy's sake, that chemise is so threadbare you can see right through it."

She cast Rhys a reproachful glance. "I know you old bachelors don't know anything about raising little girls, but you could at least have seen to it that she took a bath! Come along with me, Mina dear. We'll have a nice meal and a hot bath and then off to bed with you. And I'll see to it that you're dressed properly. I have some of my niece Linsha's old clothes packed away. I think they should just about fit you."

"Will you brush my hair for me before I go to sleep?" Mina asked. "My mother used to brush my hair every night."

"You sweet thing," said Laura, smiling. "Of course, I'll brush your hair—such pretty hair. Where is mother, dear?" she asked, as she led Mina away.

"She's waiting for me at Godshome," Mina replied solemnly.

Laura looked considerably startled at this pronouncement, then her face softened. "Ah, you sweet child," she said gently, "that's a lovely way to remember her."

Nightshade had already found a table and was discussing the evening's offerings with the waitress. Rhys looked about for Gerard, but his usual table was empty. Nightshade tucked blissfully into a large plate of corned beef and cabbage. Rhys ate a small amount, then gave the rest to Atta, who sniffed disdainfully at the boiled cabbage, but wolfed down the corned beef.

Rhys insisted on paying for their room and board by helping in the kitchen. As the night went on, he continued to look for Gerard, but the sheriff never came.

"Small wonder," said Laura, when she returned to inspect her kitchen and make preparations for tomorrow's breakfast. "There's been trouble in Temple Row lately. Oh, nothing serious, mind you. The clerics of Sargonnas and Reorx got into a shouting match and nearly came to blows. Someone threw rotten eggs at the temple of Gilean, and lewd pictures and bad words were scrawled on the walls of Mishakal's temple. Feelings are running high. The sheriff's likely out talking to people, trying to keep things calm."

Rhys listened to this in dismay. He tried to tell himself that this rivalry among the gods could not possibly have anything to do with him or his companions, but he knew otherwise. He thought of Zeboim and Chemosh, both gods trying to lure Mina to join them. Whichever side she chose—darkness or light—she would upset the balance between good and evil, tilt the scales to one side or the other.

"She's a beautiful child," said Laura, bending down to kiss the girl's forehead, as she and Rhys checked on her before going to their rest.

"She does say some strange things, though. Such a vivid imagination! Why, she said that yesterday you'd been in Flotsam!"

Rhys went thankfully to his bed, which Laura had made up in the room next to Mina's. Atta was just settling herself at his feet, when a shrill scream roused Rhys. He lit his bedside candle and hurried to Mina's room.

Mina was thrashing about the bed, arms flailing. Her amber eyes were wide open and staring.

"—your arrows, Captain!" she was crying. "Order your men to shoot!"

She sat up, gazing at some horror only she could see. "So many dead. All stacked up . . . Beckard's Cut. Killing our own men. It's the only way, you fool! Can't you see that?"

She gave a wild shout. "For Mina!"

Rhys took hold of her in his arms, trying to calm her. She fought against him, struck at him with her fists. "It's the only way! The only way we win! For Mina!"

She fell back suddenly, exhausted. "For Mina . . ." she murmured as she sank into the pillow.

Rhys remained at her side until he was certain she was once more sleeping peacefully. He asked Majere's blessing on her and then he went back to his bed.

He lay there a long time, trying to recall where he'd heard the name "Beckard's Cut" and why it struck a chill to his heart.

"Where are you going this morning?" Nightshade asked Rhys between mouthfuls of scrambled eggs and spiced potatoes.

"The Temple of Majere," Rhys replied.

"What about Mina?"

"She's in the kitchen with Laura learning to make bread. Keep an eye on her. Give me an hour or so and then bring her to me in the Temple."

"Will the monks let us in?" Nightshade asked dubiously.

"All are welcome to Majere's temple. Besides"—Rhys reached out to lightly tap the golden grasshopper the kender wore pinned to his shirt—"the god has given you his talisman. You will be an honored guest."

"I will?" Nightshade was awed. "That's really nice of Majere. Be sure and thank him for me. What are you going to tell your Abbott about Mina?" he asked curiously.

"The truth," Rhys said.

Nightshade shook his head dolefully. "Good luck with *that*. I hope Majere's monks aren't too mad at you for being Zeboim's monk for a while."

Rhys could have explained that while the monks might be sad and disappointed at his failings, they would never be mad. He realized that this concept could be difficult for his friend to understand, and he didn't have time to explain. He was in haste to go the Temple, to beg for forgiveness for his sins and turn for help to those wiser than himself. He was looking forward to being able to rest and find peace in the blessed, contemplative quiet.

Rhys had not forgotten Gerard, however, and as he was walking down the town's main street, cool beneath the dappling shadows of the vallenwood's leaves, he stopped to speak to one of the town guards.

Rhys asked where he could find the sheriff and was told that Gerard was most likely in Temple Row.

"Some sort of trouble broke out there this morning, or so I heard," the guard added.

Rhys thanked the guard for the information and continued on. Rounding a corner, he saw crowds of people—many of them bruised and bloodied—being escorted out of Temple Row by the city guard, who were pushing and shoving at stragglers and yelling at gawkers to "move along." Rhys waited until the crowds had thinned, then he made his way toward the entrance to Temple Row. Several guards eyed him askance, but, seeing his orange robes, they permitted him to pass.

He found Gerard assigning guards, giving them orders. Rhys waited quietly until Gerard had finished and was starting to move off, before addressing him.

"Sheriff—" Rhys began.

"Not now!" Gerard snapped brusquely, and kept walking.

"Gerard," Rhys said, and this time Gerard recognized his voice and, halting, turned to face him.

The sheriff was red in the face; his corn colored hair was standing all on end, for he was in the habit of running his hands through it when under duress. His intense blue eyes were narrow, their expression grim. That expression did not change when he saw Rhys. Rather it intensified.

"You," Gerard growled. "I might have known."

"It is good to see you, too, my friend," said Rhys.

Gerard opened his mouth, then shut it again. His face flushed redder. He looked ashamed and reached out his hand to clasp Rhys's hand and give it a remorseful shake.

"Forgive me. It *is* good to see you, Brother." Gerard gave Rhys a rueful smile. "It's just whenever there's trouble involving the gods, you always seem to turn up."

Rhys was trying to think how to answer this, but Gerard didn't wait for a reply.

"Have you had breakfast?" The sheriff sounded and looked tired. "I'm on my way to the Inn. You could join me." He glanced around.

"Where's your friend Nightshade? And Atta? Nothing's happened to them, has it?"

"They are both fine. They are at the Inn. I just came from there. I was on my way to the Temple of Majere to pay my respects, but I saw the turmoil and I find you here. You say there has been trouble. What happened?"

"Only a small riot," said Gerard dryly. "There's been discord brewing for some time now. The clerics and priests of all the gods have started snarling and snapping at each other like dogs over a bone. This morning a cleric of Chemosh got into a knock-down drag-out with a priest of Zeboim. Supporters from both sides rushed to help, and before long there was a pitched battle. To make matters worse, three of Kiri-Jolith's paladins took it upon themselves to try to break up the fight. At the sight of the paladins, the clerics of Zeboim and Chemosh stopped fighting each other and turned on the paladins. That brought the clerics of Mishakal to their aid. And since Reorx's worshippers like nothing better than a good brawl, they got into it, whaling on anyone they could find.

"Finally, that got boring, apparently, and someone suggested this was all Gilean's fault and they should set fire to his temple. They were headed that direction with torches blazing when I arrived with my guards. We cracked a few heads and arrested the rest and that ended the altercation. I'll let the holy fathers cool their heels in jail, then set them loose with a fine for disturbing the peace and destruction of property."

"How did the fight start?" Rhys asked. "Do you know what the quarrel was about?"

"The clerics of Chemosh refused to say. Creepy bastards. I think it was a mistake to allow them to build a temple here, but Palin Majere insisted that it is not up to us to decree which gods people choose to worship. He said that so long as Chemosh's clerics and followers don't break the law they can have their temple. So far, they've behaved. Chemosh's clerics haven't been raising the dead or raiding graveyards—at least that I know of.

"As for Zeboim, her priests were eager to talk. They're telling everyone that Chemosh is trying to take over as leader of the Gods of Darkness. What beats me is that all the clerics, even those of Kiri-Jolith, harbor resentment against Gilean. I have no idea why. His Aesthetics never take their noses out of their books."

Gerard eyed Rhys. "For months, these priests and clerics have gone about their business peacefully enough and then within the space of a fortnight, they're at each other's throats. And now you show up. You're personally acquainted with Zeboim. Something's amiss in Heaven. What is it—another War of Souls?"

Rhys was silent.

"Uh, huh. I knew it." Gerard heaved a sigh and ran his hand through his hair. "Tell me what's going on."

"I would, my friend, and gladly, but it is extremely complicated—"

"More complicated than the goddess hauling you off to fight a death knight?" Gerard asked, half-joking and half-not.

"I'm afraid so," said Rhys. "In fact, I am on my way to discuss the situation with the Abbot of my order to seek his advice and counsel. If you would like to accompany me—"

Gerard shook his head emphatically. "No thank you, Brother. I've had my fill of priests today. You go pray, and I'll go eat. I suppose Atta's keeping an eye on that kender of yours? I don't want a riot to break out in the Inn."

"Atta is with him, and I told Nightshade to meet me at the Temple." Rhys glanced uncertainly at the guards patrolling the temple district. "Will your men let him pass?"

"The guards are here to keep an eye on things, not to prohibit anyone from going to the temples. Though if this violence breaks out again . . ." Gerard shook his head. "Let's meet at my home tonight, then, Brother. I'll fix my famous stewed chicken, and you can tell me what your Abbot says."

"I would like that," said Rhys. "Thank you. One other thing," he added, as Gerard was about to depart. "What do you know of the name 'Beckard's Cut'?"

Gerard's face darkened. "Don't you recall your history lessons, Brother?"

"Not very well, I am afraid," Rhys replied.

"Beckard's Cut was a dark day in the annals of Krynn," Gerard said. "The forces of the Dark Knights of Neraka were about to lose the siege of Sanction. They were in full retreat, heading into a narrow mountain pass called Beckard's Cut. The leader of the Dark Knights gave orders for the archers to fire on their own men. They obeyed the command, firing hundreds of arrows at point blank range into their own comrades. The bodies of the fallen stacked up like cordwood, so they say, blocking the pass. The Solamnics were forced to retreat and that was the beginning of the end for us."

"Who was the leader of the Dark Knights?" Rhys asked, though he knew the answer.

"That female fiend, Mina," Gerard replied grimly. "I'll see you tonight, Brother."

Gerard went on his way, heading back down the street toward the Inn of the Last Home.

Rhys watched him go. He wondered if the sheriff would run into Mina and, if so, would he recognize her and what would happen if he did?

I was a fool to bring up Beckard's Cut, Rhys chided himself. Now he will be thinking about Mina. Perhaps I should go back . . .

Rhys looked at the green, tree-shaded grounds of Majere's temple and he felt strongly impelled to go there, as if Majere's hand had hold of his sleeve and was pulling him in that direction. Still Rhys stood undecided. He feared his own heart was leading him, not the hand of the god.

Rhys longed for the peaceful solitude, the tranquil serenity. At last he gave in, either to the command of the god or the wishes of his soul. He was in need of the Abbot's advice. If Gerard did recognize Mina and came to Rhys, demanding to know what in the name of heaven was going on, Rhys trusted the Abbot would be able to explain.

The Temple of Majere was a simple structure made of blocks of polished red-orange granite. Unlike the grand temple of Kiri-Jolith, there were no marble columns or ornate ornamentation. The door of Majere's temple was made of oak and had no lock upon it, as did the door to the temple of Hiddukel, who, being a patron of thieves, was constantly fearful that someone would steal from him. There were no stained glass windows, as in the beautiful temple of Mishakal. The windows of Majere's temple had no glass at all. The temple was open to the air, open to the sun and the sound of birdsong, open to the wind and rain and cold.

When Rhys set foot upon the well-worn path that led through the temple gardens, where the priests grew their own food, to the plain wooden door, the strength that had kept him going for so long suddenly drained out of him. Tears flowed from his eyes, as love and gratitude flowed from his heart for the god who had never lost faith in him, though he had lost faith in his god.

As Rhys entered the Temple, the cool shadows washed over him, soothing and blessing him. He asked a priest if he could beg an audience with the Abbot. The priest carried his request to the

Abbot, who immediately left his meditation and came to invite Rhys to his office.

"Welcome, Brother," said the Abbot, clasping his hand. "I understand you want to speak to me. How may I help?"

Rhys stared, struck dumb with amazement. The Abbot was an older man, as Abbots tended to be, for with age comes wisdom. He was well-muscled and strong, for all priests and monks of Majere—even Abbots—are required to practice daily the martial arts skills termed "merciful discipline." Rhys had never been in this temple or any other temple of Majere besides his own, he had never been met this man, yet Rhys knew him, recognized him from somewhere. Rhys glanced down at the Abbot's hand, which was holding his own, and noticed a white, jagged scar marring the brown, weathered skin.

Rhys had a sudden vivid memory of a city street, of priests of Majere accosting him, of Atta attacking them with slashing teeth and a priest drawing back a bleeding hand . . .

The Abbot stood quietly, patiently, waiting for Rhys to speak.

"Forgive me, Holiness!" Rhys said, guilt-stricken.

"I do forgive you, of course, Brother," said the Abbot, then he added with a smile, "but it would be good to know what for."

"I attacked you," said Rhys, wondering how the Abbot could have forgotten. "It was in the city of New Port. I had become a follower of the Goddess Zeboim. You and the six brothers who were with you sought to reason with me, to bring me back to the Temple and my worship of Majere. I . . . could not. A young woman was in terrible danger and I had pledged to safeguard her and . . ."

Rhys's voice faltered.

The Abbot was gently shaking his head. "Brother, I have traveled over much of Ansalon, but I have never been in New Port."

"But you were, Holiness," Rhys insisted, and he pointed. "That scar on your hand. My dog bit you."

The Abbot looked down at his hand. He seemed mystified for a moment, then his expression cleared. He gazed at Rhys intently. "You are Rhys Mason."

"Yes, Holiness," said Rhys, relieved. "You do remember . . ."

"Quite the contrary," said the Abbot mildly, "I have long wondered how I came by this scar. I woke one morning to find it on my hand. I was puzzled, for I had no memory of having injured myself."

"But you know me, Holiness," said Rhys, bewildered. "You know my name."

"I do, Brother," said the Abbot, and he extended his scarred hand to clasp Rhys by the shoulder. "And this time, Brother Rhys, if I urge you to pray to Majere and seek his counsel and forgiveness, you won't set your dog on me, will you?"

In answer, Rhys sank to his knees and opened his heart to his god.

4

The riot in Temple Row that morning had been staged. The fight had been carefully planned by the clerics of Chemosh on orders from the Bone Accolyte, Ausric Krell, in order to test the reaction of the sheriff and the town guard. How many men would be sent in, how would they be armed, where would they be deployed? Krell learned a great deal, and he now made ready to put his knowledge to good use in the service of his master.

Chemosh had been considerably disconcerted to discover that Mina had transformed her aspect into that of a little girl. True, Krell had told him that she was now a child, but then, Krell was an idiot. Chemosh still believed Mina was acting a part, behaving like some spurned bar wench lashing out at a faithless lover. If he could just take her away some place private, some place where she wasn't being hounded by monks or other gods, he was certain he could convince her to come back to him. He would admit to her that he'd been wrong—isn't that what mortal men did? There would be flowers and candlelight, jewelry and soft music, and she would melt in his arms. Mina would be his consort, and he would be the head of the Dark Pantheon.

As for this nonsense about her wanting to go to Godshome, Chemosh didn't believe a word of it. That was some ploy of Majere's. The blasted monk must have put the idea into her head. The monk must therefore be removed.

Chemosh was under no illusions. Gilean would take strong exception to the Lord of Death abducting Mina. The God of the Book had threatened retaliation on any god who interfered with her, but Chemosh was not overly concerned. Gilean could lecture and threaten all he wanted; he would not be able to punish Chemosh. Gilean lacked the support of the other gods, most of whom were busy with their own plans and schemes to lure Mina to their side.

The most dangerous of these gods was Sargonnas. He had some nefarious plot in the works—of that Chemosh was certain. His spies had reported that an elite troop of minotaur soldiers had been dispatched to an unknown location on some sort of secret mission. Chemosh might have thought nothing of this; the God of Vengeance was always scheming and plotting. But this troop was under the command of a minotaur named Galdar—former compatriot and close friend of Mina. Coincidence? Chemosh did not think so. He had to act and he had to act fast.

Chemosh had ordered Krell and his Bone Warriors to accost the monk while they were on the road. Chemosh was not so consumed by his desire for Mina that he had forgotten the holy artifacts the monk carried. He had ordered Krell to search the monk's body and bring anything he found to him. Krell had set up an ambush on the road, but before he could attack the party, Mina had thwarted Chemosh's plans by racing to Solace with the speed of a comet.

If she could perform such a miracle, so could Chemosh. Ausric Krell and three Bone Warriors arrived in Solace only moments behind Mina. Chemosh's orders regarding the monk and Mina were the same: kill the one and kidnap the other. While Rhys and Night-shade and Mina slept, Krell spent the night in Chemosh's temple in consultation with the priests, forming a plan of attack. The riot that morning was Phase One.

The Temple of Chemosh in Solace was the first temple honoring the Lord of Death to be built in the open. Before now, the priests of Chemosh had kept their dark doings hidden away from public view and most still did, preferring to perform the mysteries of their death rites and rituals in dark and secret places. Now that the leadership of the Dark Pantheon was within his reach, Chemosh realized that a god who wanted to be a leader of gods could not have his followers skulking about raiding tombs and cavorting with skeletons. Mortals feared the Lord of Death. What Chemosh wanted now was their respect, maybe even a little affection.

Sargonnas had achieved this. The minotaur God of Vengeance had been demeaned and reviled down through the ages. His consort, Takhisis, had sneered at him. She had used him and his minotaur warriors to fight her battles, then discarded them when she no longer had need of them. When Takhisis had stolen the world, she had left Sargonnas in the lurch, just like the rest of the gods.

All that had changed. With Takhisis gone, Sargonnas had gained power for himself and his people. His minotaurs had raided the ancient elven homeland of Silvanesti, driven out the elves, and taken over that lush land. The minotaur empire was now a force to be reckoned with. Minotaur ships ruled the oceans. The Solamnic Knights were said to be negotiating treaties with the minotaur emperor. Sargonnas had built a grand (if ostentatious) temple to himself in Solace, constructing the temple of stone shipped at great expense from the minotaur isles. His minotaur priests walked the streets of Solace and every other major city in Ansalon. Vengeance had become fashionable in certain circles. Chemosh watched the horned god's rise in jealous envy.

Thus far, the balance had not yet been disturbed. Kiri-Jolith, the god of Just War, proved an excellent counterpoint to Sargonnas. Minotaur warriors who valued honor prayed to Kiri-Jolith as well as to Sargonnas and saw no conflict in this. The priests of Mishakal, working with the mystics of the Citadel of Light, were spreading the belief that love and compassion, the values of the heart, could help ease the world's problems. The Aesthetics of Gilean were advocating and promoting education, claiming that ignorance and superstition were the tools of darkness.

Not to be outdone by his fellow gods, Chemosh ordered a temple built in Solace, constructing it of black marble. The temple was small, especially compared to that of Sargonnas, but it was far more elegant. True, not many people dared venture inside and those who did departed rapidly. The temple's interior was shadowy and dark and smelled heavily of incense that could not quite mask the foul odor of decay. His priests were a strange lot, more comfortable around the dead than the living. Still, Chemosh's temple in Solace was a start and as all men must eventually come to stand before the Lord of Death, many deemed it wise to pay him at least a courtesy call and leave a small offering.

Because of this new image, Chemosh could not allow Krell and his Bone Warriors to be seen rattling through the streets of Solace abducting small children. Another riot, larger than the first, would serve as a diversion and cover Krell's attack. Krell had to move fast, for neither he nor Chemosh knew when Mina might take it into her head to depart. One of their spies reported that Mina was staying at the Inn along with the monk. The spy overheard Rhys and Night-shade talking and confirmed that Rhys was planning a visit to the

Temple of Majere, and that the kender and the little girl were to join him there.

Krell had been thinking he might have to stage an attack on the Inn (in which case another riot in Temple Row would draw off Gerard and his forces), and he was pleased when he heard this news. He could snatch Mina and kill Rhys Mason at the same time. Krell had no fear of Majere's peace-loving priests, who went out of their way to avoid a fight, even to the point of refusing to carry weapons.

Krell was pleased with his new Bone Warriors. He had not yet seen them in action, but they looked to be formidable foes. All three of them were dead, which gave them a distinct advantage over the living. They had been hand-picked by Chemosh, who chose them from the souls who came before him, and all were trained fighters. One was an elven warrior who had died in battle against the minotaurs and whose bitter hatred of minotaurs kept his soul bound to this world. One was a human assassin from Sanction whose soul was drenched in blood, and the third was a hobgoblin chieftain who had been slain by his own tribe and who now thirsted for revenge.

Chemosh animated the bodies of the three, preserving the flesh and bone, then turning them inside out, so that their skeletons, like a ghastly semblance of armor, protected the rotting flesh. Sharp bony spikes and protrusions extending from the skeletons could be used as weapons.

Having learned his lesson with the Beloved, Chemosh made certain that the Bone Warriors were bound to him and would obey his commands, or the commands of Krell, or anyone chosen to lead them. Chemosh wanted his Bone Warriors to be intimidating, but he didn't want them to be indestructible. They could be slain, though it would take powerful magicks or blessed weapons to do it.

The Bone Warriors had one flaw Chemosh had not been able to

overcome. They had such hatred for the living that if their leader lost his hold on them, the Bone Warriors would rage out of control, venting their fury on any living being that fell into their clutches, be that person friend or foe. Chemosh's clerics might find themselves battling their god's unholy creation. A small price to pay, however.

"The monk, Rhys Mason, has entered the Temple of Majere," Krell reported to his group.

He and his Bone Warriors were safely ensconced in a secret underground chamber located beneath the Temple. Here Chemosh's clerics performed the less savory rites, those meant to be witnessed by only his most loyal and dedicated followers. The chamber was dark except for the light of a single blood red candle placed on the altar. No stolen corpses were here at the moment, though a discarded winding cloth and a burial shroud had been stashed in a corner.

The priestess of Chemosh was on hand, much to Krell's annoyance. He was convinced that Chemosh had placed her here to spy on him, and in this Krell was right. Chemosh trusted no one these days. Krell had tried a few times to get rid of the woman, but she persisted in staying and, not only that, she felt free to voice her opinion.

"We have now only to wait for Mina to arrive," Krell continued. "When I give the order, we attack the temple of Sargonnas, though we will make it appear as though his priests have attacked us."

Krell pointed to the three Bone Warriors. "Your task will be to keep the sheriff's men busy, and any others who seek to intervene, such as the foul paladins of Kiri-Jolith. I will snatch Mina and kill the monk."

The Bone Warriors shrugged their bone-armored shoulders. They had no care who or what they fought. All they sought was a chance to take out their undying rage on the living.

Having said all that was necessary, Krell was about to rise when the priestess spoke.

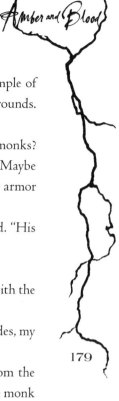

"You are making a mistake allowing Mina to enter the Temple of Majere. You should capture her before she sets foot on the grounds. Otherwise, Majere's priests will defend her."

Krell bristled. "And since when should I fear a bunch of monks? What are they going to do to me? Kick me with their bare feet? Maybe hit me with a stick?" He chortled and thumped the heavy bone armor that covered his body.

"Do not underestimate Majere, Krell," the priestess cautioned. "His priests are more powerful than you think."

Krell snorted.

"At least take me with you," the priestess urged. "I can deal with the monk while you kidnap the child—"

"I go alone!" Krell stated angrily. "Those are my orders. Besides, my fight with the monk is personal."

Rhys Mason had given Krell no end of trouble, starting from the day Zeboim had dropped the monk down on Storm's Keep. The monk had made Krell look bad in the eyes of his master, and Krell had long dreamed of the time he would have him at his mercy. Still, Krell would have been just as happy to slay Rhys in the middle of a crowded market-place as in a temple, but there was another consideration.

Chemosh had given Krell specific instructions to search the monk's body and bring to him any objects the monk might be carrying. Krell had asked point blank what Chemosh was looking for. The god had been evasive. Krell guessed the monk was carrying something valuable.

Krell tried to imagine what such an object might be—treasure valuable to a god—and at last he decided it must jewels. Chemosh probably wanted to give them to Mina.

"And why should she have them and not me?" Krell asked himself. "I do all my master's dirty work, and small thanks I get for it. Nothing but insults. He won't even make me a death knight again. If I have to be a living man, I'll be a rich living man. I'll keep the jewels for myself."

This being Krell's decision, he couldn't allow anyone—such as this high and mighty priestess—to witness the monk's death. A nice, quiet place like a temple was the perfect location for the murder. Krell had already planned what he would do with his money. He would return to Storm's Keep. Although Krell had never thought he would say this, he had come to miss the place where he had spent so many happy undead years. He would restore Storm's Keep to its former glory, hire some thugs to guard it, and spend his days terrorizing the northern coast of Ansalon.

"Krell? Are you listening to me?" the priestess demanded.

"No," said Krell sullenly.

"What I was saying is important. If this Mina is a god as Chemosh claims, how do you plan to carry her off? It seems to me," the priestess added acerbically, "that she would be more likely to carry you off—or perhaps merely suspend you from the ceiling."

The priestess was in her forties, tall for a woman and excessively thin. She had a gaunt face, protuberant eyes, and almost no lips, and she was not the least impressed with Ausric Krell.

"If His Lordship wanted you to know his plans, he would have told you, Madame," Krell answered with a sneer.

"His Lordship did tell me," replied the priestess coolly. "His Lordship told me to ask you. Perhaps I should remind you that you are counting upon my priests and followers risking their lives to assist you in this endeavor. I need to be apprised of what you have planned."

If Krell had been a death knight, he would have snapped her scrawny dried-up neck like a scrawny dried-up twig. He wasn't a death knight anymore, however, and she had been one of Chemosh's first converts. Her unholy powers were formidable.

"If you must know, I am to use these on Mina," Krell stated, and he revealed two small balls made of iron crisscrossed by golden bands. "These are magic. I'm to throw one of these at her. When the ball hits her, the gold bands will detach and bind her arms to her sides. She'll be helpless. I'll pick her up and carry her off."

The priestess laughed—screeching laughter that was like skeletal fingers clawing slate.

"This girl is a god, Krell!" said the priestess, when she could speak. Her lipless mouth twitched. "Magic will have no effect on her. You might as well bind her arms with daisy chains!"

"A fat lot you know about it," Krell returned angrily. "This Mina doesn't know she's a god. According to Nuitari, if Mina sees someone casting a magic spell on her, she falls victim to it."

"You're saying she is subject to the power of suggestion?" the priestess asked skeptically.

Krell wasn't certain he was saying that or not, since he had no clue what she meant.

"All I know is that my lord Chemosh said this would work," Krell replied in sullen tones. "If you want, you can take it up with him."

The priestess glared at Krell, then she rose haughtily and stalked out of the chamber. Shortly after that, the spy sent a message to the temple to report that Mina, accompanied by a kender and a dog, was in Temple Row.

"Time to move into position," said Krell.

5

Rhys recounted his story to the Abbot from the beginning, starting when his poor brother had come to the monastery, and continuing to the end, telling how Mina had brought them from Flotsam to Solace in a day. Rhys kept his gaze on the sunlight flickering in the distant vallenwood tree and told his tale simply, without embellishment. He freely confessed his own faults, passed lightly over his trials, and emphasized Nightshade's friendship, help, and loyalty. He told all he knew about Mina.

The Abbot listened to the monk's story without interruption, remaining relaxed and composed. Every so often he touched his fingers to the scar on the back of his hand and sometimes, especially when Rhys spoke of Nightshade, the Abbot smiled.

At length Rhys came, with a sigh, to the end. He bowed his head. He felt limp and wrung out, as though he had been drained.

At length, the Abbot stirred and spoke, "Yours is a wondrous tale, Brother Rhys Mason. I must confess I would find it hard to believe, if I had not been a part of it." He passed his hand again over the scar. "Praise Majere for his wisdom."

"Praise Majere," Rhys repeated softly.

"And so, Brother," said the Abbot, "you have made a promise to take this god-child to Godshome."

"Yes, Holiness, and I am at a loss. I do not know how to find Godshome. I do not even know where to begin to look, except that according to legend it is located somewhere in the Khalkist mountains."

"Have you considered the possibility that perhaps Godshome does not exist at all?" the Abbot suggested. "Some think Godshome is symbolic of the end of the spiritual journey each mortal takes when he first opens his eyes to the light of the world."

"Do you believe that, Holiness?" Rhys asked, troubled. "If that is true, what am I to do? The gods are vying for Mina, each wanting to claim her for his or her own. I have been accosted by Chemosh and Zeboim. The sheriff told me about the riot this morning in Temple Row. The strife in Heaven falls like poisonous rain onto the earth. We could become embroiled in another War of Souls."

"Is that the reason you risk your life and travel far to take her to a place that may not even exist, Brother?"

The Abbot did not give Rhys time to answer, but followed up that question with another. "Why do you think the god-child came to you?"

The question startled Rhys. He was silent for a moment, reflecting on it. At last he said, "Perhaps because I also know what it feels like to be lost and alone and wandering in the darkness of an endless night. Although," Rhys added ruefully, "it seems all that Mina has gained by coming to me is that the two of us are lost and wandering together."

The Abbot smiled. "That may not seem like much, but it could be everything. And in answer to *your* question, Brother, I do believe Godshome is a real place, a place mortal beings can visit. I have read the account of Tanis Half-elven, one of the Heroes of the Lance. He and his companions visited Godshome, though as I recall, he states that he does not remember how they found the place, nor does he think he could ever find it again. He and his friends were led there by a wizard named Fizban who was, in truth, Paladine—"

The Abbot's voice trailed off as a sudden thought occurred to him.

"Paladine . . ." he murmured.

"You are thinking of Valthonis," said Rhys, hope rising in him. "Do you believe he might know the way, Holiness?"

"When Paladine sacrificed himself to maintain the balance, he took on the heavy burden of mortality," the Abbot replied. "He no longer has godly powers. His mind is that of a mortal, yet he is a mortal who was once a god and that makes him wiser than most of us. If there is anyone on Krynn who might be able to guide you and Mina to Godshome, yes, it would be the Walking God."

"Valthonis is known as the Walking God because he is never stays in one place for long. Who knows where he is to be found?"

"As a matter of fact," said the Abbot, "I do. Several of our priests have chosen to travel with Valthonis, as do many others. When our brothers chance to meet any of our Order, they send reports back to me. I heard from one only last week, saying Valthonis and his followers were on their way to Neraka."

Rhys stood up, energized, renewed. "Thank you, Holiness. I am not sure I should be encouraging Mina to use her miraculous powers, but in this instance I believe I could make an exception. We could be in Neraka by nightfall—"

"You are still a very impetuous man, Brother Rhys," the Abbot remarked with gentle reproof. "Have you forgotten your history lesson of the War of Souls, Brother?"

This was the second time Rhys had been asked about history lessons. He couldn't think what the Abbot meant.

"I am afraid I do not understand, Holiness . . ."

"At the end of the War, when the gods had recovered the world and discovered Takhisis' great crime, they judged that she should be made mortal. To maintain the balance, in order that the Gods of Light would equal the number of Gods of Darkness, Paladine sacrificed himself, became mortal as well. As he looked on, the elf Silvanoshei killed Takhisis. She died in Mina's arms, and Mina blamed Paladine for the downfall of her Queen. Holding the body of her queen, Mina vowed to kill Valthonis."

Rhys sank back down into the chair, his hopes dashed. "You are right, Holiness. I had forgotten."

"The Walking God has elven warriors to protect him," the Abbot suggested.

"Mina could kill an army with a stamp of her foot," said Rhys. "This is bitter irony! The one person who can give Mina what she most wants in this world is the one person in this world she has sworn to kill."

"You say that in the form of a child she does not seem to remember her past. She did not recognize the Lord of Death. Perhaps she would not recognize Valthonis."

"Perhaps," said Rhys. He was thinking of the tower, of the Beloved, and how Mina, forced to confront them, had been forced to confront herself. "The question is: do we risk the life of Valthonis on the chance that she might not remember him?

"From all I have heard, Valthonis is honored and loved wherever he goes. He has done much good in the world. He has negotiated peace between nations who were at war. He has given hope to those in despair. Though his countenance is no longer the radiant brilliance of the god's, he yet brings light to mankind's darkness. Do we risk destroying a person of such value?"

"Mina is the child of the Gods of Light," said the Abbot, "born in joy at the moment of creation. Now she is lost and frightened. Would not any parent be glad to find his lost child and bring her home, even though her recovery came at the cost of his own life? There is a risk, Brother, but I believe it is one that Valthonis would be willing to take."

Rhys shook his head. He was not certain. There was a chance he could find Godshome on his own. Others had done so. True, Tanis Half-elven had been traveling in the company of a god, but, then, so was Rhys.

He was trying to think how he could explain his doubts when he saw the Abbot's gaze shift to the door, where one of the priests of Majere stood silently in the entrance, waiting patiently to catch the Abbot's attention.

"Holiness," said the priest, bowing, "forgive me for disturbing you, but two guests are here asking for Brother Rhys. One is a kender, and he seems most eager to speak to our brother."

"Our business is finished, isn't it, Brother?" said the Abbot, rising. "Or is there anything more I can do for you?"

"You have given me all that I required and far more, Holiness," said Rhys earnestly. "I ask now only your blessing for the difficult road that lies ahead."

"With all my heart, Brother," said the Abbot. "You have Majere's blessing and my own. Will you seek out Valthonis?" he asked, as Rhys was about to depart.

"I do not know, Holiness," said Rhys. "I have two lives to consider—that of Valthonis *and* that of Mina. I fear the consequences of such a meeting would be terrible for both."

"The choice is yours, Brother," said the Abbot gravely, "but I remind you of the old saying, 'If fear is your guide, you will never leave your house'."

Nightshade and Mina and Atta were welcomed into the Temple of Majere by one of the priests, who greeted them with grave courtesy. Every visitor to Majere's temple was met with courtesy, no one was ever turned away. All the priests asked was that the guests speak in quiet tones, so as not to disturb the meditations of the faithful. The priests themselves spoke in soft, hushed voices. Any visitors who were loud or disruptive were asked politely to leave. There were rarely any problems, for such was the wondrous serenity of the temple that all who entered felt a sense of tranquility.

Even kender were welcome, which pleased Nightshade.

"Kender are welcome in so few places," he told the priest.

"Do you require anything?" the priest asked.

"Just our friend, Rhys," Nightshade answered. "We're supposed to meet him here." He cast a sidelong glance at Mina and said in meaning-ful tones, "If you could ask him to hurry, I'd appreciate it."

"Brother Rhys is meeting with the his Holiness," said the priest. "I will tell him you are here. In the meantime, can I offer you food or drink?"

"No, thank you, Brother, I just had breakfast. Well, maybe I could eat a little something," Nightshade replied.

Mina mutely shook her head. She seemed suddenly shy, for she stood with her head ducked, stealing glimpses of her surroundings from beneath lowered eyelids. She was clean, brushed, and neatly dressed in a pretty gown with mother-of-pearl buttons up the back and long, tight-fitting sleeves. She looked the very image of the demure merchant's daughter, though she did not act the part. Her antics at the Inn and then on the way to the temple had nearly driven poor Nightshade to distraction.

Mina had grown bored making bread and Laura had sent her out to play. Once out of the Inn, she dodged around the guards and dashed up the stairs to the tree level, forcing Nightshade and a couple of guards to chase her down. When they were back on the ground and on their way again, Mina started stepping on the kender's heels trying to trip him, and stuck out her tongue at him when he scolded her.

Soon growing tried of teasing Nightshade, she had teased Atta, pulling on her tail and tugging at her ears, until the dog had lost her patience and snapped at her. The dog's teeth did not so much as break the skin, but Mina had shrieked as though she were being mauled by wolves, causing everyone in the street to stop and stare. She swiped an apple from a cart, then blamed it on Nightshade, bringing retribution from an old lady who was surprisingly spry for her age and had amazingly sharp knuckles. Nightshade was still rubbing his aching head from that encounter. By the time they reached the temple, he was worn out and could hardly wait to hand Mina over to Rhys.

The monk took them to a part of the temple known as a loggia—a kind of indoor outdoor garden, as Nightshade termed it. The loggia was long and narrow in shape, lined with stone columns allowing fresh air and sunlight to flow into the room. In the center of the loggia was a fountain made of polished stone, from which trickled clear water that had a most soothing sound. Stone benches were placed around the fountain.

The priest brought Nightshade fresh-baked bread and fruit and told them that Rhys would be with them shortly. Nightshade ordered Mina to sit down and behave herself and, to his surprise, she did. She perched on a bench and looked all around—at the water sliding over the stones, at the gently swinging chimes out-side, at the sun-dappled floor, and a crane walking with stately tread amid the wildflowers. She started to kick the bench with her feet, but stopped of her own accord before Nightshade could reprimand her.

Nightshade relaxed. The only sounds he could hear were bird calls, the musical murmurings of the water, and the wind whispering around the columns, occasionally stopping to ring silver chimes hanging from tree branches outside. Finding the atmosphere of the Temple quite soothing, but also a little boring, he thought he might just as well have a small nap in order to recover from the rigors of the morning. After eating the bread and most of the fruit, he stretched himself out on a bench and, telling Atta to watch Mina, he closed his eyes and drifted off.

Atta settled down at Mina's feet. She patted the dog on the head.

"I'm sorry I teased you," she said remorsefully.

Atta responded with a swipe of her tongue, to show that all was forgiven, then lay with her head on her paws to watch the crane and perhaps think wistfully of how much fun it would be to rush at the long-legged bird, barking madly.

Rhys found a peaceful scene when he entered the loggia: Nightshade asleep; Atta lying on the floor, blinking drowsily; Mina seated quietly on the bench.

Rhys placed his emmide alongside the bench and sat down beside Mina. She did not look at him, but watched the sunlight glistening on the water.

"Did your Abbot tell you how to find Godshome?" she asked.

"He did not know," said Rhys, "but he knew of one who might."

He thought she would ask the name of the person, and he was of two minds whether he should tell her or not. She did not ask him, however, and for that he was grateful, for he had not yet decided to seek out the Walking God.

Mina continued to sit quietly. Nightshade sighed in his sleep and flung his arm over his head and nearly rolled off his bench. Rhys carefully repositioned him. Atta stretched out on her side and closed her eyes.

Rhys allowed the soothing quiet to seep into his soul. He gave his burdens, his cares, his worries and his fears to the god. He was with Majere, seeking to attain the unattainable—the god's perfection—when a scream shattered the peacefulness of the morning. Atta leapt to her feet with a bark. Nightshade rolled over and tumbled off the bench.

The scream was followed by shouts, all coming from Temple Row. Voices cried out in anger or fear or astonishment. Rhys heard someone yell, "Fire!" and he smelled smoke. Then came the sound of many voices chanting—a cold and unearthly sound—and more screams and wails of fear and dread, clashing steel, and the angry bellowings of minotaurs calling upon Sargonnas, and human voices shouting battle cries to Kiri-Jolith.

The smell of smoke grew stronger, and now he could see ugly black billows rolling through the temple gardens in the back, starting to drift between the columns. Atta sniffed the air and sneezed. Shouts of alarm were growing louder, coming closer.

The priests of Majere, roused from their meditations, came from various parts of the temple or the gardens where they had been working. Even in this emergency, the priests maintained their calm demeanor, moving at a walk with no sense of haste or panic. Several smiled and nodded to Rhys, and their calm was reassuring. The priests gathered around the Abbot, who had emerged from his office. He sent two out to see what was going on, kept the rest with him.

Whatever was happening in the street outside the temple, the safest place to be was in Majere's hands.

Rhys could hear more screams now and a deep voice overriding them, shouting commands.

"That's Gerard," said Nightshade. Rubbing his elbow, he peered out between the columns. "Can you see? What's going on?"

A line of trees and a tall hedgerow growing in front of the temple blocked Rhys's view of the street, but he could see bright orange flames through the screen of leaves. Nightshade climbed on his bench.

"A building's on fire," he reported. "I can't tell which one. I hope it's not the Inn," he added worriedly. "It's chicken and biscuit night."

"The fire is too close to be the Inn," said Rhys. "It must be one of the temples."

Mina crowded close to Rhys, keeping hold of his hand. The sound of raised voices and clashing steel was growing louder. The smoke was thicker and caught at the throat. The two priests returned to make their report. Their expressions were grave, and they spoke rapidly. The Abbot listened for a moment, then issued orders. The priests dispersed to their cells. When they returned, they carried staves and chanted prayers to Majere. Moving together, they walked at a slow and measured pace out of

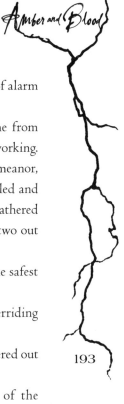

the temple, heading toward what now sounded like a pitched battle taking place in the street.

The Abbot came to speak to Rhys. "You and your friends should remain here within our walls, Brother. As I am sure you can hear, there is trouble in Temple Row. It is not safe to venture out."

An unusually loud cry caused Mina to flinch. Her face went pale, and she gave a little whimper. The Abbot looked at her and his grave expression deepened.

"What's happening, Your Monkship, sir?" Nightshade asked. "Are we at war? The Inn's not on fire, is it? It's chicken and biscuit night."

"The Temple of Sargonnas is burning," replied the Abbot. "The priests of Chemosh set it ablaze and now they are attacking the temples of Mishakal and Kiri-Jolith. Rumors have it that the priests have summoned fiends from the grave to fight for them."

"Fiends from the grave!" Nightshade repeated excitedly. He jumped down from the bench. "You'll have to excuse me. I almost never get the chance to talk to fiends from the grave. You have no idea how interesting they can be."

"Nightshade, no—" Rhys began.

"I won't be gone long. I just want to have a quick word with these fiends. You never know, I might be able to talk them into redemption. I'll be right back, I promise—"

"Atta! Guard!" Rhys ordered, and pointed at the kender.

The dog took a stance in front of Nightshade and fixed him with her intense stare. When he moved, she moved. She never took her eyes from him.

"Rhys! It's fiends!" Nightshade wailed. "Fiends from the grave! You wouldn't want me to miss that, would you?"

The smoke was thicker and they could hear the crackle of flames. Mina began to cough.

"I think perhaps you should take your charges to my chambers, Brother," said the Abbot. "The air is clearer there."

A priest came up to the Abbot and spoke to him in urgent tones. The Abbot gave Rhys a reassuring smile, then left with the priest. Mina continued to cough. Rhys's eyes were beginning to sting. Cinders and ash and soot rained down onto the garden outside the loggia, touching off small grass fires.

Rhys picked up his emmide. "Come with me, both of you—"

"Rhys, I honestly think I could help against the fiends," Nightshade argued. "Depending on what sort of fiend it is, of course. There's your Abyssal fiend and your—"

"Mina!" called a harsh voice.

She turned toward the sound of her name to see a fearsome figure clad in bone armor emerge from the coils of smoke.

"I've come for you," Krell intoned. "Chemosh sent me."

Rhys understood immediately what was going on. The battle in the street, the fire started by priests of Chemosh—all a diversion. Mina was the prize. Rhys lifted his emmide and placed himself between Krell and Mina.

"Nightshade, take Mina and run!"

The kender leaped off the bench and grabbed hold of Mina's hand. The shouts and screams, the smoke and the fire confused and frightened her. She clung to Rhys.

Clinging to his robes, she shouted at Krell, "I won't go!"

"Mina, we have to run," Nightshade urged, trying to pry her loose.

She shook her head and only held more tightly to Rhys.

Krell displayed an iron ball decorated with golden bands.

"See this, Mina? This little toy is magic. When the ball strikes you, the magic will bind you tight. You won't be able to move, and you'll have to come with me. I'll show you how it works. Watch this."

Krell flung the iron ball. Nightshade made a desperate attempt to deflect it by jumping in front of Mina. The sphere had not been aimed at Mina, however.

The ball struck Rhys on the chest.

"Bind!" Krell shouted.

Golden bands uncoiled, springing out from the sphere, and encircling Rhys, clamping over his arms and legs. He struggled against the binding bands, trying to free himself, but the more he struggled, the tighter the bands clamped down on him.

Krell, smirking beneath his skull-face helm, strode toward Mina. Atta barked at him savagely and made a lunge for him. Krell grabbed hold of one of the sharp bony protuberances from his shoulder, broke it off, and made a swipe at the dog with the sharp bone. Nightshade grabbed hold of her by the scruff of her neck and dragged the snarling dog underneath a bench.

The golden bands constricted, digging painfully into Rhys's arms, pinning his arms against his body and cutting off the circulation to his legs. Mina tried pulling and tugging on the bands with all her might, but her might was that of a child, not a god. Atta quivered in fury and continued to lunge at Krell.

Krell leered at Nightshade and jabbed at him with the spear. Laughing to see the kender cringe and the dog try to bite him, Krell stood over Mina, who was still tugging on Rhys's bands. Krell watched her with amusement.

"Never a god around when you need one, eh, Monk?" Krell jeered. He reached out with his index finger and, roaring with laughter, poked Rhys in the chest.

Rhys tottered. With his legs and arms bound, he could not keep his balance. Krell poked him again, harder this time, and Rhys went over backward. He had no way to break his fall and he landed hard, striking his head on the stone floor. Pain flared. Bright light burst behind his eyes.

He felt himself spiraling downward into unconsciousness and he fought against it, but when he hit bottom, darkness closed over him.

7

Nightshade lost his grip on Atta. The enraged dog charged out from beneath the bench and went for Krell's throat. Using the bone bracer on his forearm, Krell backhanded her across the muzzle. She slumped down beside Rhys and lay there, shaking her head, dazed. At least she was still breathing. Nightshade could see her ribs move. He couldn't say as much for Rhys.

Mina was on the floor beside him, shaking him and begging him wake up. Rhys's eyes were closed. He lay quite still.

Krell stood over Mina. He had tossed the bone spear onto the floor, and he flourished another iron ball in his hand. "Are you ready to come with me now?"

"No," Mina cried, raising her hand to ward him off. "Go away! Please go away!"

"I don't want to go away," said Krell. He was enjoying this. "I want to play catch. Catch the ball, little girl!"

He threw the iron ball at Mina. The ball struck her on the chest. Golden coils whipped out, fast as slithering snakes, and wrapped around her arms and legs. Mina lay helpless on the floor, staring up at Krell with terror-filled eyes.

"Mina, you're a god!" Nightshade cried. "The magic won't work on you! Get up!"

Krell whipped around to glare at the kender, who shrank down as small as he could manage, using the bench as cover.

Mina either didn't hear him or, more likely, she didn't believe him. She lay on the floor, sobbing.

"A god! Hah!" Krell leered at her, as she screamed in terror and tried pathetically to wriggle away from him. "You're nothing but a sniveling brat."

Nightshade heaved a resigned sigh. "I guess it's up to me. I'll bet this is the first time in the history of the world a kender had to rescue a god."

"We'll leave in a moment," Krell said to Mina. "First I have a monk to kill."

Krell broke off another bone spear and stood over Rhys. "Wake up," he ordered, jabbing Rhys in the ribs with the spear. "It's no fun killing someone who's unconscious. I want you to see this coming. Wake up!" He jabbed Rhys again. Blood stained the orange robes.

Nightshade wiped away a trickle of sweat that was rolling down his neck and then, stretching forth his sweat-damp fingers in Krell's direction, the kender began to softly sing.

"You're growing tired. You cannot smile.
You feel as though you've walked a mile.
Your muscles ache.
You start to shake.
And very soon you'll start to quake.

And as you ease down to your knees
now's the time
I end my rhyme,
you great big sleaze."

The "sleaze" term wasn't really part of the mystical spell, but Nightshade added the word because it rhymed and was expressive of his feelings. His chant had been interrupted a couple of times when smoke went down his windpipe and he had to cough, and he worried this might ruin the spell. He waited a tense moment as nothing happened, and then he felt the magic. The magic came from the water and seeped through his shoes. The magic came from the smoke and he breathed it in. The magic came from the stone, and it was cold and made him shiver. The magic came from the fire, and it was warm and exciting.

When all the parts of the magic had mixed together, Nightshade cast his spell.

A ray of dark light shot from his fingers.

This was Nightshade's favorite part—the ray of dark light. He liked it because there could be no such thing as "dark" light. But that was how the spell was named, or so his mother had told him when she taught it to him. And, in point of fact, the light wasn't really dark. It was a purplish light with a white heart. Still Nightshade could see how one might describe it as being a "dark" light. If he hadn't been so worried about Rhys and Atta, he would have really enjoyed himself.

The dark light struck Krell in the back, enveloping him in purplish white, and then the light evaporated.

Krell gave a spasmodic jerk and nearly dropped the spear. He shook his helmed head, as though wondering what had come over him, then glared suspiciously at Mina.

She lay where he'd left her, bound in the magical coils. She had quit crying and was staring in wide-eyed amazement at Nightshade.

"Don't say anything!" Nightshade mouthed. "Please for once, keep your mouth shut!" He crawled back even farther under the bench.

Krell apparently decided he'd been imagining things. He hefted his spear, getting a better grip, preparing to drive it into Rhys's chest. Nightshade knew then that his spell had failed, and he gnashed his teeth in frustration. He was about to hurl his own small body at Krell in what would probably be a fatal attempt to knock him down, when Krell suddenly swayed on his feet. He took a few staggering steps. The bone spear slipped from his hand.

"That's it!" Nightshade cried gleefully. "You're feeling tired. Really, really tired. And that armor is really, really heavy . . ."

Krell sagged to his knees. He tried to stand up again, but the bone armor weighed him down, and he toppled to the floor. Encased in the bone armor, he lay helpless on his back, feebly flapping his arms and legs like an overturned turtle.

Nightshade crawled out from his hiding place. He didn't have much time. The spell would not last long.

"Help!" he shouted, coughing in the smoke. "Help me! I need help! Rhys is hurt! Abbot! Someone! Anyone!"

No one came. The priests and the Abbot were out in the street, fighting a battle that was, by the sounds of it, still raging and growing worse. The fire, too, appeared to be spreading, for the chamber was now obscured in smoke, and he could see flames shooting up over the tops of the trees.

Nightshade grabbed hold of the bone spear. Krell was glaring at him from out of the eye sockets of his helm and cursing him roundly. Nightshade searched for a fleshy place he could skewer with the spear, but the bone armor covered every bit of the man's body. In desperation,

Nightshade struck Krell on his helmed head. Krell blinked at the blow and snarled a nasty word and flailed about, trying to grab the kender. Krell was still under the effects of the mystic spell, however, and he was too exhausted to move. He sank back weakly.

Nightshade bashed Krell in the head again, and Krell groaned. The kender hit Krell until he quit groaning and quit moving. Nightshade would have continued hitting Krell except the spear broke. Nightshade eyed him. The kender didn't think his foe was dead, just knocked senseless, which meant that Krell would come around eventually and when he did, he'd be in an extremely bad mood. Nightshade knelt beside Rhys.

Mina was wriggling about on the floor, trying to claim his attention, but he'd get to her in a minute.

"How did you do that?" Mina demanded. "How did you make that purple light?"

"Not now," Nightshade snapped. "Rhys, wake up!"

Nightshade shook his friend by the shoulder, but Rhys lay unmoving. His skin was ashen. Nightshade took hold of Rhys's scrip, intending to use it as a pillow. But when he lifted Rhys's head, Nightshade saw a pool of blood on the floor. He drew back his hand. It was covered in blood. Nightshade knew another mystical spell with healing properties and he tried calling it to mind, but he was flustered and upset and couldn't remember the words. The Dark Light chant kept running through his head, like an annoying song that once you've heard it, you keep on hearing it no matter how hard you try not to.

Hoping the words might pop unexpectedly into his head if he thought about something else, Nightshade turned to Atta, who lay on her side, her eyes closed. He rested his hand on Atta's chest and felt her heart beating strongly. She lifted her head and rolled over. Her tail thumped the floor. He gave her a hug and then sat back on his heels and looked sorrowfully at Rhys and tried desperately to remember his healing spell.

"Nightshade—" Mina began.

"Shut up!" Nightshade told her, sounding quite savage. "Rhys is hurt really bad and I can't remember my spell and . . . and it's all your fault!"

Mina began to cry. "These bands are pinching me! You have to get them off."

"Get them off yourself," Nightshade returned shortly.

"I can't!" Mina wailed.

Yes you can, you're a god! Nightshade wanted to shout back at her, but he didn't because he'd already tried that and it hadn't worked. But there might be another way . . .

"Of course *you* can't!" Nightshade said disdainfully. "You're a human, and humans are too fat and too stupid for words. Any kender could do it. *I* could wriggle out of those bonds like that!" He snapped his fingers. "But since you're a human *and* a girl, I guess you're stuck."

Mina quit crying. Nightshade had no idea what she was doing, and he didn't care. He was too worried about Rhys. Then Nightshade thought he heard Krell move or snort, and he cast a fearful glance at him, afraid he was waking up. Krell continued to just lay there like a big bone-covered lump, but it was only a matter of time. He shook his friend on the shoulder and called out his name.

"Rhys," he said anxiously, "can you hear me? Please, please wake up!"

Rhys moaned. His eyelids fluttered, and Nightshade felt encouraged. Rhys opened his eyes. He winced and gasped in pain, and his eyes rolled back in his head.

"Oh, no!" Nightshade cried, and he grabbed hold of Rhys's robes. "Don't go passing out on me again! Stay with me."

Rhys gave a wan smile and his eyes remained open, though they looked odd; one pupil was bigger than the other. He seemed to have trouble focusing.

"How do you feel?" Nightshade asked.

"Not too well, I'm afraid," Rhys answered weakly. "Where's Mina? Is she all right?"

"I'm here, Rhys," Mina answered in a small voice.

Nightshade jumped at the sound, which had come from over his shoulder. His ploy had worked. The golden bands were still in place, still coiled on the floor, but Mina was no longer inside them.

She stood gazing down sorrowfully at Rhys. Her face was puffy from crying, her cheeks grubby with tears and soot.

"You're right, Nightshade," she said. "This is my fault."

She looked so frightened and unhappy that Nightshade felt lower than a worm's belly.

"Mina, I didn't mean to yell at you—" he began.

Mina wasn't listening. She knelt down and kissed Rhys on his cheek. "You'll feel better now," she said softly. "I'm sorry. So sorry. But you won't have to take care of me anymore."

And, before Nightshade could do or say anything, she grabbed up the scrip with the blessed artifacts and ran off.

"Mina!" Nightshade cried after her. "Don't be stupid!"

Mina kept running, and he lost sight of her in the smoke.

"Mina!" Rhys called. "Come back!"

His voice was strong. His eyes were alert and clear, and he was gaining some color back into his face.

"Rhys! You're better!" Nightshade cried gleefully.

Rhys tried to stand up, but he was still bound by the magical golden bands and he fell back, frustrated.

"Nightshade, you have to go after Mina!"

Nightshade just stood there.

Rhys sighed. "My friend, I know—"

"She's right, Rhys!" Nightshade stated. "The fire, the fiends from the grave, Krell hurting you—it's all her fault. The fighting, the dying—that's her fault, too! And I'm not leaving you to go after her. Krell will wake up any minute and even though your head's healed, you're still stuck in these magical bands. And Krell said he was going to kill you!"

Rhys looked up at him. "You're the only one I can count on, my friend. The only one I can trust. You must find Mina and bring her back here to the temple. If I'm . . . not around . . . the Abbot will know what to do."

Nightshade's lower lip started to tremble. "Rhys, don't make me—"

Rhys smiled. "Nightshade, I'm not *making* you do anything. I'm asking you—as a friend."

Nightshade glared at him.

"That's not fair!" he said crossly. "All right, I'm going." He shook his finger at Rhys. "But before I go chasing after that brat, I'm going to find someone to help you! *Then* I'll look for Mina. Maybe," he added under his breath.

He cast a quick glance at Krell, who was still unconscious, but probably wouldn't be for much longer. Once the spell wore off, Krell would feel strong as ever and twice as mad, and three times more determined to kill Rhys.

"Atta, you stay with him," Nightshade said, petting the dog.

"Atta, go with Nightshade," Rhys ordered

The dog sprang to her feet and shook herself all over. Nightshade cast Rhys one last glance, begging him to reconsider.

"Don't worry about me, my friend," Rhys said, reassuring. "I am in Majere's care. Go find Mina."

Nightshade shook his head and then ran off. He followed the direction Mina had taken, which was, of course, the very worst direction possible. She'd run out the front of the temple, heading right for the street and the battle.

Nightshade raced heedlessly through the garden, with Atta running behind, both of them trampling the flowers and vegetables that were all covered with soot anyway. He could barely see anything in the smoke, and it made him cough. He kept running, coughing and waving his hand at the smoke. Atta was snorting and sneezing.

When he reached the street, he was thankful to find the air was clearer. The wind was blowing the smoke in a different direction. Nightshade searched for Mina and, more important, someone to save Rhys.

That was going to prove difficult. Nightshade came to a dead stop and stared in dismay. Temple Row was clogged with people fighting, and things were in such confusion he couldn't make out which side was which. Men wearing the livery of the town guard were trying to bring down a raging minotaur. Not far from them, paladins of Kiri-Jolith in their shining armor battled spell-chanting clerics wearing black robes and hoods. All around him, people lay on the ground, some of them shrieking in pain, others not moving.

The fires still burned. As Nightshade watched, the temple of Sargonnas collapsed in a heap of burning rubble and flames flared from the roof of the temple of Mishakal.

Nightshade looked for Mina, but what with the crowd and the melee and the confusion and the lamentable fact that he was about eye-level with people's bellies, he couldn't see her anywhere.

"If she had any sense, she wouldn't run out there in the midst of a raging battle. But then," he reminded himself glumly, "this is Mina we're talking about."

And Rhys was lying, bound and helpless, in the temple, and Krell might be awake by now.

A minotaur soldier fighting a black-robed cleric hurtled toward him, making Nightshade scramble backward to avoid being clubbed, and he fell into the gutter. Lying here, he concluded that lying on the ground was safer than standing, and he rolled behind a hedge. Atta hunkered down with him. He was angry with himself. He was supposed to be finding Mina and saving Rhys and instead he was languishing in a gutter. Gerard must be out here somewhere. Or the Abbot. There had to be a way to find help. If only he could get a better view of the street! He might climb a tree. He was starting to think about getting up out of the gutter when he felt something crawling down the back of his neck. He reached around and grabbed hold of it and there was a grasshopper.

And that gave Nightshade an idea. He looked down at the grasshopper pin on his chest.

"Mina said something about jumping. I guess it can't hurt to try. I wonder if I'm supposed to pray? I hope not, because I'm not very good at it."

Nightshade unpinned the little golden grasshopper and clasped his hand tightly around it. He bent his knees and jumped.

Looking around, he found himself high above the roof of the temple. He was so astonished and excited that he forgot what he was supposed to be doing, and he was heading downward before he remembered. He was afraid that the landing was going to be rough, but it wasn't. He landed lightly as a grasshopper.

Nightshade jumped again, finding it immensely exhilarating. He went higher this time, way above the temple roof, and as he looked down on the bloody turmoil in the streets with what he imagined was a god's-eye view, he thought, "Wow, don't we look stupid." He waved at

ot see them, but he did see a person wearing red robes standing calmly beneath a tree, watching the battle with interest.

Nightshade couldn't see the person clearly, due to the smoke, but he hoped it might be one of the priests. Once back on the ground, Nightshade gave the grasshopper a "thank-you" pat and thrust it into a pocket. Then he dashed toward the person in red, shouting "help" as he ran, and waving his arms.

The person saw him coming and immediately raised both hands. Blue lightning crackled from the fingers, and Nightshade skidded to a halt. This was not a priest of Majere. This was a Red Robe wizard.

"Don't come any closer, kender," the wizard warned in dire tones.

The wizard's voice was a woman's, deep and melodious. Nightshade couldn't see her face, which was shadowed by her cowl, but he recognized the sparkling rings on her fingers and the sumptuous red velvet of her robes.

"Mistress Jenna!" he cried, limp with relief. "I'm so glad it's you!"

"You're Nightshade, aren't you?" she asked, astonished. "The kender Nightstalker. And Lady Atta." She greeted the dog, who growled and wouldn't come near her.

The lightning shooting from her fingers had ceased to crackle, and she held out her hand to him to shake. But Nightshade regarded her doubtfully and put his hands behind his back, just in case any flesh-sizzling magic was left over.

"Mistress Jenna, I need your help—" he began, when she interrupted him.

"What in the name of Lunitari is going on here?" she demanded. "Have the people of Solace gone stark, raving mad? I was looking for

Gerard, and I was told I might find him here. I heard there was trouble, but I had no idea I was walking onto a battlefield. . ."

She shook her head. "This is quite remarkable! Who is fighting whom over what? Can you tell me?"

"Yes, ma'am," said Nightshade. "No, ma'am. That is, I could, but I can't. I don't have time. You have to go save Rhys, Mistress! He's in the temple and he's tied up with magical gold bands and there's a death knight who has sworn to kill him. I would help him myself, but Rhys told me I had to find Mina. She's a god, you know, and we can't have her running about loose. Thanks so much! Sorry I can't talk. I have to run now. Bye!"

"Wait!" Jenna cried, grabbing Nightshade by the collar as he was preparing to dash off. "What did you say? Rhys and magical bonds and a *what?*"

Nightshade had used up all his breath relating his tale once. He didn't have breath enough to do it again and, just at that moment, he caught a glimpse of what looked like Mina's dress disappearing in a swirl of smoke.

"Rhys . . . temple . . . alone . . . death knight!" he gasped. "Go save him, Mistress! Run!"

"At my age, I don't *run* anywhere," Jenna said severely.

"Then walk fast. Please, just hurry!" Nightshade cried, and with a twist and a wriggle, he broke free of Jenna's grip, and went haring off down the street, with Atta racing behind.

"Did you say a *death* knight?" Jenna called after him.

"*Former* death knight!" Nightshade yelled over his shoulder, and, pleased with himself, he kept on going, now free to search for Mina.

"Former death knight. Well, that's a relief," Jenna muttered.

Thoroughly perplexed, she stood wondering what to make of all this. She might have dismissed Nightshade's story as a kender tale (a god running around loose?), but she knew him, and Nightshade was not your run-of-the-mill kender. She'd met Nightshade the last time she'd been in Solace—that disastrous time when she and Gerard and Rhys and a paladin of Kiri-Jolith had tried and failed to capture one of the Beloved.

Jenna had come to respect and admire the soft-spoken, gentle monk, Rhys Mason, and she was aware that Rhys himself thought highly of the kender, which was a mark in Nightshade's favor. And she had to admit that Nightshade had accorded himself well during that last crisis, acting sensibly and rationally, which couldn't be said for most kender, no matter what the circumstances.

Jenna concluded, therefore, that Rhys might well be in danger as Nightshade claimed (though she did admit to having her doubts as to the existence of a death knight, former or otherwise). Conceding the need for haste, she drew her cowl over her head, spoke a word of magic, and whisked herself calmly and with dignity through time and space.

As Jenna had told the kender, at her age, she didn't run anywhere.

8

*B*ound by the magical golden bands, Rhys lay helpless on the Temple floor, unable to do anything except watch the smoke from the fire drift past the columns. The pain in his head was gone, his injury healed by Mina's kiss. He thought of the strange and terrible irony—the kiss that had slain his brother had healed him.

Nearby, Krell was groaning, starting to regain consciousness.

The temptation to struggle against his magical bonds was strong, but the struggle would have been futile and wasted his energy. He prayed to Majere, asking the god's blessing, asking the god to grant him courage and wisdom to fight his foe and the strength to accept death when it came, for Rhys was well aware that although he was determined to fight, he could not win.

His prayer concluded, Rhys maneuvered his prone body into position and then there was nothing more to do except wait.

Krell grunted and raised his aching head. He tried to stand up, slumped over, and groaned in pain. Muttering that his helm was too tight, he wrestled with it and managed after some difficulty to remove it. Flinging it to the floor, he groaned again and put his hand to his forehead. He had a large knot over his left eye, and his left cheek was swollen. The skin was not broken, but he must be suffering from a pounding headache. Krell gingerly touched the bruised areas and swore viciously.

Krell picked up his helm and thrust it on his head, then rose ponderously to his feet. He saw Rhys, still lying bound on the floor, and the empty golden bonds that had once held Mina.

Krell broke off another bone spike from his shoulder and stomped back to confront Rhys.

"Where is she?" Krell raged. "Tell me, damn you!"

He tried to stab the monk, but Rhys flipped his body over and, rolling across the floor, slammed into Krell, driving his shoulder into the man's bone-covered shins. Krell toppled headlong over Rhys and landed on the stone floor with a thud that shook the columns.

Krell gargled a moment, then clamored onto his hands and knees and, from there, with the help of the stone bench, pushed himself to a standing position. He picked up the bone spear and slowly hobbled about to face Rhys, who lay on the floor, breathing hard.

"Think you're clever, don't you, Monk." Krell picked up his bone spear. "See if you can dodge this!"

He was about to hurl the weapon when a woman dressed in red robes materialized out of the smoke-tinged air right in front of him. Her sudden and unexpected appearance rattled Krell. His hand jerked, throwing off his aim. The spear missed its mark and clattered to the floor.

Mistress Jenna nodded her cowled head at Rhys, who was staring at her with as much astonishment as Krell.

"For a monk, you lead the most interesting life, Brother," Jenna said coolly. "Please, allow me to assist you."

Speaking a word of magic, she waved her hand in a dismissive gesture and the golden bands that bound Rhys sprang off him, freeing him. A motion from Jenna sent the bands and the iron ball bounding off into the fountain. Freed from his bonds, Rhys grabbed up his emmide and turned to face Krell.

The former death knight had considered himself up to the task of fighting an unarmed monk, a kender, and a little girl. No one had said anything about a wizardess. Seeing that he was outflanked, Krell summoned help. Hearing his master's urgent call, a Bone Warrior left off battling the clerics of Mishakal and came to Krell's aid.

Rhys caught sight of movement out of the corner of his eye and called out a warning.

Jenna turned to see a minotaur warrior come roaring in from the garden. At first startled glance, it seemed as if the minotaur had been turned inside out. He wore his skeleton over his flesh and matted fur. Blood oozed ceaselessly from hideous, gaping wounds. His entrails spewed out. His throat had been cut, and one eye dangled hideously from the eye socket of the minotaur's skull that was now his helm. He carried a bloody sword in his hand and, shrieking in rage and torment, he came rushing straight at Jenna.

215

She let go of the spell she had been about to cast, for it would not work against this undead monstrosity.

"A Bone Warrior," she remarked to herself. "Chemosh must be growing desperate."

An interesting observation, but not much help. Jenna had never fought a Bone Warrior before and she had only seconds to figure out how to destroy it before it destroyed her.

Confident that the annoying wizardess would no longer be a concern, Krell prepared to finish the monk. He picked up his spear and was disconcerted to see Rhys pick up his staff. Krell remembered that staff, remembered it vividly. When the monk had been Krell's "guest" on Storm's Keep, the staff had transformed itself into a praying mantis. The bug had flown at Krell, wrapped its horrid legs around him, and sucked on his brain. Krell had been a death knight at the time, and the staff hadn't done any real damage, but Krell loathed bugs and the experience had been terrifying. He still suffered nightmares over it.

He snarled in fury. The only way to insure the staff didn't turn into a bug again was to kill its monk-master. Krell hurled his spear at the monk, and this time his aim was true.

Jenna could not concern herself with the living. She had to concentrate on the dead. She had read about Bone Warriors, but that had been years ago, in the course of her studies. No Bone Warrior had been seen on Krynn since the days of the Kingpriest, and damn few had been around then. She assumed the textbooks must have told how to destroy these undead but, if so, she couldn't recall it. And she didn't have time to give the matter a lot of consideration.

The minotaur bone warrior was in front of her now. Raising an enormous battle axe over his head, he brought the blade slashing down, intending to cleave her skull. He would have succeeded, but her skull did not happen to be there at the moment. The minotaur's sword sliced through an illusion of Jenna.

The real Jenna had swiftly moved to position herself behind the minotaur, as she continued to try to figure out how to slay the fiend. She hoped the minotaur warrior would continue attacking the illusion and give her time to think. Her hope was well founded, for generally undead weren't very smart and would hack away at an illusion without ever realizing the truth. Chemosh must have found the means to make improvements to his undead, however. When his first blow failed to slay the wizardess, the Bone Warrior whipped around and began searching for his foe.

The minotaur spotted her immediately and, swinging his sword, came roaring in her direction. Jenna stood her ground. The brief respite had given her time to prepare her spell, time to think of the words, time to recall the correct hand motions. Casting this spell was risky, not only to her—if it failed she would have neither the time nor strength to cast another—but also to Rhys, who might suffer residual effects. Hoping to Lunitari she didn't accidentally blind the monk, Jenna thrust out her hand and began to chant words of magic.

Rhys was dimly aware of Jenna battling the fiendish creature Krell had summoned. The monk could do nothing to help the wizardess, not with his own daunting foe to fight and he guessed she would not appreciate his help anyway. Most likely, he would just get in her way.

Rhys gripped his staff firmly, faced his enemy fearlessly. Krell was armored in bones and, to Rhys's mind, they were the bones of all those Krell had slain. His hands were stained with blood. He stank of death, his soul as foul and rotting as his body.

Majere is known to be a patient god, a god of discipline, who does not give way to emotion. Majere is saddened by the faults of man, rarely angered by them. Thus he teaches his monk to use "merciful discipline" to stop those who would harm them or others, to prevent those intent on evil from committing acts of violence without resorting to violence. Punish, deter, do not kill.

Yet, there are times when Majere knows rage. Times when the god can bear no longer bear to see the suffering of innocents. His rage is not hot and wayward. His wrath is directed, controlled, for he knows that otherwise it will consume him. Thus, he teaches his followers to use their anger as they would use a weapon.

Do not let your anger master you, his monks are taught. If you do, your aim will be off, your hands will shake, your feet will slip.

Though months had passed since that terrible time, Rhys remembered vividly how he had been consumed by his anger as he stood gazing in horror at the bodies of his murdered brethren. His rage had choked him with its bitter bile. His anger had blinded him, then cast him into hellish darkness. He knew anger now, but this anger was different. The god's anger was cold and pure, bright and blazing as the stars.

Jenna intoned the last word of her spell. The rampaging minotaur was so close to her that she gagged at the foul odor of corruption from his putrefying body, as she waited tensely for the magic to work.

She reveled in a rush of warmth, a tingling thrill that shot through her body. The magic foamed and bubbled and surged in her blood. She seized it, directed it, cast it forth. The magic splintered. Beams of colored light shot from her fingers.

As though she had grabbed a rainbow from the sky and flung it at the minotaur, seven blazing streams of red and orange, yellow and green, blue, indigo, and violet light splashed over her foe.

The yellow beams shot jolts of energy into his body, disrupting the unholy magic that gave the corpse the hideous semblance of life. His limbs jerked. The minotaur twitched and writhed. The red beam

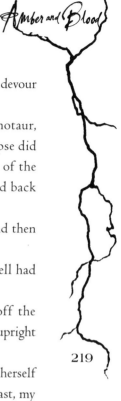

struck his battle axe, setting it ablaze. The orange ray began to devour what was left of his hideous flesh.

The green ray, poison, would have no effect on the minotaur, and apparently the blue failed, as well, for the animated corpse did not turn to stone. Jenna prayed to Lunitari that the power of the violet ray would work, for it was supposed to carry the fiend back to his creator.

The minotaur shrieked hideously, stumbled toward her, and then vanished.

Jenna sank down limply onto the bench. The powerful spell had drained her, leaving her weak and trembling.

She hoped to heaven Rhys Mason managed to finish off the gruesome-looking object he was fighting. She could barely sit upright on the bench, much less fling any more magic.

"At your age, you really should know better," she scolded herself wearily. Then she smiled. "But that was a beautiful spell you cast, my dear. Truly lovely . . ."

Krell's spear flew toward him. Rhys leaped high into the air, and the spear whistled harmlessly beneath his feet. Still in midair, Rhys arched his back, flipped over, and landed lightly on his feet in front of the astounded Krell. Rhys shifted his hold on the emmide. Lunging forward, he struck Krell's bone breast-plate with the end of his staff. The force of the blow cracked the breastplate and the collarbone beneath, and sent Krell staggering backward.

Armored by his god in the bones of the dead, Krell had smugly thought himself invulnerable to sword and spear and arrow, and now he'd been hurt by a stick-wielding monk. He was in pain and, like all bullies, he was terrified. He wanted this encounter to end. Using his good arm, Krell broke off another sharp spike. Wielding it like a sword, roaring curses, he charged at Rhys, hoping to frighten the monk and overwhelm him by sheer brute strength.

The emmide flicked out and shattered the bone sword. Twirling the staff in his hands, Rhys began to weave a deadly dance around Krell, attacking him from the front and the sides and the back, striking him on the helm and the breastplate, hitting him on the shoulders and the arms, battering his legs and thighs. The emmide sheared off the bony spikes on the shoulders and broke one of the ram's horns. Everywhere the emmide touched the bone armor, it cracked and split wide open.

Rhys drove the emmide through the cracks, widening them. Parts of the armor began fall off, and the emmide struck the soft, flabby flesh beneath. Bones cracked, but now they were Krell's bones, not those of some wretched corpse. Another blow split the helm wide open, and it fell off and rolled about on the floor.

Krell's face was purple and swollen. Blood streamed from his wounds. In agony, bruised and bloodied, he slumped to the floor on his knees and, kneeling in a sodden bloody heap at Rhys's feet, Krell blubbered and slobbered.

"I surrender!" he cried, spitting up blood. "Spare me!"

Breathing hard, Rhys stood over the hulking brute quivering at his feet. He could be merciful. He could give Krell his life. Rhys had inflicted the lesson of merciful discipline. But Rhys knew with the clarity of the god's cold anger that being merciful to Krell would be an indulgence on Rhys's part, one that would make him feel just and righteous, but which would send forth this monster to murder and torture other victims.

Rhys saw Krell watching him from the corner of his swollen eye.

Krell was certain of himself, certain Rhys would be merciful. After all, Rhys was a good man, and good men were weak.

Rhys lifted up the emmide. "We are told that the souls of men leave this realm and travel to the next, learning from mistakes made in this life, gaining in knowledge until we come to the fulfillment of the soul's journey. I believe that this is true of most men, but not all. I believe there are some like you who are so bound up in evil that your soul has shrunk to almost nothing. You will spend eternity trapped in darkness, gnawing on the remnant of yourself, consuming, yet never consumed."

Krell stared at him, his eyes wide and terrified.

Rhys struck Krell in the temple with the emmide.

Krell toppled over dead onto the blood-smeared floor. His eyes were wide and staring. A bloody froth drooled from his flaccid lips.

Rhys remained standing over the brute, his emmide poised to strike again. He knew Krell was dead, but he intended to make certain Krell stayed dead. He did, after all, serve a god who was known to bring the dead back to a hideous pretence of life.

Krell did not so much as twitch. In the end, even Chemosh abandoned him.

Rhys relaxed.

"Well done, Monk," said Jenna weakly.

Her face was haggard, her skin pale. Her shoulders slumped. She seemed too exhausted to move. Rhys hastened to her side.

"Are you hurt, Mistress? What can I do to help?" Rhys asked.

"Nothing, my friend," she said, managing a smile. "I am not injured. The magic exacts its toll. I just need to rest a little while."

She regarded him intently. "What about you, Brother?"

"I am not hurt, praise Majere," he said.

"You did the right thing, Brother. Killing that brute."

"I hope my god agrees with you, Mistress," Rhys said.

"He will. Do you know what I was fighting, Brother? A Bone Warrior of Chemosh. Such fiends have not been seen on Krynn since the days of the Kingpriest."

She pointed to the corpse. "That lump is . . . or was . . . a Bone Acolyte. Chemosh seized the minotaur's wretched soul, using his rage to ensnare him. And there are probably more than one. The Acolyte would have had as many Bone Warriors serving him as he thought he could control. And these warriors are deadly, Brother.

"Perhaps your brethren are fighting them now," she added somberly. "By slaying the Acolyte, you have made it easier for those fighting the Bone Warriors to destroy them. The Acolyte controls them and once he is dead, the warriors will go berserk and fight in a blind fury."

The smoke had died away. The fires were being brought until control, but they could both hear the sounds of battle still raging outside. Rhys worried about Nightshade and Mina being caught in the chaos. He was anxious to go after them, but he did not like to leave Jenna, especially if there were more Bone Warriors about.

She read his thoughts and patted his hand. "You are concerned about your kender friend. He is safe, at least he was the last time I saw him. He was the one who sent me to your aid. Lady Atta was with him, and they were both pursuing Mina."

Jenna paused, then said, "I have heard some strange tales regarding her, Brother. That is why I came to Solace to seek out Gerard, who once met her, or so I was told. I will not waste your time asking for details. You must go find her, of course. But is there some way I can be of help?"

"You have done more than enough for me, Mistress. I would be dead by now if it were not for you."

She laughed. "Brother, I would not have missed this for the world. To think—I fought a Bone Warrior of Chemosh! Dalamar will be quite green with envy."

Jenna gave his hand a mock slap. "Go find your little god, Brother. I will be fine. I can take care of myself."

Rhys stood up, but still he hesitated.

Jenna raised her eyebrows. "If you do not leave, Brother, I will begin to think that you consider me a helpless and infirm old lady, and I will be extremely insulted."

Rhys bowed to her in profound respect. "I think you are a very great lady, Mistress Jenna."

She smiled in pleasure and waved him away.

"And, Brother," Jenna called after him, as he was leaving, "I still want that kender-herding dog you promised me!"

As Rhys hastened off, he made a promise to himself that Mistress Jenna should have the finest puppy in Atta's next litter.

9

By the time Rhys made his way through the gardens and across the front lawn to the street, the town guard had managed to regain some semblance of control. Rhys halted, shocked at the sight of the carnage. The street was littered with bodies, many of them stirring and groaning, but some lying dead. The cobblestones were slippery with blood. The fires had been doused, but the stench of burning stung his nostrils. The guards had blocked off the street and now that the battle had ended, they had their hands full holding back frantic friends and relatives seeking their loved ones.

Rhys did not know where to begin to search for Nightshade and Mina and Atta. He roamed up and down the street, calling Nightshade's name, calling Mina, calling Atta. There was no answer. Everyone he saw was covered in soot and dirt and blood. He could not tell the identity of a victim simply by looking at the clothes and whenever he saw the body of a kender-sized person lying the street, his heart clogged his throat.

Even as Rhys searched, he did what he could to aid the wounded, though—not being a priest—there was little he could do except offer comfort and ease their fear by assuring them help was on the way.

Ordinarily the wounded would have been taken to the temple of Mishakal, for her priests were skilled in healing. Her temple had been damaged by the fire, however, and the Temple of Majere was opened to the victims, as were the Temples of Habbukuk and Chislev. The priests of many gods worked among the injured, ministering to friend and foe alike, making no distinction.

In this the priests were aided by mystics, who had hastened to the site to offer their help, and with them came the herbalists and physicians of Solace. The bodies of the dead were taken to the Temple of Reorx, where they were laid in quiet repose until family and friends came to undergo the sorrowful task of identifying and claiming them for burial.

Rhys came across the Abbot organizing litter-bearers. Many of the wounded were in dire condition, and the Abbot was exceedingly busy, for lives hung in the balance. Rhys hated to interrupt his work, but he was growing desperate. He had still not found his friends. Rhys was about to take a brief moment to ask the Abbot if he had seen Mina, when he caught sight of Gerard.

The sheriff was splattered with blood and limping from a wound to his leg. A guardsman walked alongside him, pleading with him to seek treatment for his wound. Gerard angrily ordered the man off, telling him to help those who were really hurt. The guardsmen hesitated, then—seeing the sheriff's baleful expression—returned to his duties. Once the man was gone and Gerard thought no one was watching, he sagged against a tree, drew in a deep and shivering breath and closed his eyes and grimaced.

Rhys hurried to his side. Hearing footfalls coming toward him, Gerard abruptly straightened and tried to walk off as though nothing was the matter. His injured leg buckled beneath him and he would have fallen, but Rhys was there to catch him and ease him to the ground.

"Thank you, Brother," said Gerard grudgingly.

Ignoring Gerard's insistence that the wound was merely a scratch, Rhys examined the gash in Gerard's thigh. The cut was deep and oozing blood. The blade had sliced through the flesh and muscle and perhaps cracked the bone. Gerard winced as Rhys's fingers probed, and he swore softly beneath his breath. His intense blue eyes glinted more with anger than with pain.

Rhys opened his mouth to start to shout for a priest. Gerard didn't wait to hear him, however.

"If you say one prayer, Brother," Gerard told him, "if you utter one single holy word, I'll shove it down your throat!"

He gasped in agony and leaned back against the tree, groaning softly.

"I am a monk of Majere," Rhys said. "You need not worry. I do not have the gift of healing."

Gerard flushed, ashamed of his outburst. "I'm sorry I shouted at you, Brother. It's just that I'm fed up to here with your gods! Look at what your gods have done to my city!"

He gestured to the bodies lying in the street, to the clerics moving among the wounded. "Most of the evil done in this world is done in the name of one god or the other. We were better off without them."

Rhys could have responded that much good was done in the name of the gods, as well, but this was not the time to enter into a theological argument. Besides, he understood Gerard. There was a time Rhys had felt the same.

Gerard eyed his friend, then heaved a sigh. "Don't pay any attention to me, Brother. I didn't mean what I said. Well, not much. My leg hurts like hell. And I lost some good men today," he added grimly.

"I am sorry," Rhys said. "Truly sorry. Sheriff, I hate to trouble you now, but I must ask. Did you"—Rhys felt his throat go dry as he asked the question—"did you see Nightshade anywhere—"

"Your kender friend?" Gerard shook his head. "No, I didn't see him, but that doesn't mean much. It was sheer bloody chaos out there, what with the smoke and fire and those horrible undead fiends slaughtering every person they came across."

Rhys sighed deeply.

"Nightshade's got more sense than usual for a kender," Gerard said. "Is Atta with him? That dog's smarter than most people I know. He's probably back at the Inn. It's chicken and biscuit night you know—"

He tried to grin, but he drew in a sharp breath and rocked back and forth, swearing under his breath. "That hurts!"

The best place for Gerard would in be one of the Temples, but Rhys knew how that suggestion would be received.

"At least let me help you back to the Inn, my friend," Rhys suggested, knowing Gerard would be in safe hands with Laura to care for him. Gerard agreed to this, and he reluctantly allowed Rhys to help him to his feet.

"I have a recipe for a poultice that will ease the pain and allow the wound to heal cleanly," Rhys told him, putting his arm around him.

"You won't whip a prayer into it, will you, Brother?" Gerard asked gruffly, leaning on his friend.

"I might say a word or two to Majere on your behalf," Rhys replied, smiling. "But I'll make sure you don't hear me."

Gerard grunted. "Once we reach the Inn, I'll put out the word about the kender."

They had gone only a short distance when it became clear that Gerard could not continue without more help than Rhys could give him. Gerard was by this time too weak from loss of blood weak to put

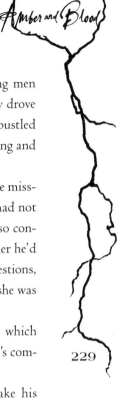

up a fight, and Rhys summoned assistance. Three stout young men came immediately to his aid. Hoisting Gerard onto a cart, they drove him to the Inn and carried him up the stairs to a room. Laura bustled about, fussing over him, helping Rhys make the poultice, cleaning and bandaging his wound.

Laura was deeply concerned to hear that Nightshade had gone missing. In answer to Rhys's question, she replied that the kender had not returned to the Inn. She hadn't seen him all morning. She was so concerned over the kender that Rhys didn't have the heart to tell her he'd lost Mina, as well. He said in response to Laura's worried questions, that Mina was with a friend. This wasn't quite a lie. He hoped she was with Nightshade.

Gerard complained bitterly about the smell of the poultice, which he swore would kill him if the wound didn't. Rhys took Gerard's complaints for a sign the sheriff was feeling better.

229

"I will let you get some rest," Rhys said, preparing to take his leave.

"Don't go, Brother," Gerard said fretfully. "Between the stink of that glop you put on me, and the pain, I won't be able to sleep. Sit down and talk to me. Keep me company. Take my mind off things. And stop pacing about the room. We'll hear word of your kender soon enough. What's in that goo you put on me anyway?" he asked suspiciously.

"Plantain, bayberry, bark, ginger, cayenne pepper and cloves," Rhys replied.

He hadn't realized he'd been pacing, and he forced himself to stop. He felt as though he should be out there, actively searching, though he was the first to admit he had no idea where to begin to look. Gerard had told his guardsmen to be on the lookout for the kender and the dog and to spread the word among the populace. The first news they had of the missing, they would communicate that news to Gerard.

"Once I find the kender, I don't want to have to go chasing you down," Gerard told Rhys, who conceded that this was logical.

Rhys drew a chair near Gerard's bedside and sat down.

"Tell me what happened on Temple Row," Rhys said.

"The priests and followers of Chemosh started it," Gerard replied. "They set fire to the Temple of Sargonnas and then tried to burn down Mishakal's temple by throwing flaming brands inside, while others started killing. They summoned two fiends that were like some horror out of a fever-dream. They wore armor made of bones with their insides falling out, killing anything that moved. A priestess of Chemosh led them. It took the paladins of Kiri-Jolith to finally destroy them, but only after the undead monsters had turned on the priestess and hacked her to pieces."

Gerard shook his head. "What I find damn odd is why Chemosh's followers did all this in broad daylight. Those ghouls generally work their evil under the cover of darkness. Almost seems as if it was meant as some sort of diversion . . ."

Gerard paused, regarding Rhys intently.

"It was a diversion, wasn't it?" Gerard slammed his hand down on the coverlet. "I *knew* this must have something to do with you. You owe me an explanation, Brother. Tell me what in the name of Heaven is going on."

"That's a good way to put it. I will explain"—Rhys gave a rueful sigh—"though you will find my story difficult to believe. The tale does not start with me. It starts with the woman you know as Mina . . ."

He related the story, as much as he knew. Gerard listened in amazed silence. He remained quiet until Rhys had reached the end of his tale, telling how he had killed Krell, and then Gerard shook his head.

"You're right, Brother. I'm not sure I do believe it. Not that I doubt your word," he added hastily. "It's just . . . so implausible. A new god? That's all we need! And a god who's gone crazy at that! So what—"

They were interrupted by a knock on the door.

Rhys opened it to find one of the town guard in company with an older woman dressed in traveling clothes.

The guardsman touched his forehead respectfully to Rhys, then spoke to Gerard, "I have some information on that kender you were looking for, Sheriff. This lady saw him."

"I did, Sheriff," said the woman briskly. "I'm a recent widow. My husband and I had a farm north of here. I sold it—too much for me to handle, and I am moving to Solace to live with my daughter and her husband. We were on the road this morning, and I saw a kender like the one described. He was traveling with a black-and-white dog and a little girl."

"Are you sure it was them, Madam?" the sheriff asked.

"I am, Sheriff," said the woman, complacently folding her hands beneath her cloak. "I remember because I thought it was odd to see such a strange trio, and the kender and the girl were standing in the middle of the road arguing about something. I was going to stop to see if I could help, but Enoch—he's my son-in-law—he said I shouldn't speak to kender, not unless I wanted to be robbed blind. Whatever the kender was up to, it was probably no good and none of our affair.

"I wasn't sure about that. I'm a mother, and it looked to me like the little girl was running away from home. My daughter did the same when she was that age. She packed up her little things in a gunny sack and set out. She didn't go far before she got hungry and came back, but I was half dead with fright. I remember how I felt, and the first thing I did when we reached Solace was to tell the guard what I'd seen. He said you were searching for this kender, and so I figured I'd come tell you what I saw and where I saw it."

"Thank you, Madame," said Gerard. "Did you happen to see if they continued on the road north?"

"When I looked back the little girl was walking along the highway, heading north. The kender and the dog were trailing behind."

"Thank you again, Madame. May Majere's blessing be on you," Rhys said, and he picked up his staff.

"Good luck, Brother Rhys," said Gerard. "I won't say it's been a pleasure knowing you, because you've brought me nothing but trouble. I will say it's been an honor."

He reached out his hand. Rhys took it, pressing it warmly.

"Thank you for all your help, Sheriff," he said. "I know you don't believe in the gods, but—as someone once told a friend of mine—they believe in you."

Rhys stopped on his way out to tell Laura that Nightshade had been located and that he, the kender, and Mina were going to resume their travels.

"She's a dear, sweet child. Try to see to it that she has a bath every now and then, Brother," Laura told him, and she sent him on his way with a hug and tears and as much food as he could carry and would consent to take.

Gazing out his window, Gerard watched the monk in his shabby orange robes make his unobtrusive way among the crowds, taking the highway that led north.

"I wonder if I'll ever know how this strange tale ends?" Gerard asked himself. He sighed deeply and lay back among the pillows. "I don't see any good coming of it, that's for sure."

He was just about to try to get some sleep when a guardsmen came to inform the sheriff that an angry mob was taking out their fury on the Temple of Chemosh.

BOOK III

GODSHOME

*N*ightshade traipsed along down the road after Mina, muttering to himself and scuffing his boots in the dust. Mina walked several paces ahead of him, her head held high, her back stiff. She was taking no notice of him, pretending she didn't know him. Atta trotted along at the kender's side, though she would stop every so often and look back wistfully down the road, searching for Rhys.

"I hope he's all right," Nightshade said for the thousandth time. He glared at Mina and kicked irritably at a rock and said loudly, "If it wasn't for *some people,* I could be back there seeing for myself and maybe helping to save him after some people *ran away and left him!"*

Mina flashed him an angry glance over her shoulder, and stubbornly kept on walking.

At least they had managed to escape the battle in Temple Row.

The brutality of the fighting, the sight of so many dead and wounded had completely overwhelmed Mina. She was confused by the noise, horrified by the carnage. Nightshade and Atta finally located her crouched under a bush, her eyes squinched shut, her hands over her ears to drown out the screams.

Nightshade persuaded her with some difficulty to come with him, only to nearly lose her to a black-robed, hooded priest of Chemosh, who stumbled across them by accident. Nightshade recited his rhyme for his exhaustion spell and the last he'd seen of the priest, he was lying on his back in the middle of the street taking an unexpected snooze.

Running around the back of the temple of Zeboim and cutting through an alley, they found themselves in the relative quiet of a residential area. The citizens, hearing the sounds of battle and fearing it might spill over into their neighborhood, had all barred their doors and were staying inside.

Nightshade stopped to catch his breath and get rid of a painful stitch in his side and try to figure out what to do. He decided to take Mina to the Inn and leave her in the care of Laura, then go back to find Rhys. Nightshade and Atta started off in the Inn's direction, only to find Mina going the opposite way.

"Where are you going?" Nightshade demanded, halting.

Mina stood in the middle of the road, holding fast to the scrip with the artifacts in it. The scrip was dirty and stained, for when it grew heavy, she let it drag on the ground. Her face was covered in grime and soot, her hair was wet with sweat, her red braids starting to come undone. Her dress was splattered with blood stains.

"Godshome," Mina replied.

"No, you're not," Nightshade scolded her. "You're going back to the Inn. We have to wait for Rhys!"

"I won't." Mina returned. "I have to go to Godshome or the fighting will only get worse."

Nightshade didn't see how matters could get much worse than they already were, but he didn't say that. Instead, he said crossly, "Then you're going the wrong direction. Godshome is north, and you're going west. We're on the road to Haven." He pointed. *"That's* the road north."

"I don't believe you," Mina told him. "You're lying, trying to trick me."

"I am not," Nightshade returned angrily.

"Are so."

"Am not!"

"Are so—"

"You've got the map," Nightshade shouted at last. "Look for your-self."

Mina blinked at him. "I don't have the map."

"You do too," Nightshade said. "Remember? I spread it out on the rock back there near Flotsam and then you decided we were going to go for a fast walk and—"

He stopped talking. Mina was biting her lip and digging the toe of her shoe into the dirt.

"You didn't!" he said, groaning.

"Shut up," she said, glowering.

"You left my map back there! *Way* back there! Halfway around the world back there!"

"I didn't leave it there. You did. It was your fault!" she flared.

Nightshade was so taken aback by this accusation that he was reduced to spluttering.

"You were supposed to pick up the map and bring it with us," Mina continued. "The map was your responsibility because it was your map. Now I don't know which road to take."

Nightshade looked to Atta for help, but the dog had flopped onto her belly in the dirt and lay there with her chin between her paws. When Nightshade calmed down enough to speak without spitting all over himself, he stated his case.

"I would have taken the map, but you ran away with me so fast I didn't have a chance."

"I don't want to talk about it anymore," Mina said petulantly. "You lost the map so what are you going to do about it?"

"I'll tell you what we're going to do. *You're* going back to the Inn and *I'm* going to find Rhys and then we're all going to have a good dinner. After all, it is chicken and——"

But Mina wasn't listening. She walked over to a group of idlers hanging about the street outside a tavern with mugs of ale in their hands, arguing drunkenly about whether they should or should not go to see what the ruckus was about.

"Excuse me, sirs," Mina said. "Which road do I take to go north?"

"That way, sis," one of the young men told her with a belch and a vague wave of his hand.

"Told you," Nightshade said.

Mina picked up the scrip, slung it over her shoulder, and walked off.

Nightshade immediately realized he'd made a mistake. What he should have said was that he didn't know the way north and they should wait for Rhys. Too late for that now. He watched her walk off, alone and forlorn, and considered leaving, but he knew Rhys wouldn't want him to abandon her. Though Nightshade didn't know what good he could do. She never listened to him anyway.

He looked at Atta, who was sitting on her haunches, looking at him. The dog offered no advice. Heaving a deep sigh, Nightshade trudged after Mina and now here they were together, heading north towards Godshome without Rhys.

Nightshade continued to try to persuade Mina to go back to the Inn, but she continued to adamantly refuse. The argument carried them several miles out of Solace, at which point Nightshade finally gave up and saved his breath for walking. He was at least thankful for one mercy—since they didn't have the map, Mina couldn't very well run off at a god's pace. She had to walk like an ordinary person.

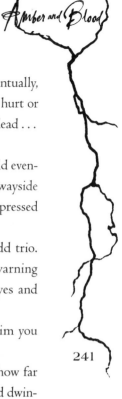

Nightshade could only hope that Rhys would find them eventually, though the kender didn't see how. Rhys would believe they were hurt or dead or hiding somewhere . . . Maybe Rhys himself was hurt or dead . . .

"I won't think about that," Nightshade told himself.

They walked a long, long time. Nightshade hoped Mina would eventually grow tired and want to rest and, whenever they came to a wayside inn, he hinted strongly that they should stop. Mina refused and pressed on, dragging the scrip along in the dirt behind her.

Travelers they met along the way stopped to stare at the odd trio. If anyone tried to approach Mina, Atta would growl at them, warning strangers to keep their distance. Nightshade would roll his eyes and spread his hands to indicate he was helpless in the matter.

"If you meet a monk of Majere named Rhys Mason, tell him you saw us and we're going north," he would call out.

The road went on, and so did they. Nightshade had no idea how far they'd come, but he couldn't see Solace anymore. The highway had dwindled to a road and not a very good road at that, and then, without warning, the road heading north ended. A large mountain stood in the way, and the road went around it, branching off to the east and the west.

"Which way do we go?" Mina asked.

"How should I know?" Nightshade grumbled. "You lost the map, remember? Anyway, this is a good place to stop to rest— What are you doing?"

Mina put her hand over her eyes and began twirling around and around in the middle of the road. When she made herself dizzy, she staggered to a stop and thrust out her hand, her fingers pointing east.

"We'll go this way," she said.

Nightshade stood staring at her, dumbfounded.

"For a gnome nickel, I'd leave you to be eaten by bugbears," he told her, then added in a mutter, "But that would be mean to the bugbears."

He glanced to the west, where the sun was sinking rapidly out of sight, as though it couldn't get away fast enough. Shadows were slithering over the road.

Nightshade began wandering up and down the side of the road, looking for largish rocks. When he found one, he picked it up and lugged it over to where Mina was standing and dropped it down at her feet.

"What are you doing?" Mina demanded, after he came back with the fourth rock.

"Marking the trail," Nightshade said, hauling over rock number five. He threw it down, then began arranging the rocks, stacking four on top of each other and placing the fifth to the east of the stack. "This way Rhys knows which direction we've taken at the crossroads, and he can find us."

Mina stared at the stacked rocks, and suddenly she ran at them and began to kick at them in frenzy, knocking Nightshade's neat pile all askew.

"What you are doing?" Nightshade cried. "Stop that!"

"He's not going to find me!" Mina shouted. "He's never going to find me. I don't want him to find me."

She picked up a rock and threw it, almost hitting Atta, who leaped to her feet in shock.

Nightshade grabbed hold of Mina and hauled off and swatted her a good one on the rear portion of her anatomy. The blow couldn't have hurt very much, because he encountered nothing but petticoat. His swat shocked her immensely, however. She stood gaping at him, and then she burst into tears.

"You are the most spoiled, selfish little kid I ever met in my life!" Nightshade yelled at her. "Rhys is a good man. He cares about you more than you deserve, because you've been a real brat. And now you've run off, and he's probably worried sick—"

"That's why I ran away,' " Mina gulped between sobs. "That's why he must never find me. He *is* a good man. And I almost got him killed!"

Nightshade gaped at her. She had *not* run off to escape Rhys. She'd run off to protect him! Nightshade sighted. He was almost sorry he'd spanked her. Almost.

"There now, Mina." Nightshade began to thump her on the back to help her quit crying. "I'm sorry I lost my temper. I understand why you did it, but you still shouldn't have run away. As for almost getting Rhys killed, that's nothing. I've almost gotten Rhys killed a couple of times and he's almost gotten me killed a bunch. It's what friends are for."

Mina looked extremely startled at this, and even Nightshade had to admit his explanation didn't sound as good when it came out of his mouth as it had when it was in his head.

"What I mean, Mina, is that Rhys cares about you. He won't stop caring just because you've run off. And now you've added worrying and wondering to caring. As for you putting him in danger"—Nightshade shrugged—"he's known all along that he would be in danger when he decided to take you to Godshome. The danger doesn't make any difference to him. Because he cares."

Mina regarded him intently, and it seemed to Nightshade that her tear-shimmering amber eyes would swallow him whole. She reached out a tentative hand.

"Is it the same with you?" she asked meekly. "Do you care about me?"

Nightshade was bound to be truthful. "I'm not as good a person as Rhys, and maybe for a moment or two back there I didn't care much at all, but only for a moment . . . Or two."

He took hold of her hand and squeezed it. "I do care, Mina. And I am sorry I spanked you. So help me stack up these rocks up again."

Mina helped him arrange the rocks and then they continued on, heading east. The road led through fields of tall grass, past a small pond, over a couple of creeks. By this time, the sun was barely a red smear in the sky. From the top of a hill, they could see the road dip down into a valley and disappear into a forest.

Nightshade considered their options. They could camp here, by the roadside, out in the open. Rhys would be able to find them, but then, so would anyone else including thieves and brigands, and while Mina, being a god, could take care of herself, would she take care of Night-shade and Atta? Having seen her in action in the temple, Nightshade didn't much like the odds.

If they camped in the forest, there would be lots of places—hollowed logs, thickets, and so forth—where they could rest close to the road and yet remain hidden. Atta would alert them if Rhys came along.

Having made up his mind, Nightshade started down the road leading into the forest. Mina, being on her best behavior after their fight, kept close to his side and Atta padded behind them. The sun slipped away to wherever it went to spend the night and left the world a lot darker than one might have imagined it could be. Nightshade had hoped for a moon or two to give some light, but the moons were apparently off on other business, for they didn't make an appearance and the stars were obscured by the thick leaves of the overarching tree branches.

Nightshade had been in a lot of forests, and he couldn't recall having been in one quite this dark or this gloomy. He couldn't see hardly anything, but he could hear quite well and what he heard was a lot of slinking, skulking, and sneaking noises. Atta didn't help matters by glaring into the woods and growling, and once she made a lunge at something and snapped her teeth and the something growled and snapped back, but it went away.

Mina took hold of his hand, so as not to lose him in the darkness. She was obviously frightened, but she never said a word. She seemed to be trying to make up for being a brat, which gesture touched Nightshade. He was thinking that his idea of camping in the forest had not been one of his best. He had been keeping an eye out for a place to spend the night, but he couldn't find anything, and the forest was growing darker by the moment. Something dove at them from a tree and soared over their heads with a cawing shriek, causing Mina to scream and crouch into a ball and Nightshade fell and twisted his ankle.

"We have to stop and make camp," he said.

"I don't want to stop here," said Mina, shivering.

"I can't see my nose in front of my eyeballs," Nightshade told her. "We'll be safe enough—"

Atta gave a blood-curdling bark and attacked something and wrestled with it briefly. Whatever it was yelped and loped off. Atta stood panting and Mina's lower lip quivered. So did Nightshade's heart.

"Well, maybe just a little farther," he said.

The three continued on along the road; Mina walking close to Nightshade and Nightshade shuffling along in the dark, with Atta growling at every other step.

"I see a light!" said Mina, stopping suddenly.

"No, you don't," Nightshade said crossly. "You couldn't. What would a light be doing out here in a dark old forest?"

"But I do see a light," Mina insisted.

And then Nightshade saw it, too—a light shining amongst the trees. The light shone from a window and a window meant a house and a house with a light in the window meant someone living here in the woods in a house with a light in the window. What's more, he smelled the most wonderful smell—the tantalizing scent of bread or cake or pie hot out of the oven.

"Let's go!" said Mina excitedly.

"Wait a moment," said Nightshade. "When I was a little kender, my mother told a story about a horrible old witch who lured the children into her house and stuffed them into her oven and baked them into gingerbread."

Mina made a gasping sound and clutched his hand so tightly he lost all feeling in his fingers. Nightshade sniffed the air again. Whatever was being cooked smelled really, really good, not at all like baked children. And spending the night in a soft bed would be far preferable to sleeping in a hollow log, providing he could find one.

"Let's go see," he said.

"Go see a horrible old witch?" Mina quavered, hanging back.

"I'm pretty sure I was wrong about that," Nightshade replied. "It wasn't a witch. It was a beautiful lady and she baked gingerbread *for* the children, not the other way around."

"Are you sure?" Mina wasn't convinced.

"Positive," said Nightshade.

The odd thing was, however, that he could have sworn the moment he mentioned it that he did smell gingerbread.

Mina made no further argument. Keeping tight hold of his hand, they walked up to the house. Nightshade ordered Atta to stay by his side, since he was forced to admit privately that they were far more likely to find horrible witches living in dark and gloomy forests than beautiful ladies. Atta had quit growling, and Nightshade took that for a good sign.

As they drew closer to the light, Nightshade grew more and more hopeful. He could see the light came from a snug little cabin of maybe two or three rooms. A candle stood in the window, gleaming through white curtains and lighting their way along a neat flagstone path lined with flowers whose petals drooped drowsily and filled the air with sweet perfume.

All this boded well, but Nightshade was a cautious kender, and he had a spell prepared for use, just in case.

"If this turns out to be a horrible witch," he whispered to Mina, "I'll yell 'run' and you run. Don't worry about me. I'll catch up with you."

She nodded nervously. He had to pry her hand loose, because he was going to need one of his hands to knock at the door and the other hand to cast his spell in case a witch answered.

"Atta, you be ready," he warned the dog.

Reaching the door, Nightshade gave it a brisk rap.

"Hullo!" he called out. "Is anyone home?"

The door opened and light poured out. A woman stood in the door-way. Nightshade couldn't see her very well, for bright light dazzled his eyes. She was dressed all in white, and he had the impression she was kind and gentle and loving and yet strong and powerful and command-ing. He didn't know how anyone could be all these things at once, but he felt it was so, and he was a little fearful.

"How do you do, madam," he said. "My name is Nightshade and I'm a kender Nightstalker and I know some very powerful spells, and this is Mina and this is Atta, a biting variety of dog. Her teeth are quite sharp."

"How do you do, Mina and Nightshade and Atta," the woman said, and she held out her hand to the dog. Atta sniffed at her and then, to Nightshade's immense astonishment, the dog stood up on her hind legs and put her paws on the woman's chest.

"Atta! Don't do that!" Nightshade commanded, shocked. "I'm sorry, ma'am. She's not supposed to jump on people."

"She's all right," said the woman, and she smoothed the fur on Atta's head with a gentle hand and smiled at Nightshade. "You and your little friend look tired and hungry. Won't you come in?"

Nightshade hesitated, and Mina wasn't budging.

"You're not going to shove us in your oven, are you?" she asked warily.

The woman laughed. She had wonderful laughter, the sort that made Nightshade feel good all over.

"Someone has been telling you fairy tales," the woman said, with an amused glance at the kender. She held out her hand to Mina. "By a strange chance, however, I have baked some gingerbread. If you come in, you can share it with me."

Nightshade thought this a *very* strange chance, maybe a sinister strange chance. Atta had already accepted the invitation, however. The dog trotted into the house and, finding a place near the fire, she curled up, wrapped her tail around her feet, buried her nose in her tail, and settled herself comfortably. Mina took hold of the woman's hand and allowed herself to be led inside, leaving Nightshade by himself on the stoop with the tantalizing aroma of fresh-baked gingerbread pummeling his stomach.

"We can only stay a little while," he said, inching his way across the threshold. "Just until our friend, Rhys Mason, finds us. He's a monk of Majere and quite handy with his feet."

The woman cut a piece of gingerbread, placed it in a bowl and handed it to Mina, along with a spoon. The woman poured sweet cream over the gingerbread. She cut another large piece and held it out to the kender.

Nightshade gave in.

"This is remarkably good, ma'am," he mumbled, his mouth full. "It may be the best gingerbread I've ever eaten. I could tell for certain if I had another piece."

The woman cut him another slice.

"Definitely the best," said Nightshade, wiping his mouth with his napkin and accidentally stuffing the napkin and the spoon in his pocket.

Mina had fallen asleep with her gingerbread half-eaten. She lay with her head pillowed on her arms on the table. The woman gazed down at her, smoothing the auburn hair with a gentle hand. Night-shade was feeling sleepy himself. One of the first rules of traveling was that you didn't fall asleep in a strange house in the middle of a dark forest, no matter how good the gingerbread. His eyes kept trying to close, and so he propped the eyelids open with his fingers and began to talk, hoping the sound of his own voice would help keep him awake.

"Do you live here by yourself, ma'am?" he asked.

"I do," she replied. She walked over to a rocking chair that stood near the fire and sat down.

"Isn't it kind of scary?" Nightshade asked. "Living in the middle of a dark forest? Why do you do it?"

"I give shelter to those who are lost in the night," said the woman. She reached down to pet Atta, who lay beside the chair. Atta licked her hand and rested her nose on the woman's foot.

"Do many people find their way here?" Nightshade asked.

"Many do," the woman said, "though I wish more would find me."

She began to rock back and forth in her chair, humming a soft song.

Nightshade felt warm and safe and peaceful. He couldn't hold up his head any longer, and he lay it down on the table. His eyelids seemed determined to close no matter what. He realized that he didn't know the woman's name, but that didn't seem important now. Not important enough to wake out of his warm comfort to ask her.

He was dimly aware of the woman standing up from the chair and walking over to Mina. He was dimly aware of the woman gathering the slumbering child up in her arms and holding her close and kissing her.

As sleep stole over Nightshade, he thought he heard the woman whisper lovingly, "Mina . . . My child . . . My own . . ."

R hys walked the highway leading north out of Solace, confident he was on the trail of his friends. Not only had the matron seen the kender and the child and the dog, he'd met others along the route who had also seen them. The three were together and well and they were traveling north.

He was cheered to learn that although the three had been on the road several hours before he had started in pursuit, they were not far ahead of him. He had been afraid that Mina might take it into her head to walk to Godshome at a god's pace, but apparently she and the kender and the dog were ambling along, moving slowly. He half-expected to find them sitting somewhere alongside the road, footsore and tired of arguing.

Time passed, and he did not run into them. He began to wonder if they were still ahead of him. He had no way to know for sure. He no longer ran into many travelers. Night was coming on and he'd seen no sign of them. Thinking he might have to search for them after dark, he had borrowed a lantern from Laura, and now he lit the candle inside and flashed it about as he went along. He knew from past experience with lost sheep that searching done by night was tedious and difficult and often fruitless. He might walk right past them in the dark and never know.

The search would have been easier if he'd had Atta with him. Without his dog, he wondered if it wouldn't be safest to stop and wait to resume his search in the morning. Then he thought of the three of them alone and benighted in the wilderness, and he pressed on.

He came to the place where the road split. The stacked-up rocks were clearly visible in the lantern light, and Rhys breathed easier. He could reasonably assume that they had been left by the kender to indicate the direction they were traveling, an assumption born out by the fact that Rhys saw Atta's paw prints at one point and a smallish boot print at another.

He took the road east and entered the forest and soon came to the house, although he did not immediately know it was a house. He was walking slowly, keeping watch on the road, looking for signs of the missing. Every so often he would pause and during one of these times he saw the tiny pinprick of light, shining in the night like a steadfast star.

He continued on until he came to a place where trampled brush and broken sticks indicated his friends had left the road and gone into the woods. They were traveling in the direction of the light, which he judged came from a candle in a window, a beacon left to guide those who wander in the night.

He walked the flagstone path. The flowers had closed up in slumber. The small house was wrapped in stillness. On the road, he had heard the sounds of animal movement in the forest, the calls of night birds. Here all was silence, sweet and restful. He felt no unease, no sense of threat or danger. As he came closer, he saw the curtains in the window had been drawn aside. The candle stood in

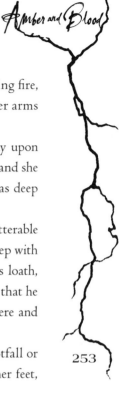

a silver candle holder on the window sill. By the light of a dying fire, he could see a woman sitting in a rocking chair, holding in her arms a slumbering child.

The woman rocked slowly back and forth. Mina's head lay upon the woman's breast. Mina was too big to be rocked like a baby and she would have never permitted it, had she been awake. But she was deep in sleep and would never know.

The expression on the woman's face was one of such unutterable sorrow that it struck Rhys to the heart. He saw Nightshade asleep with his head on the table and Atta slumbering by the fire. He was loath, suddenly, to knock, not wanting to disturb any of them. Now that he knew his friends were in safe-keeping, he would leave them here and return for them in the morning.

He was starting to withdraw when Atta either heard his footfall or sniffed his scent, for she gave a welcoming woof. Leaping to her feet, she ran to the door and began to whine and scratch on it.

"Come in, Brother," the woman called. "I have been expecting you."

Rhys opened the door, which had no lock, and entered the house. He patted Atta, who wagged not only her tail, but her entire back end in joyous greeting. Nightshade had jumped at Atta's bark, but the kender was so worn out that he went back to sleep without waking.

Rhys came to stand before the woman and bowed deeply and reverently.

"You know me, then," she said, looking up at him with a smile.

"I do, White Lady," he said softly, so as not to wake Mina.

The woman nodded. She stroked Mina's hair and then kissed her gently on the forehead. "Thus I would comfort all the children who are lost and unhappy this night."

Rising to her feet, the White Lady, as some knew the goddess Mishakal, carried Mina to bed. Mishakal laid the child down and covered her with a quilt. Rhys tapped Nightshade gently on the shoulder.

The kender opened one eye and gave a large yawn. "Oh, hullo, Rhys. I'm glad you're alive. Try the gingerbread," Nightshade advised, and went to back to sleep.

Mishakal stood gazing down at Mina. Rhys was overcome with emotion, his heart too full for speech, even if he knew what words to say. He felt the sorrow of the goddess, forced to place the child born of joy in the moment of the world's creation in eternal slumber, knowing her child would never see the light that had given her birth. And then had come the more terrible knowledge that when her child had first opened her eyes, she had not looked on light, but on cruel darkness.

"It is not often a mortal pities a god, Brother Rhys. It is not often a god deserves a mortal's pity."

"I do not pity you, Lady," Rhys said. "I grieve for you and for her."

"Thank you, Brother, for your care of her. I know you are weary, and you will find rest here as long as you require. If you can stave off your weariness for a little longer, Brother, we must talk, you and I."

Rhys sat down at the table on which were still scattered crumbs of gingerbread.

"I am sorry for the destruction and loss of life in Solace, White Lady," Rhys said. "I feel responsible. I should not have Mina brought there. I knew Chemosh was seeking her. I should have foreseen he would try to take her—"

"You are not responsible for the actions of Chemosh, Brother," Mishakal said. "It was well you and Mina were in Solace when Krell attacked. Had you been alone, you could not have fought off him or his Bone Warriors. As it was, my priests and Majere's and those of Kiri-Jolith and Gilean and others were there to assist you."

"Innocents died in that battle . . ." Rhys said.

"And Chemosh will be made to account for their lives," Mishakal said sternly. "He flouted the decree of Gilean by trying to abduct Mina. He has brought the wrath of all the gods down upon him, including the anger of his own allies, Sargonnas and Zeboim. A minotaur force is already marching on Chemosh's castle near Flotsam with orders to raze it. The Lord of Death has fled this world and is now entrenched in the Hall of the Dead. His clerics are being hunted and destroyed."

"Will there be another war?" Rhys asked, appalled.

"None can say," Mishakal replied gravely. "That depends on Mina. Upon the choices she makes."

"Forgive me, White Lady," Rhys said, "but Mina is not fit to make choices. Her mind is deeply troubled."

"I am not so sure of that," Mishakal said. "Mina herself made the decision to go to Godshome. None of us suggested that to her. Her instinct draws her there."

"What does she hope to find?" Rhys asked. "Will she truly meet Goldmoon, as she expects?"

"No," said Mishakal, smiling. "The spirit of my blessed servant, Goldmoon, is far from here, continuing her soul's journey. Yet Mina does go to Godshome in search of a mother. She seeks the mother who brought her into joyous being, and she seeks the dark mother, Takhisis, who brought her to life. She must choose which she will follow."

"And until she makes her decision, this religious strife will continue," Rhys said unhappily.

"That is sadly true, Brother. If Mina could be given an eternity of time to decide, eventually she would find her way." Mishakal sighed softly. "But we don't have eternity. As you fear, what has started as strife will devolve into all-out war."

"I will take Mina to Godshome," said Rhys. "I will help her find her way."

"You are her guide and her guardian and her friend, Brother," said Mishakal. "But you cannot take her to Godshome. Only one may do that. One with whom her fate is inextricably bound. *If* he chooses to do so. He has the power to refuse."

"I don't understand, White Lady."

"The gods of light made this promise to man: mortals are free to choose their own destiny. *All* mortals."

Rhys heard the gentle emphasis on the word "all" and thought it strange, as if she were including one mortal who might otherwise be singled out as exceptional. Wondering what she meant, he thought back on her words and suddenly he understood her.

"*All* mortals," he repeated. "Even those who were once gods. You speak of Valthonis!"

"As Mina goes to Godshome seeking her mother, so she also seeks her father. Valthonis, who was once Paladine, is not bound by the edict of Gilean. Valthonis is the only one who can help her find her way."

"And Mina has sworn to kill him—the one person who could save her."

"Sargonnas is clever, far more clever than Chemosh. He plans to give Mina a choice—darkness or light. Gilean cannot very well interfere with that. And Sargonnas gives Valthonis a choice, as well. A bitter dilemma for Mina, for Valthonis, for you, Brother," said Mishakal. "On the morrow, I can send you and Mina and those who choose to go with you to meet with Valthonis if you are still resolved upon this course. I will give you the night to consider, for I may well be sending you to your death."

"I do not need the night to think about this, White Lady. I am resolved," said Rhys. "I will do what I can to help both Mina and

Valthonis. And do not fear for him. He does not walk alone. He has the Faithful, self-appointed guardians, who are sworn to protect him . . ."

"True," Mishakal said with a radiant smile. "He is watched over by many who love him."

And then she sighed and said softly, "But the choice is not theirs. The choice must be Valthonis's choice and his alone . . ."

3

*T*he Wilder elf named Elspeth had been with Valthonis since the beginning. She was one of the Faithful, though one who was often overlooked.

When Valthonis had elected to exile himself from the pantheon of gods, he had done so to maintain the balance, disrupted after the banishment of his dark counterpart, Takhisis. Choosing to be mortal, he had taken the form of an elf, joining these people in their own bitter exile from their ancestral homelands. He did not ask for followers. He meant to walk his hard road alone. Those who accompanied him did so of their own accord, and people called them the Faithful.

All the Faithful had vivid memories of their first meeting with the Walking God—recalling even the hour of the day and whether the sun was shining or the rain was falling, for his words had touched their hearts and changed their lives forever. But they had no memory of meeting Elspeth, though they knew she must have been with him then, simply because they could not recall a time she hadn't been.

A woman of indeterminate age, Elspeth wore the simple, rough tunic and leather breeches favored by the Wilder elves, those elves who have never been comfortable in civilization and live in lonely and isolated regions of Ansalon. Her hair was long and white and hung down about her shoulders. Her eyes were blue crystal. Her face was lovely, but impassive, rarely showing emotion.

Elspeth maintained her isolation even in company with the other Faithful. The Faithful understood the reason why—or thought they did—and they were gentle with her. Elspeth was mute. Her tongue had been cut out. No one knew how she had come by this terrible injury, though rumors abounded. Some said she had been assaulted, and her attacker had cut out her tongue so that she could not name him. Some said the minotaur rulers of Silvanesti had mutilated her. They were known to cut out the tongues of any who spoke out against them.

The most terrible rumor, and one that was generally discounted, was that Elspeth had cut out her tongue herself. No one knew why she would do such a thing. What words did she so fear to speak that she would mutilate herself to prevent their utterance?

The members of the Faithful were always kind to her and tried to include her in their activities or discussions. She was painfully shy, however, and would shrink away if anyone spoke to her.

Valthonis treated Elspeth as he treated the other Faithful—with reserved, gentle courtesy, not aloof from them, yet set apart. A barrier existed between the Walking God and the Faithful that none could cross. He was mortal. Being an elf, he did not age as did humans, but his constant journeying took its toll. He always slept outdoors, refusing shelter in house or castle, and he walked the road every day, walked in wind and rain, sun and snow. His fair skin was weathered and tanned. He was lean and spare, his clothes—tunic and hose, boots and woolen cloak—were travel-worn.

The Faithful regarded him with awe, always mindful of the sacrifice he had made for mankind. In their eyes, he was still almost a god. What was he in his own eyes? None knew. He spoke of Paladine and the Gods of Light often, but always as a mortal speaks of the gods—worshipful and reverent. He never spoke as having been one of them.

The Faithful often speculated among themselves whether or not Valthonis even remembered that he had once been the most powerful god in the universe. Sometimes he would pause in a conversation and look far away, into the distance, and a frown would mar his forehead, as though he was concentrating hard, striving to recall something immensely important. These times, the Faithful believed, he had seen some glimmering of what he had once been, but when he tried to retrieve the memory it slipped away, ephemeral as morning mist. For his sake, they prayed he would never remember.

At such times, the Faithful noted that Elspeth always drew a little nearer to him. Any who chanced to look at her would see her sitting still, unmoving, her eyes fixed upon Valthonis, as if he was all she saw, all she ever wanted to see. His frown would ease, and he would slightly shake his head and smile and continue on.

The numbers of the Faithful changed from day to day, as some decided to join Valthonis on his endless walk and others departed. Valthonis never asked them to remain, nor did he ask them to leave. They swore no oath to him, for he would not accept it. They came from all races and all manner of life, rich and poor, wise and foolish, noble or wretched. No one questioned those who joined, for Valthonis would not permit it.

The Faithful all remembered the day the ogre emerged from the woods and fell into step beside Valthonis. Several clapped their hands to their swords, but a glance from Valthonis halted them. He went on speaking to those around him, who found it hard to listen, for they could not take their eyes from the ogre. The gigantic brute lumbered along, scowling balefully at all of them and snarling if any ventured too close.

Those who knew ogres said he was a chieftain, for he wore a heavy silver chain around his neck and his filthy leather vest was adorned with innumerable scalps and other gruesome trophies. He was huge, topping the tallest among them by chest, head, and shoulders, and he stank to high heaven. He remained with them a week and in all that time he spoke no word to any of them, not even to Valthonis.

Then one evening, while they were sitting around the fire, the ogre rose to his feet and stomped over to Valthonis. The Faithful were immediately on their guard, but Valthonis ordered them to sheathe their weapons and resume their seats. The ogre drew the silver chain from around his neck and held it out to the Walking God.

Valthonis placed his hand upon the chain and asked the gods to bless it and gave the chain back. The ogre grunted in satisfaction. He hung the chain about his neck and, with another grunt, he left them, lumbering back into the forest. Everyone breathed a sigh of relief. Later, when stories began to filter out of Blöde how an ogre wearing a silver chain was working to ease the misery of his people and trying to bring an end to violence and bloodshed, the Faithful remembered their ogre companion and marveled.

Kender often joined them on the road, jumping about Valthonis like crickets and pestering him with questions, such as why frogs have bumps but snakes don't and why cheese is yellow when milk is white. The Faithful rolled their eyes, but Valthonis answered all questions patiently and even seemed to enjoy having the kender about. The kender were a trial to his followers, but they strove to follow the example of the Walking God and show patience and forbearance, and they reconciled themselves to the theft of all their possessions.

Gnomes came to discuss schematic layouts of their latest inventions

with the Walking God, and he would study them and try as diplomatically as he could to point out the design flaws most likely to result in injury or death.

Elves were always with Valthonis, many remaining with him for long periods. Humans were also among the Faithful, though they tended to stay for shorter periods of time than the elves. Paladins of Kiri-Jolith and Solamnic knights would often come to speak to Valthonis about their quests, asking for his blessing or forming part of his entourage. A hill dwarf traveled with them for a time, a priest of Reorx, who said he came in memory of Flint Fireforge.

Valthonis walked all roads and highways, stopping only to rest and sleep. He ate his frugal meals on the road. When he came to a town, he would walk its streets, pausing to talk to those he met, never remaining in one place long. He was often asked by clerics to give sermons or lectures. Valthonis always refused. He talked as he walked.

Many came to converse with him. Most came in faith, to listen and absorb. But there were also those who came as skeptics, those who wanted to argue, mock, or jeer at him. The Faithful had to practice restraint at these times, for Valthonis would permit intervention only if people became violent, and then he was far more concerned about the safety of those around him than he was for himself.

Day after day, the Faithful came and the Faithful went. But Elspeth was always with him.

This day, as they walked the winding roads through the Khalkist mountains, somewhere in the vicinity of the accursed valley of Neraka, the silent Elspeth startled the Faithful by leaving her customary place on the fringes of the group and, creeping close to Valthonis, fell into step behind him. He took no notice of her, for he was conversing with a follower of Chislev, discussing how to reverse the depredations of the Dragon Overlords on the land.

The Faithful noted Elspeth's action and thought it odd, but took no further notice of her. Only later did they look back and wish, to their sorrow, that they had paid more heed.

Galdar had mixed feelings about his assignment. He was going to be reunited with Mina, and he wasn't certain how he felt about that. On the one hand, he was glad. He had not seen her since their enforced separation at the tomb of Takhisis, when she had given herself into the arms of the Lord of Death. He had tried to stop her, but the god had torn him from Mina's side. Even then, he would have searched for her, but Sargas had given Galdar to understand that he had more important work to do for his god and his people than chase after a silly chit of a human.

Galdar had heard news of Mina after that, how she had become a High Priestess of Chemosh, beloved of the Lord of Bones, and Galdor had scowled and shaken his horned head. Mina's turning priestess was a grievous waste. Galdor could not have been more shocked if he'd heard that the renowned minotaur war hero, Makel Ogrebane, had become a druid and gone about healing baby bunnies.

Because of this, Galdar was reluctant to meet Mina again. If the woman who had boldly and courageously ridden with him on dragon back to do battle with the dread Dragon Overlord Malys was now a bone-waving, spell-chanting, grave-robbing follower of the sly and treacherous Chemosh, Galdar wanted nothing to do with her. He didn't want to see her like that. He wanted his memories of her to be of the conquering soldier, not some lying priest.

He disliked this assignment for another reason. It involved gods and Galdar'd had a belly full of gods during the War of Souls. Like his old enemy-turned-friend, Gerard, Galdar wanted as little to do with gods as possible. His feelings were so strong that he had almost refused to take the assignment, even though this would have meant saying "No," to Sargas, something not even the god's own children dared.

In the end, Galdar's faith in Sargas (and his fear of him) and his longing to see Mina won out. He reluctantly agreed to accept the assignment. (It should be noted that Sargas did not tell Galdar the truth—that Mina was a god herself. The Horned God must have considered that too great a test for his faithful follower.)

Galdar and the small minotaur patrol under his command spent considerable time scouting the enemy, determining their numbers, appraising their skill. A cautious and intelligent leader, Galdar did not immediately assume, as did some of his race, that just because they were dealing with elves his soldiers would have an easy time of it. Galdar had fought elves during and after the War of Souls, and he had come to respect them as a warriors even if he didn't think much of them in any other regard. He impressed upon his troops that elves were skilled and tenacious fighters, who would fight all the more fiercely because of their loyalty and dedication to their Walking God.

Galdar laid his ambush in the wilds of the Khalkist mountains. He chose this region because he calculated that once the Walking God was far from civilization the numbers of his followers would dwindle. When Valthonis traveled the major highways of Solamnia, he might have as many as twenty or thirty people accompanying him. Here, far from any major city, close to Neraka, a region of Ansalon most people still considered cursed, only the most dedicated remained at his side. Galdar counted six elven warriors armed with bow and arrow and sword, a Wilder elf who bore no weapons, and a druid of Chislev clad in moss green robes who would probably attack them with holy spells.

He set the time for the ambush at twilight, when the shadows of night stealing among the trees vied with the last rays of the sun. At this time, tricks of the waning light could fool the eye, make finding a target difficult even for elven archers.

Galdar and his troops hid themselves among the trees, waiting until they heard the party moving along the trail, which was little more than a goatherd's path. The small band was still some distance away, time for Galdar to give his minotaur band some last-minute whispered orders.

"We are to take the Walking God *alive*," he said, laying heavy emphasis on the word. "This command comes from Sargas himself. Remember this—Sargas is the god of vengeance. Disobey him at your peril. I for one am not prepared to risk his wrath."

The other minotaurs agreed wholeheartedly and some glanced uneasily at the heavens. Sargas's retribution against those who thwarted his will was known to be as swift as it was brutal.

"What if this so-called Walking God chooses to do battle, sir?" asked one. "Will the Gods of Wimps fight for their own? Should we expect lightning bolts to strike us down?"

"Gods of Wimps, is it, Malek?" Galdar growled. "You lost the tip of your horn to a Solamnic knight. Was she a wimp, or did she kick your sorry ass?"

The minotaur looked chagrined. His fellows grinned at him, and one nudged him with an elbow.

"So long as we threaten no harm to the Walking God, the Gods of Light will not intervene. So the priest of Sargas assured me."

"And what do we do with this Walking God once we have him, sir?" asked another. "You haven't told us that yet."

"Because I don't want to burden your brain with more than one thought at a time," Galdar told him. "All you need worry about now is capturing the Walking God. Alive!"

Galdar cocked an ear. The voices and the footfalls were drawing nearer.

"Take up your positions," he ordered and dispersed his men, sending them running to the ditches on either side of the road. "Don't move a muscle and keep upwind of them! These blasted elves have a nose for minotaur."

Galdar crouched behind a large oak tree. His sword remained sheathed. He hoped he would not have to use it, and rubbed the stump of his missing arm. The wound was an old one. The arm was fully healed, but sometimes, strangely, he felt pain in the limb that was not there. This evening the arm burned and throbbed worse than usual. He blamed it on the damp, but he had to wonder if it hurt because he was thinking of Mina, recalling their first meeting. She had reached out her hand to him and her touch had healed him, given him back his severed limb.

The limb he'd lost again, trying to save her.

He wondered if she remembered, if she ever thought of their time together, the happiest and proudest time of his life.

Probably not, now that she was a high muckety-muck priestess.

Galdar rubbed his arm and cursed the damp and listened to the voices of elves coming closer.

Hunkering down among the dead leaves and shadows, the minotaur soldiers gripped their weapons and waited.

Two elven warriors walked in front, four came behind. Valthonis and the druid of Chislev walked in the center of the group, absorbed in their conversation. Elspeth kept very close to him, almost at his heels. Usually she would have been far in the rear, several paces behind the rear guard. This sudden change added to the uneasiness the others felt at being so near the accursed valley of Neraka where the Dark Queen had once reigned. They had questioned Valthonis about why he had chosen to come here, to this dread place, but he would only smile and tell them what he always told them in answer to their questions.

"I do not go where I want to go," he would say. "I go where I need to be."

Since they could elicit no information from the Walking God, one of the Faithful took it upon himself to question Elspeth, asking her in a low voice what was wrong, what she feared. Elspeth might have been deaf, as well as mute, for she did even glance his way. She kept her gaze fixed upon Valthonis and, as the elf later reported to his fellows, her face was drawn and tense.

Already uneasy and nervous about their surroundings, the elven warriors were not quite caught off guard by the sudden attack. Something struck them as wrong as they passed beneath the leaves of the overhanging tree limbs. Perhaps it was a smell; minotaur have a bovine stench that is not easy to conceal. Perhaps it was the breaking of a stick beneath a heavy boot, or the shifting of a large body in the underbrush. Whatever it was, the elves sensed danger, and they slowed their pace.

The two in front drew their swords and fell back to take up positions on either side of Valthonis. The elves following nocked their arrows and raised their bows and turned to stare intently into the shifting shadows in the trees.

"Show yourselves!" one of the elves shouted harshly in Common.

The minotaur soldiers obeyed his command, clambering up out of the ditches and surging onto the road. Steel clanged against steel. Bowstrings twanged and the druid began to chant a prayer to Chislev, calling on her for blessed aid.

Valthonis's voice cut through the chaos, ringing out loudly and forcefully. "Stop this! Now."

He spoke with such authority that all the combatants obeyed him, including the minotaurs, who reacted to the commanding tone out of instinct. A heartbeat later they realized that it was their intended victim who had ordered them to cease and, feeling foolish, sprang again to the attack.

This time Galdar roared, "Stop in the name of Sargas!" The minotaur soldiers, seeing their leader striding forward, reluctantly lowered their swords and fell back.

The elves and the minotaurs eyed each other balefully. No one attacked, but no one sheathed his blade. The druid was still praying. Valthonis placed a hand upon the man's shoulder and spoke a soft word. The druid cast him a pleading glance, but Valthonis shook his head, and the prayer to Chislev ended in a sigh.

Galdar raised his only hand to show he bore no weapon and walked toward Valthonis. The Faithful moved to interpose their own bodies between the Walking God and the minotaur.

"Walking God," said Galdar, speaking over the heads of those who blocked him, "I would speak to you—in private."

"Stand aside, my friends," said Valthonis. "I will hear what he has to say."

One of the elves tried to argue, but Valthonis would not listen. He asked the Faithful again to stand aside and this they did, though reluctantly and unhappily. Galdar ordered his soldiers to keep their distance and they obeyed, though with lowering looks at the elves.

Galdar and Valthonis walked into the trees, out of earshot of their followers.

"You are Valthonis, once the god Paladine," stated Galdar.

"I am Valthonis," said the elf mildly.

"I am Galdar, emissary of the great god known to minotaur as Sargas, known to those like yourselves as Sargonnas. My god bids me speak these words: 'You have unfinished business in the world, Valthonis, and because you have chosen to 'walk' away from this challenge there is new strife in heaven and among men. The great Sargas wants to bring this strife to an end. This matter must be brought to a swift and final resolution. To facilitate this, he will bring about a meeting between you and your challenger.' "

"I hope you do think I am being argumentative, Emissary, but I am afraid I know nothing about this strife or the challenge of which you speak," Valthonis replied.

Galdar rubbed his muzzle with the side of his hand. He was uncomfortable, for he believed in honor and in honesty, and in this he was being less than honest, less than honorable.

"Perhaps not a challenge from Mina," Galdar clarified, hoping his god would understand. "More of a threat. Still," he went on before Valthonis could reply, "it hangs between the two of you like noxious smoke, poisoning the air."

"Ah, I understand now," Valthonis said. "You speak of Mina's vow to kill me."

Galdar glanced about uneasily at his minotaur escort. "Keep your voice down when you mention her name. My people consider her a witch."

He cleared his throat and added stiffly, "I was told by Sargas to say that the Horned God wants to bring the two of you together, that you may resolve your differences."

Valthonis smiled wryly at this, and Galdar, embarrassed, kept on rubbing his muzzle. Sargas had no intention the two should resolve their differences. Galdar had no love for any elf, but he scorned to lie to this one. He had his orders, however, and so he said what he'd been told to say, though he was making it clear he wasn't the one to say it.

The two were interrupted by one of the Faithful, who called out, "You have no need to parlay with this brute, sir. We can and will fight to defend you—"

"No blood will be shed because of me," said Valthonis sharply. He cast a stern glance at the Faithful. "Have you walked the road with me all this time and listened to me speak of peace and brotherhood and yet heard nothing I have said to you?"

His voice rasped, and his followers were abashed. They did not know where to look to avoid his angry gaze, and so averted their faces or stared at the ground. Only Elspeth did not look away. Only she met his gaze. He smiled at her in reassurance and then turned back to Galdar.

"I will accompany you on the condition that my companions be allowed to leave unharmed."

"Those are my orders," said Galdar. He raised his voice so that all could hear. "Sargas wants peace. He does not want to see blood spilled."

One of the elves sneered at this, and one of the minotaurs growled, and the two leaped at each other. Galdar flung himself at the minotaur and socked him in the jaw. Elspeth grasped the sword arm of the elven warrior and pulled him back. Startled, the warrior immediately lowered his weapon.

"If you will walk with us, sir," Galdar said, shaking out his bruised knuckles, "we will act as your escort. Give me your vow that you will not try to escape, and I will not chain you."

"You have my word," said Valthonis. "I will not escape. I go with you of my own free will."

He bade goodbye to the Faithful, giving his hand to each and asking the gods to bless them.

"Do not fear, sir," said one softly, speaking Silvanesti elven, "we will rescue you."

"I have given my word," said Valthonis. "I will not break it."

"But, sir—"

The Walking God shook his head and turned away, only to find Elspeth blocking him. It seemed she longed to speak, for her jaw trembled and low, animal sounds came from her throat.

Valthonis touched her cheek with his hand. "You need say nothing, child. I understand."

Elspeth grasped hold of his hand and pressed it to her cheek.

"Take care of her," Valthonis ordered the Faithful.

He gently freed his hand from her grasp and walked to where Galdar and the minotaur guard stood waiting for him.

"You have my word. And I have yours," said Valthonis. "My friends depart unharmed."

"May Sargas take my other arm if I break my oath," said Galdar. He entered the forest, and Valthonis followed. The minotaur guard closed in around them both.

The Faithful stood on the path amidst the gathering gloom, watching their leader depart. Their elven sight allowed them to keep track of Valthonis for a long while and, then, when they could not see him, they could hear the minotaur crashing and hacking their way through the brush. The Faithful looked at one another. The minotaur had left a trail a blind gully dwarf could follow. They would be easy to track.

One started after them. The silent Elspeth stopped him.

"He gave his word," she said, using signs, touching her hand to her mouth, then to her heart. "He made his choice."

Grieving, the Faithful began to trace their steps, returning the way they had come. It was some time before any of them realized that Elspeth was not with them. Mindful of their promise, they began to

search for her and at last they found her trail. She walked the same
path the Walking God had been traveling—the road to Neraka. She
refused to turn aside, and mindful of their promise to care for her, the
Faithful accompanied her.

273

Rhys was dreaming that he was being watched and he woke with an alarmed start to find his dream was true. A face hovered over him. Fortunately, the face was one Rhys knew, and he closed his eyes in relief and calmed his racing heart.

Nightshade, chin in hand, was sitting cross-legged beside Rhys, peering down at him. The kender's expression was gloomy.

"About bloody time you woke up!" Nightshade muttered.

Rhys sighed and kept his eyes closed a moment longer. Until his dream, his slumber had been deep and sweet and easeful, and he let go of sleep with regret. All the more so since it appeared by the glimpse he'd had of Nightshade's grim expression that waking would not be nearly so pleasant.

"Rhys." Nightshade poked at him with his finger. "Don't you dare go back to sleep. Here, Atta, slobber on him."

"I'm awake," said Rhys, sitting up and ruffling Atta's fur, for the dog was unhappy and she pressed her head into his neck for comfort. Still soothing Atta, Rhys sat up and looked about.

"Where are we?" he asked, amazed.

"I can tell you where we're *not*," stated Nightshade glumly. "We're *not* in the house of the pretty lady who makes the best gingerbread in the world. Which is where we both were yesterday, and the day before that and we were there when I went to sleep last night, and that's where we should be this morning, only we're not. We're here. Wherever 'here' is. And I don't mind telling you," the kender added in a tense tone, "that I'd rather be somewhere else. Here is *not* a nice place."

Rhys gently put Atta aside and rose swiftly to his feet. The forest was gone, as was the small house, where, as Nightshade had said, he and the kender, Atta and Mina had spent two days and two nights—days and nights of blessed tranquility and peace. They had intended to set out upon the final stage of their journey this morning, but it seemed Mishakal had forestalled him.

They looked out upon a desolate, barren valley slung between the charred ridges of several active volcanoes. Tendrils of steam drifted up from the blackened peaks, trailing into a sky that was a stark and empty blue. The air was chill, the sun small and shrunken and impotent, radiating no warmth. Their shadows straggled across the trackless gray stone floor of the valley and dwindled to nothing. The air was thin and sulpherous, difficult to breathe. Rhys could not seem to take in enough to fill his lungs. Most awful was the silence which had a living quality to it, like an inhaled breath. Watchful, waiting.

Strange rock formations littered this valley. Enormous black crystals, jagged-edged and faceted, thrust up out of the stone. Some standing twenty feet high or more, the monoliths were scattered about the valley at random. They were not a natural formation, did not appear to have sprung up out of the ground. Rather, it seemed they had been cast down from heaven by some immense force whose fury had driven them deep into the valley floor.

"The least you could have done is bring the gingerbread with you,"

Nightshade said. "Now we don't have any breakfast. I know I agreed to come with you to find the Walking God, but I didn't know the trip was going to be quite so sudden."

"I didn't either," Rhys said, then added sharply, "Where's Mina?"

Nightshade jerked a thumb over his shoulder. Mina had waited with him beside the slumbering Rhys until she'd grown bored and wandered off to investigate. She stood some distance away, gazing at her reflection in one of the crystalline monoliths.

"Why are you looking all tense like this?" Nightshade demanded. "What's wrong?"

"I know where we are," said Rhys, hurrying over to fetch Mina. "I know this place. And we must leave at once. Atta, come!"

"I'm all for leaving. Though leaving doesn't look to be as easy as coming," Nightshade stated, breaking into a run to keep up with Rhys's long strides. "Especially since we have no idea how the 'coming' happened. I don't think it was Mina. She was asleep on the ground when I woke up and when she woke up, she was as startled and confused as I was."

Rhys was certain the White Lady had sent them to this terrible place, though he could not imagine why, other than that it was said to be close to Godshome.

"So, Rhys," said Nightshade, his boots thunking on the stone and causing dust to swirl in small, slithering eddies over the floor like sidewinding snakes, "where are we? What is this place?"

"The valley of Neraka," Rhys replied.

The kender gasped, his eyes going round. "Neraka? *The* Neraka? The Neraka where the Dark Queen built her dark temple and was going to enter the world? I remember that story! There was a guy with a green jewel in his chest who murdered his sister, only she forgave him and her spirit blocked the Dark Queen's entry, and she lost the war and the brother came back to his sister and together they blew up the temple and . . . and this is it!" Nightshade stopped to stare with excitement into one of the black monoliths. "These ugly rocks are pieces of Takhisis's temple!"

"Mina!" Rhys called out to her.

She didn't seem to hear him. She was staring fixedly at the rock, seemingly mesmerized. Rhys slowed his pace. He didn't want to startle or alarm her by accosting her suddenly, without warning.

Meanwhile Nightshade was mulling things over. "Neraka had something to do with the War of Souls, too. That war started when Takhisis became the One God and she was going to keep all the souls imprisoned here. Poor souls. I spoke to a good many of them, you know, Rhys. I was glad for them when the war was over and they were finally free to depart, though the graveyard was awfully lonely after that . . ."

"Mina," called Rhys softly.

Motioning for Nightshade to keep back, Rhys walked slowly toward her. The kender caught hold of Atta and both of them stopped, both of them panting in the thin air.

"Neraka. War of Souls. Neraka," Nightshade muttered. "Oh, yes, now I remember it all! Neraka was where the war started and . . . Omigod! Rhys!" he shouted. "This is where Mina came to start the War of Souls! Takhisis sent her out of the storm . . ."

Rhys made a stern, emphatic gesture, and Nightshade gulped and fell silent.

"I guess he already knew that," the kender said and put his arms around Atta's neck and held onto her tightly—just in case the dog was scared.

Rhys came up to stand behind Mina.

"Who is she?" Mina demanded, frightened. She pointed at her reflection in the black crystal.

Rhys's breath caught in his throat. He could not speak. The Mina that stood beside him was the child, Mina, with long red braids and freckles on her nose and guileless eyes of amber. The Mina reflected in the black crystal was the woman of the soul-imprisoning amber eyes, the warrior woman who had been born in this valley, the woman who had worshipped the One God, the Dark God, Takhisis.

Mina flung herself in sudden fury at the black rock, kicking it and beating it with her fists.

Rhys seized hold of her. The sharp rock had already cut her hand. Blood trailed down her arm. He hauled her back from the rock. She jerked free of his grip and stood panting and glaring at the rock, and wiped the blood from her cut onto her dress.

"Why does that woman stare at me like that? I don't like her! What has she done with *me?*" Mina cried in anguish.

Rhys tried to soothe her, but he was shaken himself by the sight of the hard-faced, amber-eyed woman gazing back at them from the black crystal.

"Woo boy," said Nightshade. Coming up to stand beside Rhys, the kender stared at Mina, then he stared at the reflection in the crystal monolith and rubbed his eyes and scratched his head. "Woo boy," he said again.

Shaking his head in perplexity, he turned to Rhys.

"I hate to add to our problems, especially since they appear to be real doozies, but you should probably know that there's a large group of minotaur soldiers up on that ridge."

The kender squinted, shaded his eyes with his hand. "And I know this sounds strange, Rhys, but I think they have an elf with them."

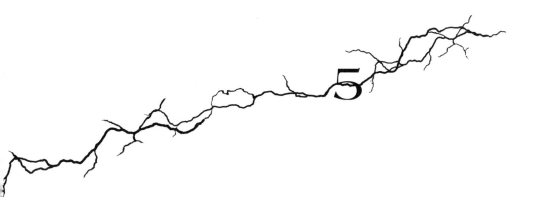

*G*aldar was plagued by ghosts. Not ghosts of the dead, as during
the War of Souls. Ghosts of himself, of his own dead past. Here, in
Neraka, Mina had walked into this valley and into his life and forever
changed him. He had not been in the valley since that night which had
been both terrible and wonderful. He had not been back in Neraka
until now, and he was not happy to return. Time had healed the wound
The scar tissue had grown over his stump. But his memories ached and
throbbed and tormented him like the pain of his phantom arm.

"The dwarves call this place *Gamashinoch*," Galdar said. "It means
'Song of Death'. Guess they don't call it that now, 'cause the singing's
stopped, Sargas be praised," he added.

He talked to the only person with him—Valthonis—and Galdar
wasn't talking to Valthonis because he enjoyed conversing with the elf.
The racial hatred between minotaur and elves went back centuries, and
Galdar saw no reason why the hatred shouldn't last a few more. As for
this elf being the 'Walking God', Galdar had himself been witness
to the transformation so he knew the tale was true. What he didn't
understand was why everyone was making such a fuss over him. So

he'd once been a god? What of it? He was a man now and had to take a crap in the woods like everyone else.

Galdar was mainly talking because he had to talk or else listen to the eerie silence that blanketed the valley. At that, Galdar had to admit the silence was better than that horrible singing they'd heard when he'd last been here. The lamenting souls of the dead had finally departed.

Galdar and Valthonis entered the valley alone; Galdar having ordered his men to stay on the ridge. His soldiers protested the decision. They even dared to argue with him, and no minotaur ever argued with his commanding officer. If Galdar insisted upon entering this accursed valley, his men wanted to come with him.

The minotaur soldiers admired Galdar. He was plain-speaking and blunt, and they liked that in a commander. He shared their hardships, and he made no secret of the fact that he didn't like this assignment any better than they did, especially coming to the accursed valley of Neraka.

Takhisis had been Sargas's consort, but there had been no love lost between them. Her favored race, the ogres, had long been enemies of the minotaur, at one time enslaving and brutalizing them. Sargas had pleaded their cause, but she had laughed at him and mocked him and his minoyaur race. She was now dead and gone, or so people claimed. The minotaurs did not trust Takhisis, however. She'd been banished once by Huma Dragonbane and she'd come back. She might rise again, and no one wanted to walk the dark valley where she had once reigned.

"If you're not back by noon, we're coming in to get you, sir," stated his second-in-command, and the other minotaurs raised their voices in agreement.

"No, you won't," Galdar said, glaring around at them. "If I'm not back by sunset, return to Jarek. Make your report to the priests of Sargas."

"And what do we say, sir?" his second demanded.

"That I did as Sargas commanded," Galdar answered proudly.

His men understood him, and though they did not like it, they no longer argued. They left the ridge and returned to the foothills, to while away the time with a game of bones, in which none took much pleasure.

Galdar and the elf continued making their way down what was left of a road. Galdar wondered if it was the road he'd walked that night, the night of the storm, the night of Mina. He didn't recognize it, but that wasn't surprising. He'd gone out of his way to try to forget that nightmarish march.

"I first came here with a patrol the night of the great storm," Galdar explained as they left the road and entered the valley. "We didn't know it at the time, but the storm was Takhisis, announcing to the world that the One God was back and this time she meant to have it all. We were under the command of Talon Leader Maggit, a bully and a coward, the sort of commander that would always run from a battle, only to pull some stupid stunt to try prove how brave he was and get half his men killed in the process."

Talon Leader Magitt dismounted his horse. "We will set up camp here. Pitch my command tent near the tallest of those monoliths. Galdar, you're in charge of setting up camp. I trust you can handle that simple task?"

His words seemed unnaturally loud, his voice shrill and raucous. A breath of air, cold and sharp, hissed through the valley, sent the sand into dust devils that swirled across the barren ground and whispered away.

"You are making a mistake, sir," said Galdar in a soft undertone, to disturb the silence as little as possible. "We are not wanted here."

"Who does not want us, Galdar?" Talon Leader Magitt sneered. "These rocks?" He slapped the side of a black crystal monolith. "Ha! What a thick-skulled, superstitious cow!"

"We made camp," said Galdar, his voice low and solemn. "In this valley. Among the blasted ruins of her temple."

A man could see his reflection in those glossy black planes, a reflection that was distorted, twisted, yet completely recognizable as being a reflection of himself. . . .

These men, long since hardened against every good feeling, looked into the shining black plane of the crystals and were appalled by the faces that looked back. For on those faces they could see their mouths open to sing the terrible song.

Galdar glanced at the black crystalline monoliths that littered the valley, and he could not repress a shudder.

"Go ahead, look into one of them," he said to Valthonis. "You won't like what you see. The rock twists your reflection, so that you see yourself as some sort of monster."

Valthonis stopped to stare at one of the rocks. Galdar halted, too, thinking it would be amusing to see the elf's reaction. Valthonis gazed at his reflection, then glanced at Galdar. The minotaur stepped up behind the elf to see what he was seeing. The elf's reflection glistened in the rock. The reflection was the same as the reality—an elf with a weathered face and ancient eyes.

"Hunh," Galdar grunted. "Maybe the curse on the valley has been lifted. I haven't been here since the war ended."

He elbowed Valthonis aside and stood before the rock and gazed boldly at himself.

The Galdar reflected in the rock had two good arms.

"Give me your hand, Galdar," Mina said to him.

At the sound of her voice, rough, sweet, he heard again the song singing among the rocks. He felt his hackles rise. A shudder went through him, a thrill flashed along his spine. He meant to turn away from her, but he found himself raising his left hand.

"No, Galdar," said Mina. "Your right hand. Give me your right hand."

"I have no right hand!" Galdar cried out in rage and anguish.

He watched his arm, his right arm, lift; watched his hand, his right hand, reach out trembling fingers.

Mina extended her hand, touched the phantom hand of the minotaur.

"Your sword arm is restored . . ."

Galdar stared at his own reflection. He flexed his left hand, his only hand. His reflection flexed both hands. Burning liquid stung his eyes, and he turned swiftly and angrily away and began to scour the valley, searching for some sign of Mina. Now that he was here, he was impatient to get this over with. He wanted to get past the awkward first meeting, endure the pain of disappointment, leave her with the elf, and go on with living.

"I remember when you lost the arm Mina had given you," Valthonis said, the first words he'd spoken since he'd been taken captive. "You fell defending Mina from Takhisis, who accused her of conspiring against her and would have slain her in a rage. You shielded Mina with your body and the Dark Queen cut off your arm. Sargas offered to restore your arm, but you refused—"

"Who gave you permission to speak, elf?" Galdar demanded angrily, wondering why he'd let the yammering go on so long.

"No one," Valthonis said with a half-smile. "I will be silent if you like."

Galdar didn't want to admit it, but he found the sound of another voice soothing in this place where only the dead had once spoken, so he said, "Waste your last breaths if you want. Your preaching won't have any effect on me."

Galdar halted to stare squint-eyed into the valley. He thought he'd caught sight of movement, of people down there. The pale sunlight seemed to be playing tricks on his eyes, and it was difficult for him to tell if he'd actually seen living beings walking about, or ghosts, or only the strange shadows cast by the loathsome monoliths.

Not shadows, he determined. Or ghosts. There are people down there and they must be those I was told to meet.

There was the monk in the orange robes who was said to be Mina's escort. But, if so, where was Mina?

"Blast and damn this cursed place!" Galdar said in sudden anger.

He'd been assured Mina would be with the monk, but he saw no sign of her. He hadn't understood why she should be traveling with a monk anyway. He hadn't liked this from the beginning and he was liking it less and less.

Removing a length of rope from his belt, Galdar ordered Valthonis to hold out his hands.

"I gave you my word I wouldn't try to escape," Valthonis said quietly.

Galdar grunted and tied the rope securely around the elf's slender wrists. Tying the knot wasn't easy for the one-armed minotaur. Galdar had to use his teeth to finish the job.

"Bound or not, I can't escape her," Valthonis added. "And neither can you, Galdar. You've always known Mina was a god, haven't you?"

"Shut up," Galdar ordered savagely.

Grasping the elf roughly by the arm, Galdar shoved Valthonis forward.

The next lightning flash was not a bolt, but a sheet of flame that lit the sky and the ground and the mountains with a purple white radiance. Silhouetted against the awful glow, a figure moved toward them, walking calmly through the raging storm, seeming untouched by the gale, unmoved by the lightning, unafraid of the thunder.

"What are you called?" Galdar demanded.

"My name is Mina." . . .

He had sung her name. They had all sung her name. All those like himself who had followed her to battle and glory and death.

"You did this," Takhisis raved. "You connived with them to bring about my downfall. You wanted them to sing your name, not my own."

Mina . . . Mina . . .

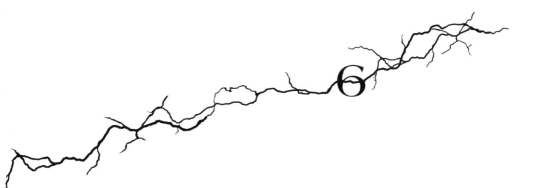

Keeping one hand on Mina's shoulder, Rhys glanced around to where Nightshade was pointing. He could see the minotaur troops, now leaving the ridgeline, marching away. Two people entered the valley. One was a minotaur wearing the emblem of Sargonnas emblazoned on his leather armor. One was an elf whose hands were bound.

Too late to flee, even if there had been any place to go. The minotaur had spotted them.

The minotaur was armed with a sword, which he wore on his right hip, for his right arm—his sword arm—was missing. He had not drawn his weapon, but he kept his left hand hovering near it. His keen eyes fixed a suspicious gaze on Rhys, then left him and flicked over the rest of the group. His scowl deepened. The minotaur was searching for Mina.

The elf wore simple clothing—green cloak and tunic, well-worn boots, dusty from the road. He was not armed, and though he was obviously the minotaur's prisoner, he walked with his head up, taking long, graceful, purposeful strides, as one who is accustomed to walking many roads.

The Walking God. Rhys recognized Valthonis, and was about to call out a warning, when he was drowned out by the minotaur's roar.

"Mina!"

Her name rang out across the valley and bounded off the Lords of Doom, who cast it back in eerie echoes, as though the bones of the world were crying out to her.

Galdar!" Mina gave a glad shout.

She knocked Rhys aside, hitting him a blow that was like being hit by a lightning bolt. He sagged, stunned, to the ground, unable to move.

"Galdar!" Mina cried again, and ran to him with outstretched arms..

She tried to wrench free and when Rhys tried to stop her, she struck him a blow with her hand that was like being hit by a lightning bolt. He crumpled to the ground and lay there, paralyzed and stunned, unable to move.

Mina was no longer a child. She was a girl, seventeen years old. Her head was shorn like a sheep at shearing. She wore the breastplate of those who called themselves Knights of Neraka, and it was charred and dented and stained with blood, as were her hands and arms up to the elbows. Reaching Galdar, she flung her arms around him and buried her face in his chest.

The minotaur clasped her with his good arm, held her close. Two furrows in the fur on either side of his snout marked the overflow of his feelings.

Seeing that they were both occupied, Nightshade crept over to kneel beside Rhys.

"Are you all right?" Nightshade whispered.

"I will be . . . in a moment." Rhys grimaced. He was starting to regain some feeling in his hands and feet. "Don't let go of Atta!"

"I have her, Rhys," Nightshade said. He had wound his hand in the long fur at her neck. To his surprise, the dog had not tried to attack the grown-up Mina. Perhaps Atta was now as confused as the kender.

Galdar held Mina tightly and glared at them all defiantly, as though daring any of them to try to take her from him.

"Mina!" he said brokenly, "I came to find you— That is, Sargas sent me—"

"Never mind that now!" Mina said sharply. She pulled away from him, looked up at him. "We have no time, Galdar. Sanction is under siege. The Solamnic knights have it surrounded. I must go there, take command. I will break the siege."

Her amber eyes flared. "Why do you just stand there? Where is my horse? My weapon? Where are my troops? You must fetch them, Galdar, bring them to me. We don't have much time. The battle will be lost . . ."

Galdar blinked in astonishment. "Er . . . don't you remember, Mina? You won the battle. You broke the siege of Sanction. Beckard's Cut—"

She frowned at him and said sharply, "I don't know what's got into you, Galdar. Stop wasting my time with such foolery and obey my command."

"Mina," Galdar said uneasily, "the siege of Sanction happened long ago during the War of Souls. The war is over. The One God lost. Don't you remember, Mina? The other gods cast Takhisis out, made her mortal—"

"They killed her," Mina said softly. Her amber eyes glittered beneath sharply slanting brows. "They were jealous of my Queen, envious of her power. The mortals of this world adored her. They sang her name. The other gods couldn't allow that, and so they destroyed her."

Galdar tried to speak a couple of times without success, then he said awkwardly, "They sang *your* name, Mina."

Her amber eyes shone, illuminated from within.

"You're right," she said, smiling. "They did sing my name."

Galdar licked his lips. He looked about, as though seeking help. Finding none, he cleared his throat with a rumble and launched into a much-rehearsed speech, talking quickly, without inflection, in haste to reach the end.

"This elf is Valthonis. He used to be Paladine, the leader of the pantheon of gods, the instigator of the fall of Queen Takhisis. My god, Sargas, hopes that you will accept Valthonis as his gift and that you will take your just revenge upon the traitor who brought down . . . your . . . our Queen. In return, Sargas hopes you will think well of the him and . . . and . . . that you will . . ."

Galdar stopped. He stared at Mina, stricken.

"That I will what, Galdar?" Mina demanded. "Sargas hopes I will

think well of him and I will what?"

"Become his ally," Galdar said at last.

"You mean—become one of his generals?" Mina asked, frowning. "But I can't. I am not a minotaur."

Galdar couldn't answer her question. He looked about again for help, and this time he found it.

Valthonis answered him. "Sargas want you to become the Queen of Darkness, Mina."

Mina laughed, as though at some rich jest. Then she saw no one else was laughing. "Galdar, why do you look so glum? That's funny. Me? The Queen of Darkness!"

Galdar rubbed his muzzle and blinked his eyes rapidly and gazed out somewhere over her head.

"Galdar!" said Mina, suddenly angry. "That is funny!"

"Is the minotaur right, Rhys?" Nightshade asked in a smothered whisper. "Is that elf really Paladine? I always wanted to meet Paladine. Do you think you could intro—"

"Hush, my friend," said Rhys softly. He rose to his feet, moving fluidly, quietly, trying not to draw attention to himself. "Keep hold of Atta."

Nightshade took a firm grip on the dog. Eyeing the Walking God, the kender whispered into Atta's ear, "I expected him to be a lot taller—"

Rhys picked up the emmide and the scrip. He tied the scrip to the top of the staff, then padded across the stone floor, the dust slithering beneath his feet. He came to stand to one side and a little in front of Valthonis.

"This man knows the way to Godshome, Mina," Rhys said.

Mina's amber eyes, laden with trapped souls so that they were almost black, shifted to Rhys. Her lip curled in scorn. "Who are you? Where did you come from?"

Rhys smiled. "Those are the very questions you asked of me, Mina, when we first met. The riddle the dragon posed to you. 'Where did you come from?' You told me that I knew the answers. I did not know then, but I know now. And so do you, Mina. You know the truth. You have to accept it. You can no longer hide from it. Valthonis is your father, Mina. You are his child. You are a god. A god born of Light."

Mina went livid. Her amber eyes widened, grew large.

"You lie," she breathed. The words were soft, barely a whisper.

"Men sang your name, Mina. As did the Beloved. If you kill this man, commit this heinous crime, you will take your place among the Dark Pantheon," Rhys told her. "The balance will shift. The world will slide into darkness and be consumed. That is what Sargonnas wants. Is that what *you* want, Mina? You have walked the world. You have met its people. You have seen the misery and destruction and upheaval that is war. Is that what you want?"

Mina's form altered again and this time she was the Mina of the

Beloved, the Mina who had given them the lethal kiss. Her auburn hair was long. She wore black and blood red. She was confident, commanding, and she regarded Valthonis with frowning intensity. Her expression hardened, her lips compressed.

"He killed my Queen!" Mina stated coldly.

She brushed past Galdar, who stared at her with gaping mouth and white-rimmed eyes, his frame trembling in fear. Mina walked over to Valthonis and gazed at him for a long moment, trying to draw him, another insect, into the amber.

He stood calmly under her scrutiny.

Does his mortal mind retain something of the mind of the god? Rhys wondered. Does some part of Valthonis remember that burst of joy at creation's dawning that brought forth a child of joy and light? Does he remember the searing pain he must have felt upon realizing he had to sacrifice the child for the sake of that very creation?

Rhys did not know the answer. What he did know, what he could see on the elf's ravaged face, was the grief of the parent who sees a loved child succumb to dark passions.

"Let me help you, Mina." Valthonis held out his hands to Mina: his bound hands.

Mina stood over him. She held out her hand. "Galdar, give me your sword."

Galdar looked uneasily at the fallen Valthonis. The minotaur's hand went to his sword's hilt. He did not draw the weapon.

"Mina, the monk is right," Galdar said, anguished. "If you slay this man, you will become Takhisis. And that's not who you are. You prayed for your men, Mina. Wounded and exhausted, you walked the battlefield and prayed for the souls of those who gave their lives for the cause. You care about people. Takhisis didn't. She used them, just as she used you!"

"Give me your sword!" Mina repeated angrily.

Galdar shook his horned head. "And at the end, when Takhisis had been cast out of heaven, she blamed you, Mina. Not herself. Never herself. She was going to kill you in a spiteful, vindictive rage. That was Takhisis. Spiteful and vindictive, cruel and vicious and self-serving. Nothing mattered to her except her own aggrandizement, her own ambition. Her children hated her and worked against her. Her consort despised and distrusted her and rejoiced in her downfall. Is this what you want, Mina? Is this what you want to become?"

Mina stood regarding him scornfully. When Galdar paused for breath, she said with a sneer, "I don't need a sermon. Just give me the damn sword, you stupid, one-armed cow!"

Galdar paled, the pallor visible even beneath his dark fur. A spasm of pain wrenched his body. He cast a glowering glance at heaven, then he drew his sword. He did not give it to Mina. Going to the unconscious Valthonis, the minotaur sliced the bonds that bound the elf's wrists.

"I'll have nothing to do with murder," Galdar said with quiet dignity.

Slamming his sword into the sheath, he turned and started to walk away.

"Galdar! Come back!" Mina shouted furiously.

The minotaur kept walking.

"Galdar! I command you!" Mina cried.

Galdar did not look around. He wound his way among the black monoliths, remnants of dark ambition.

Mina glared at his retreating back, then suddenly sprang after him, running swiftly across the windswept floor. Rhys called out a warning. Galdar turned, just as Mina caught up with him. Ignoring him, she grasped the hilt of the sword and yanked it out of its sheath.

Galdar caught hold of her wrist and tried to wrench his sword from

293

her hand. Mina lashed out in a blind rage, striking him with the hilt of the sword and with the flat of the blade.

Galdar tried to fend her off, but he had only one hand and Mina fought with the strength and fury of a god.

Rhys ran to the minotaur's aid. Dropping his staff, he grabbed hold of Mina and tried to drag her off Galdar. The big minotaur collapsed, bloodied and groaning, onto the ground. Mina jerked free of Rhys. Shoving him backward, off-balance, she returned to the assault on Galdar, kicking him and hitting any part of him still moving. The minotaur quit groaning and now lay still.

"Mina—" Rhys began.

Mina snarled and slammed her fist deep into Rhys's diaphragm, so deep the blow stopped his breathing. He tried to draw in air, but the muscles were in spasm and he could only gasp. Mina smashed him in the jaw with her fist, shattering his jawbone. His mouth flooded with blood. Mina stood over him, the minotaur's heavy sword in her hand, and there was nothing Rhys could do. He was choking on his own blood.

Nightshade tried his best to keep hold of Atta, but the sight of Rhys being attacked was more than the dog could bear. She wrenched free of the kender's grasp. Nightshade made a grab for her and missed, went sprawling onto his belly. Atta launched herself into the air and smashed bodily into Mina, knocking her down, knocking the sword from her grasp.

Snarling, Atta went for Mina's throat. She fought the dog, using her hands to try to fling her off. Blood and saliva flew.

Nightshade staggered to his feet. Rhys was spewing up blood. The minotaur was either dead or dying. Valthonis lay unconscious on the ground. The kender was the only man standing, and he didn't know what to do. His brain was too flustered to think of a spell, and then he realized that no spell, even the most powerful spell cast by the most powerful mystic, could stop a god.

The cold, pale sun flashed off steel.

Mina had managed to grab hold of the sword. Raising it, she slashed at the dog.

Atta collapsed with a pain-filled yelp. Her white fur was stained with blood, but she still struggled to get up, still snapped and snarled. Mina raised the sword to stab her again, this time going for the kill.

Nightshade clasped hold of the little grasshopper pin and gave a galvanized leap. He sailed over one of the black monoliths, and smashed into Mina, knocking the sword from her grasp.

Nightshade landed hard on the ground. Mina recovered herself and both of them dove for the sword, each scrabbling to seize hoold of it. Rhys spit out blood and half-crawled, half-flung himself into the fray.

But he was too late.

Mina seized hold of the kender's topknot of hair and gave a shrp, twisting jerk. Rhys heard a horrible snapping and crunching sound. Nightshade went limp.

Mina let loose his hair and the kender slumped to the ground.

Rhys crawled to his friend's side. Nightshade stared at him, unseeing. Tears filled Rhys's eyes. He did not look for Mina. She was going to kill him, too, and he couldn't stop her. Atta whimpered. The sword had laid open her shoulder to the bone. He gathered the suffering, dying dog close to him, then reached out a blood-stained hand to close Nightshade's eyes.

A little girl with red braids squatted down beside the kender.

"You can get up now, Nightshade," said Mina.

When he did not move, she shook him by the shoulder.

"Stop pretending to be asleep, Nightshade," she scolded. "It's time to leave. I have to go to Godshome, and you have the map."

Mina's voice quivered. "Wake up!" the child gulped. "Please, please wake up."

The kender did not move.

Mina gave a heart-broken wail and flung herself on the body.

"I'm sorry I'm sorry I'm sorry!" she cried over and over in a paroxysm of grief.

"Mina . . . " Rhys mumbled her name through the blood and bone and broken teeth, and her name echoed back from the Lords of Doom.

"Mina, Mina . . . "

She stood up. The little girl gazed down sorrowfully at Nightshade, but it was the woman, Mina, who gently closed the staring eyes. The woman, Mina, walked over to Galdar. She laid a hand on him and whispered to him. The woman came back to Atta and petted her gently. Then Mina knelt down beside Rhys. Smiling sadly, she touched him on the forehead.

Amber, warm and golden, slid over him.

7

Mina, the woman, sat next to Valthonis on the hard, windswept
stone. She was not wearing armor, nor the black robes of a priestess
of Chemosh. She wore a simple gown that fell in folds about her
body. Her auburn hair was gathered in soft curls at the back of her
neck. She sat quietly, watching the Walking God, waiting for him
to regain consciousness.

Valthonis finally sat up, looked about, and his expression grew grave.
Rising swiftly, he went to tend to the wounded. Mina watched him
dispassionately, her face impassive, unreadable.

"The kender is dead," she said. "I killed him. The monk and the
minotaur and the dog will live, I think."

Valthonis knelt beside the kender and, gently arranging the broken
body into a more seemly form, he spoke a quiet blessing.

"Shake off the dust of the road, little friend. Your boots have stardust on them now."

Removing his green cloak, he laid it reverently over the small
corpse.

Valthonis bent over Atta, who feebly wagged her tail and gave his hand a swipe with her tongue. He brushed back the black fur that was covered with blood, but he could not find a wound. He stroked her head and then went to see to her master.

"I think I know the monk," Mina said. "I've met him before. I was trying to recall where, and now I remember. It was in a boat . . . No, not a boat. A tavern that had once been a boat. He was there and I came in and he looked at me and he knew me . . . He knew who I was . . ." She frowned slightly. "Except he didn't. . . ."

Valthonis raised his head and looked into her amber eyes. He saw no longer the countless souls, trapped bug-like within. He saw in her clear eyes terrible knowledge. And he saw himself, reflected off the shining surface.

"The monk was sitting next to a man . . . He was a dead man. I don't know his name." Mina paused, then said with a catch in her voice, "So many of them . . . and I didn't know any of their names. But I know the monk's name. He is Brother Rhys. And he knows my name. He knows me. He knows who and what I am. And yet, he walked with me anyway. He guided me." She smiled sadly. "He yelled at me . . ."

Valthonis rested his hand on Rhys's neck, felt the lifebeat. The monk's face was bloody, but Valthonis could not find any injuries. He said nothing in response to Mina. He had the instinctive feeling she did not want him to speak. She wanted, needed, to hear only herself in the deathlike silence of the valley of Neraka.

"The kender knew me, too. When he first saw me, he began to weep. He wept for me. He wept out of pity for me. He said 'You are so sad'. . . And the minotaur, Galdar, was my friend. A good and faithful friend . . ."

Mina shifted her gaze from the minotaur to the barren, ghastly sur-roundings. "I hate this place. I know where I am. I am in Neraka, and awful things have happened because of me . . . And more awful things will happen . . . because of me . . . "

She shifted her gaze to Valthonis, looked at him, pleading.

"You know what I mean. Your name means 'the Exile' in elven. And you are my father. And both of us—mortal father, wretched daughter—are exiles. Except you can never go back." Mina sighed, long and deep. "And I must."

Valthonis walked to over the minotaur. He placed his hand on the strong, bull-like neck.

"I am a god," Mina said. "I live in all times simultaneously. Though," she added, a frown line again marring her smooth forehead, "there is a time before time I do not remember, and a time yet to come I cannot see . . . "

The wind whistled among the rocks, as through rotting teeth, but Valthonis did not hear anything except Mina. It was as if the physical world had dropped out from beneath him, leaving him suspended in the ethers and there was only her voice and the amber eyes that, as he watched, filled with tears.

"I have done evil, Father," Mina said, as the tears spilled over and slid slowly down her cheeks. "Or rather, I do evil, for I live in all times at once. They say I am a god born of light and yet I bring forth darkness. Thousands of innocents die because of me. I slaughter those who trust me. I take away life and give back living death. Some say I am duped by Takhisis, and that I do not know I am doing wrong."

Mina smiled through her tears, and her smile was strange and cold. "But I know what I am doing. I want to hear them sing my name, Father. I want them to worship me—Mina! Not Takhisis. Not Chemosh. Mina. Only Mina."

She made no move to wipe away the tears. "The two who were mothers to me both died in my arms. When Goldmoon was dying, she looked at me from the twilight, and she saw the truth, the ugliness inside me. And she turned from me."

Mina rose to her feet and ran over to the minotaur. She crouched beside him but did not touch him. She rose and walked over to where the kender's body lay beneath the green cloak. Reaching down, she carefully replaced a corner the wind had blown askew. Her empty amber eyes shimmered.

"I can fix him," she said. She stood up and flung her arms wide, encompassing the wounded and the dead, encompassing the blasted temple, the accursed valley. "I am a god! I can make all this as if it never happened!"

"You can," said Valthonis. "But to do that you would have to go back to the first second of the first minute of the first day and start time again."

"I don't understand!" Mina cried, perplexed. "You speak in riddles."

"All of us would start over if we could, Mina. All of us would wipe out past mistakes. For mortals this is impossible. We accept, we learn, we go on. For a god, it is possible. But it means wiping out creation and beginning again."

Mina looked rebellious, as though she didn't believe him, and Valthonis feared for one frightening moment that she was in such pain she might actually try to ease her own suffering by plunging herself and the world into oblivion.

Mina sank to her knees and lifted her face to heaven.

"You gods! You pull at me and tug me in all directions!" she shouted. "You each want me for you own ends. Not one of you cares what *I* want."

"What *do* you want, Mina?" Valthonis asked.

She looked about, as though wondering herself. Her gaze went to the kender, lying broken and lifeless beneath the green cloak. Her gaze went to the unconscious Galdar, loyal friend. Her gaze went to Rhys, who had comforted her when she woke crying the night.

"I want to go back to sleep," she whispered.

Valthonis's heart ached. His own tears blurred his vision, choked off his voice.

"But I can't." Mina said brokenly. "I know. I have tried. They call my name and wake me . . ."

She gave a sudden, anguished cry. The tears flooded her amber eyes, so that the Walking God's reflection seemed to be drowning.

"Make them stop, Father!" she begged, rocking back and forth in her terrible agony. "Make them stop!"

Valthonis crossed the stone floor of the valley of Neraka and came to stand beside his daughter. She knelt before him, clutched at his boots. He took hold of her and raised her up.

"The voices will not stop," he said. "For you, they will never stop—until you answer them."

"But what do I say?"

"That is what you must decide."

Valthonis handed her the scrip Rhys had carried for so long. Mina regarded it, puzzled. Unwrapping it, she looked inside. Her two gifts lay there, the Necklace of Sedition, the crystal Pyramid of Light.

"Do you remember these?" Valthonis asked.

Mina shook her head.

"You found them in Hall of Sacrilege. You were going to give them as gifts to Goldmoon when you came to Godshome."

Mina gazed long at the two artifacts, one of consuming darkness, one of enduring light. She wrapped them back up, reverently and carefully.

"Is the way to Godshome far, Father?" she asked. "I am so very tired."

"Not far, daughter," he answered. "Not far now."

301

A hairy finger pried open one of Rhys's eyelids, causing him to wake with a start, startling Galdar who nearly poked out Rhys's eye. The minotaur withdrew his hand and grunted in satisfaction. Sliding an enormous arm beneath Rhys's shoulders, he heaved Rhys to a sitting position and thrust a vial between Rhys's lips, dumping some sort of foul-tasting liquid into his mouth.

Rhys choked and started to spit it out.

"Swallow!" ordered Galdar, giving him a thump on the back that caused Rhys to cough and sent the liquid trickling down his throat.

He gagged and wondered if he'd just been poisoned.

Galdar grinned at him, showing all his teeth, and grunted, "Poison tastes a lot better than this stuff. Sit still for a moment and let it do its work. You'll be feeling better soon."

Rhys obeyed. He didn't ask questions. He didn't feel strong enough yet to be prepared for the answers. His jaw ached and throbbed, though it was no longer broken. His diaphragm was sore, every breath hurt. The potion seeping through his body began to ease the pain of his wounds, if not the pain in his heart.

Galdar, meanwhile, took hold of Atta's muzzle, gripping it tightly while another minotaur in soldier's harness, bearing the emblem of Sargas, deftly smeared brown glop over her wound.

"You'd like to bite my hand off, wouldn't you, mutt?" said Galdar, and Atta growled in response, causing him to chuckle.

When the minotaur was finished with his ministrations, he nodded to his companion. Galdar released the dog and both minotaurs sprang back. Atta rose, somewhat wobbly, to her feet. Keeping a distrustful eye on the minotaur, Atta came to Rhys to be petted. Then she limped over to the green cloak. She sniffed at it and pawed the cloak and looked back at Rhys and wagged her tail, as though saying, "You'll fix this, Master. I know you will."

"Atta, come," Rhys said.

Atta stayed where she was. She pawed again at the cloak and whined.

"Atta, come," Rhys repeated.

Slowly, her head and tail drooping, Atta limped painfully over to Rhys and lay down at his side. Putting her head on her paws, she heaved a deep sigh.

Galdar squatted beside the body. He moved slowly and stiffly. His blood-matted fur was slathered with the same brown goop his men had spread on Atta. Galdar lifted a corner of the green cloak and looked down at Nightshade.

"Sargas commands us to honor him. He will be known among us as *Kedir ut Sarrak.*[2]"

Rhys smiled through his tears. He hoped Nightshade's spirit had lingered long enough to hear that.

The minotaur soldiers gathered up their belongings, making ready to leave. No one wanted to stay in this place any longer than necessary.

"Are you fit to travel, Monk?" Galdar asked. "If so, you are welcome

2 Kender with Horns

to come with us. We will help you carry your dead and the mutt, if she won't bite," he added gruffly.

Rhys gave grateful assent.

One of the minotaur lifted the small body in strong arms. Another picked up Atta. She barked and struggled, but at Rhys's command, she quit fighting and allowed the minotaur to carry her, though she growled with every breath.

"I want to thank you for your help—" Rhys began

"I had nothing to do with it," Galdar interrupted. He waved his good hand at his soldiers. "You can thank this mutinous lot. They disobeyed my command and came after me, even though I had ordered them to stay behind to wait for me."

"I'm glad they disobeyed," said Rhys.

"If you must know, so am I. Go on ahead," Galdar told his men. "The monk and I cannot walk as swiftly. We will be safe enough. There are only ghosts left in this valley now, and they cannot harm us."

The minotaurs didn't appear to be too certain of this, but they did as Galdar commanded, though they did not move quite as swiftly as they could have, but kept within shouting range of their commander.

Galdar and Rhys walked together, both of them limping. Galdar grimaced and pressed his hand to his side. One of the minotaur's eyes was swollen shut and blood trickled from the base of one of his horns. Rhys's stomach and jaw both hurt, making breathing difficult and painful.

"Where will you go now?" Rhys asked.

"I will return to Jelek to resume my duties as ambassador to you humans. I doubt you want to go *there*," he added with a wry glance at Rhys. "But my men and I will not abandon you. We will wait with you until help arrives."

"Help may be long in coming." Rhys spoke with an inward sigh.

"You think so?" Galdar asked, and a smile flickered on his lips. "You should have more faith, Monk."

Rhys had no idea what the minotaur meant, but before he could ask, Galdar's smile vanished. He glanced back into the valley of stone and black crystal.

"Mina went with him, didn't she? She went with the Walking God."

"I hope so," Rhys replied. "I pray so."

"I'm not much for praying," Galdar said. "And if I did pray, I'd pray to Sargas, and I would guess the Horned God is not feeling kindly disposed toward me at the moment."

He paused, then added somberly, "If I did pray, I would pray that Mina finds whatever it is she seeks."

"You forgive her for what she did to you?" Rhys was astonished. Minotaurs were not known as a forgiving people. Their god was a god of vengeance.

"I suppose you could say I got into a habit of forgiving her." Galdar rubbed the stump of his arm, grimacing. Strange that the pain of a missing arm was worse than the pain of cracked bones. He added half-ashamed, half-defiant, "What about you, Monk? Do you forgive her?"

"I walked my road once with hatred and revenge gnawing at my heart," Rhys said. His gaze went to the minotaur who was carrying the small body, to the green cloak that fluttered in the still air. "I will not do so again. I forgive Mina and my prayer is the same as yours—that she finds what she seeks. Though I am not certain I should be praying for that."

"Why not?"

"Whatever she finds will tip the scales of balance one way or the other."

"The scales might tip in your direction, Monk," Galdar suggested. "You'd like that, wouldn't you?"

Rhys shook his head. "A man who stares at the sun too long is as blind as one who walks in pitch darkness."

The two fell silent, saving their laboring breath for the climb out of the valley. The minotaur under Galdar's command stood waiting for them among the foothills of the Lords of Doom. The minotaur looked grim, for the Faithful were also waiting there. Led by silent Elspeth, they had come to the valley, though too late to find Valthonis.

Galdar scowled at the elves. "You gave your oath," he told them.

"We did not break faith with you," said one of the elves. "We did not try to rescue Valthonis."

The elf pointed to the cloak that covered the body of the kender. "That belongs to Valthonis! Where is he?" The elf glared at Galdar. "What have you done with him? Have you basely murdered him?"

"On the contrary. The minotaur saved Valthonis's life," Rhys replied.

The elves scowled in disbelief.

"Do you doubt my word?" Rhys asked wearily.

The leader of the Faithful bowed.

"We mean no offense, Servant of *Matheri*," the elf said, using the elvish name for the god, Majere. "But you must understand that we find this difficult to comprehend. A monk of *Matheri* and a minotaur of *Kinthalas* walk together out of the Valley of Evil. What is going on? Is Valthonis alive?"

"He is alive and unharmed."

"Then where is he?"

"He helps a lost child find her way home," Rhys replied.

The elves glanced at other, mystified, some clearly still disbelieving. And then silent Elspeth walked over to stand in front of Galdar. One of the elves sought to stop her, but she thrust him aside. She reached out her hand to the minotaur.

"What's this?" he demanded, frowning. "Tell her to stay away from me."

Elspeth smiled in reassurance. As he watched, tense and frowning, she lightly brushed her fingers across the stump of his arm.

Galdar blinked. The grimace of pain that had twisted his face eased. He clasped his hand over the stump and stared at her in astonishment. Elspeth walked past him and came to kneel beside the body of the kender. She tucked the cloak around him tenderly, as a mother tucks a blanket around her child, then lifted the body in her arms. She stood waiting patiently to depart.

Galdar glanced at Rhys. "I told you help would find you."

The elves were now more mystified than before, but they obeyed Elspeth's silent command and made preparations to leave.

"I hope you will honor us with your company, Servant of *Matheri*," said the leader to Rhys, who gave his grateful assent.

Galdar held out his left hand, grasped Rhys's hand in a crushing grip. "Farewell, Brother."

Rhys clasped the minotaur's hand in both his own. "May your journey be a safe one and swift."

"It will be swift, at least," Galdar stated grimly. "The faster we're away from this accursed place, the better."

He bellowed orders that were quickly obeyed. The minotaur soldiers marched off, as eager as their commander to leave Neraka.

But Galdar did not immediately follow them. He stood still for a moment, gazing west, deep into the mountains.

"Godshome," he said. "It lies in that direction."

"So I have been told," Rhys said.

Galdar nodded to himself and continued to stare into the distance, as if trying to catch some last glimpse of Mina. Sighing, he lowered his gaze, shook his horned head.

"Do you think we will ever find out what happens to her, Brother?" he asked wistfully.

"I don't know," Rhys answered evasively

In his heart, he feared very much that they would.

9

Valthonis and Mina walked slowly to Godshome, taking their time, for each knew that no matter what happened, what choice Mina made, this would be their final journey together.

The two had talked of many things for many hours, but now Mina had fallen silent. Godshome was only about ten miles from Neraka, but the road was difficult, steep and winding and narrow—a rock-strewn, desolate track forced to pick its way among steep canyon walls, constrained by strange rock formations to take them in directions they did not want to go.

The sky was dark and overcast, obscured by the steamy snortings of the Lords of Doom. The air stank of sulfur and was hard to breathe, drying the mouth and stinging the nostrils.

Mina soon grew weary. She did not complain, however, but continued walking. Valthonis told her she could take her time. There was no hurry.

"You mean I have all eternity before me?" Mina said to him with a twisted smile. "That is true, Father, but I feel compelled to go on. I know who I am, but now I must now find out why. I can no longer rest easy in the twilight."

She carried with her the two artifacts she had brought from the Hall of Sacrilege. She held them fast in her hand and would not relinquish them, though their burden sometimes made traversing the steep trail difficult for her. When she finally gave in and sat down to rest, she unwrapped the artifacts and gazed down at them, studying them, taking up each in turn and holding it in her hands, running her fingers over them as would a blind man trying to use his hands to see what his sightless eyes cannot. She said nothing about her thoughts to Valthonis, and he did not ask.

As they drew nearer Godshome, the Lords of Doom seemed to release their hold on the travelers, sanctioning their going. The path grew easier to walk, led them down a gentle slope. A warm breeze, like spring's breath, blew away the sulfur fumes and the steam. Wild flowers appeared along the trail, peeking out from beneath boulders, or growing in the cracks of a stone wall.

"What is wrong?" Valthonis asked, calling a halt, when he noticed that Mina had begun to limp.

"I have a blister," she answered.

Sitting down on the path, she drew off her shoe, looking with exasperation at the raw and bloody wound.

"The gods play at being mortal," she said. "Chemosh could make love to me and receive pleasure from the act—or so he convinced himself. But in truth, they can only pretend to feel. No god ever has a blister on his heel."

She held up the blood-stained shoe for him to see.

"So why do *I* have a blister?" she demanded. "I know I am a god. I know this body is not real, I could leap off this cliff and plummet onto the rocks below and no harm would come to me. I know that, but still"—she bit her lip—"my foot hurts. As much as I would like to say it doesn't really, it really does!"

"Takhisis had to convince you that you were human, Mina," said Valthonis. "She lied to you in order to enslave you. If you knew the truth, that you were a god, she feared you would become her rival. You had to be made to believe you were human and thus you had to feel pain. You had to know illness and grief. You had to experience love and joy and sorrow. She took cruel pleasure in making you believe you were mortal. She thought it made you weak."

"It does!" flashed Mina, and the amber eyes glittered in anger. "And I hate it. When I take my place among the pantheon, I cannot show weakness. I must teach myself to forget what I have been."

"I am not so sure," said Valthonis, and he knelt down before her and regarded her intently. "You say the gods play at being mortal. They do not 'play' at it. By taking an aspect of mortality, a god tries to feel what mortals feel. The gods try to understand mortals in order to help and guide them or, in some cases, to coerce and terrorize them. But they are gods, Mina, and try as they might, they cannot truly understand. You alone know the pain of mortality, Mina."

She thought this over. "You are right," she said at last, thoughtful. "Perhaps that is why I am able to wield such power over mortals."

"Is that what you want? To wield power over them?"

"Of course! Isn't it what all we all want?" Mina frowned. "I saw the gods at work that day in Solace. I saw the blood spilled and the bodies stacked up in front of the altars. If mortals will fight and die for their faith, why should they not go to their deaths singing *my* name as well as another?"

She slipped her shoe back on her foot and stood up and started walking. She seemed bound to try to convince herself that she felt nothing and tried to walk normally, but she could not stand it. Wincing in pain, she came to a halt.

"You were a god," she said. "Do you remember anything of what you were? Do you remember the moment before creation? Does your mind yet encompass the vastness of eternity? Do you see to the limits of heaven?"

"No," Valthonis answered. "My mind is that of a mortal. I see the horizon and sometimes not that, if the clouds obscure it. I am glad for this. I think it would be too terrible to bear otherwise."

"It is," said Mina softly.

She yanked off both her shoes and threw them off the side of the cliff. She started walking barefoot, stepping gingerly on the path, and almost immediately cut her foot on a sharp pebble. She gasped and came up short. She clenched her fists in frustration.

"I am a god!" she cried. "I have no feet!"

She stared at her bare toes, as if willing them to disappear.

Her toes remained, wriggling and digging into the dust.

Mina moaned and sank down, crouched down, huddled into herself.

"How can I be a god if I will always be a mortal? How can I walk among the stars when I have blisters on my feet? I don't know how to be a god, Father! I know only how to be human . . ."

Valthonis put his arms around her and lifted her up. "You need walk no farther, daughter. We are here," he said.

Mina stared at him, bewildered. "Where?"

"Home," he replied.

In the center of a smooth-sided, bowl-shaped valley, nineteen pillars stood silent watch around a circular pool of shining black, fire-blasted obsidian. Sixteen pillars stood together. Three pillars stood apart. One of these was black jet, one red granite, the other white jade. Five of the remaining pillars were of white marble. Five were of black marble.

Six were made of marble of an indeterminate color.

Once twenty-one pillars had guarded the pool. Two of them had toppled to the ground. One, a black pillar, had shattered in the fall. Nothing remained of it but a heap of broken rubble. The other fallen pillar was still intact, its surface shining in the sunlight, swept free of dust by loving hands.

Mina and Valthonis stood outside the stone pillars, looking in. The sky was cloudless, achingly blue. The sun teetered precariously on the peaks of the Lords of Doom, still casting its radiant light, though any moment it would slide down the mountain and fall into night. The valley was filled with the twilight; shadows cast by the mountains, sunlight gleaming on the obsidian pool.

Mina gazed with rapt fascination on the black pool. She walked toward it, prepared to squeeze her way through the narrow gap between two pillars, when she realized Valthonis was no longer at her side. She turned to see him standing near the small crack in the rock wall through which they had entered.

"The pain will never end, will it?" she asked.

His answer was his silence.

Mina unwrapped the artifacts of Paladine and Takhisis and held them, one in each hand. She lay the scrip that had belonged to the monk at the foot of a pillar of white marble streaked with orange, then walked between the pillars and stepped onto the pool of shining black obsidian. Lifting her amber eyes, she stared into the heavens and saw the constellations of the gods shining in the sky.

The gods of light, represented by Branchala's harp, Habbakuk's phoenix, the bison's head of Kiri-Jolith, Majere's rose, the infinity symbol of Mishakal. Opposing them were the gods of darkness, Chemosh with his goat's skull, Hiddukel's broken scales, Morgion's black hood, Sargonnas's condor, Zeboim's dragon turtle. Separating darkness and light, yet keeping them together was Gilean's Book, the creation-forging hammer of Reorx, the steadfast burning planets of Shinare, Chislev, Zivilyn, Sirrion. Nearer to mortals than the stars were the three moons: the black moon of Nuitari, the red moon of Lunitari, the silver moon of Solinari.

Mina saw them.

And they saw her, all of them.

They watched and waited for her to decide.

Standing in the center of the pool, Mina raised up the artifacts, one in each hand.

"I am equal parts of darkness and of light," she cried to the heavens. "Neither holds sway over me. I may side sometimes with one and sometimes with the other. And thus the balance is restored."

Mina held up the Necklace of Sedition of Takhisis; the necklace that could persuade good people to give way to their worst passions, and then she cast it onto the obsidian pool. The necklace struck the dark surface and melted into it and vanished. Mina held the crystal pyramid of Paladine in her hand a moment longer, the crystal that could bring light to a benighted heart. Then she cast it down as well. The crystal sparkled like another star in an obsidian night, but only briefly. The light went out, the crystal shattered.

Turning her back, Mina walked out of the obsidian pool. She walked away from the circle of stone guardians. She walked across the floor of the empty, barren valley, walked barefoot, her cut and blistered feet leaving tracks of blood.

She walked until she came to a place in the valley known as Godshome where the shadows vied with the sun and here she stopped. Her back to the gods, she looked down at her feet, and she wept and left the world.

In the valley known as Godshome, a pillar of amber stood alone and apart in a still pool of night-blue water.

No stars were reflected in the water. No moons or sun. No planet. No valley. No mountains.

Valthonis, looking into the pool, saw his own face there.

Saw the faces of all the living.

10

Rhys Mason sat beneath an ancient oak tree near the top of a green, grass-covered hill. He could see in the distance the smoke rising from the chimneys of his monastery, the home to which he had returned after his long, long journey. Some of the brothers were in the field, turning over the ground, awakening the earth after its winter slumber, making it ready for planting. Other of the brethren were busy around the monastery, sweeping and cleaning, repairing the stonework that had been gnawed and worried by the bitter winter winds.

The sheep were scattered about the hillside, grazing contently, glad to be eating the tender green grass after the stale hay on which they'd subsisted during the cold months. Spring meant shearing time and lambing and then Rhys would be busy. But, for the moment, all was peaceful.

Atta lay by his side. She had a scar on her flank where her fur would not grow, but otherwise she had recovered from her injuries, as Rhys had recovered from his. Atta's gaze was now divided between the sheep (always a worry) and her new litter of pups. Only a few months old, the pups were already showing a strong interest in herding, and Rhys had started training them. He and the pups had worked all morning, and the exhausted pups were now sleeping in a furry black and white heap, pink noses twitching. Rhys had marked one already—the boldest and most adventuresome—to give to Mistress Jenna.

Rhys sat at his ease, his emmide resting in the crook of his arms. He was wrapped in a thick cloak, for though the sun shone, the wind still nipped with winter's teeth. His mind floated free among the high, feathery clouds, touching lightly on many things and passing on to others; in all things honoring Majere.

Rhys was alone on the hillside, for the sheep were his care and his responsibility, and he was therefore startled to be lured from his reverie by a voice.

"Hullo, Rhys! I'll bet you're surprised to see me!"

Rhys had to admit he was surprised. Surprised was hardly the word, in fact, for sitting calmly by his side was Nightshade.

The kender grinned gleefully at Rhys's shock. "I'm a ghost, Rhys! That's why I look washed out and wobbly. Isn't it exciting? I'm haunting you."

Nightshade grew suddenly concerned. "I hope I didn't scare you."

"No," Rhys said, though it took him a moment to find his voice.

Hearing her master speak, Atta lifted her head and glanced over her shoulder to see if she was wanted.

"Hi, Atta!" Nightshade waved. "Your puppies are beautiful. They look just like you."

Atta's eyes narrowed. She sniffed the air, sniffed again, thought things over, then, dismissing what she did not understand, rested her head on her paws and went back to watching her charges.

"I'm glad I didn't scare you," Nightshade continued. "I keep forgetting I'm dead and I have an unfortunate tendency to drop in on people suddenly. Poor Gerard." The ghost heaved a sigh. "I thought he was going to have an apologetic fit."

"Apoplectic," Rhys corrected, smiling.

"That, too," said Nightshade solemnly. "He went extremely white and started wheezing, and then he vowed he would never touch another drop of dwarf spirits as long as he lived. When I tried to cheer him up by assuring him I wasn't a hallu— a halluci— that he wasn't seeing things and that I was real live ghost, he began to wheeze even harder."

"Did he recover?" Rhys asked.

"I think so," Nightshade said cautiously. "Gerard scolded me soundly after that. He told me I'd taken ten years off his life and then he said he had enough trouble with living kender and he wasn't about to be plagued by a dead one and I was to go back to the Abyss or wherever it was I'd come from. I told him I wasn't in the Abyss. I'd been on a world tour, and that I understood his feelings perfectly, and I'd just stopped in to say 'thank you' for all the kind things he said about me at my funeral.

"I was there, by the way. It was really lovely. So many important people came! Mistress Jenna and the Abbot of Majere and the Walking God and the elves and Galdar and a minotaur delegation. I especially enjoyed the fight in the bar afterward, though I guess that wasn't really part of the funeral. And I like having my ashes scattered underneath the Inn. Makes me feel that part of me will never leave. Sometimes I think I can smell the spiced potatoes, which is odd, since ghosts can't smell. Why do you suppose that is?"

Rhys had to admit he didn't know.

Nightshade gave a shrug, then frowned. "Where was I?"

"You were talking about Gerard—"

"Oh, yes, I told him I'd come to good-bye before I started on the next stage of my journey, which, by the way, is going to be extremely exciting. I'll tell you why in a minute. It has to do with my grasshopper. Anyway, Gerard wished me luck and escorted me to the door and opened it to let me out. I said he didn't need to open the door because I can whisk right through doors and walls and even ceilings. He told me I wasn't to go whisking through his door or his wall. He was quite stern about it, so I didn't. And I don't think he was serious when he said he going to swear off dwarf spirits, because after I left I saw him grab the jug and take a big swig."

"Did you say good-bye to anyone else?" Rhys asked, considerably alarmed at the thought.

Nightshade nodded. "I went to visit Laura. After what happened with Gerard, I thought I'd sneak up on Laura gradually—you know, give her time to get used to me." The ghost sighed. "But that didn't

make any difference. She screamed and threw her apron over her head and broke a whole stack of dirty dishes when she fell into the wash basin. So I thought it would be best if I didn't stick around. Now I'm here with you, and you're my last stop, and then I'm off for good."

"I am glad to see you, my friend," said Rhys. "I have missed you very much."

"I know," said Nightshade. "I felt you missing me. It was a good feeling, but you mustn't be sad. That's what I came to tell you. I'm sorry it took so long for me to get here. Time doesn't have much meaning for me anymore and there were so many places to visit and so much to see. Do you know there's a whole 'nother continent! It's called Taladas and it's a very interesting place, though that's not where I'm going on my soul's journey— Oh, that reminds me. I have to tell you about Chemosh.

"The ghosts I talked to when I was a Nightstalker told me how when you die your soul goes before the Lord of Death to be judged. I was looking forward to that part and it was very exciting. I stood in line with a whole bunch of other souls: goblins and draconians, kender and humans, elves and gnomes and ogres and more. Each soul goes up before the Lord of Death, who sits on an enormous throne—very impressive. Sometimes he tries to tempt them to stay with him. Or sometimes they're already sworn to follow him or some other god, like Morgion, who is *not* a nice person, let me tell you! And sometimes other gods come to tell Chemosh that he's to keep his hands off. Reorx did that for a dwarf.

"So I was standing there in the back of the line, thinking it was going to take me a long, long time to reach the front, when suddenly the Lord of Death bolts up from his throne. He walks down the line and comes to stand in front of me! He glares at me quite fiercely and looks very angry and tells me I can go. I said I didn't mind staying; I was visiting with some friends, and that was true. I'd run into some dead kender and we were talking about how interesting it was being dead, and we described how each of us had died and they all agreed that none of them could top me since I'd been killed by a god.

"I started to explain this Chemosh, but he snarled and said he wasn't interested. My soul had already been judged, and I was free to go. I looked around, and there was the White Lady and Majere and Zeboim and all three moon gods, and Kiri-Jolith in his shining armor and some other gods I didn't recognize and even Sargonnas! I wondered what they were all doing there, but the White Lady said they'd come to honor me, though Zeboim said *she'd* come just to make sure I was really dead. The gods all shook my hand, and when I came to Majere, he touched the grasshopper that was still pinned to my shirt, and he said that it would let me jump forward to see where I was going and then jump back to say goodbye. And I was just telling Mishakal how much I liked her gingerbread and I was about ready to leave when who do you think came to see me?"

Rhys shook his head.

"Mina!" said Nightshade, awed. "I was going to be mad at her, for slaying me, you know, but she came to me and she put her arms around me and she cried over me. And then she took me by the hand and walked with me out of the Hall of Judgment and she showed me the road made of star dust that will take me onward past the sunset when I am ready to leave. I was glad for her, because she seems to have found her way, and because she's not crazy anymore, but I was sad, too, because she looked so very sad."

"I think she always will be," said Rhys.

Nightshade heaved a deep sigh. "I think so too. You know, in my travels I've seen the little shrines people are starting to build to honor her and I was hoping those would cheer her up, but the people who come to her shrines always look so sad themselves that I don't think it helps her much."

"She wants the people to come to her," said Rhys. "She is the God of Tears and she welcomes all who are unhappy or sorrowful, especially those consumed by guilt or regret, or struggling against dark passions. Any person who feels that no one else can understand his pain can come to her. Mina understands, for her own pain is constant."

"Woo, boy," said the ghost.

Nightshade was never downhearted for long, however. After gathering up a few ghostly pouches, he bounced to his feet.

"Well, I'm off," he said, adding cheerfully, "As Zeboim said, it's time for me to go annoy the poor, unfortunate people in some new world."

Nightshade reached down to pat Atta. His ghostly touch caused the dog to jerk awake and stare about, puzzled. Nightshade held out his hand to Rhys. He felt a soft whispering touch, like the fall of a feather on his skin.

"Farewell on your journey, my friend," Rhys said.

"So long as there's chicken and dumplings, I'll be happy!" Nightshade replied, and he waved and whisked himself through the oak tree—just because he could—and then he was gone.

A bell ringing out from the monastery called the monks to evening meditation. Rhys stood up and smoothed the folds of his orange robes. As he did so, he felt something fall to the ground. A gold grasshopper lay at his feet. Rhys picked up the grasshopper and pinned it to his robes and sent a silent prayer of well-wishing along the stardust road after his friend. Then he whistled to Atta, who sprang to her feet and raced down the hill, herding the sheep.

Her pups chased after her, barking frantically and making little darting runs at the sheep in imitation of their mother. And though Atta cuffed them for getting in her way, her eyes shone with pride.

Rhys picked up one of the pups, the runt of the litter, who was having trouble keeping up. He tucked the pup under his arm and continued down the hill, taking his flock safely to the fold.

APPENDIX

AMBER
AND
BLOOD

by Jaymie Chambers and Cam Banks

MINA

Goddess of Tears

Lesser Deity

Symbol: An amber teardrop.

Celestial Symbol: None.

Home Plane: Ethereal Plane/Krynn.

Alignment: Neutral good or neutral evil.

Portfolio: Grief, loss, mortality.

Worshipers: The desperate and the abandoned; the grief-shattered; those feeling trapped, suicidal; those who have lost all hope.

Colors: Black, purple, yellow.

The embodiment of the sorrow of the gods in the face of the world's many tragedies, Mina (*mee*-na) is a mysterious divine agency who does not stand among the other gods of Krynn. Once the divine power of innocence, Mina was corrupted by and subsequently liberated from the plots of Takhisis and the other gods of Darkness during the Age of Mortals. Her trials have irrevocably changed her. Now, she is the patron of the faithless, the hopeless, and those who, either through their own fault or despite their best efforts, have lost what they hold most dear. She brings comfort in the face of sorrow, yet she is a constant reminder to the grieving that their pain is a real and necessary part of a mortal's existence.

History

Mina is the daughter of Mishakal, Goddess of Healing, and Paladine, the Platinum Dragon. She was born out of their sheer joy in the creation of the world. Sister to Kiri-Jolith and Solinari, Mina was not counted among those gods who brought forth the world during the Age of Starbirth. Indeed, her existence was known only to her divine parents and to their wise counselor, Majere, who knew that if she joined them in the pantheon of Light, her existence would upset the divine Balance between Good, Neutrality, and Evil. Such an imbalance would be an excuse for the Queen of Darkness to manipulate events to her advantage, and thus Paladine and Mishakal bade Majere hide Mina away, safe in eternal slumber deep within Krynn's primal oceans. Her divine essence was thus housed within Krynn itself, unseen and unknown, until the world was stolen by Takhisis after the Chaos War. Takhisis, thinking herself alone, felt Mina's holy power, and set out to find her. She awakened the god-child and tricked her into believing herself mortal. Thus began the sequence of events that led to the War of Souls and the rise of the Beloved.

Relationships

As a goddess, Mina sets herself apart from the other gods. Chemosh opposes her, though her relationship to the other gods of Darkness is less clear; most would like to recruit her into their pantheon if they could. Among the gods of Light, she is respected and supported by Mishakal, Majere, and their mortal agents, but she does not forget their role in her eons-long slumber, and cannot join them in Light after the pain and sorrow she has endured as a mortal. Nor is she aligned with the Gods of Balance, though Gilean and his fellow neutral gods accept her presence in the universe, and he has added her to the roll of Krynn's divine powers.

Mina in Your Campaign

Mina is a special case, much like the Highgod and Chaos. She is a goddess who has no clerics and does not grant clerical powers to those who worship or give offerings to her. Instead, she appears to those who need her, regardless of their alignment or their ethos, usually in the form of an aspect. Her blessings are rarely given, but always to those who truly need her help. She does not discriminate between those who walk in light and those who dwell in darkness. No matter what evil deeds a mortal has committed, if that mortal comes to her, she will listen without judgment and try to assist. She is both black and white. She may urge those who are suffering to accept and embrace their fates. She may urge them to rebel against fate. She has a vigilant eye open not only to the innocent victims of war, crime, and violence, but also to the perpetrators. Thus, she makes an exceptional element of an adventure in which the consequences of these tragic events are explored or witnessed or enacted by the player characters. When Mina gets involved, it is almost always because somebody has appealed to her, perhaps at one of the numerous roadside shrines that have sprung up across Ansalon, or they have "hit bottom" in the moment of deepest despair. The heroes may be present when Mina manifests, either as neutral witnesses to her involvement or as active participants in whatever events transpired to summon her. Although she will not usually direct her godly powers against mortals, she is not above altering the circumstances of the situation to spur the activity of those who might support her cause.

Mina's Aspects

During the course of her time as a mortal, Mina took several forms, all of them characterized by her red hair and amber eyes. Mina's aspects are always female, and usually human, though she is as likely to appear a member of another race if the circumstances demand it. The aspect may appear, physically, to be that of a young girl, about six years old, or as a mature warrior woman as she was during the War of Souls. She will never appear as a priestess of

Chemosh, for she wants nothing to do with the Lord of Bones. Mina can appear innocent or she may exert her power and seem terrifying and vengeful. Mina's aspects are always appropriate to the situation at hand. Although Mina has no clerics, her aspects may embody the clerical domains of Charm, Liberation, Meditation, or Protection.

Note: Mina's dual alignment reflects her unique nature, outside of the strict divisions of the Gods of Light, Darkness, and Balance. Although she is not one of them, she is yet bound by the edicts of the Highgod, and thus she exists as a counterpoint to herself. In this way, she does not upset the Balance of powers in Krynn's universe.

DISCIPLES OF BONE

The War of Souls created a vacuum in the seats of power among the pantheons of both good and evil. Unrest in the realms both divine and infernal has forced the gods to take a far more active role in the world than they have since the earliest days upon Krynn.

The Lord of Death, Chemosh, made the enigmatic Mina his prophet and messenger, creating the nearly unstoppable undead creatures known as the Beloved. Unfortunately for Chemosh, the Beloved proved to be something of a failed experiment. Though Mina created them in Chemosh's name, the power that created them turned out to be hers. Chemosh found he could not control the undead[3]. Fortunately for the people of Ansalon, few Beloved are now found roaming Krynn.

After the debacle with the Beloved, Chemosh decided to return to a more tried and true model of disciple, one whose loyalty he could ensure.

Bone Warriors

Bone Warriors are fearsome opponents, extremely difficult to control, even by those who summon them to service. Their undead remains are covered and protected by bone armor. Their souls are bound to the Lord of Death in hatred and anger over their fate. If not controlled by a strong and powerful will, they will attack every living being in sight until there is no one left to kill.

3 For more information on the Beloved, refer to the Appendix in *Amber and Iron*, Volume 2, *Dark Disciple*.

Creation

Among his other duties, the Lord of Death serves an important role as adjudicator of souls. The souls of all who have lived upon Krynn must pass under his watchful eye. Those who strived to do good with their lives pass on to the next stage of the journey. Some may be bound to the service of other gods (such as Morgion) and proceed on to whatever fate awaits them. Some souls who cannot bear to be parted from life—for whatever reason—Chemosh claims for his own. These anguished dead might return to the world as an unquiet spirit, a ghost, or a specter. They might include a husband who comes back to watch over his wife or man who returns to haunt the place where he was murdered.

A Bone Warrior is one of these unquiet undead. In their case, they are warriors who died on the field of battle and who are so filled with hatred of the enemy that they refuse to quit the fight. Their one desire is to return to the world to inflict revenge on those they believe mistreated them. Chemosh will offer them the chance and, if they agree, he will seize them and force the rage-filled spirits to become Bone Warriors in his service.

It is interesting to note that even servants of Light may become Bone Warriors. For example, an elven warrior fighting minotaur in Silvanesti despises her enemy so much that her hatred lives on even after her death. If she cannot let go of her rage, her soul may well fall victim to Chemosh.

Appearance & Personality

The Lord of Death allows the fallen warrior to keep his original body and the skills that go with it. Thus an elven swordsman will still retain his deadly grace, the ogre bandit his brutish strength. Those who knew the Bone Warrior in life will not likely recognize him in death, for Chemosh has quite literally turned the Bone Warrior inside out.

Through a slow and painful process, the soft and meaty innards of the Bone Warrior are drawn inside its skeleton while the bones are re-shaped and strengthened to form a hard carapace that protects every part of the body. Chemosh allows his new disciple to feel every moment of this terrible ordeal, constantly reliving the moment of its death, thus reinforcing the rage that binds him to this plane.

A Bone Warrior "lives" in constant, burning agony. It hates the living, viewing them all as the enemy. It knows only pain and rage. It does not require food, drink, sleep, or shelter. Though it still under-stands the languages it knew in life, the horribly deformed mouth and tongue utters nothing except inarticulate cries of fury.

The Bone Warriors are extremely dangerous. If uncontrolled, the Bone Warrior will attack every living being in sight, making no dis-tinction between friend and foe, until it is finally destroyed. And if the Bone Warrior ever encounters those it counted as its enemy, it will focus on that enemy to the exclusion of all others.

Since mindless rage does little to serve the Chemosh's purpose, how-ever, a Bone Warrior will almost always be under the control of one of his living servants—either a powerful dark cleric or a Bone Acolyte.

Bone Warrior Powers

Like other undead, a Bone Warrior remains unaffected by many physical and magical attacks. These include: sleep, poison, paralysis, disease, or spells that affect the mind. A Bone Warrior's bone armor has the hardness of Solamnic plate mail, and it covers the entire body—with only the smallest openings to allow the flesh to move underneath the bone. Swords and arrows do little damage to a Bone Warrior's armor. The rare weapon that manages to pierce it causes no more pain than the undead warrior already endures.

The pain-fueled anger is the key which grants the Bone Warrior supernatural strength. It is significantly stronger in death than it was in life, though any magical spells or abilities it once possessed are lost in the transformation, and it is incapable of taking any actions that require much in the way of focus or concentration.

Though it does not understand complex strategies, it does retain the warrior's mind it possessed in life and can utilize battlefield tactics with cunning. Many enemies assume Bone Warriors to be mindless, a mistake a Bone Warrior gladly uses to its advantage. A Bone Warrior follows the orders of the person to whom it is bound, though it will constantly struggle against the will of those who control it, blaming them for keeping it bound to this terrible existence. If a Bone Warrior breaks free, it will first attempt to slay its master.

Bone Acolyte

The Bone Acolyte is a living disciple of the Lord of Death. Protected by unholy skeletal armor, the Bone Acolyte possesses a number of powers granted by Chemosh.

Bone Acolytes were known during the Age of Dreams, and there was a brief (though largely forgotten) time in which they were among the most feared servants of any evil god. Only the Plague Knights of Morgion rivaled the Bone Acolytes in the dark tales spun by the bards of that age. So feared were they that warriors and wizards and clerics devoted themselves to destroying them. Chemosh determined they were not worth the time and effort, and moved on to other schemes. After all these ages have passed, however, the tales of the Bone Warriors are known to only a few wizards and historians. The Lord of Death believes that the time is right for these fearsome undead to return to work his will among the living.

Creation

A Bone Acolyte is a powerful servant of Chemosh. Though he or she might be a dark cleric who calls upon the Death Lord for greater power, the Bone Acolyte is often a warrior of Darkness willing to trade his soul for the power granted to him by Chemosh. The unholy bone armor grants special abilities, though unlike that of the Bone Warrior, the bone armor allows the Acolyte to still enjoy the pleasures of the living.

Typically, one who wants to gain the power of a Bone Acolyte must perform a profane ritual that involves the sacrifice of an elf, an ogre, and a human. The flesh is boiled from these victims to retrieve the true goal—the bone. A terrible craft is required to magically shape the skeletal remains into armor made specifically to fit the Bone Acolyte.

With the armor in place, the initiate must offer his life and his soul to Chemosh and adjure the Lord of Death to grant to him the powers of the Bone Acolyte. If Chemosh deems the candidate unworthy, the best that can be hoped for is a swift, yet painful death. Those who are deemed worthy are granted both dark secrets and divine magical abilities.

Chemosh might, however, grant a warrior in his direct service, such as Ausric Krell, the gifts of a Bone Acolyte without the need of special ritual and craft. But there is a price for anything, and the Lord of Death will claim his servant's soul should he fall.

Appearance & Personality

A Bone Acolyte is still alive, and without the benefit of his armor he has all the same physical characteristics, strengths and weakness, as before. But when he dons the bone armor, he becomes a nightmare figure. His armor is made of whitish-yellow bone, with unnaturally long spikes protruding from the shoulders, elbows, knuckles and knees, serving to protect the joints. These spikes, being imbued with the divine magic, do not interfere with the Bone Acolyte's movement. In some instances, they may even enhance it.

The exact appearance of the Bone Acolyte's armor is specific to person, fitting his personality and history. The only thing all have in common is the symbol of Chemosh, the tattoo of a skull above the Bone Acolyte's heart.

The Lord of Death provides direction for a Bone Acolyte's actions, though the Acolyte's own passions and agenda certainly play a part—as they do for all mortals. A Bone Acolyte might be found guarding a temple or stronghold of Chemosh or on the field of battle, fighting in the name of his god.

Powers

A Bone Acolyte's primary power is related to his armor. Created with unholy magic, the armor can be summoned or discarded with nothing more than a simple prayer to Chemosh.

The armor enhances the strength of the wearer, making him a fearsome opponent without even considering his other abilities. It also provides nearly complete protection against mundane attacks.

But it is the Bone Acolyte's ability known as *boneshaping* that makes him a terrifying enemy. The armor may alter, grow, and change at the direction of the Acolyte. A novice Bone Acolyte may grow a bone blade from his wrist if he is disarmed. A more experienced and powerful Acolyte may draw his opponent into an embrace, then grow a dozen bony spikes to impale the enemy.

Once a Bone Acolyte has acquired mastery of his true powers, he can use his power over bones and direct it at the enemy. By magically exerting his will against a foe, he is able to snap bones from a distance—causing a warrior's sword arm to become useless or render a wizard unable to use the somatic components of a spell. This gruesome ability can demoralize an entire enemy force. It is fortunate for Chemosh's enemies, however, that those of great strength or exceptional will can resist this power of the Bone Acolyte.

The legends from the Age of Dreams state that a truly powerful Bone Acolyte in Chemosh's service gains one final, terrible power—the ability to liquefy all of the bones of a single opponent in an instant. With no structure to support the body, the unfortunate victim dies almost instantly, leaving behind only a soft and fleshy mound. This dread power can only be used rarely.

Bone Acolytes gain an advantage over others such as dark clerics when attempting to control a Bone Warrior. In addition, a Bone Acolyte may choose his Bone Warrior from the undead army of Chemosh, thus enabling the Bone Acolyte to select a warrior to suit his needs. (A minotaur Bone Warrior who hates elves to fight elves, for example.)

There is one drawback. If the Bone Acolyte does lose control of his Bone Warriors, he will almost certainly be destroyed by them. Chemosh has no use for weaklings.

The Future

Though his Bone Acolytes and Warriors have been defeated for the time being, Chemosh was pleased with them and toys with plans to keep creating them. His goal is to supplant Sargonnas as head of the Dark Pantheon and thus his dark clerics will require the aid and protection of strong warriors, while his armies need generals and powerful troops.

With the destruction of Ausric Krell, there are now no more known death knights in Krynn. Chemosh's Servants of Bone could become some of the most terrifying foes to cast their fearsome shadows over the world. They will undoubtedly be seen again.